THE CAT MAN

"What's wrong, femina?" he demanded in a silky, seductive voice. "Having trouble dealing with your desire for me, are you?"

Rissa flushed crimson and twisted frantically in his grasp. "I feel nothing for you but disgust! You're just so . . . so fascinatingly ugly—"

Morigan wrenched her up against himself. "Disgust? Ugly?" He gave a low, harsh laugh. "Sorry, femina, but those were hardly the emotions I saw in your eyes or felt emanating from you. You forget I can look into your mind—and I know a woman in heat when I see one!"

"In-in *heat?* Why you-you—"

Before Morigan could guess her intent, Rissa's free hand lifted. Only the quickest of Cat reflexes saved him from a stinging blow to the side of his face. He caught her hand only millimeters away, halted it, then slowly brought it to rest along the side of his beard-stubbled cheek. His fingers entwined in hers, imprisoning them there. Morigan turned his head then, bringing his mouth in contact with the palm of Rissa's hand.

At the touch of his full, soft lips, Rissa gasped. Fear rocketed through her. Fear of his intent, of the unknown—and fear of the intense surge of emotions his action had roused . . .

READ ON FOR EXCITING QUOTES
ON THIS FASCINATING FUTURISTIC ROMANCE

HEART'S SURRENDER

KATHLEEN MORGAN

PINNACLE BOOKS
WINDSOR PUBLISHING CORP.

PINNACLE BOOKS are published by

Windsor Publishing Corp.
850 Third Avenue
New York, NY 10022

First Printing: November, 1994

Printed in the United States of America

It is difficult to fight against anger; for a man will buy revenge with his soul.

Heraclitus, as quoted in Aristotle's *Politics*

Prologue

Early autumn, the planet Agrica

Ashes. Everything lay in ashes. His home . . . his dreams . . . and what little remained of his heart.

Morigan, heir to the throne of the Cat People, surveyed the scene of smoking ruins, charred bodies, and scattered possessions—and felt like his life had just been slammed against a wall of sudden and shocking brutality. There was nothing left of him. Nothing save a quivering mass of muscle and bone and agonized, shattered soul.

Their snug, skin-covered lodges—hundreds of them—lay in smoldering shambles. Food and belongings had been dragged out and rifled before they, too, were destroyed. Cat People—men, women, and children—sprawled where they'd been cut down, some dying in futile attempts at defense, others slaughtered as they fled. Their species, in one premeditated and cold bloodedly executed massacre, had been all but wiped out.

Gone were the happy days of a simple, yet fulfilling life. Gone were the dreams of growing in wisdom and maturity under the wise tutelage of Bardock, his father, until the time came to assume his own place on the Cat Throne. Gone was the anticipation of living out a peaceful, happy existence with his beloved mate, Winna, and of watching his children grow, of guiding them into a good and honorable adulthood.

As Morigan gazed out on the utter devastation that had once been the forested winter home of the Cat People, the swirling breeze carried the taint of wood smoke and burnt flesh to him. It was too much to bear. He wanted to turn, to run as fast and far as he could. Yet such desires were but empty, self-serving acts at a time like this. Self-serving . . . and not the way of one such as he.

His family and people, those few who remained, needed him. Until his father could be found—if he indeed still lived—Morigan must rally the others of his hunting party and set in motion a search among the mutilated bodies. A search Morigan feared would reveal more than any son—or husband and father—could ever be prepared to deal with. A sick dread churning in his gut, he waved over Naren, his friend since boyhood, a good, dependable, and unusually levelheaded Cat Man.

The tall, black-maned man strode lithely to his side. Horror burned in his tear-filled eyes. "Wh-who did this? Who would slaughter innocent people? And for what reason?"

"Bellatorians need no reason," Morigan snarled bitterly. "None save the one that has set them against us for the past thirty cycles. They want Agrica at all costs. The rules, without our even being aware of it, have changed. We're now the prey . . ."

His gaze snared on a tiny babe who lay but ten meters away. Morigan bit back an anguished curse. The infant was still wrapped in his swaddling cradle, his small form bloody and lifeless. Beside him, her hand still clutched in the cradle's carrying strap, lay the brutalized remains of his mother.

The Cat Man swallowed hard, fiercely blinking back his own hot surge of tears.

"What are we to do?" Naren's voice pierced the mist that swam before him. "Their weapons, their technology, are far too advanced ever to hope—"

"We'll fight on as we have before!" Morigan snapped, cutting off his compatriot's words before Naren gave utterance to thoughts of defeat. This wasn't the time to show weakness or indecision, no matter how ravaged his heart and mind felt. "The Bellatorian victory—*if* it ever comes—will be dearly bought. They'll not subjugate the Cat People as easily as they have the rest of Agrica." He gripped Naren by the arm. "But enough of that. It's time we saw to our own."

"You're right. Bellator can be dealt with later." Naren hesitated, bewilderment clouding his eyes. "I don't know where to begin. What would you have me—"

"My Lord!" the low cry pierced the heavy gloom of the smoke-tainted forest.

Morigan turned. There, borne by four Cat Men, was his father's lifeless body. He went rigid, every muscle of his big, powerfully built frame going taut with dread. They carried Bardock over to where Morigan stood, then gently, reverently, laid their lord and leader at his son's feet.

For a long moment, Morigan stared down at the body. Bardock was all but unrecognizable, his face little more than a charred mass of flesh thanks to a Bellatorian blaster's fiery barrage. Additional weapon blasts had left gaping, scorched wounds in his chest and upper torso. He hadn't had a chance.

With a low moan, Morigan sank to his knees and gathered his father to him. He stroked back the tangled remnants of the silver-threaded brown mane and kissed his sire tenderly on the forehead. The scent of burnt flesh and singed hair filled Morigan's nostrils. Nausea roiled and swelled in the pit of his stomach.

He forced down the gorge that rose in his throat and lowered his father back to the ground. With infinite care, Morigan slipped the aureum chain with its single aureum Cat's claw from about his father's neck and placed it over his own head.

As the badge of his newly inherited office settled in the middle of his breast, he glanced down at it. Glinting a dull gold in the crisp furring of his dark chest hair, the claw still felt warm with life—his father's life, Morigan thought with a searing pain—and so very, very heavy. As heavy as the terrible burden that had just been placed on his shoulders.

The realization wrenched him back to reality. In a lithe bunching of Cat-potent muscles, Morigan rose, flung back his own long mane of thick, dark-brown hair, and squared his massive shoulders. Green-gold eyes swept the faces of the men standing before him.

"Each of you gather forty males and have them search for any survivors. That includes the surrounding forest. I'll take another twenty to build the funeral pyres. There are far too many to bury this night. Naren," Morigan added, turning to him, "you take the rest and go through the lodges. Gather any usable bedding, clothing, weapons, and foodstuffs. We'll need everything we can find for where we're going."

"And where is that, my Lord?" his friend asked, rendering him the title of respect for his new office. "Where will we next make our lair?"

Morigan's gaze swung north. Through the dense forest that had long been their favorite lair in their nomadic way of life, past the lush farmlands and plains, his memory flew, envisioning their destination. "The Serratus Mountains," he replied hoarsely. "They are abundant with thousands of caves and a myriad of virtually hidden valleys, a land unfriendly and unforgiving to all who venture into them. Yet as dangerous as they may be to us, they'll be even more hazardous to any Bellatorians who dare follow. The mountains are our only hope."

He motioned to his men. "Go now. Daylight is fast waning, and we must be gone before darkfall. Not even one night more in these woods is safe for us. Not tonight . . . and perhaps never again."

Somberly, they nodded and strode off. Morigan joined in the building of the funeral pyre. The wood felt rough, its texture harsh and uncomfortable in his arms, a discordant wrench back to reality in an otherwise unreal time. He clutched it to him, grinding the logs into his bare chest and arms in the futile hope that the physical pain would mute some of his soul's anguish.

As the dead were carried over, he helped lay them on the huge pile of tinder and wood. The pyre grew in height until it towered above them. They were forced to build three more to accommodate the volume of bodies.

And still his mother, his beloved mate, and two-year-old son, Calder, were not among the slain brought forward. Though he knew it unwise to hope for it, Morigan's mind began to consider other possibilities. Perhaps they'd managed to escape into the forest when the attack came. Perhaps they were out there even now, afraid to return to their forest lair. Perhaps . . .

Then, there was nothing left to hope for. The forest stilled, the leaves of the trees calming to hang limp and lifeless— mournful, waiting. His mother was found hiding in a dense stand of bushes, alive but hovering on the brink of madness.

Morigan was quickly summoned. In her arms, Sarna

clutched the lifeless body of his son; at her side lay Morigan's dead wife.

He knelt beside her. "Mother, give Calder to me," he whispered, his voice raw and rusty with the strain. "It's over for him. There's no more you can do."

The elderly Cat Woman shook her head and instead began to rock the child. At the blank, glazed look in her eyes, Morigan choked back a groan. With a gentle, careful touch, he pried Sarna's fingers loose and took back his son.

Then, with Calder clasped to his breast, Morigan turned to his wife, his sorrow so deep he thought he'd go mad from the pain. He inhaled deeply, struggling to capture the sweet essence of her one last time. Smoke and the scent of singed flesh filled him instead.

His gut heaved. Only the staunchest of efforts kept him from vomiting. With the most exquisite tenderness, Morigan stroked away a damp leaf clinging to Winna's face, a face flawlessly beautiful still, before trailing his fingers down the side of her neck, over her chest, to the gaping black blaster wound in her abdomen.

She'd been eight months pregnant. The Bellatorian who had killed her had meant to take not only her life, but their unborn child's as well. Sheer, unmitigated, heartless butchery—that's all it was. And he hadn't been there to protect her . . . to protect anyone.

Agonizing impotence welled in Morigan's heart, searing a gaping hole of its own in the acrid surge of frustration and despair. He felt drained, as weak as a babe, without even the strength to lift his head, much less move.

His mother whimpered, uttered a small cry, and began to keen the ritual song of mourning. Morigan jerked in recognition, his body turning hard as stone.

Rage poured into the empty hole that had once been his

heart. With a groan so loud and tormented it was little more than an animalistic howl, Morigan lamented with her. Gone . . . all gone. His family, his once simple but happy life, his people . . .

With a wracking shudder, he shoved the pain away into some dark, distant corner of his heart. Morigan rose, lifting Winna and Calder in his arms. Back to the funeral pyres he went, his mind seething with desperate thoughts and brutally unyielding plans. There was too much left to be done to squander time on the luxury of mourning the dead, no matter how dear.

No time to deal with the emotional consequences, no time to form new dreams, or to find some way to ease the pain.

His energies were better spent on salvaging what could be salvaged—and on vengeance. A vengeance that would not only punish the enemy where it would hurt the most, but ensure the continued survival of his species.

Fingers of deepening twilight threaded their way through the trees as the last of the Cat People were laid to rest upon the funeral pyres. Eight hundred and forty Cat Women, one thousand four hundred children, and five hundred Cat Men mercilessly slaughtered. Save for the fifty females out gathering berries or washing clothes down by the river, about thirty children of various ages who'd managed to escape and hide in the forest, and the three hundred or so Cat Men who'd been out on the annual autumn hunting trip, their lair was all but wiped out. Over twenty-seven hundred people—gone, annihilated.

The Bellatorians had been brutally thorough. So thorough it would be next to impossible for the Cat People to reproduce themselves fast enough ever to have hopes of rebuilding their nation. Fifty females for over three hundred males. The inbreeding itself would be devastating after but a few generations.

If they were fortunate enough to elude the Bellatorians long enough *to* reproduce, Morigan thought despairingly as he laid his wife and son upon the last funeral pyre.

Naren walked forward with a flaming brand. Morigan forced himself to step up and take the torch from him. As Lord of the Cat People, it was his duty to set fire to the funeral pyres. As he must guide them into existence, sanction their life matings, and sit as judge over all their conflicts, he must also be there in their life departures. Yet even in his worst imaginings, Morigan had never thought to witness such a slaughter.

He strode back to the pyre that held Winna and Calder, hesitated but a moment, then touched the torch to its base. The fire grew quickly into red tongues of flame, consuming the mass of wood and bodies in but the short span of minutes.

Morigan watched the conflagration briefly, then moved to the next pyre and lit it, then the next, and the next. Smoke rose to billow into the night, wending its way through the dense canopy of leaves high overhead. The fire grew, hot and searing. And the scent . . .

It was finally more than Morigan could bear. He shoved the still flaming brand into Naren's hand and strode away. Into the depths of the forest he went, needing, no, demanding a few precious minutes of solitude. There was no way to block out the images, though.

No way, he thought in rising anguish, crushing his face into his fisted hands. He'd never forget, never be able to sleep again without having even his dreams permeated with the horrible scenes. The present reality was too much to endure. His father and most of his people dead, his pregnant wife and son murdered . . .

He was now his people's only hope at the worst crisis in their long and glorious history. How could they go on? How could *he* go on?

Yet, how could he not?

The Cat Man shoved to his feet, swayed for a brief instant, then righted himself. His personal sorrow was no greater than the rest of his people's. All had lost loved ones. All must go on.

With a determined resolve burning in his heart, Morigan returned to the pyres. He stood apart until the flames died and a hush settled once more over the forest. Then, he stepped forward.

"The Bellatorians think they've won a major victory," Morigan cried, his voice strong and clear. "They think the threat of the Cat People is over, as our existence soon will be. They think wrong.

"They'll pay—and pay dearly—for their brutal error this day. And this," he rasped, his voice momentarily breaking as, with claws bared, he indicated their forest lair and the smoldering ruins of the funeral pyres, "will be paid for as well. Paid in like manner.

"We'll have our revenge, and their own kind will bear the burden, dearly borne though it may be," Morigan roared, his anger and bitter despair fueling his words until they reverberated in the cool night air. "This I vow, this I swear, as Lord of the Cat People!"

One

One cycle later

"What a hellish planet!" Rissa Lindatees blew a damp lock of curling, flaxen blond hair out of her eyes and glanced up at the huge sun blazing overhead. Though it was well into the early phase of Agrica's short fall and winter season, here, on the rolling grasslands, the days were still quite sultry.

Her pale blue-green riding jacket clung damply to her back. Beneath the matching, snug-fitting breeches and brown, knee-high boots, her skin was sweat-drenched and chafed. She felt hot, dirty, and thoroughly miserable.

A maddeningly persistent apis bug buzzed noisily about the small, prick ears of the Bellatorian-imported, tan-colored equs she rode. Finally, with an irritated snort, the large, normally docile animal flung up its head.

Startled, Rissa jerked on the reins and grabbed hold of the stiff, domare-hide saddle horn. She bit back an exasperated curse at the unfortunate fate that had required that she and the eleven other women who'd accompanied her on this pioneering mission to Agrica travel in this merchants' caravan. If only this backwater planet hadn't possessed just a single transport station, four long and dusty days' journey from the

Bellatorian-held Agrican capital of Primasedes, she wouldn't have been forced to endure such uncomfortable, primitive, and dangerous conditions.

By the five moons of Bellator! Riding an equs in this day and age to get anywhere! Curse this backward planet for failing to keep up with even the most minimal semblance of civilization!

"You could have ridden in one of the wagons," Diona, her personal serving maid observed, noting Rissa's aggravated expression as she urged her own mount up alongside her mistress's. "Considering your lack of expertise with the beasts, there was no reason to risk your life on an equs."

Rissa shot her a black look. "I may be inexperienced, but I'm not helpless. And riding in the wagons is no less hot and dusty. At least out here I get full benefit of the breeze, however niggardly it has blown today." She sighed. "If only my father had sent some skim crafts to fetch us."

"That *would* have made for a far quicker and more pleasant trip," Diona agreed, flipping her long braid of light brown hair back over her shoulder, "but since they lack the range for such an extended journey . . ."

"Yes, I know." Rissa nodded her glum agreement. "And I know, as well, I shouldn't complain so. It isn't at all the kind of behavior my father would appreciate."

"Well, I couldn't say, never having met your father. He may be the Lord Commander of the Bellatorian forces on Agrica, but how can even you really speak for his opinions? You've not seen him in over ten cycles."

A troubled frown creased Rissa's forehead. "It *has* been a long time, I suppose, considering I was barely ten when my parents separated . . ." She inhaled a steadying breath. "I just remember how proud he used to be of me. I don't want to disappoint him."

Rissa peeled the front of her riding jacket free from her clammy skin, the sweltering sun overhead once more foremost in her mind. "By the five moons, what a cursedly hot day!"

"Well, I don't care if it is a bit hot. It's a lovely day. Even this far into autumn, Agrica has the most agreeable weather," her serving maid offered blithely, attempting to change the conversation to a more cheerful topic. With the wasting sickness and death of her mother, Rissa had been through enough heartache and upheaval in the past cycle. This journey to Agrica was intended to be the start of a new and happier life. There was no point in stirring doubts and fears prematurely.

"And the adventure of traversing such a primeval planet!" Diona hurried on, her glance scanning the verdant, grassy plains, slashed at intervals by river-carved ravines where water ran as clear a blue-green as the prized turcas stones her mistress wore at her throat and dangling from her ears. "For all its wild, untamed character, I find Agrica quite beautiful. I look forward to an exciting life helping to colonize this planet—*and* taming its men."

Rissa shot her a disbelieving look, opened her mouth to tell her exactly what she thought of that last, particularly inane remark, then thought better of it. "Strange, but I was under the distinct impression you were along to assist me in adapting to my new life," she muttered wryly instead. "Now, the truth is out. You've come to Agrica to find a man."

Diona shrugged. "What if I have? Isn't that part of the reason you agreed to transport here? Didn't your father not only offer you a new home and life, but also the assurance of a life mating to one of his high ranking military officers, one destined for a great and glorious political career? Don't deny me my simple aspirations. You stand to do even better in the bargain, my friend."

Rissa rolled her eyes, then shook her head in weary resignation. Diona was an excellent serving maid, honest and true as the day was long, but her forthright manner galled a bit at times. Yet, when the truth of her words was faced, she *was* right.

For the past cycle, Rissa had been at a loss as to what to do with her life. Her beloved mother was gone, she had no other relatives nearby, and she quickly found the fine, pampered existence of a Bellatorian gentlewoman was no longer enough. Indeed, she now realized only the companionship of her mother the past few cycles had kept the growing restlessness at bay. Though still of a tender age, Rissa already craved more than the daily walks through the lush flower gardens, the pointless entertainments, and the shallow, spoiled suitors who coveted her hand for the wealth and position she'd bring them as the daughter of an important Bellatorian official.

She had a mind, curse them all, and dreams of contributing something useful to society. She wanted to do brave and noble things. If the young officer her father had in mind for her didn't suit, she still envisioned an influential position at her father's side, advising and aiding him in the peaceful and successful colonization of Agrica. Bellator stood to gain greatly from the agricultural bounty of this planet, as did its simpleminded if hardworking inhabitants. Indeed, the entire Imperium stood to profit.

Rissa smiled. She liked the mental image of herself as diplomat and advisor very much. She wanted what she did in life to matter, to possess some lasting good. And, as far as a life mating went, she definitely yearned for a higher purpose than serving as a pretty decoration in some man's home and bed. She wanted to *matter* to him—and she wanted to be loved for who she was, not for what she symbolized or possessed.

"No, I'll not do badly if I can find the right man," Rissa admitted, drawn back to the reality at hand by the sweltering sun beating down on them. "Or," she added, "the right position of usefulness at my father's side. Either way, I'd be happy. I just want to banish this empty feeling, this pointless floundering my life seems, of late, to have become mired in. It's time, Diona, I became a woman."

Her serving woman grinned, a knowing glint in her eyes. "Ah, yes, becoming a woman. But that, my naive young mistress, generally requires the help of a man. And you haven't had many of those, have you?"

Rissa flushed crimson. "I haven't had *any* of those, and well you know it! I'd thank you not to taunt me about it just because *you're* a few cycles older and far more experienced in such matters. I'll find a man soon enough," she continued with more conviction than she actually felt. "I always get what I set my mind to—sooner or later."

"As you most certainly will in Primasedes," Diona hastened to agree. "It's common knowledge there's a shortage of women there. With your delicate beauty, well-curved form, and luxurious blond hair, you'll soon have most of the men in the garrison vying for your favors. You're just fortunate you'll have me nearby to assist in their assessment. I know a lusty lover when I see one. And you'll definitely need a strong, virile mate to tame you."

"Will I now?" Rissa turned away with an impudent flounce of her long tresses. "We'll just see who tames whom. I need no man controlling me. I want an equal relationship, respect for my ideas, my talents, and what I have to offer.

I'll never be some man's chattel, just a breeder for his children and a receptacle for his lust. Never!"

"And isn't being the mate of a fine, handsome man and bearing him strong, healthy children enough for any woman?"

Once more, Rissa frowned. "It would seem so to many, but still I suspect there must be more. *Should* be more."

Diona cocked a speculative brow. "Well, a man who treats me kindly and thrills me in bed is quite enough for me. The more animal, the better, in fact." She paused, a gleeful light dancing in her eyes. "Speaking of animals, have you heard the tales of the infamous Cat Men? They're said to be one of Agrica's most exotic species, half-humanoid and half-animal."

She shuddered in horrified delight. "There are rumors of their wildly uncontrollable sexual urges on the night the Agrican triple moons align. Think how exciting the mating would be with one of them . . ."

"Those tales are revolting!" Rissa snapped, half-sickened, half-fascinated by her serving woman's description of the legendary Cat Men. "Besides, they're hardly a problem anymore. Father assured me the Bellatorian campaign to eradicate that odious race is all but complete. He wouldn't have let me come if it wasn't."

"Yes, I suppose you're right." Diona sighed, glancing about her sadly. Up ahead, the caravan headed down onto a narrow trail running beside a fast-flowing river that cut through yet another ravine. Stands of mighty robur trees grew in clumps along both rims of the ravine. Some, almost as if seeking to span the distance to the other side, thrust their massive trunks and leafy branches out at precarious, gravity-defying angles. Still others had boldly chosen to take root alongside the river itself.

"They were quite a threat to the Bellatorian colonization attempts for a time, though," the servant rambled on. "Still, I'd have liked just one glimpse of a Cat Man. They're said to be quite powerful and hairy, have long, lethal claws and possess the most amazing psychic powers. Can you imagine what it would be like to have one of them in your—"

A strangled scream silenced whatever observations Diona had been about to make. The two women exchanged anxious glances, then leaned forward and craned their necks in an attempt to see to the front of the caravan.

"What do you think that was?" Rissa's hand slipped to the dagger hanging at her side.

Her maid shrugged, shooting her a wry grin. "Nothing to concern yourself about, I'm sure. A few of the soldiers consumed a bit too much of the merchants' imported Moracan ale last night. One of them probably just paid for it by falling asleep, tumbling off his equs, and receiving a big hoof in the side for his efforts."

"Well, perhaps," Rissa muttered and, when no further sound or commotion was forthcoming, relaxed and settled back on her equs. As she did, an animalistic snarl jerked her attention overhead.

The two women's gazes snapped upward. There, glaring down at them from the ravine ledge high above, was a being so feral and hirsute its presence was the very embodiment of all the horrible tales they had ever heard of the dreaded Cat Men.

Morigan watched the caravan wend its sinuous way across the grassy plains and smiled grimly. There were surprisingly few Bellatorian soldiers set to guard the train of merchants' wagons and travelers mounted on equs. Unless there were more hidden within the gaily colored, flag-emblazoned wagons, the caravan was virtually defenseless. One way or another, from their vantage above the wagons as the vehicles made their way through the narrow river gorge, it would be an easy thing for the Cat Men psychically to detect any additional humanoid presence within the wagons. If there were more soldiers, they'd know soon enough.

The seemingly defenseless caravan could well be a trap meant to lure any remaining Cat survivors of the forest massacre, but, somehow, Morigan doubted it. He had taken too great a care in the past cycle to hide their presence in the Serratus Mountains. Not that his efforts had been enough to prevent further tragedy or deaths.

As the painful memories once more rushed into his mind, Morigan's hands clenched and his jaw tightened. No, the suffering of the Cat People hadn't been over even then. One of the harshest and longest winters in memory had settled over the Serratus Mountains soon after they arrived. They'd barely escaped starvation. In the desperation of people forced into a land where they were ill-prepared to survive, forty-three good Cat Men had been lost in blizzards while out hunting in frequently unsuccessful attempts to find food.

Five of the Cat Women pregnant at the time of the massacre had lost their young. Several more who had become pregnant later miscarried. And only a few females since then had conceived. The future looked grim, their survival—

"It's not your fault."

Morigan exhaled a weary breath and glanced over at Naren. He must be more tired than he realized, to lower his mind shield enough for another Cat Man to slip in.

With an effort, he strengthened his psychic defenses. He was leader. It served no purpose for the others to know how discouraged he really was. Not even his closest friend.

The black-maned Cat Man, now his second-in-command, resolutely met his shuttered look. "It isn't your fault, no matter how much you seek to carry that burden as well. If it hadn't been for your choice of those hot spring caves scattered through the mountains for our lairs, we'd have frozen to death from the cold. If you hadn't divided us up into smaller units last winter more easily to hide our presence from the Bellatorian patrols, they'd have found us all. And if you hadn't finally ordered our females to avoid mating during their fertile cycles, in order to conserve their own health until spring, we'd have lost not only more babes, but Cat Women as well."

"Yet, spring and summer have passed. We're all together again," Morigan rasped, unable to keep the anguish from his voice, "and only three females have conceived. I fear the stress has left the rest of them infertile. Permanently."

"We all fear that. Why else would we be here on such a mission, turning to such desperate measures?" Naren grasped his arm and gave it a reassuring squeeze. "You were right once again in proposing this. Don't doubt yourself. None of us does."

His lord grimaced. "None, you say? Have you so quickly forgotten my cousin Cradoc?" Morigan sighed and shifted restlessly. "Gods, but I haven't my father's wisdom and experience. I don't deserve—"

He paused, shamed to silence by his friend's searing look. "Fine. Deserving or not, it *is* my responsibility now. But the consideration of taking helpless females and chemically inducing them against their wills, if need be, to mate with us fills me with loathing. Though sexual enslavement of the enemy's women may have long been one of the rights of conquest throughout the Imperium, it goes against everything the Cat People believe in."

"It is an accepted act as spoils of war."

"Granted, but how much better are we, if we follow th[e] lead of the rest of the Imperium in this? Greed, treachery and the takeover of other planets, not to mention the slaughte[r] of innocent people, have never been Agrica's way—nor ours!

Naren said nothing.

Morgan turned back to gaze out over the plains, a deep bitter frustration filling him. Neither of them liked the grad ual decline they saw in their own belief and value systems nor the threat to ancient customs and laws. Yet, despite ev erything, it was happening.

With its wealth of fertile farmland and long, tranquil sum mers, Agrica historically had been content with its role a[s] the breadbasket of the Imperium. Then, after the mysteriou[s] theft of the Imperial judicial unit known as the Knowing Crystal and in the absence of its fair judgments and govern ing practices that all had come to depend upon, life—an[d] morality—had gradually declined. Bellator, always aggres sive and warlike under the best of circumstances, had evolve[d] into the galaxy's rapacious dictator.

The only surprise had been how long it had taken Bellato[r] to turn to Agrica. Now, after just thirty cycles, the Imperia[l] warriors all but controlled the big, agricultural planet an[d] worked slavishly to colonize it with Bellatorian substation[s] and settlers intent on raping the land of its wealth of food And no one save the Cat People had raised protest or resisted

The caravan drew closer. From his psychically cloake[d] concealment that no humanoid save his species could see Morgan's acute Cat's vision now could make out the form[s] and faces of individual travelers. A quick mental scan of th[e] wagon interiors found no additional soldiers hidden within only a single female reclining inside each of four of the wagons. He counted six more females riding with the wagon drivers and another two on equs near the back of the train.

Twelve females. All relatively young and of breeding age. Their capture would be a significant addition to their own females and a decided victory on their first attempt at abduction. At least some of the Cat Men would have a soft body to warm them through the fast approaching winter nights. And come next summer, the first of the half-Cat, half-Bellatorian babies would be born . . .

Mating with a female outside one's species. The thought sickened him. Morigan knew their captives would have just as much to overcome in accepting Cat Men as mates. The aversion was hardly one-sided.

The Cat People were a proud, ancient bloodline whose original evolution was lost in the mists of antiquity, but the purity of Cat's blood had remained untainted for thousands of cycles. Now to be forced to mix it with that of another species, to corrupt and perhaps even dilute the wondrous abilities and powers that coursed through their veins, was akin to sacrilege. A sacrilege that would perhaps annihilate them—one way or another—in the long run.

But there *was* no other choice. The future was too hard to see in times such as these. Survival of the species came first. They were just that desperate. The consequences would have to be dealt with later.

He only prayed he'd made the right decision.

The first wagons filed into the ravine and made their way down alongside the river. Morigan signaled to his men, their presence cloaked as well, who were lined up and down both sides of the gorge. They had their orders. The entire caravan must be allowed to enter the ravine before they attacked. The soldiers would be taken care of first, then any of the merchants who chose to resist. And not one of the females must

be allowed to escape or be harmed. Not one—each was in
valuable and must be conserved.

He would have ample opportunity to test his plan, Morigan
thought glumly. As Lord of the Cat People and now withou
a mate of his own—or heirs, for that matter—he had felt i
only fair to add his name to the drawing to determine which
Cat Men would be among the first to take a Bellatorian fe
male as mate. Though he hadn't been pleased when his name
had been chosen, Morigan didn't feel right asking his people
to do anything he wasn't willing to do.

The thought of taking another mate so soon after Winna's
death disgusted him. Winna would understand, wherever she
now resided in the vast, spiritual cosmos of space, loving
her people as she always had. But the disloyalty of the act
the implied devaluation of their life mating, was almost more
than Morigan could bear. He felt sordid, shamed beyond endurance, and secretly wondered how he'd ever be able to
rouse his emotions strongly enough even to touch, much less
mate with, the female he must take for his own.

Curse the Bellatorian invaders for driving him and his people to this! He would never forgive, never be free again of
the seething, bitter hatred their heartless slaughter had
wrought, no matter how long his span of cycles ran.

The last of the caravan entered the ravine. Morigan gave
a low whistle, attuned only to highly sensitized Cat hearing,
signaling the attack. One of the Cat Men stationed up ahead
used a confiscated stunner to take out a soldier. The man
toppled from his equs with a strangled scream.

For a minute, everything went still. Then, snarling savagely, the Cat Men uncloaked from their psychic concealment and flung themselves into battle.

* * *

With a loud cry, their attacker leaped from the cliff above them, his net unfurling as he fell. Rissa grabbed for her dagger. Her equs gave a snort of surprise and reared. Rissa's equestrian skills weren't sufficient to the challenge. With a startled gasp, she tumbled off.

Huge cloven hooves stomped around her as her mount leaped about, and Diona fought to control her own wildly shying equs. Her serving maid screamed, then went suddenly silent.

Rissa struggled to her feet, flung her hair out of her eyes, and swung about just in time to be struck by Diona's equs and knocked back to the ground. The brief glimpse of the horrible alien wrestling with Diona, who was now wrapped within the net, was enough to set Rissa's innate Bellatorian battle instincts aflame. Once more, she shoved herself to her feet, grabbed for her dagger, and dodging the chaotically milling, panicked equs, attacked Diona's captor.

He must have possessed some sixth sense which warned him of her assault. In a lightning quick move, the alien wheeled about, grabbed Rissa's raised arm, and halted the downward trajectory of her dagger. A dagger now aimed straight for his heart.

Suddenly, Rissa was immobilized—and totally at his mercy. The creature's strength seemed as superhuman as his reflexes. With a quick flick of his hand, he snapped her wrist down, sending her dagger sailing away. Then, pulling Rissa to him, the alien jerked her arm behind her back and shoved her beneath his net to join the shrieking Diona.

A sharp tug on the rope gathered the net at their feet. The two women fell heavily to the ground. Diona continued to scream and sob, flailing wildly at the net.

"Stop that yowling!" Rissa grabbed hold of the other woman's face with both hands to help her regain her rapidly waning hold on reality. She shot their captor a quick look to see if he overheard. His attention was elsewhere as he shouted something unintelligible to what must have been another one of his compatriots. "It'll do no good. We need to find some way to escape, not scream ourselves senseless!"

With a hysterical whimper, Diona calmed. "Wh-what do you want to d-do?" she hiccuped.

A glint of metal caught Rissa's eye. The dagger! There must be someway to—

Their captor began dragging them forward. They rolled and tumbled about in the net but, blessedly, headed in the general direction of the dagger.

"Diona!" she gritted as her back struck an unexpected stone, "roll over with me to the right until I tell you to stop. Now!"

"What are you—?" the other woman began, then did as requested as Rissa's own body tumbling atop hers began the process.

As they were simultaneously pulled forward by their captor's determined efforts, the two women moved in an awkward, rolling, sideways manner across the ground. When they neared the spot where the dagger lay, Rissa managed to thrust her hand through the netting. Just . . . one more . . . turn, she thought with a grunt as her head made jarring contact with another stone jutting from the ground.

Then, she was once more atop a softly groaning Diona and reaching desperately for the dagger. Still . . . too far . . . away, she realized in despair as her fingers grasped and missed by millimeters. In one last, frantic effort as she began to roll beneath Diona once again, Rissa made a wild lunge forward.

Something hard and long touched her palm. Her fingers

clenched around the object, felt its familiar contours, and jerked it back to her. The dagger!

Rissa pulled the weapon within the confines of the net and clutched it to her. "St-stop!" she gasped out the command. "Stop your rolling, Diona! You're k-killing me!"

"No more than you're d-doing to me," her maid servant hissed, stilling her movements. "You have the b-boniest elbows!"

"It has never been a problem up until now," Rissa hissed back, as one of Diona's own bony elbows rammed into her side. As they continued to slide over what seemed to be every rock in the ravine, she seriously considered using the dagger to slice through the netting in an attempt to escape. But, as they made their confined and increasingly dirty way to the head of the caravan, where all the activity seemed to be, Rissa soon decided the act would be futile.

The place was covered with the wild, hirsute aliens, fleeing merchants, and the dead bodies of the few soldiers sent along to guard the caravan. From the sounds of the hysterical screams and indignant shrieks of the other women in their party, it was apparent all the females were being taken to the same area. Better, Rissa thought, to hide the dagger and save it for a more opportune moment. Or a more desperate one, if that were indeed possible.

Finally, blessedly, their ruthless captor drew to a halt. There, standing before them, were the other ten women, all equally disheveled and terrified, but unharmed. Rissa breathed a sigh of relief and used the opportunity to hide the dagger inside her jacket.

She and Diona were jerked to their feet, the noose loosened, and the net pulled away. They quickly smoothed down their torn, dirty riding garments and glanced up at the other women. Rissa managed a smile of wobbly reassurance. Taking Diona by the arm, she stepped forward to join them.

When she turned to face the strange aliens, however, she nearly fainted from the sight. It seemed the work of securing the caravan was complete. At least thirty or forty of the hairy, unkempt beast men now had gathered to eye her and the other women. Some looked bored, others angry, but the majority stared back with predatory, calculating gazes.

"What are they thinking, do you imagine?" Diona asked hoarsely from behind her. "I feel like a haunch of meat being contemplated for dinner."

"Indeed?" Rissa shot back. "From the way that black-haired one in front is staring at my breasts, I'd have thought instead they'd more carnal ideas in mind."

There was a long pause from her serving maid, then a slow exhalation of air. "Yes, I see the look myself now. Perhaps, you'd be wise to get behind *me.*"

Rissa forced a semblance of cool nonchalance into her voice, even as her heart pounded in her chest. "A noble sentiment, but at this particular moment, I think I'm the best equipped to defend the lot of us." Deciding it time to assume a more aggressive stance, she withdrew her dagger and waved it in a manner she hoped was both lethal and menacing. For her efforts, all she gained was a twist of the black-haired alien's mouth that might possibly be construed as a smile.

"He hardly seems impressed," Diona muttered, moving to stand beside her. "Perhaps, my plan is a better choice."

"Are you that hungry for a man that you'd throw yourself at the first inhabitant you meet? I'd give it a few more days and hope something better comes along," Rissa said, eyeing the alien more closely.

He was definitely humanoid—tall, broad of shoulder, and

long of limb, with the usual facial features and body parts. His face, however, framed by hair that extended out from his hairline in a lush flow of black mane, bore a distinctly leonine appearance from the slightly flattened nose and almond-shaped gray eyes to the more pronounced browline. He was definitely in fine physical condition, lean and muscular with a luxurious furring of body hair. He wore only a brief, leathern, tan-colored loincloth and soft, knee-high boots.

The other aliens grouped behind him, Rissa noted, wore identical clothing and possessed similar feline characteristics and amounts of body and facial hair. But was it possible these beings could really be some of the horrible Cat Men? They were all supposed to be dead, weren't they? And didn't they possess virtually superhuman powers, powers few could ever hope to overcome?

Well, Rissa thought grimly, there was only one way to find out. She gestured to the black-haired alien who seemed to be their leader. "Are you . . . are you Cat Men?" she asked, speaking in the Imperial Common Language.

The black-haired one studied her for a moment, then nodded.

"Ah, good, you understand me." Rissa bit her lip, considering how to phrase her next questions so as to be construed the least offensively. No good would come of angering them, and yet, it was difficult—

"Put down your dagger. It is useless against us."

Her gaze jerked up to lock with the Cat Man's. "Indeed? I don't see you rushing me to gain possession of it. Why is that?"

"Certainly not because I fear any danger to me, femina," he replied, apparently trying to soften his words with the gentle form of address. "I worry only about damaging you in the struggle." His glance slid down the length of her body.

"And you're far too well-built and healthy to risk your child-bearing on any injury. No, you'll serve us too well as a breeder to consider harming you."

Rissa's eyes narrowed. "If you think I intend to let you touch me or any of the other women, you'll soon learn the error of that thought." To emphasize her point, she took a step forward and made a stabbing motion at him.

He didn't move, just cocked a dark brow, scrutinized her for a moment more, then laughed. The action startled Rissa. Then, anger rushed in to drive away the surprise.

Suddenly, she saw the true seriousness of her situation. These beasts stood to destroy all her plans, all her hopes and dreams for a new life here in one swift, violent act. They had come for more than the booty the caravan possessed. They had come for more than revenge against Bellator.

They had come to take her and the other women back to their hiding places as mates!

"It won't happen," she cried. "I'll die before I let that happen!"

He eyed her for a moment longer, his gaze narrowing. In that instant, Rissa felt a strange warmth ripple through her mind. Then, it was gone.

As was the black-haired Cat Man. He turned on his heel and strode away, leaving Rissa and the other women staring down the Cat Men who remained. Cat Men who were far more powerful and better armed than they, she realized in helpless fury. And her puny dagger notwithstanding, there was nothing she could do until their captors made their next move.

Morigan shook his head in disgust. The endless bolts of fabric being unloaded from the wagons were largely the same. Fine, expensive serica cloth meant for rich females and luxurious homes. And of little use to them.

He motioned to the meager pile of more sturdy lana cloth. "Take those. Perhaps our Cat Women can make some use of that material. The rest," he said, indicating the serica cloth, "burn. We don't need such a frivolous thing, and I certainly don't want the Bellatorians profiting from it in any way."

The Cat Man, leading the looting of the wagons, nodded. "There was little more in the other wagons, my Lord. The personal items of the females, some casks of Moracan ale, and a fine set of Nadrygean daggers, meant as a gift, I'd wager, but not much else." He cocked his shaggy head. "I know we'll enjoy the ale and find some use for the daggers, but shall we bring along the females' belongings as well?"

Morigan considered the request. It might ease the females' captivity a bit if they retained some of their personal items . . .

Finally, he shook his head. "No, we'll have our hands full enough with the booty and with them. For all practical purposes, their former life is over. The sooner they accept that, the better. Mementos from home will only slow that process."

His compatriot nodded and turned back to the task of sorting and assigning bearers for the booty. Morigan watched for a few minutes more, then turned. As odious as the duty was, it was past time for him to see how the division of the captured females among his men was going.

Each male chosen by lot would pick a female, in order of the number he'd earlier drawn. He would then be totally responsible for her care and safe journey back to their mountain lair, an undertaking which hopefully, in the process, would begin the establishment of some sort of positive relationship between them. It was also hoped, in time, that the

Cat Men's abilities to psychically attract, combined with their renowned sexual prowess, would win over the alien females. Or, at least, that was the theory.

"My Lord."

Morigan's head jerked up. Naren strode toward him, a wryly amused expression on his face. The Lord of the Cat People frowned. Naren was supposed to be supervising the selection of the females. Something must be wrong.

"Having problems, are you?" he demanded as his second-in-command drew up before him. Time was of the essence now. There was no sense wasting any more of it with conversational preliminaries.

Naren grinned. "Only a minor difficulty. A certain yellow-haired female is defending the others against us. I thought you might like to come and convince her of the error of her ways."

Morigan's mouth tightened in exasperation. "We haven't time for games. Is she so heavily armed you fear for your safety in disarming her?"

"She sports a pretty nasty looking little dagger, which she swears she'll use if one of us approaches too closely."

Green-gold eyes narrowed in sudden suspicion. "And your powers are inadequate for such a simple task? I think not, Naren. What game do you play with me?"

His friend shrugged, a small smile glimmering on his lips. "None, my Lord. But the choosing of the other women cannot commence until we deal with her."

"So, deal with her!"

"I thought you might prefer to do so," Naren said, pretending a sudden interest in the blaster strap hanging from his shoulder, "considering how important first impressions can be."

With the greatest of efforts, Morigan contained the impatient anger that welled inside him. "And pray, why are her first impressions of me so important?"

The black-maned Cat Man glanced up, grinning now from ear to ear. "You said to choose a mate for you. I have done so. And the yellow-haired female, as alien as she is to us, is as fiery and beautiful as they come. I think she will suit you quite nicely. Quite nicely, indeed."

Two

He should have known better, Morigan thought in disgust as he accompanied Naren back to where the females had been gathered. In his naive attempt to distance himself from the odious obligation of choosing one of the Bellatorian females for his own, he had thought to allow his friend to assume the responsibility for him. He should have known that Naren would spare no effort to glean the maximum amount of pleasure he could from that task—and all of it at *his* expense.

"I said to take whatever female was left," he snarled over at his friend. "I said to let the others have first pick. It matters not to me who I take as mate, as long as she's healthy and fertile."

"You want heirs to the Cat Throne, don't you?" Naren shot back, not at all shaken by his lord's aura of simmering anger.

"Yes. It seems imperative, does it not, considering the times and circumstances? If anything should happen to me—"

"My point exactly," his compatriot cut him off. "And your heirs can only come from a life mating. Whomever you took this day couldn't be yours for just a few cycles. A temporary mating, lawful as it is, wouldn't have been sufficient for you."

"I fail to see the point of all this," Morigan gritted. "Any female would have sufficed."

"No, any wouldn't have." Naren grasped him by the arm and pulled him to a halt. "Would you so willingly condemn yourself to living the rest of your days with a dull, ugly female just for the sake of heirs? Would you so easily give up the chance to love again?"

"Gods!" Morigan's jaw tightened with anger. "Don't speak to me of love, not so soon after Winna's—"

"She's been dead over a cycle now! Life must go on. She'd want that for you. Winna wasn't the kind of Cat Woman who'd begrudge you happiness just because she no longer could be there for you."

A hard look glittered in the depths of Morigan's eyes. "I don't expect nor want any love from this mating. The female is Bellatorian! She is and will always be my enemy. Even the remotest consideration of having to rouse my desire—" He broke off. "Don't push it, Naren," he whispered hoarsely, his gaze dropping. "There is only so much a man can bear, and I've sufficient challenge in just keeping our people alive. I trust your judgment to choose an appropriate mate for me. Let it go at that."

Naren's hand fell from his friend's arm. "And I have, my Lord. The best of the lot, by far. Come now," he added gently. "We can't finish until you claim her as your own. And I'm sure the other lucky winners grow restless even as we linger here."

"Indeed?" Morigan glanced up, a sardonic twist to his mouth. "Then, let's be done with it. I've more important matters to concern me than who'll warm my bed this winter."

He strode off, leaving Naren behind. The black-haired man stared after him for a moment, then chuckled. "Poor fool," he muttered half to himself as he stepped out after his friend.

"If only you knew what lies in store for you with this particular female. If only you knew . . ."

"Rissa," Diona whispered from behind her. "Perhaps you should just surrender your dagger to them. They look none too pleased with you and escape seems hopeless at any rate. There are too many of them, and you're no better with a weapon than you are on an equs. Give it up. Please."

"Hold your tongue, Diona," her mistress ordered tautly. "They'd know nothing of my abilities—or lack of them—if you'd just keep quiet. And what have I to lose? If they truly mean to take us back with them as mates . . ." She inhaled a shuddering breath. "Let them kill me now, I say. I won't let one of those filthy, disgusting beasts take control of my . . ."

Her voice faded as two Cat Men strode up, the black-haired one and another she'd never seen before. Briefly, her glance assessed the newest arrival. He looked in the prime of life, perhaps twenty-seven or twenty-eight cycles old. He was as tall as his companion, broad-shouldered and massively built, and graced with a thick, unruly, shoulder-length mane of dark-brown hair. His skin was sun-bronzed, and his muscular chest and rippling abdomen were covered with a luxurious furring of dark hair. Like the others he, too, wore only a simple, tan-colored domare-hide loincloth and soft, knee-high boots.

There was nothing commonplace about the Cat Man's face, however. Though feline in features, the exotic combination of piercing green-gold eyes, bold spade of a nose, high cheekbones, and full, sensual lips formed a most striking and virile countenance. His beard-shadowed jaw was firm, his throat powerful and pulsing with life, and the single, aureum Cat's claw dangling in the middle of his breast gleamed with a body-warmed luster.

This was their leader, Rissa realized, locking gazes with the strangely unnerving Cat Man, not the black-haired one. She swallowed hard, knowing her next words were crucial if they were to have any hope—

"Well, what do you think, Morigan?" the black-maned Cat Man asked. "Is she not everything I said she was? She'll make an excellent mate and fine breeder, once she's tamed."

Rissa shot the black-haired one a furious look. "Stop talking about me as if I were a piece of livestock on the auction block, you ignorant sandwart! I have a mind and voice of my own. I can talk for—"

"Give me the dagger."

She stopped short, startled by the unexpected demand from the green-eyed Cat Man. Her wary gaze swung to his. Once more, she lifted her weapon in a threatening gesture. "No. For the present, it's the only advantage I have." She paused. "Isn't there someplace we could go to speak privately? I'm certain we could work out—"

The merest hint of irritation flickered in his eyes—the only warning Rissa had. The next instant, in a blinding flash of unleashed agility, he had the dagger wrenched from her grasp and her arms twisted behind her back.

Her surprise expelled on a furious rush of air. "How dare you? Let me go, you big, slime-ridden crock of barsa dung! Let me go, I say!"

To add a decided emphasis to her pretty plea, Rissa commenced to squirm wildly in his arms, her booted feet flailing back to kick at his domare hide-covered shins. Though her hands were caught in his grip, she clawed frantically. A lucky downward swipe made contact with his abdomen, raking a deep furrow through hair-roughened skin.

Morigan inhaled a sharp breath and went rigid. "Stop this useless struggling," he rasped angrily. "And keep your claws sheathed, or I'll show you what a real pair of claws can do." To add further emphasis to his words, he secured both of her hands in the big clasp of one of his and brought his free hand around to her face.

As the female continued to fight against him, Morigan unsheathed first one, then each of the rest of his claws. The female gasped, then froze, her gaze fixed on the lethal looking talons that had sprung from his fingertips. "That's better," he growled. "Much better."

He hadn't expected anything quite like her. She was small but exquisitely curved, her snug-fitting, blue-green riding clothes molding sensuously to her slender body. Her pale gold hair, brushed back from her face with a soft peak in the middle of her forehead, was as long and lush as any Cat Woman's.

Rare turcas stones set in silvery argentum metal dangled from her ears and hung from a twisted argentum chain about her neck. Her eyes, rich brown and flecked with gold, were shadowed by the longest, thickest dark brown lashes he'd ever seen. And her delicately boned face, set off by a pert little nose and full, rose-pink lips, bloomed with the most becoming flush of battle.

The realization he found the Bellatorian female attractive startled Morigan. He hadn't thought . . . never imagined such a possibility.

And what did it matter at any rate? She would serve her purpose well, whether pretty or plain. A breeder was a breeder.

Shoving aside further consideration of the female's unsettling physical attributes, Morigan signaled over the Cat Man who held the bonds each of the females would be secured in for the journey. He held her hands out from her body and indicated that she be bound.

The touch of the domare-hide thongs winding about her wrists jerked Rissa from her horrified fascination with the Cat Man's claws. "Nooo," she moaned. "Don't do this. We are free women, bound for Primasedes. You have no right to—"

The task of tying her complete, the tall Cat Man turned her back around to face him. He retracted his claws and grasped her arms. With a rough motion, he pulled her hard up against him.

Rissa gasped. In that first instant of contact, something electric, something wildly unexpected and shamefully exciting, arced between them. Gazing up into his eyes, she knew he'd felt it just as surely, just as strongly as she. Puzzlement, then shock, flashed in those green-gold depths before he recalled himself and that feline, inscrutable mask of his settled down in place once more.

"Listen to me, and listen well," the Cat Man named Morigan snarled. "I care not who you are, what you are, or where you were bound. I have you now, and nothing will ever be the same again. You and the other women are going with us."

He glared down at her with all the ferocity he possessed, thinking that fear would best control her. The look of utter horror gleaming in her tawny brown eyes, however, was almost his undoing. Morigan swallowed hard, recalled the splintering fragments of his self-control, and forced himself to forge on.

"Thanks to *your* men," he savagely enunciated the word, "most of us are now without mates. You and the other females, however, will soon begin to remedy that little shortcoming. Don't fight what you've no hope of prevailing against. Accept, and you'll be treated kindly. Resist, and you'll suffer my wrath."

He shoved her from him then, his breath strangely ragged, his heart thundering. She stared up at him, transfixed, her soft lips parted slightly, her pale hair a wild tumult about her.

A rage, sprung from some place he'd not known existed, flamed within Morigan. By the three moons of Agrica, how he hated her! She was everything he despised in Bellatorians—arrogant, self-engrossed, and fully expecting that all would acquiesce to her demands. She was also exquisitely, unexpectedly beautiful. That, more than anything else, astounded—and angered him.

He grabbed her by the arm, wheeled her around, and shoved her at Naren. "Finish the selection of the females. We leave in a half hour's time." With that, Morigan turned on his heel and strode away.

"And what am I to do with this yellow-haired she-cat?" Naren called after him.

"Do what you want with her! I've more important matters to concern myself with!"

The black-haired Cat Man stared after his retreating lord, a befuddled look on his face. Then, at the realization of what Morigan's strange behavior signified, he gave a low laugh. "I chose well, did I not, my friend?" he whispered. "Indeed, far beyond my wildest expectations."

With that, he turned back to the group of frightened, huddled females, smiled reassuringly at them, and signaled for the Cat Men to begin the selection of their mates.

They wouldn't let her near Diona who, after Rissa, had been the first woman to be chosen. They wouldn't let her near any of the women. After the choices had been made and the sobbing, panicked women had been led away by their new owners—or rather, new mates, as the black-haired Cat Man who finally introduced himself as Naren firmly corrected her—Naren had apologetically tied her hands over her head to a stout tree branch, explaining that Morigan, *her* new mate, would come for her when it was time to leave.

Her new mate, indeed, Rissa had fumed, humiliated beyond words at being bound like some common slave awaiting the whim of her lord and master. She would *never* submit to his commands, no matter if he slashed her to pieces with his revolting, deadly claws! And she would never, ever, be a mate to him!

He was filthy, covered with days of sweat and dirt. He was nearly naked and as hairy as some animal. He had claws. He was disgusting, loathsome—and she hated him!

Desperately, Rissa twisted in her bonds, yielding little for her efforts but an additional abrasion of her wrists. Frustration, then rising hysteria at her utter helplessness, rose in her. She felt sick and lightheaded, as if she were teetering on the edge of madness.

This couldn't be happening. One moment she was on the way to her father and a new, far happier life. The next, she was a prisoner of some half-human beast man, destined to become his breeder.

She wanted to scream, to cry, to beg them to let her go. Anything, if only it would end this waking nightmare. Yes, that's indeed what it had become . . . a nightmare.

Yet, Rissa knew, even as she wished it weren't so, that this was no dream. The thongs cut too deeply into the raw flesh of her wrists not to be real. The soft sobs of the other women, standing nearby, were too heartrending not to be real. The taint of death, of burning wagons, of the hot sun, and dry, strength-sapping breeze were . . . too . . . real . . .

After a time, everything dulled. The intensity of her fear, her frustration, her rage, drained Rissa of all will to fight. She hung there, bound to the tree, and waited.

As the sun dimmed in the sky and began its downward descent far off in the western expanse of rolling plains and distant farmlands, the Cat Men began to gather their belongings. The women, hands bound behind their backs, were led away, the booty shouldered by the aliens not encumbered by women, and the trek begun.

And, still, Rissa hung there, tied to the tree. Panic briefly surged through her at the thought of being left behind, then a fierce elation. Leave me here, she mentally defied them. Anything is better than going with you! Anything, even dying here tied to this tree.

Then, something caught the edge of her vision. A tall, lithe form—the Cat Man, curse him—swung into view. The Cat Man named Morigan.

He strode up to stand before Rissa. His glance, as full of loathing as hers, raked down her body. For a heart-stopping instant as his piercing gaze appeared to linger at the swell of her small, taut breasts, Rissa feared he'd strip her and take her right then and there. His eyes smoldered, turning to smoky jade. His unshaven jaw clenched and his mouth tightened.

Then, his head lifted. Eyes, now flat and supremely indifferent, locked with hers.

"I'd leave you here if your breeding potential didn't mean so much to my people," he finally said. "I know you despise me, see me as little more than a disgusting animal not worthy of your regard, much less anything more intimate. But hear me, and hear me well," he added, his voice pitched low, so harsh and grating it sent shivers down her spine. "I despise the thought of touching you, of joining bodies with you as much as you despise the thought of joining with me. I want *nothing* to do with you.

"But your people, *your* men," Morigan continued fiercely, as if driven by some personal demon, "have taken that choice from me and therefore, have taken it from you as well. Don't ever forget that—and don't forget what I'll do to you if you cause me any more problems. We may never be friends or lovers, but I'd like to think we can at least live out our lives together in some semblance of peace."

As he spoke, he leaned so close Rissa felt the heat emanating from his big, powerful body and smelled his musky scent which was disturbingly pungent, yet, surprisingly, not unpleasant. His presence, so potent, so primal, encompassed her until Rissa felt as if she was being swallowed alive by the sheer, overwhelming strength of the man. Her resistance crumbled, shredding into fleeting wisps of petty defiance before his masterful, mind-drugging control.

Her mind, Rissa thought dreamily, a warm lethargy weighting her thoughts and responses. That was it. Somehow, some way, he had found entrance into her mind.

The realization frightened her. Frightened her enough to sweep away the encroaching mists of her submission. Her father. He must not find out about—

The fierce Bellatorian blood, the blood of warriors, pumped more quickly, more heatedly, through her veins. Rissa jerked back, clamped shut her eyes and mentally shoved him away. "St-stop it!" she gasped. "Get out of my mind! You have no right. St-stay away!"

Morigan went taut. He dragged in a long, unsteady breath and took a step back from her. Gods, what had he done? Never had he used his psychic powers to manipulate, to control as he had just been doing with this female. He had too much respect for the freedom of the mind ever to attempt such a thing.

He stared down at her, shattered beyond belief at what she, in the short span of time since he'd first met her, had wrought in him. She stood there, helpless, her arms tied to the tree above her, trembling uncontrollably but her face resolute, fighting him in every way she could. He was struck with the sudden realization that, for all the frailty of her slender form, she possessed a spirit as indomitable as his.

The faintest ember of respect for the Bellatorian female flared in Morigan's heart. With a savage curse, he crushed it out. Untying her hands from the tree, he flung her over his shoulder and strode off in the dying light.

The journey home had begun. Home. The lair. His people. Somehow, Morigan sensed this particular journey would set into action events and emotions he'd be far wiser to turn from—if only he'd had the choice.

She couldn't take it much longer. She just couldn't. If this insolent, hardhearted, thickheaded Cat Man didn't put her down soon, Rissa didn't know what she'd do. The constant jarring from his bounding stride and rock-solid shoulder had long ago sent her abdomen and lower chest into spasms of muscle-twisting agony. When, oh, when, would they halt for a rest?

He'd not spoken to her since he'd flung her over his shoulder two hours ago. He'd never once asked as to her condition, situated as embarrassingly—and uncomfortably—as she was atop his unnerving height. They'd left behind the rest of his band, the Cat Men splitting up into smaller groups of five or six to take alternate routes back to wherever their foul and nefarious hideout must be.

The black-haired one named Naren had accompanied them, along with two other Cat Men, one young and blond and the other of middle age with gray-streaked, sandy brown hair. All but Morigan carried a large bundle of booty strapped to their backs. He, quite obviously, had his hands full with her.

As they strode along, the deepening twilight of the waning day eased gently into inky blackness, save for brilliant bits of twinkling starlight overhead. Bouncing about on her precarious perch, Rissa considered and discarded several possible approaches to dealing with her captor.

Reason wouldn't work. He was too thickheaded for that. Threats were out of the question. He was too arrogant to be intimidated by a mere woman. And appealing to his humanity was by far the most hopeless plan of all. He wasn't at all human, despite the outward similarities.

Frustration welled in Rissa. There seemed only one other recourse left her, and even the merest contemplation of it sickened her. She could try to win him over with her feminine charms and seduce him into treating her better. As inexperienced as she was in such matters, she knew, despite all the Cat Man's overt hostility toward her, that she stirred him. There was no mistaking the strange, heated response that had flared between them that time they'd touched, when standing close to each other.

But to play such a game was worse than dangerous. It invited what he'd already promised he would do. No, she didn't want to attract him further. She wanted to drive him away.

There was nothing left to do but grit her teeth and bide her time, Rissa realized, the admission only miring her deeper in misery. Bide her time, and await the first opportunity to escape. *If* she lived that long . . .

The night passed and still the Cat Men slogged on. Rissa, now all but semiconscious from the pain, found after a time she no longer cared whether she lived or died. If only the misery would leave her, she'd gladly relinquish her hold on life. It wouldn't be so bad to join her mother, wherever her spirit now called home. Her sweet, beautiful, gentle mother . . .

The memory of her, so happy, so full of life before the cruelly debilitating illness had struck her down, wrung a moan from Rissa's lips that no amount of physical pain could ever induce. And it was finally enough to bring an end to her own, unrelenting torment.

The sound, so soft and anguished, pierced the seething mists of Morigan's anger. He stopped short, suddenly acutely aware of the human burden he carried slung over his shoulder like some sack of supplies. His hands moved, grasping her more firmly, then he swung her down.

As the female's feet touched ground, his grip momentarily loosened. She sagged, her head tumbled back. She would have fallen if not for his quick reaction. With a puzzled curse, Morigan grasped her behind her legs and lifted her up in his arms.

Naren, signaled by his leader's sudden halt that something was amiss, stepped forward. "What's wrong?"

Morigan frowned and shook his head. "The female." Rising irritation threaded his voice as she sighed deeply and her head flopped down upon his chest. "She appears to be sick."

His friend peered down at her, his enhanced night vision piercing the gloom. "Perhaps, but I'd wager it has more to do with the way you were carrying her for the past four hours." He prodded her abdomen gingerly. At his touch, Rissa winced and moaned again.

"She's far too soft," Morigan growled, tamping down the swell of guilt that rose at his unthinkingly harsh treatment of her. "A Cat Woman—"

"You would've had difficulty enduring being carried head first over someone's shoulder with your hands tied behind you for four hours!" Naren snapped. "So don't blame it on the femina. I should have thought to say something a long while ago, but waited instead for her to complain." He eyed her with grudging respect. "But she's not the kind to complain, nor beg, for that matter. You've got your hands full with this one, my friend."

"I don't need your dire warnings." Morigan hefted the female more snugly to him. "Just tell me what to do to help her. I don't want her dying because of me."

The black-haired Cat Man shrugged. "Untie her." He scanned Rissa's face intently. "She looks quite comfortable now. With her hands free, I'll wager she'll sleep until daybreak."

"Do you, now?" Morigan couldn't quite keep the sarcasm from his voice. He did as his friend suggested, though. Lowering Rissa gently to the ground, he rolled her on her side and unsheathed a single claw. With one swipe of the razor-sharp talon, the thongs fell away. Ever so carefully, Morigan brought her arms around to her sides. It was then he saw the cruel gouges in her wrists, scabbed over now with her blood.

"By the three moons! Lisan," he commanded, beckoning over the young Cat Man who'd just seen his first battle today. "Bring the pack with our medical gear. This female needs her wrists cared for before they start to fester."

Lisan did as ordered. As his young assistant removed bandages and a healing salve from the pack, Morigan poured water from his flask over Rissa's wounds. The water must have stung, for she moaned again and tried to pull away. With the gentlest touch, Morigan anchored her hands in place, finishing the job of flushing out the angry red gouges, then quickly applied the smelly gray salve and bandaged her wrists.

"You really must take better care of your female," Naren chided softly as he leaned over Morigan's shoulder to inspect his handiwork. "At this rate, she'll never make it back to the lair, much less survive a night of mating with you."

Morigan shot him a black look. "Perhaps you'd do better with her? Care to give it a try?"

His friend gave a wry laugh. "A tempting offer, to be sure, but I wouldn't want to deprive you of heirs. As Lord of the Cat People, your need for offspring is far greater than mine."

"Then keep your remarks to yourself!"

Naren held up his hands in mock submission as Morigan gathered Rissa back into his arms and rose. "As you wish, my Lord. I only thought to preclude a mistake you might long regret."

"The only thing I regret is ever allowing you to choose a mate for me!" came the savage rejoinder. "Now, let's be off. We've several hours more to journey before we reach the healer's hut. And I mean to be there before sunrise."

With that, Morigan strode off into the night, the slight weight of the living burden in his arms inconsequential in comparison to his sudden realization of this newest burden of responsibility that had been added to his heart. He didn't want a female and especially not this particular one. She promised to be the worst, the most troublesome, of the lot.

Though he'd meant her no harm in carrying her slung over his shoulder, the longer he'd traveled, the more angry at her he'd become. Even carried as she'd been, treated as a virtual possession, she'd still worked her feminine wiles on him.

Her soft breasts had pressed into his back, rubbing to and fro until her nipples hardened into taut little peaks that jutted impudently against the thin fabric of her jacket. Her long hair had brushed against the backs of his legs, silky, teasing, the gossamer strands clinging to his skin like the golden webs of the famed Aranean mutant weaving spiders. And her scent, heady and haunting as the rare valleria flower that grew in the hidden mountain valleys, wafted up to him, permeating his being with her essence . . . and the unmistakably blatant reminder of her femininity.

He hadn't thought ever to desire any female again, not after having loved Winna so totally, so passionately. He'd thought any mating thereafter, necessary as it might be, would be emotionless, empty, tepid. But this female, this Bellatorian, this *enemy,* roused him as he'd never been roused before.

It was only his hatred for her that stirred him so, Morigan tried to convince himself. It was only the anticipation of the pleasure the symbolic venting of his anger at her men would give him that fired his lust. It was only the total power and control of the act, in a time when he no longer felt in control of anything, that attracted him.

He *had* to believe that. To accept any other answers would leave him vulnerable, wanting, and as malleable as clay in her hands. Hands that, in the end, were still as evil and treacherous as any other Bellatorian's.

His fingers tightened, digging into the soft flesh of her body. The female stirred and murmured something unintelligible. Her arms snaked up his chest to entwine about his neck. Then, with a drowsy, contented sound she snuggled close, her soft lips grazing the Cat's claw that hung about his neck, and fell back to sleep.

Morigan's breath caught in his throat. His heart leapt beneath his breast, began a wild beat, then finally steadied.

Curse her, he thought, his loins responding to the feel of her soft woman's body. Curse her, he implored any merciful god who might be listening. He wanted her, desired her with every fiber of his being. Wanted a female whom, though he must ultimately possess to propagate his species, he must never allow himself to need or trust. A female he had sworn never to allow to touch his emotions in any way—not even in the act of mating.

Rissa woke to the scent of man filling her nostrils. She sniffed appreciatively, never before realizing how sense-stirring that unique combination of warm flesh and masculine essence could be. She rubbed her face against the cushion of springy hair and broad, firm muscle, reveling in the comfort, the heady contentment of a rhythmically thudding heart.

Her dreams had been just as pleasant, if not more so. A wild, longhaired man, leonine of features and green-gold of eyes, had held her. He'd smiled down at her, tenderly, lovingly, as if he cherished her above all else. Not since her mother had been alive had Rissa felt such joy, such a fierce, searing love. And, yet, this love, as deep, as heartfelt as that from her mother, was different as well.

Her mother's love had been acceptance, understanding, peace. This man's love was fire, ardent desire, and an all but insatiable need that even as it satisfied, threatened never to be filled.

He was of her heart, her soul, her body. Her completion; even as she knew to love him was always to go on striving, to seek the fulfillment of one's highest aspirations.

He was everything she'd ever wanted, dreamed of, in a man.

"If you don't stop rubbing your body like that against mine," a strained voice gritted from above her, "I won't be responsible for the consequences."

The rough words, vibrating against Rissa's ear, were finally enough to jerk her to full wakefulness. Her head swung up, slamming into a hard jaw. Her fingers, locked behind a powerful neck, clenched in a spasm of fear. Her nails dug into flesh, scoring it.

"By the three moons!"

A voice, the Cat Man's voice, had ground out the harsh exclamation. Rissa's eyes snapped open. There, glaring down at her, was the man of her dreams—and her waking nightmare.

She shoved herself back, in her haste inadvertently dragging her nails down along the sides of his neck. He flinched, sucked in a deep breath, then he grasped her hands, pulled them away from him, and lowered her to her feet.

"I've had about all I can take of your claws." A deadly edge crept into his voice. "I haven't even known you a day, and already I bear the wounds of a battle like none I've ever experienced."

Rissa tossed back the hair that had tumbled into her face at his abrupt release and lifted her chin. "I didn't mean to scratch you that time. You just startled me and—"

"Fine. Your apology is accepted." He made an impatient motion for her to precede him. "Now get on with you. We've another hour of travel before we reach our destination, and the sun is already beginning to rise. You've slept most of the night away. Let's see if you can make up for it on the trail."

"A-apology? Make up for it?" Rissa's fists clenched at her sides. She took a step toward him, her chin lifting to an even more pugnacious tilt. "I'll have you know, you son of a subterranean slime worm, I've done *nothing* to make up for! On the contrary, *you're* the one who needs to apologize and make amends!"

Morigan eyed her, a thunderous expression hardening his features. "Femina, don't start."

She paused, suddenly realizing her temerity in daring to threaten a man of his size and strength. She also realized, albeit belatedly, that Naren and the other two Cat Men were watching their heated interchange with barely contained amusement.

Anger surged through her. Curse him. Curse him and all his kind! Then, with every bit of dignity she could muster, Rissa tossed her hair aside in a haughty gesture of contempt, turned on her heel, and promptly tripped over a protruding tree root. With a strangled cry, she tumbled forward, only to have her arm all but wrenched from its socket by her captor's quick reaction in halting her fall.

"Going somewhere?" he inquired silkily as he pulled her back to her feet.

"Yes." She struggled to free herself of his clasp. "Just as far away from you as I can get!"

His grasp on her arm tightened. "I think not, *sweet femina*. Not now or ever."

Rissa met his frigid gaze with an equally icy one of her own, then smiled slowly. "We'll just have to see about that, won't we?"

The hard, ruthless light glittering in the depths of his green-gold eyes was her only warning of what was to come. With a brutal jerk, the Cat Man pulled her to him. "I suppose we shall," he growled, his words low and rough and deep. "And I'm beginning to think neither of us will particularly enjoy the experience."

Three

For what seemed an eternity, they battled, eyes clashing, bodies pressing tightly together. Neither gave ground, their minds melding to slam repeatedly, one against the other. Though her mental powers were no match for his own, Rissa fought the Cat Man valiantly. Fought him until his psychic forces finally wore her down.

He was so strong. She had never met a being so powerful, so resolute—and so hateful! His essence entwined about her, warm, shamefully alluring—and relentlessly mind-seeking.

Her defenses crumbled. Her will to resist disintegrated, razed by abilities so far advanced than her own. A strange lethargy filled her.

Submit, the word echoed repeatedly in Rissa's head. *Submit, and no harm will come to you.* But even as she acquiesced, a small voice within her cried out in distress.

She was Bellatorian. Defeat was unheard of, unacceptable. She must fight back even if death were the only recourse left her. Fight . . . to the end.

Morigan sensed her decision, felt her gather all the life force left within her for the final, decisive battle—and somehow knew he'd kill her if he pressed her further. Her will was invincible; her pride was fierce. There was no hope of using his psychic abilities to bend her spirit to his.

And no way to ease the agony of the conflicts to come.

With a shuddering sigh, Morigan withdrew from the female's mind. Their mental communion, however violent, had been far too intimate for him to think of her impersonally ever again. He, too, had paid a painful price in the vicious battle of minds. Morigan now saw her more clearly, more intensely, than he'd ever seen anyone before. He vowed never to probe into her mind again, no matter the need or cause.

He stepped away when she steadied and her vision focused once more. His hands fell from her arms. And, still, she stood there, gazing up at him.

Confusion gradually transformed to realization in the tawny brown orbs lifted to him, then growing anger. "You're the most unfair, cowardly, and underhanded man I have ever met!" she gasped out finally.

Morigan's mouth twisted. "Indeed? And how so?"

"Isn't that obvious? You can't face me or fight me as one humanoid to another. Instead, you only feel safe using your vile Cat powers against me!"

"On the contrary, femina," he replied, using all the self-control at his command to contain his freshly roused anger. "Whatever is vile about me is most definitely humanoid. Like the emotions of hatred and revenge and the need to manipulate the lives of others. Perhaps I erred in using my Cat's powers in such a vilely humanoid attempt to subdue you, but it was only a momentary lapse in my more tender *Cats'* inclinations toward mercy. An inclination, you can be certain," he added acidly, "I'll try to contain in the future."

"Mercy?" Rissa cried. "You call what you just attempted mercy? Why, I've felt more mercy at the hands of a—"

"A most interesting topic, this discussion of mercy," Naren interjected dryly as he strode over to stand before them. "But be that as it may, you two will have the rest of your lives to debate who is at fault and for what. In the meanwhile, the rest of us are exhausted and would like to reach Zada's some-time today. Preferably before it's light enough for any Bel-latorian patrols to spot us."

Morigan swung around, a stinging retort hovering on his lips. Then, as he noted his friend's raised brow and amused twist to his mouth, thought better of it. He motioned over Lisan.

The blond Cat Man ran up, his blue eyes bright with eager expectation. "Yes, my Lord? How can I be of service?"

For an instant, Morigan nearly regretted his decision to foist the female on the younger man. Lisan was but eighteen cycles, fully grown in body, but his heart was as yet untem-pered in life's harsh forge. If she had a mind for it, she could flay him alive.

But his own tolerance was at an end, and he feared for his control. He'd gone over twenty-four hours without sleep, led and fought a battle, and then had to endure the company of the most unsettling and upsetting female he'd ever had the misfortune to encounter. There was only so much a man could bear. Lisan would have to fend for himself for the next hour.

"The female is your responsibility until we reach Zada's," Morigan rasped, indicating her. "Have a care. She's a crafty one and intent on escaping."

The young Cat Man's eyes widened, then he bobbed his head in avid assent. "I'll guard your mate with my life, my Lord. No harm will come to her while on my watch."

At the word "mate," Morigan saw the female's eyes nar-row, but she didn't say a word. Instead, she extended a hand to Lisan. "My name is Rissa," she purred sweetly. "And yours?"

Puzzlement clouded the young Cat Man's eyes, and he shot Morigan a questioning glance. Then, quickly composing himself, he took Rissa's hand in both of his own and patted it. "Lisan. My name is Lisan, my Lady. Your devoted servant."

She shot Morigan a triumphant look. He scowled back, then turned and strode away. Taking the lead, Morigan motioned for Naren to fall into step beside him. When they were sufficiently out of earshot of Rissa and Lisan, with the fourth Cat Man, Brandar, bringing up the rear, Morigan glanced over at his friend. "Are you happy yet? I'd thought my life was already sufficiently in turmoil but, in just the course of one day, you've managed to all but send me plummeting into the depths of madness."

Naren chuckled. "You've just forgotten the sweet insanity of dealing with a comely female. In time, you'll adapt to it again."

"But you don't seem to realize," Morigan gritted, "I don't *want* to adapt. I despise her. We will never be compatible. Never!"

"Then, enjoy her for the pleasures of her delectable body."

"*Enjoy* her? Are you mad?"

His friend shrugged. "Do you deny you don't find her attractive? That she hasn't already stirred your blood?"

Morigan flushed. "Oh, she stirs my blood all right. To a murderous rage."

"I can see we've touched on a delicate subject here. One that bears further discussion."

"There'll be no more discussion on this subject, do you hear me? You've already meddled far more than is tolerable!" With that the Lord of the Cat People thundered off, leaving the rest of his party far behind.

As sunrise brushed the rolling hills and valleys in delicate shades of rose and lilac, they came upon the solitary hut of Zada the healer. Morigan paused in the shelter of a thick grove of robur trees to allow the others to join him, all the while taking the greatest care not to glance Rissa's way. "Lisan," he said when the young Cat Man drew to a halt before him, "cloak yourself and scout out the hut and surrounding area. We'll wait here until your return."

The Cat Man nodded, wheeled about, and loped away, his form gradually fading from view. Rissa stared after him, her eyes widening in disbelief as Lisan disappeared. She turned back to discover Morigan's gaze upon her.

"You find our powers unnerving."

She bristled at his calm, flat statement. "Who wouldn't? Everything about you Cat People is shocking."

His mouth drew into a ruthless, forbidding line. "At least we don't use them against those less gifted for purposes of treachery and murder."

"Indeed?" Rissa arched a dark blond brow. "And what do you call the use of your powers to attack our caravan? An act of charity?"

"A necessary means to an end. No more, no less."

"And that end is?" she asked, casually glancing away.

"Survival."

The heavy lashes shadowing Rissa's cheeks flew up. Her gaze swung back to him. "Survival? I don't understand?"

"Don't you?" Just then, Lisan uncloaked a few meters away. "Well," Morigan snapped, "that's another story. One I've no patience for today."

With that, he walked off to meet his young compatriot, effectively dismissing her. "What did you find?" he demanded of Lisan when the Cat Man drew up before him.

"Just the healer Zada, humming to herself over some simmering pot of herbs. If my keen sense of smell served me well, the other pot on the fire held a fine lepus stew. And no one else seemed about for kilometers. It's safe for us to approach."

"Good." Morigan motioned the others forward. "Let's go. I've a need for rest, but first, a bowl of Zada's savory stew would set well with me."

"As it would with all of us," Naren agreed cheerfully, taking Rissa by the arm to urge her after his leader.

She shot the black-haired Cat Man an irritated glance, then, with a sigh, accepted his presumptuous handling. She'd better get used to it, Rissa reminded herself glumly. There would most likely be a lot more unwanted hands on her before she finally made good her escape.

Priorities being what they were, however, a bowl of lepus stew sounded pretty appealing right now. In all the excitement, she'd not eaten in almost a day. And, since it now appeared she was going to live, she might as well keep up her strength. There was no telling when she'd next need it.

After a hearty meal of stew, rich with thick chunks of roast lepus and several varieties of tasty root vegetables, fresh baked bread, and some unfermented uva juice, the four Cat Men took up guard positions outside the windows and doors of the hut and promptly fell asleep. As the sun rose into the heavens and the day burned on, Rissa sat there, too angry to rest, and watched old Zada work.

The Cat Men meant to guard more than their own lives by sleeping where any unexpected sound would rouse them, Rissa fretted. Their positions also blocked all escape routes from the hut. All *her* escape routes, to be exact. Sound asleep as they were, Rissa knew they'd immediately waken if she moved one hair past the threshold of the door or sill of the three windows. She'd seen enough in the short time she'd been with them to have the utmost respect for their Cat powers.

There must be some way to escape, though. Rissa only

wished she'd stumble upon it soon, before she drew even further from Primasedes. There was nothing she could do for the other women, save reach the capital as soon as possible and bring back help. Yet, to leave them for even a short time to such a fate . . .

Rissa glanced up at the sky. By the position of the sun, she calculated they had journeyed almost due north from the Agrican capital. If her hunch was right, they were headed toward the distant mountains. It would seem the perfect environs for a hideout.

And nearly impossible to be found in, once she was taken there.

But how to take the crafty Cat Men unawares, much less make good an escape? Rissa's glance swung back to where the old healer labored, crushing dried herbs into a fine powder between two stones. The woman was definitely of a fully humanoid Agrican race, her skin tanned to a deep, leathery bronze color from years beneath the unrelenting sun, her close-cropped hair bleached white. Where, Rissa mused, did her loyalties lie?

Rissa picked up the stool she sat upon and moved closer to Zada and the table. "Er, how long have you known the Cat Men?"

Zada graced her with a quick look, then went back to her herbs. "These in particular, or the Cat People in general?"

That question gave Rissa pause. She shrugged. "The Cat People, I suppose."

"All my life. Every spring and summer their various clans would pass by my hut in their periodic moves to follow the game. And, then in the autumn, I'd see most of them once more as all the clans headed to the forest to make their big winter camp." The healer smiled sadly. "I even stayed with them one winter, when a grass fire burned down my home.

The next spring, a band of Cat Men ventured out and rebuilt my hut. It was a grand time for me, though, spending long winter evenings snug in their lodges deep in the forest. I remember well the feasting, the storytelling, singing, and dancing."

She glanced back up at Rissa. "They were once a huge nation, proud and free, harming none and taking only what they needed to survive. Then the Bellatorian invaders came to Agrica."

Warmth flooded Rissa's face. "I'm Bellatorian, you know."

Something flickered in the old woman's eyes. "Yes, I suspected that. Why are you with them?"

"I didn't come willingly, if that's what you're thinking," Rissa hotly replied. "They attacked the merchants' caravan I was traveling with to Primasedes. The Cat Men were vicious, killing every Bellatorian soldier, driving off the merchants, and looting and burning the wagons. And they took all the women—twelve of us—captive."

"Indeed?" Zada paused to open a pottery bowl and pour her ground herbs into it. She covered it with a lid, wiped clean the grinding stones, then laid a fresh supply of dried leaves between the two stones. Once more, her hands moved in the rhythmic, rolling motion that crushed the herbs. "I wondered what the solution to their tragic problem would be. This action of theirs doesn't surprise me. Desperate people do desperate things."

Rissa's brow furrowed in puzzlement. "What do you mean? What tragedy befell the Cat People?"

"He didn't tell you then, did he?"

"Who?"

"Morigan, the Lord of the Cat People. Ever since the death of his father a cycle ago, he has been their leader."

"No," Rissa replied slowly, "he didn't. He doesn't care to tell me much of anything." Her gaze lifted. "Will you?"

Zada shrugged. "If you wish." Her rheumy gray eyes clouded for a moment with memories. Then, she sighed. "A cycle ago the Cat People gathered at their winter sanctuary in the Ardennen Forest. They put up their lodges, gathered in the grain and foodstuffs they'd traded for all summer, and then a large party of Cat Men, about three hundred strong, left for the annual autumn hunt. It was then they always brought back the game to be put up to last the winter.

"While they were away the Bellatorian army attacked the winter camp, slaughtering every man, woman, and child who had remained behind, burning their lodges, and destroying almost all of their food supplies. Morigan returned to find his family dead, as well as almost twenty-seven hundred of his people. Returned as well, to assume the leadership of the remaining four hundred or so Cat People."

The blood drained from Rissa's face. "Are you saying my people cold-bloodedly murdered all those Cat People? But my fa—"

She stopped herself before she revealed that her father had been Lord Commander of Agrica a cycle ago when this slaughter was supposed to have taken place. "There must have been some terrible mistake. The Bellatorian Lord Commander would never permit such a horrible thing to happen. Perhaps the Cat Men lied. Perhaps they were the ones who attacked the Bellatorians and instigated the battle . . ."

"You can believe what you wish." The healer's calm gaze locked with Rissa's. "I saw the remains of their forest home. I saw what was left of the bodies and the funeral pyres. And I am Agrican. Of course, I will view things differently than you."

"Do you view the abduction and intended rape of innocent

women to aid in the Cat People's procreation differently as well?" Rissa demanded, rising to her feet. "Do you think my body should be sacrificed to some slavering Cat Man because of a war between Bellator and Agrica?"

Zada stared up at her. "Aren't women always the innocent victims when men go to war? But no, I don't think it's right, not in this case or ever."

A wild hope sprang in Rissa's breast. "Then, you'll help me? You won't let them take me back to their lair?"

The healer frowned. "You ask me to make a choice between you and the Cat Men. I won't do that. I understand their need. It is deep and desperate."

"And what of my need, my desperation?"

The old woman put down her stone. "What are you afraid of? The Cat People are good and kind."

"I don't want to be forced to mate with—with some loathsome stranger against my will!" Rissa whispered hoarsely. "And I don't want to bear an alien's child! How will I ever be able to go back to my own kind with a half-breed babe at my breast?"

Zada considered that for a long moment. "It *would* be very difficult." She rose from the table and walked over to a wooden cabinet. Opening the door, she extracted another covered pottery jar.

"The Cat People are my friends. I refuse to interfere in their efforts to rebuild their nation." She turned back to Rissa. "I will, however, give you something to suppress your fertility for a time." Zada smiled kindly. "Or, at least, suppress it long enough to allow you the opportunity to learn more of these people and come to love your mate."

"Never!" Rissa exclaimed in horror. "I'll never, *ever* come to love Morigan! And I'll never submit to him as my mate!"

"Well, be that as it may, this powder will keep you sterile

for five to six weeks." The old woman poured a small amount into a cup and added a healthy splash of water. After mixing it thoroughly, Zada handed the cup to Rissa. "Drink. It may not be much, but it is all I can or will do for you. If things don't work out between you and the young lord, at least you won't leave carrying his child."

Rissa accepted the cup. This concoction, if it truly worked, could buy her up to six weeks of infertility. Not the full extent of what she needed, but some control of her fate nonetheless. No matter what the Cat Lord did to her, he wouldn't be able to get her pregnant. And that mattered to him more than anything else.

She downed the contents of the cup, then placed it back on the table. "I thank you for your kindness. This will at least grant me additional time."

"Yes, I suppose it will." Zada hesitated. "There is one favor I would ask of you in return."

"And that is?"

"Give Morigan a chance. Give his people a chance. They are not so very different when the physical dissimilarities are set aside. Observe with your heart instead of your mind. The heart can be a potent arbitrator in determining what's of value and what's worthless."

"It's hard to feel kindly toward some alien who thrusts himself into your life, treats you harshly, and then flatly informs you he intends to force himself on you for the sole purpose of getting you with his child." For the first time since the caravan had been attacked, tears stung Rissa's eyes. "He has all but ruined my life—and I've absolutely no say, no control anymore! I-I can't help it. I hate him!"

She swiped away the tear that trickled down her cheek, both angry and frightened by her sudden display of weakness. Now wasn't the time to lose her nerve. *He* would like it all too well if she broke down and became a frail, weepy female. He would have won the first victory in the battle for her ultimate submission. And she'd die before she ever surrendered to him—in any way.

"I'm weary. My tolerance is at an end." Rissa glanced around. "Is there somewhere I might make a bed? The Cat Men are sure to set out as soon as it grows dark."

"And sure to travel all night as well," Zada smilingly added. She motioned to a small alcove enclosed by a threadbare curtain. "My boxbed is yours to use, if you wish. I will waken you when the Cat Men rouse."

Rissa's smile was warm with gratitude. "My thanks. Your bed would be most welcome." She walked over to the alcove, then turned. "I don't wish you to think I haven't taken your words to heart, Zada. I cannot promise, though, I'll ever make peace with the Cat Man Morigan." A troubled light flared in her eyes. "There is just something about him . . ."

The old woman nodded. "Indeed there is. Something that has been deeply and most painfully buried for the past cycle. Something, it seems," she added wonderingly, "you have stirred to life once again."

"I hope you rested well," Morigan snapped six hours later as they made preparations to set out once more. "We've a hard night of travel and mean to reach the foothills of the Serratus Mountains by dawn."

Rissa stiffened, stung by the tone of contempt she was certain she heard in his voice. "Think I'm too soft to keep up, do you?"

"More or less," came the dry rejoinder. "Care to prove me wrong?"

She laughed. "In most instances, yes. But, in this case, if

I begin to lag behind, feel free to go on without me. I'd hate to jeopardize your strict timetable."

"Indeed?" Unexpectedly, a lazy smile lifted the corners of the Cat Man's mouth. "You'd like that, wouldn't you? But I think not, femina. If the pace gets to be too much for you, I'll just heft you back over my shoulder like before. You did enjoy that, didn't you?"

Rissa scowled. "You know I didn't, you foul-minded, sleazy—"

Morigan turned to his second-in-command. "Unappreciative little she-cat, isn't she? Lucky for her, I'm in a better mood after a good rest and meal in my belly. And feeling very generous in sharing her sweet company with my friends." He indicated Rissa. "Why don't you begin the journey by guarding her, Naren? You two should have a lot to talk about, shouldn't you?"

The black-haired Cat Man cocked his head in consideration. "Yes, I suppose we do. Like you, for instance."

His friend's smile thinned. "Just try and remember whose side you're on, will you?"

Naren's gray eyes lit in amusement. "But of course, my Lord. It *is* the Cat People's, is it not?"

A muscle twitched in Morigan's jaw. "Yes, always." He wheeled around and strode over to Zada. "Fare you well, old friend." He smiled down at her in tender leave-taking. "Your hospitality, as always, was deeply appreciated."

"It is here for you whenever you desire it." Zada paused, her glance flitting briefly to where Rissa stood. "The femina. Go gently with her. She is proud, but beneath her defiance she is afraid, unsure. You have all the power. Wield it with compassion, and you may reap more than you ever dared dream possible."

At her words, a haunted look flared in Morigan's eyes,

then was firmly extinguished. "There is nothing left me to dream about, much less reap, save the rescue of my people from certain extinction. That, and my revenge. I want only her obedience. Once she learns that, she'll find our treatment of her far more humane than her people's treatment of us ever was."

"Yet, what will you have in the end if you succeed as you envision?" the old healer asked. "A spirit-broken female who lies submissively beneath you each time you mate? A mother of your children who has nothing of the joy of life left to share with them? A Lady of the Cat People who bears them no love or concern?" Her hand gripped his arm. "Is that what you want, Morigan? Is that truly enough for you?"

Beneath her fingers, the Cat Man's arm tightened, his hand fisting, the muscles bulging with the effort to contain himself. Zada's glance lifted once more to eyes gone storm dark with the wild emotions that roiled within the man. She stood there a moment longer, struck by the intense anguish that drove such an inward battle. Then, with a sad sigh, Zada stepped away.

"You must let it go, sooner or later," she whispered, "or buy that dearly desired revenge with your very soul. Remember that, my friend."

A hard, wracking shudder vibrated through Morigan, then was gone. He forced a wan smile to his lips. "I'll remember, Zada. I swear."

"Good." She patted him on the cheek. "Then, I know the femina will be safe with you."

At the reminder of Rissa, Morigan shook his head in wry amusement. "You always were the optimist."

Zada laughed. "Get on with you now. You've a long journey ahead, and I've herbs yet to gather."

Morigan dipped his head once more in farewell, then

turned and strode away. Passing Naren and Rissa, he paused to retrieve one of the large packs of booty, then continued on.

The black-maned Cat Man smiled. "You disturb him, you know," he said, turning to Rissa.

"Do I, now? Then all my efforts haven't been in vain." She shot him a self-satisfied glance. "Shall we be going?"

"Most definitely." Naren motioned her forward, then fell into step beside her.

They walked in companionable silence for a time, enjoying the deepening shadows that crept across the grassy hills and the mellow warmth of the setting sun sinking beyond the distant horizon in the west. It was a tranquil, breeze-softened evening.

Rissa was struck by the realization that, even in some of life's most trying times, there were still unexpected moments of peace and beauty. Moments to cling to when life's harsher, more unsettling aspects reared their ugly heads, she thought, catching a quick glimpse of the Cat Lord's tall, broad shouldered form up ahead before he once more vanished from sight down the far side of yet another hill.

"Tell me of yourself." Naren's deep voice intruded into her suddenly glum reverie. "Why did you come to Agrica?"

Rissa shot him a startled glance. "And why would you care? Isn't it enough I serve my purpose as a breeder? I'm the enemy, after all."

"As our females and children were enemy to Bellator?"

"Precisely."

Naren smiled and shook his head. "Before we captured you, you were enemy. Now, you are one of us. We will protect you and care for you as we would one of our own females. And you, above all, because you are the mate of our lord."

The impulse to tell him exactly what she thought of that singular honor rose to Rissa's lips, but she squelched the harsh rejoinder. As naive as Naren was in imagining his simple explanation was sufficient to ease her concerns—or negate her intent to escape—he meant it as an overture of friendship. The black-haired Cat Man was as unlike his lord as any two of the same species could be. Where Naren appeared easygoing, kind, and open-minded, Morigan was tense, bitter, and as unyielding as they came.

"He wasn't always that way, you know."

Rissa's head snapped around. She stared up at her companionable guard in puzzlement. Then, realization dawned.

"Really," she muttered, flushing crimson, "I do wish you'd stay out of my head. It's not . . . not moral to intrude into another's thoughts without her permission."

Naren had the good grace to flush in turn. "I beg pardon, femina. It's just so easy, and I was curious as to your feelings about Morigan. I was the one responsible for choosing you for him, you know. I can't help but hope your mating will be successful."

"I suppose it will be," Rissa sighed, "if my opinion on the matter isn't an issue. Which, of course, it never has been, has it? You men put your heads together long ago and made that decision for us women, didn't you?" She cocked her head as they walked along, her curiosity getting the better of her. "Are you Cat Men always so arbitrary?"

"Only when we've no other choice. Only when we're desperate."

"Do you know how sick and tired I am of hearing that? What about my choice? My desperation? Contrary to what you may believe, mating with a Cat Man, no matter how royal he may be, isn't my concept of the ideal life."

"One's concepts can change," Naren replied calmly, "given the right circumstances—and male."

"Well, it most certainly isn't your fine and haughty lord,

let me assure you! Sorry to prick a hole in that little dream," Rissa burst out in sudden exasperation at the Cat Man's stolid conviction to the contrary, "but if you'd bothered to consult me, I could have told you that from the start."

Naren shrugged. "Perhaps I erred, but my hope is still intact until you and Morigan have more of an opportunity to spend time together, relax, and get to enjoy each other's company. Then, we'll talk more on this subject. In the meanwhile, I ask again. Why did you come to Agrica?"

"Why else?" Rissa muttered, ready to answer his question and drop the whole unpleasant subject. "To start a new life."

The Cat Man grinned. "Good. And start one you shall, if not in a manner quite to your original plans. You see, it *was* fate that brought us to your caravan. We needed you and you were ready—"

A low whistle attuned only to his ears pierced the stillness. Naren stopped, pulling Rissa to a halt.

"What is it?" she asked, noting the look of tense vigilance on his face.

"A signal. Morigan has come upon some danger and alerted us to it."

"Who? Where?" A sudden thought struck her. It could be Bellatorians out searching for her. Before her captor realized her intent, Rissa swung about and rammed her elbow deep into his abdomen. The Cat Man gasped, doubled over, releasing her arm.

It was all the opportunity she needed. Grabbing his blaster, Rissa swung it into position, backed off several steps, and aimed it at the three Cat Men. They froze, eyeing her warily.

"Let me pass," Rissa said. "I mean you no harm. I only want to return to my people."

"W-we can't let you go, femina," Naren gritted, straightening. "You're our l-lord's mate. We vowed to guard you with our life. Use the blaster, or surrender it."

She hadn't meant to hurt him so badly, Rissa thought in sudden and surprising remorse, noting the strained look on Naren's face, but there was no other choice. *They* had given her no other choice. Just as their stubborn refusal now to move aside forced her to kill them.

Rissa lifted the blaster and slid her finger over the firing mechanism. Her gaze locked with Naren's. A mixture of resolute determination and disappointment gleamed in his gray eyes. Determination to uphold his word to Morigan, disappointment in her.

Anger flooded Rissa. How dare he look at her that way? How dare he be disappointed in her? She was Bellatorian. What did he expect her to do? Indeed, what else *could* she do?

Give them a chance. Zada's words echoed suddenly in Rissa's mind. *They are not so very different . . .*

The anger fled her in one debilitating rush. Her shoulders sagged. "I can't do it," she muttered, disgusted at her lack of heart for a warrior's task. "I—"

A strong arm snaked about her waist, jerking her back into a rock-hard body. The blaster was ripped from her clasp and flung aside. Rissa froze, knowing him even before she turned to look into his face, recognizing the deep voice that snarled harshly in her ear.

"By the three moons," Morigan ground out, "we all stand in the gravest danger, and you choose this moment to attack my men? I swear to you. Just as soon as I get the chance, I'm going to teach you something of obedience you'll not long forget!"

Four

Morigan flung Rissa to Lisan. "Bind and gag her. A camp of Atrox trackers lies just over the next hill, and it's obvious to me none of you are capable of controlling her any other way." Then, he wheeled about to lock gazes with Naren. "Why didn't you give the command to cloak? She could have killed you all!"

Naren shrugged. "It was a risk. I know that. But if we'd cloaked, I'd never have had the opportunity to test the depths of her humanity or discover how far she'd have followed her Bellatorian teachings. Now, I know."

"And an earthshaking revelation it was, I'm sure," his lord snarled. "From now on, save your study of Rissa until we're safe in the lair. These experiments of yours are fast becoming far too dangerous."

His friend glanced over at a bound and gagged Rissa, who glared indignantly back at him. "Perhaps you're right. I just feel a responsibility . . ." Naren let the words die. Squaring his shoulders, he swung back to Morigan. "How many Atroxes await us? I assume you plan to eliminate them?"

"Fifteen," Morigan muttered. "There are fifteen and they're heavily armed. And evidently out on some tracking mission. I'd wager the bounty on the Cat Men has suddenly risen again."

A frustrated anger filled him. Would it never end? Would they never be able to live in peace without the constant worry of vicious trackers finding and attacking them? The Atroxes were some of the most dangerous hunters on Agrica, huge, swarthy, wolfish-faced mutants renowned for their savage cruelty and peerless tracking abilities, and for the fact their loyalty always lay with the highest bidder. The Lord Commander, Fautor Lindatees, had sent them. There was no other reason for the Atroxes to be out here, so close to the Serratus Mountains.

"We have to kill them," Morgan forced himself to continue. "The others of our battle party are out there with the females. We may be the only ones who know of the Atroxes. And, because of that, the only ones who have a chance against them."

Naren frowned. "Well, four against fifteen are rather heavy odds. We've only three blasters between us."

"Only three of us are going after the Atroxes. Lisan will stay behind with Rissa. I want her taken back to the lair. Not one of the twelve females must be lost, no matter what happens to us."

The black-haired Cat Man eyed him. "It would be better if you stayed behind with her. You are Lord—"

"Lisan is too unseasoned yet to take on Atroxes!" Morgan cut him off angrily. "And Lord or no, I'll not sit back here and passively await the outcome of a battle. You need me, Naren, and well you know it!"

"Yes, we need you," his friend admitted. "But we need you to lead us as well. Despite your doubts to the contrary, you're the living symbol of our people, of our pride, and fierce determination to survive at all costs. If, on top of everything else that has befallen us of late, something should happen to you . . ."

Morigan stepped closer to grasp Naren by the arm. "I know. But I know as well I cannot stand back and let others carry the burden. We need every Cat Man we have, and while I'm still young and strong and able . . ."

Their gazes met and held for the span of several seconds, then Morigan released Naren's arm. "Lisan." He gestured to the small stand of boulders nearby. "Take Rissa over there and hide her. Stand guard until we come back. If we don't, set out with her by another route and get her to the lair. Get her to the lair at all costs."

The young Cat Man nodded his acquiescence. "It will be done as you ask, my Lord."

"Good." Morigan motioned for Brandar to join them. "We should be back within a few hours, if we're coming back." He spared one final glance at Rissa, standing beside Lisan, then turned and loped away.

She watched as the three Cat Men climbed the first hill and disappeared slowly from view. Anger filled her. Anger at the gross unfairness of her fate, at being bound and gagged, at Morigan of the arrogant mien and piercing, unnerving eyes.

In that last moment before he'd turned away, the look he'd given her had sent a current of intense awareness rippling through Rissa. His eyes, for the briefest moment, had warmed once more to smoky jade. Then there'd followed a smoldering farewell, a puzzled regret, a haunted hunger.

Rissa shuddered at the memory. It was too much to fathom, much less bear. Life had suddenly become so intense and confusing, sending her emotions spinning wildly, chaotically out of control. And all thanks to the most infuriating, enigmatic, and frightening of Cat Men.

* * *

It was deep into the night before Brandar came for them, appearing out of the darkness without sound or movement. Lisan, who had evidently been aware of his approach, rose and walked over to speak with him. Their voices were pitched too low for Rissa's ears, but from the tension threading them, she knew something had gone wrong.

Finally, Lisan returned and helped her to her feet. "We must go. The Atroxes have been destroyed, but Naren was severely injured. Brandar will take us to them."

They immediately set out, both men shouldering the bags of booty and supplies. Lisan walked on one side of her, Brandar on the other. Through the blackened night they went, traveling as quickly as Rissa's pace would allow. They skirted the edge of the Atrox camp, the dying embers of a fire illuminating the gory scene of death and destruction.

Some of the mutant trackers had been killed where they sat about the campfire, most likely anticipating a slice of the side of domare still roasting there. Others, alerted in time by the deaths of their compatriots, had opportunity to reach their blasters and take cover, though, they, too, had fallen to the Cat Men's determined assault.

The last few bodies lay far from camp and were the ones they passed closely by as they moved along. Those, Rissa suspected from the claw marks that slashed their bodies, had met the Cat Men in hand-to-hand combat. With a shudder of revulsion, she turned away and hurried past.

A kilometer beyond the Atrox camp, Brandar motioned them off to the right. There, its mouth half-hidden by a large boulder and thick stand of bushes, lay a cave. As they drew close to its entrance, Rissa caught a faint glow emanating from within. Then, she was being pulled inside, around a sharp turn and into a large cavern.

A perpetual light box illuminated the stone-hollowed

room, bathing its occupants in a soft, blue-violet light. Rissa's glance swept the cave and found Morigan bending over a body.

She squirmed in the two Cat Men's clutches, begging, with her eyes, to be unbound and released. Lisan eyed her uncertainly. "My Lord." His gaze lifted to where Morigan knelt. "Your lady wishes us to free her. Is it permissible?"

The Cat Lord turned. An anguished pair of green-gold eyes met Rissa's, saw the honest concern burning there, and nodded. "Yes, free her. Perhaps she has some knowledge of healing we can use."

The gag was removed, the bonds fell away, and Rissa was at Morigan's side. Sinking to her knees, she gazed down at Naren. He was unconscious, which was a blessing Rissa quickly realized as she scanned his blood-smeared body. His face was slashed and several gaping wounds on his arms and legs, crudely bandaged, oozed continuously. But it was the charred blaster injury to Naren's chest, Rissa realized as she gingerly lifted the cloth that hid it from view and peeked beneath, that was the most severe—and potentially fatal.

Nausea roiled through her. She dropped the bandage back in place as if burned. Her gaze met Morigan's. In their tormented depths, she saw the confirmation of her own fears.

"He took the blast meant for me," the Cat Man rasped. "It was aimed at my head and . . . and he threw himself in front of me just as the Atrox fired. Naren lives still, though barely. I would have died instantly." He grabbed her arm, his grip tight. "Can you save him? Do you know the healing arts?"

A sense of utter helplessness flooded Rissa. He didn't understand the life she'd once lived, pampered, her every whim seen to, and her education limited to the skills deemed necessary for a lady of breeding. Skills that had never included soiling one's hands in another's blood or other body secretions.

Rissa shook her head. "No, I've no knowledge of the healing arts. I'm sorry. But, if you tell me what to do, I'll help you."

Disappointment flared in Morigan's eyes, then was shuttered behind a thick wall of frustrated fury. "You're not of much use for anything, are you, save to cause trouble?"

She reared back as if struck. By the five moons, would he never cease his cruelties toward her? It wasn't her fault she lacked the knowledge . . .

"I wasn't meant for the harsh life you've so callously thrust me into," Rissa snapped. "And you've only yourself to blame for that. But, now that you have, it's your responsibility to teach me what I need to know to survive in your world. Not continue to berate and abuse me for it!"

Shame filled Morigan. As much as he hated to admit it, Rissa was right. And she, despite her ignorance in such things, despite what they'd done to her, had been willing to help. Instead of accepting whatever she could give, he'd flung her offer back in her face.

His eyes lowered, his long hair cascading about his face. "Fine," he hissed through clenched teeth, the act of even appearing to need a Bellatorian's assistance making his gut clench, "I can use the help." He lifted his gaze. "He's my best friend."

Rissa inhaled a ragged breath. The raw, primitive grief burning in Morigan's eyes tore through her. With the greatest of efforts, she recalled who he was and the true reality of her situation. They were enemies, alien one to the other. To attempt to bridge the chasm between them would only set into motion the most fearful of consequences—for the both of them.

She acknowledged his grudging acceptance of her help with a clipped nod of her head. "Fine. Why don't we just forget the personal hostilities for the time being and direct our efforts to Naren?" She motioned toward the bandages and containers lying nearby. "What have you done so far?"

"Not much," he admitted. "When I attempted to cleanse his wounds, it caused him so much pain I feared going on. He just blacked out a few minutes ago. I suppose it's best if we clean and treat him now."

"Yes, that would seem the most likely course of action." Frantically, Rissa searched her memory for any shred of information that might be useful. "I think it best, as well, to cut away any ruined flesh," she added, recalling something mentioned in passing after one particular vicious battle against the planet Aguilan when she was a child, "then flush the wounds well with water and apply a healing powder."

Rissa shot a quick glance over her shoulder at the packs. "Do you have more of that powder you used on my wrists?" She held up her hands, the skin of her wrists all but healed. "It has worked wonders. Surely, it would help Naren as well."

"Yes, we do in that tan pack over there." Relief flooded Morigan at having the burden of Naren's care shared. He managed a quick, taut smile. "You seem to know more than you realize. We'll do exactly as you suggest."

Rissa clamped down on an answering smile and rose to retrieve the healing powder and additional bandages from the pack as well as a domare-hide flask of water. Together, they worked on Naren's wounds. An hour later, he lay there cleansed and freshly bandaged.

With a deep sigh, Rissa rocked back on her heels and flung the sweat-damp locks off her face. "We've cared for him as best we can. I only wish there was something we could give him for the pain when he wakens. His wounds . . . they will hurt him fiercely."

Morigan considered her statement. "It would be too difficult, not to mention extremely dangerous, to take Naren back to Zada's. Before we attacked the Atroxes, we overheard them talking about other tracking parties about in the area. The sooner we get to the safety of the mountains, the better. But I'll send Brandar back to Zada's for additional supplies— and some potion to ease Naren's pain. We're only three hours from the healer's hut, and we won't be moving anywhere for some time."

He motioned over the older Cat Man, uttered a few terse commands, then sent Brandar on his way. Then, after several more minutes of intense thought, Morigan called on Lisan.

The blond Cat Man hurried over. "Yes, my Lord?"

"Naren is too badly injured to travel, and there aren't enough of us to move him through the mountains. Go to the lair and bring back four more Cat Men, a litter, and the healer, Agna. Warn the lair, as well, of the other Atrox tracking parties about. We'll await you here."

Lisan leaped to his feet, a fierce excitement burning in his deep blue eyes. "It will be as you ask, my Lord. I won't fail you!"

"Lisan, a moment," Morigan cautioned, climbing to his feet. He strode over and grasped his young compatriot by the shoulders. "Have a care. A heavy responsibility lies on you—Naren's life and perhaps ours, as well—that you bring back help as quickly as possible. But in no way endanger the secrecy or safety of the lair in your attempt to aid us. Do you understand? And if you're captured—"

"I know what I must do, my Lord," Lisan cut him off proudly. "I won't betray our lair—or your trust in me."

"Good." Morigan released him and stepped back. "I knew I chose well in bringing you along." He extended his hand in the traditional Imperium salutation. They clasped, arm to arm, held tightly for a brief instant, then released each other. Lisan turned and left the cave.

"You sent him out there alone, with nothing, not a blaster or even a water flask!" Rissa protested. "How can you expect him—"

"He's a Cat Man, one of the finest of our young," Morigan silenced her. "He can find water easily whenever he needs it, and the blaster would only slow him down. It also," he added, "can't be cloaked, if Lisan needs to do so. And his cloaking ability, combined with his acute hearing and vision, are the best protections he has. He'll be all right."

A sudden thought struck him. "You seem surprisingly concerned after our welfare of late. Why is that?"

Heat flooded Rissa's face. "I wish you no harm. Besides," she mumbled, averting her gaze, "Naren and Lisan have been kind to me."

"Not like my treatment of you has been."

She jerked her head up and met his piercing look squarely. "No, not like you have treated me."

Morigan eyed her for a long, heated moment, then turned away. He walked over and sat beside Naren, leaning back against the cave's rock wall. "I've my reasons. Reasons for which I certainly don't owe you, a Bellatorian, an explanation."

"And entirely justifiable they are, I'm sure," Rissa mockingly agreed. "After all, neither I nor the other women are anything to you but pieces of chattel. There's no need to consider our feelings in any of this."

He shot her a narrowed glance. "Don't start, femina. I can't deal with your sharp little tongue just now. You've helped me with Naren. For that I am grateful. But if you continue to prick at me, I swear I'll gag and bind you again.

"Why not take out a few blankets from one of the packs and get some rest?" he asked, trying to modulate the harshness of his voice as he struggled with his rising anger. "It's been a trying time for the both of us, these past two days. Just let it be, at least for now."

Morigan was exhausted, more emotionally than physically, Rissa realized, and near the end of his tolerance. She knew a few more well-chosen words could easily send him past the limits of his control. Something inside her was tempted to push him, to see what he'd do, to stir that barely contained fire that smoldered so close to the surface. She wanted him to suffer the same full measure of her own torment. Yet, the more prudent part of her shied from prodding further.

No good would be served, at any rate. They'd made progress of a sort in the past hour, working together for a common cause, Naren's recovery. The almost palpable sense of loathing and mistrust he bore for her had lessened. And had lowered his guard.

That was the way to deal with him, Rissa realized in a sudden flash of insight. Not by reason, not by seduction, not by threats. She must appear to work with him, to cooperate, to lead him to believe she understood and sympathized with the Cat People's plight. She must win his trust.

Then, at long last, she might find some way to escape.

The realization filled Rissa with equal portions of elation and guilt. Strangely, the guilt wended through her the most strongly. She'd never been a deceitful person, given to treachery or manipulation of others. Her mother had taught her too well the innate value of another's trust and good regard, that all were worthy of consideration and respect, no matter their species or social standing.

But her mother had never had to teach her how to extricate herself from such an untenable, frightening situation, either. Somehow, Rissa sensed the rules of a cultured, civilized people didn't always apply in such primitive circumstances. Especially not when someone held you captive with the intent to control and change every aspect of your life—and all of it against your will.

"Fine," Rissa whispered hoarsely. "We did agree to a temporary truce because of Naren, didn't we?" She rose and stalked over to the packs and dug out two blankets. They were thin, threadbare, and would afford little protection from the stone cold of the cave, but they were all the Cat Men had.

Rissa wondered how they'd managed to survive with such a meager amount of life's basic necessities at their disposal. She guessed she'd soon find out more than she ever cared to know on that subject, if she made it to their lair. The thought wasn't at all comforting.

She carried the blankets over to the opposite side of the cave, as far from Morigan as she could get, and wrapping herself in them, settled down for a nap. She wasn't really all that tired, Rissa told herself, but even a feigned attempt at sleep was better than enduring the Cat Man's searing looks. With a deep sigh, she closed her eyes, leaned back against the rough, uncomfortable surface of the cave wall, and resigned herself to several hours of boredom. Five minutes later, she was asleep.

The low rumble of masculine voices woke Rissa from a deep slumber. She moved restlessly, banged her head against a sharply protruding rock, and grimaced in pain. Her lids lifted, her eyes drowsily scanning the unfamiliar scene. Confusion grasped her in a misty disorientation. Then, the movement of Morigan, leaning over Naren, snapped Rissa back to reality.

An impulse to rise and see how the injured Cat Man was doing filled her but, as the conversation of the two men drifted over to her, she decided more might be served by a surreptitious eavesdropping. Rissa closed her eyes and pretended continued sleep.

"How do you feel?" Morigan was asking Naren. "Think you'll live?"

"It's a definite p-possibility," the black-haired Cat Man croaked. He moved his limbs carefully and winced in pain. "Then, again . . ."

"I sent Brandar to Zada's for more medicine. He should be back in another few hours. We'll have something to ease your pain then. Lisan, in the meanwhile," Morigan added, "has gone to the lair for additional men and a litter. They'll bring back Agna as well."

Naren managed a wan smile. "You shouldn't r-risk so much for me. There are more Atroxes out there. You should've f-finished me off and headed out . . ." He paused to inhale a steadying breath. "With Lisan and Brandar gone, y-you're too vulnerable here. Rissa and your safety is m-more important than the l-life of one Cat Man."

"We're far too short of Cat Men to waste even one," Morigan smilingly chided. "Even one as troublesome and aggravating as you."

"Still a-angry at my choice of Rissa, are you?" Naren shifted in an attempt to ease his discomfort. "By the three moons!" he groaned, then caught himself as his friend leaned over him in immediate concern. "It-it's nothing. Just a s-small twinge of pain, now past."

His hand gripped Morigan's. "P-promise me you'll not let our f-friendship endanger the lair. If it comes down to l-leaving me to save yourselves, promise me you'll do it. No good will be served in s-sacrificing your life and the others for me."

Morigan's head dipped. "I don't know if I could do it,

Naren. No matter the circumstances, I don't think I could bring myself to—"

"To kill me in order to p-protect the lair?" his friend finished grimly for him. "What other c-choice is there, for any of us? You know you c-could do it . . . and would. The welfare of many . . . f-far outweighs the plight of a single Cat Man . . ."

His voice faded. Morigan jerked his head up in terror, only to find that Naren had drifted back off to sleep. Ever so gently, he pried Naren's fingers free and laid his hand at his side. Then, glancing up, Morigan caught Rissa's horrified gaze upon him.

He put a silencing finger to his lips, rose, and walked over to her. "Come," he said, offering his hand. "Naren sleeps. A breath of fresh air would be most welcome now."

She eyed his proffered hand warily before accepting it. In a quick, effortless motion, Morigan pulled Rissa to her feet. The blankets fell away but, for several breathless seconds, they continued to stand there, staring at each other.

His eyes blazed hot and scalding, holding Rissa in a heated prison of bitter confusion and fearful desire. Something heavy, smothering, encompassed her, squeezing her chest until Rissa could barely drag in a breath. Her heart pounded. A crazed urge to step closer to Morigan filled her. To join bodies, to feel the hard length of him press against her. To taste his mouth upon hers . . .

With a gasp, Rissa jerked back, her eyes gone wide, her mouth dry. His hand, however, maintained its grip.

"What's wrong, femina?" he demanded in a silky, seductive voice. "Having trouble dealing with your desire for me, are you?"

Rissa flushed crimson and twisted frantically in his grasp.

"I feel nothing for you but disgust! You're just so . . . so fascinatingly ugly—"

Morigan wrenched her up against him. "Disgust? Ugly?" He gave a low, harsh laugh. "Sorry, femina, but those were hardly the emotions I saw in your eyes or felt emanating from you. You forget I can look into your mind—and I know a woman in heat when I see one!"

"In-in *heat?* Why you-you—"

Before Morigan could guess her intent, Rissa's free hand lifted. Only the quickest of Cat reflexes saved him from a stinging blow to the side of his face. He caught her hand only millimeters away, halted it, then slowly brought it to rest along the side of his beard-stubbled cheek. His fingers entwined in hers, imprisoning them there. Morigan turned his head then, bringing his mouth in contact with the palm of Rissa's hand.

At the touch of his full, soft lips, Rissa gasped. Fear rocketed through her. Fear of his intent, of the unknown—and fear of the intense surge of emotions his action had roused.

Her lids lowered, her head sagged back, and her woman's curves, almost in some instinctive response, pressed against his own tautly strung body. He was seducing her, in as much with the strength of his unique psychic powers as he was with his body, and she didn't want it. Gods, she didn't *dare* let herself want it!

"P-please," Rissa breathed. "D-don't. I don't want—"

"You don't know what you really want, femina," Morigan groaned softly. "And I . . . I know this is not at all what I *should* be wanting." His lips slid down the length of her hand, alternately caressing, then gently nipping her with his strong white teeth. "But I'm a male and have a male's needs. Needs that haven't been satisfied in over a—"

He stopped short, went rigid, then pushed her slowly back

from him. The most intense battle raged in his eyes. A battle of wild desire and raw anguish.

After a time, Morigan relaxed, the bow-strung tension easing from his big body. With a deep, unsteady breath, he released her and stepped back. "We were going outside, were we not, before we became sidetracked?" Morigan managed a tight little smile and motioned her ahead of him. "Would you still like to do so?"

"Y-yes." Rissa turned and hurried down the short tunnel that led outside. Stepping from the cave, she glanced around her and, with a deep sigh of relief, threw back her head.

Stars, brilliant pinpoints of light in the ebony canopy of the heavens, twinkled back at her. Two moons, one full and high overhead, one rising close to the horizon, little more than a slender crescent, filled the night sky. The third apparently had yet to rise. Alien and so very different from the nighttime display back on Bellator, the scene was still somehow strangely comforting. At least there were still a few things in life that remained constant, predictable.

Not like her perpetually changing emotions when it came to the Cat Man, Morigan.

Rissa wheeled around, acutely aware of him standing directly behind her. Less than a meter away, he stared at her, his expression shuttered. In the light of the single full moon, an eerie green glow seemed to emanate from his eyes. She shuddered.

Morigan stepped closer. "What's wrong, femina?"

She clasped her arms about her and fiercely shook her head. "Nothing. Nothing's wrong. I've just seen so much violence and bloodshed of late. I-I'm worried about the other women, especially my friend, Diona. And now . . ." Her voice broke. Her head dipped. She inhaled an unsteady breath and forced herself to go on. "And now, Naren."

Tawny brown eyes swung up to his. "If things don't go well, you mean to kill him, don't you, before you leave here?"

Morigan's mouth drew into a tight, forbidding line. "If absolutely necessary, yes."

Utter disbelief twisted Rissa's features. "You haven't a shred of compassion or mercy in you, have you? In your own way, you Cat Men are as brutally ruthless as you claim we Bellatorians are. How can you call yourself Naren's friend one minute and then the next speak of murdering him?"

The Cat Lord's hands fisted at his sides. His shoulders went rigid. "How? Because, my shortsighted little femina, if we were forced to leave him behind, and he was captured, the Bellatorians would use their most painfully efficient ways of extracting information from him. Eventually, no matter how valiantly Naren resisted, they'd discover the location of our lair. To preclude that eventuality, all of us, Cat Man and Woman alike, have taken a vow to kill ourselves if captured. It's the only way to protect our people.

"So speak to me not of our brutality," Morigan snarled, his anger a heated, palpable aura about him. "We do the best we can with what life has dealt us. And we *will* survive, no matter what it takes. No matter what!"

Rissa stared up at him, struck vividly by the true reality of the Cat People's plight. Any people forced to go into hiding, kidnap females of other species to help propagate themselves, and take a vow to commit suicide if captured were surely doomed. Especially when they pitted themselves against a planet as powerful and determined as Bellator. Three or four hundred people against Imperium-renowned Bellatorian warriors. They didn't stand a chance.

Yet, still they fought on, refusing to surrender. Fleetingly, Rissa wondered if even surrender would save their lives. She knew her people and their fierce single-mindedness when it came to achieving a goal. So long as any Cat Man survived, they would remain a threat to Bellator's Agrican objectives. And what were three or four hundred animalistic aliens in comparison to an entire planet of people?

They were half-naked savages. They possessed little worth and were deemed a great obstacle to further, peaceful settlement of Agrica. No, there'd be no mercy shown the Cat People, whether they surrendered or were systematically hunted down and slaughtered. And, as a loyal Bellatorian, raised to unthinking, unquestioning obedience, she must accept whatever her planet determined appropriate. It was, and always had been, the safest course.

A soft breeze caressed Rissa's cheek, recalling her attention to the night around her. But, only a few moments ago, she'd found it comforting, found it reassuring once more to be outside.

Now . . . now, the moonlight, the air, the sounds pressed down on her, rife with danger, ominous, inconstant and unpredictable. As unpredictable and frightening as her life had suddenly become. There were no easy answers anymore. No simple solutions.

She was caught in an ever blurring morality between one species' military prerogative and another's right to survive, between loyalty to one's self and one's heritage, and the even more ancient pull of powerful, primal mating urges. It was a struggle, Rissa realized, that in many ways, on many levels, could be one of life—and death.

Five

Brandar arrived two hours later, his pack laden with bandages, herbal poultices, additional healing powders, and a strong narcotic to ease Naren's pain. Wisely, Zada had also sent instructions along on how to best care for the Cat Man's injuries.

The narcotic was gratefully swallowed; the herbal poultices were soaked in water warmed on the small campfire and laid directly on the wounds to draw out infection and any foreign objects the earlier cleansing hadn't removed. Then, fresh bandages were applied.

Rissa attempted a nourishing broth from some dried meat sticks, seasoning, and water heated over the campfire, but even the ever considerate Naren couldn't hide his distaste for the noxious brew. Morigan, noting his friend's pained expression as he tried to force himself to drink it all down, grabbed the cup from him and tasted it himself.

"B-by the three moons!" he sputtered, spewing out the mouthful of broth in outrage. "What did you do to this? Are you trying to poison him?"

"Poison him?" Rissa cried. "I did nothing but attempt the same sort of broth I once watched my nursemaid brew. It seemed simple enough to make . . ." She shot Naren an uncertain look. "Was it really that bad?"

He smiled up at her wanly. "I'm afraid so, femina. But I'm sure you'll get better with practice."

Morigan rose and doused the campfire with the remainder of the soup. "I doubt that. How could anyone ruin something as simple as broth? Of all the females we captured, I'd wager none are as unskilled as this one." He glared down at his friend. "Once again, Naren, I congratulate you on your un-paralleled ability to choose a mate for me."

"Well, if you're so displeased with me," Rissa countered furiously, climbing to her feet to stomp over to him, "why not just let me go? Surely, a woman as stupid and unskilled as I isn't worthy of mating with one of your precious Cat Men, much less bearing a Cat Child. Think how slow and ignorant any offspring of mine would be, having a mother like me!"

She stood on tiptoe in an attempt to meet him eye-to-eye, her small hands fisting at her sides. "Well, my great and glorious Lord? What do you have to say now?"

Morigan shot Naren a quick glance. The black-haired Cat Man was looking pointedly away, his lips twitching. Brandar, however, standing guard near the doorway, seemed to lack the proper degree of social grace to hide his amusement. A wide grin split his grimy, hirsute face. With a growl of dis-gust, Morigan turned back to Rissa.

"There's hope a good dose of Cat's blood would improve the limited intelligence of any offspring of yours," he snarled. "It's worth a try, at any rate." He took her by the arm and turned her back toward the packs. "There are additional meat sticks, journey bread and dried fruit in the packs. See if you can manage to find them and lay them out for our supper. No cooking or additional preparation is required, so you should be able to handle that, shouldn't you?"

She jerked her arm from his grasp with an expression of

utter distaste. "Yes, I should, but why don't you just get them yourself? That way we'll preclude any further culinary accidents or covert poisoning attempts." With that, Rissa stalked back across the cave and sat down, her back turned to Morigan.

He scowled, wavering between the urge to walk over, jerk her to her feet, and force her compliance to his orders, or just giving it up as a lost cause. Once the initial onslaught of anger had passed, Morigan decided on the latter. As furious as Rissa could make him, he knew he couldn't raise a hand against her.

Cat Men never struck their females. The few that ever did were severely punished, their mates given to another. And now that females, in their scarcity, were an even more precious resource, no one could dare be permitted to harm one. Even one such as Rissa, who dearly needed a lesson in respect, not to mention obedience.

"Fine," he gritted. "If you refuse to help prepare the meal, you can just do without it. It's as simple as that."

"Fine," she hissed from over her shoulder. "I wasn't hungry anyway."

Morigan motioned to Brandar, who headed swiftly to the packs to retrieve their food. Five minutes later, the three Cat Men were hungrily consuming their Spartan meal.

As Morigan paused to cut the dried meat sticks into smaller bites for Naren, his friend managed a wry grin. "You brought on all that yourself, you know."

His friend cocked a dark brow. "Indeed? How so?"

"Rissa's proud. You insulted her one time too many. When will you learn to go gently with her? She's a female, after all. They respond best to honeyed words and compliments, not criticisms."

"I haven't the time for such things," Morigan muttered,

doggedly sawing through more of Naren's meat stick. "Even if I *had* the inclination, which I most certainly don't."

"Still, you were in the wrong here. She was trying to help. The intent matters more than the results."

Morigan shoved a hand through his mane, totally exasperated. "Gods, Naren, this isn't at all what I envisioned it would be like! What do you suggest I do to ease those prickly feelings of hers? Honeyed words and compliments have never been a particular talent of mine."

"No, they haven't," Naren chuckled softly. "Why not offer her a bath instead? The hot springs down below the cave looked quite appealing. And females love to bathe."

Morigan considered the suggestion, then shook his head. "No, it wouldn't be safe, not with other Atroxes possibly out there."

"I wasn't advising you to let her go there alone. Take a blaster and post Brandar at the mouth of the cave to guard the valley and hot spring. He'll be far enough away not to see much of Rissa, and you'll be close by to defend her if necessary."

"And close enough to watch her." Morigan's mouth twisted. "She'll never agree to it. She's not going to bathe naked in front of me."

Naren shrugged. "Perhaps not, but you won't know if you don't offer. Besides, the point of this whole thing is to make amends, not entertain yourself at her expense. You don't have to watch *everything* she does."

"Nor do I want to," his friend growled. He added the chopped up meat sticks and a chunk of rehydrated fruit to Naren's platter. "It's not as if I would find any particular pleasure viewing her nudity. When it comes to sheer, animal attractiveness, she can never hope to compare to even the plainest Cat Woman."

The black-haired Cat Man eyed him with disbelief, then shrugged. "I suppose you're right. So the only problem that remains is convincing Rissa she's totally safe in your hands. Isn't that so? Eh, Morigan?"

Green-gold eyes swung down to his friend. "Of course. The female's in no danger from me, at least not until we get back to the lair and I'm required to do my procreative duty by her." Morigan rose. "My thanks for your suggestion. It's at least worth a try."

Yet, as he walked across the cave to confront Rissa, Morigan wasn't all that certain Naren's idea was prudent after all. Even as his friend had blithely agreed with him that Rissa was far too unattractive to compare to any of their Cat Women, the memory of his heated response to her but a few hours ago had flooded Morigan's mind.

He'd wanted her. She'd wanted him. And the fire that had blazed between them was both unexpected and intensely disturbing. Morigan had never thought it possible to desire a female of another species, especially a female of the enemy. Yet, when he recalled the exciting sensations the feel of Rissa's soft hand against his mouth had stirred . . . Even now, he could almost smell the sweet essence of her, taste the heady flavor of her skin . . .

Morigan swallowed a savage curse. This wasn't at all what he'd intended to remember. Such recollections were best forgotten. Rissa must remain as she'd been intended—an object to be used in the ongoing quest to ensure his people's survival. An object . . . a *Bellatorian* object.

There was no time for desire, and certainly none for love. His ability to love had died with Winna . . . and little Calder. He meant to keep it that way. Emotion accomplished naught but to weaken and distract one from what must be done. Any hope of happiness left to him in life lay in the prospect of saving his people. That had to be enough. It would take everything he possessed to see even that much to fruition.

Somehow, though, that resolve angered Morigan. As he drew up before Rissa and squatted before her, another cutting remark rose to his lips. He squelched it with the greatest of efforts.

She eyed him with suspicion. "What do you want now? Thought up some fresh insults to hurl at me, have you?"

"No. My remarks were uncalled for. You were trying to help. Naren most bluntly pointed that out to me."

"And whatever will you do when you no longer have him around to do your thinking for you?"

"Why," he gave a wry chuckle, "then I'll have you, won't I? Fate, it seems, has determined never to leave me without an advisor of some kind or another." He offered his hand. "Come. I know a hot springs nearby you might like to bathe in. Zada included a container of cleansing sand and a few toweling cloths in the pack Brandar brought back."

Excitement flared in Rissa's eyes, then was quickly extinguished. "No, I couldn't do that."

"Why not? You're quite safe from my disgusting advances, if that's what you're worried about. I'm only coming along to guard you."

"Guard me?" Carefully, consideringly, Rissa wet her lips. She desperately needed a bath and the hot springs sounded wonderful. "And how close is this guarding to be?"

"I'll be watching you almost the entire time," Morigan said in exasperation, filling in the unspoken aspects of her question. "If you'd like, I'll turn my back while you disrobe and enter the water, as well as when you leave it, but the rest of the time I'll have my eyes on you. And if you think to grab a stone while my back's turned and attack me with it, give up that idea right now. If you haven't figured it out by now, my hearing and reflexes are far too quick for you to get away with anything that aggressive."

"Actually, I'd something more in mind like seducing you into the water and drowning you," she muttered sarcastically. "Cat Men don't know how to swim, do they?"

"We love the water. Does that answer your question?" His mouth tightened in impatience. "Well, what's it to be? It's almost sunrise, and you're wasting valuable bathing time. Are you interested or not?"

Rissa hesitated a brief moment more, then placed her hand in his. "Yes, definitely."

"Good." Morigan pulled her to her feet. "You were getting to be a bit pungent for a Cat Man's sensitive nose."

"Pungent?" She jerked her hand from his grasp. "You, of all people, have the nerve to comment on my—"

He gave a low bark of laughter. "Calm yourself, femina. I was only joking. Your scent is not the least offensive. I but thought you'd enjoy the pleasures of the hot springs, that's all."

"Well, I suppose that's all right," she huffed. "I just find your humor rather lacking when it comes to my personal cleanliness. I don't particularly enjoy being so filthy, you know."

"No, I imagine not," Morigan agreed, his tone grave. "We've several hot springs in our lair and make regular use of them ourselves. As surprising as it might be to you, Cat People are generally quite fastidious about their appearances."

Her glance swung down the length of his body. "Forgive me for saying so, but that does come as somewhat of a surprise. You're filthy. And you definitely do have a strong odor."

He shot her a faintly amused look. "My apologies. I'll see what I can do about my sorry personal hygiene before we bed down tonight. Is that acceptable?"

She glanced toward the packs, missing the suddenly heated look that flared in his eyes. "Shall we get the cleansing sand and towels, then, and be on our way? Though I can't say I relish you as an audience, I must admit to an eager anticipation of a bath."

Morigan nodded. After procuring the necessary equipment, they headed across the cave. Naren grinned at Morigan as they passed by his bed. In reply, the Lord of the Cat Men simply rolled his eyes.

He'd never seen a female disrobe so quickly. In less than a minute, Rissa had her boots, jacket, and breeches off and was in the water. Briefly, Morigan speculated on whether she'd worn anything beneath that blue-green garment of hers. Then he shoved that consideration aside. It stirred too many images of Rissa's body for comfort.

As it was, his physical comfort was rapidly waning, he realized glumly as he watched her cavort like some sleek white sea creature in the bubbling, steaming waters, the early rays of the rising sun setting her aglow. Though initially wary of him and careful to keep all but her head and neck submerged, as time went on and the warm waters relaxed her, Rissa became more playful. She swam about, dove beneath the water, then burst to the surface, her blond hair darkening to the deep gold color of apis honey with the repeated dunkings.

She was carefree, delightful, laughing in girlish abandon as she swam as close to him as she dared, then turned and sped away. Morigan grimaced and shook his head. Rissa was the most unpredictable, disconcerting female he'd ever met. One moment she was a defiant, sharp-tongued she-cat, the next a sensuous, exquisitely desirable woman, and the next, a teasing, mischievous little girl.

And he suddenly wasn't so sure he'd ever know how to handle her.

The thought angered him. With a frown, Morigan tossed the container of cleansing sand to Rissa. It sank beneath the water, then bobbed to the surface to float beside her. "Time to finish your bath. We can't linger here. The sun will soon be high and make us far too exposed and vulnerable out here."

She made a small moue of distaste, then opened the container and proceeded to wash her hair, face, shoulders, and arms. Then, glancing down at herself, Rissa hesitated. Her gaze lifted to Morigan. "Will you please turn while I complete my bath?"

He considered her request and made an uncharacteristic decision to toss all propriety, all honor to the winds. Perhaps it was the result of her earlier behavior in the spring. Perhaps he wanted her to experience just a small bit of the frustration he felt. "No. Just finish and be done with it." He squatted at the water's edge. "You're in no danger from me out here. I'd be a fool to take you now, with Atroxes roaming about."

Rissa's eyes narrowed in anger—and at the implied challenge in his words. Something hard, intense, something that slipped past the cycles of breeding and customary sanctions, filled her.

She hated him. He angered her, confused her, frustrated her. And he thought her too shy to bare her body to him. He thought her foolish to imagine he was so lust-crazed he'd risk their lives for a quick and sordid mating. He thought he had her cowed.

He thought wrong.

Rissa grabbed the container of cleansing sand. In two

quick strides, she moved toward him until her torso was bared. Then, with a defiant lift of her chin and toss of her long hair, she opened the container, scooped out a generous amount of cleansing sand, and began to lather her breasts and belly.

Morigan watched, every muscle in his body going taut and rigid. One hand moved to fist upon his thigh, the other gripped the side of the tree whose branches hung over the spring. And, the longer he watched, the farther his claws unsheathed, digging into his hand and the bark of the tree.

The barely leashed tension emanating from the Cat Man wasn't lost on Rissa. She saw the hunger glitter in his eyes, sensed the smoldering emotions, felt his desire. His excitement stirred something equally fevered in her. Something that both attracted and frightened her.

But she refused to back down, refused to let him control or intimidate her in even this most basic of ways. He was a male, bigger and stronger than she. But there was a certain power in her own femininity as well. Rissa had seen the impact of a beautiful woman on a man time and again. And, though she'd never had any inclination to use it, she suddenly wanted, needed, to see what effect her own feminine attributes would have upon the Cat Man.

It was wrong, unfair, and dangerous, but Rissa no longer cared. She was tired of Morigan having all the power, all the control. Just once, she wanted to control him, if only for a few brief moments bathing naked in the spring. The consequences be damned. Just once, she wanted to torment him the way he tormented her.

She arched back her head, unabashedly reveling in the spray of warm water misting her face and body, the slick sensation of the cleansing sand as it lathered into a rich foam, and the cool caress of the predawn breeze that tingled across her skin and tightened her pink nipples to taut little buds. And reveled, as well, in the heated glance of Morigan raking her body, searing her flesh again and again.

When the washing of her upper body was complete, Rissa lowered herself into the water until only her head remained exposed. She rinsed, then stood and strode yet closer to him, pausing when the water caught her at mid-thigh.

There was no mistaking the heated intent in his green-gold eyes as his gaze dipped past her flat belly to the golden thatch of her woman's mound. She proceeded to soap herself there and spread the foaming lather down her thighs and around to her buttocks. He glistened now with a fine sheen, but whether from sweat or from the warm mist of the hot springs, Rissa didn't know. And the sudden tautness to his loin cloth at the juncture of his thighs was but further evidence of the effect she was having on him.

For the first time since she'd determined to set out on this seductive game, Rissa's resolve faltered. A memory, of Diona's words, speaking of the Cat Men, filtered into her mind . . . *their wildly uncontrollable sexual urges* . . .

What if Morigan truly did lose control, even out here in the open, where they stood in danger of attack by Atroxes? He was half-animal, after all. Where did reason fade and bestial instincts take over? Suddenly, she didn't want to know.

Heat flooded her, but this time it was of shame for her shocking, totally uncharacteristic behavior. Rissa dipped beneath the water to rinse herself, then caught the floating container of cleansing sand and motioned to Morigan. "I'm finished with my bath. If you'd please turn around, I'd like to get out and dress now."

He stared down at her, silent, a muscle twitching wildly in his beard-shadowed jaw. An errant breeze caught a lock of his dark hair and whipped it into his face. He seemed oblivious to it.

"Morigan?" An edge of uncertainty threaded her voice. "Did you hear what I said?"

"Yes. I heard." His reply was no more than a low, harsh rasp. "Finished with your little game, are you?"

"I-I don't know what you're talking about," she prevaricated. "I only wished to bathe—"

"Liar! You and I both know what you intended to do. And you succeeded, didn't you?"

As he spoke, Morigan rose. Her gaze dropped, riveting on his groin. Even to Rissa's inexperienced eyes, his loincloth-covered manhood was now bulging and blatant.

"You're quite an accomplished seductress, aren't you?" the Cat Man snarled. "I'd thought your youth precluded any prior experience, but I find I was wrong. You've lain with other males, haven't you?"

He cocked a dark brow, his mouth twisting in disgust. "Perhaps that was why you and the other females were so intent on reaching Primasedes. There were plenty of imperials to be made in that male-dominated Bellatorian fortress, weren't there? Plenty of money from female-starved men."

As Rissa stared up at him in growing horror, Morigan gave a self-deprecating laugh. "Once more, it seems, the Bellatorians have turned the tables on us. We thought to punish them by stealing their females, and all we seem to have accomplished was the abduction of a group of alley walkers. Females soiled and shameless on whom, in our desperation, we're still forced to breed our children. And the most shameless, the most sordid of them all, it seems, is the one I must take to mate."

Outrage rushed through Rissa, sending hot blood pumping to her limbs and heart. Her former regret at her outrageous behavior dissipated in the freshened onslaught of wounded honor. She threw the container of cleansing sand at him with all the fury and strength of a woman wronged. Thanks to his Cat reflexes, Morigan easily dodged the blow.

Grimly, he smiled down at her. "Care to try again, femina? Why not come out of the water and use those vicious little claws on me? See if you can draw blood this time?"

Fists clenched at her sides, Rissa made a move toward him, then thought better of the foolhardy attempt. He was livid, spoiling for a fight, a fight she'd no hope of winning. A fight *she* had instigated.

Let him think of her what he wanted. Perhaps it would work to her advantage. Perhaps it would kill his desire for her, keep her out of his bed for a time longer. She definitely needed more time if she were to make good her escape. Though far too belated, the thought strengthened her resolve.

It took all the will Rissa possessed, however, to lower her gaze and shake her head, to play the meek little captive. "No," she muttered at last, hating the words, hating him for goading her into all of this. "I don't want to fight, much less get near you right now. Just let me come out of the water and dress. That's all I ask."

"Ask?" Morigan gave a harsh laugh. "And since when have you ever *asked* anything of me? Do you fear I won't mate with you, now that I know the truth? But I'm only a savage, barely human Cat Man. Surely, you don't think I can afford to be particular? I have to take whatever leavings the Bellatorians offer. Even," he added with a curl of his lip, "their most disreputable of females."

"Fine!" Rissa cried, her own tolerance at an end. She strode out of the water and, with a sharp motion, jerked up a toweling cloth, rubbed it fiercely over her body to dry herself, then snatched up her clothes and donned them. "Take whatever leavings you want, you big, thickheaded son of a blind Arborian warthog! Just look elsewhere, whatever you do. You're the most despicable, insulting man I've ever met, and I want nothing from you! Nothing!"

With that, Rissa plopped down on the nearest rock, dragged on her boots, then rose. In a flounce of waterlogged tresses, she stomped off in the direction of the cave.

Morigan watched her stalk away, then shouldered the blaster he'd laid against the tree and gathered up the bathing supplies Rissa, in her outrage, had left behind. Snarling a scalding string of Agrican curses, he followed after her.

Naren immediately knew something was wrong. Rissa had returned alone, stalked over to the other side of the cave without a word, and sat down with her back turned to him. She had then proceeded to finger comb her wet hair of its tangles, her movements jerky and agitated. When the task was complete she surveyed the results and, apparently not at all pleased, burst into tears.

"Rissa, femina," he said, levering himself painfully to one arm. "What's wrong. I know we brought along no hair combs but once we get to the lair—"

"It's not a c-comb!" she sobbed, burying her face in her hands. "It's—it's just e-everything!"

"Come here, femina," Naren entreated softly. "I would come to you if I could, but I fear I haven't the strength even to sit up, much less crawl over to you."

Rissa wheeled around, her eyes huge, her face tear streaked. "No . . . don't. You'll tear open your wounds." When she saw he hadn't made a move toward her, she sighed and shook her head. "It doesn't concern you anyway. It's nothing more than I should have expected."

The black-haired Cat Man scowled. "What has he done to you this time? By the three moons, I thought Morigan's offer to take you for a bath would ease things between you, not make them worse!"

"He's the most despicable, hardhearted man I've ever had the misfortune to know!" Rissa swiped the moisture from her face, her recollection of their battle at the spring sending a fresh surge of anger to dry up her tears. "He . . . he accused me of being an . . . an alley walker!"

"He what?" Naren's face went white with shock. "Morigan has always had the utmost respect for females. He's never insulted them. Why would he now turn on you? Bellatorian or no, you're still a female."

Rissa hesitated. She knew she wasn't blameless in the sorry outcome of their latest interaction. Far from it. Her head dipped, the long hanks of her water-damp hair tumbling down to hide her rising flush. "I teased and taunted him with my . . . nakedness when he refused to turn away while I finished my bath. I must have driven him past the limits of his control."

"Do you still have your maidenhood?"

She blinked in confusion, then flushed even darker. "Not that it's any of your business, but yes, I do. What does that have to do with this?"

"Then you didn't drive Morigan past the limits of his control. He'd have had you on the ground and been rutting between your legs if you'd truly driven him over the edge." Naren chuckled. "I think you just angered him to the point at which he had to strike back at you. And since he couldn't rape or beat you, words were all he had left."

Rissa's head jerked up, anger sparking once more in her eyes. "You and Morigan are two of a kind, aren't you? Crude and totally disparaging of the value of a woman save for her ability to pleasure you and bear your children." She paused, suddenly recalling something else Naren had said. "And what do you mean, he couldn't rape or beat me? I thought forcing me to mate with him *was* his ultimate goal."

"Rissa, Rissa." Naren sighed and, his strength ebbing, lay back on his bed. "Haven't you figured it all out yet? Have we laid one hand on you since you've been captured, save for the sometimes necessary expediency of binding and gagging you? Despite what you may have heard about the Cat People, we're not slavering savages, out raping and pillaging at every opportunity. We're but simple beings, albeit a bit different from your kind, driven by the same needs and goals.

"We love and cherish our mates, are proud of our children, respect our elders, and obey our laws," he continued, his eyes gleaming with a tender warmth. "We laugh, we sing, we dance. We cry and mourn as well. But, until your people came to Agrica, intent on stealing its special wealth, we lived in peace."

"Bellator didn't come to steal anything," Rissa hotly defended her planet. "They were invited here to assist in upgrading Agrica's agricultural technology. Your planet was so backward that most of its vast resources were being squandered. And we were welcomed here by all, save you Cat People."

"No," Naren corrected her quietly, "that's not quite true. The Cat People were the only Agrican inhabitants who cared enough to watch the Bellatorians, to look beneath the surface of all the diplomacy and gifts to discern their real motives. Bellator desires total dominance of Agrica so as to fatten its coffers and spread its military rule throughout the Imperium. Do you realize the strategic significance of controlling the primary food source of the entire Imperium? Do you, Rissa?"

"I'm not some naive schoolgirl," she bristled, stung by his prodding. "Of course, I know any planet that controls Agrica could well control the Imperium. But I can't believe your people are entirely blameless in this war with Bellator, either."

"And what would be our motive to dare go up against the military might of Bellator?" He arched a dark brow. "We never aspired to wealth or many possessions, knowing them too great a hindrance to our beloved way of life. We never desired dominance over other races, well aware our Cat powers already made us superior to all. Yet, someone still seemed convinced we were a threat. If not Bellator directly, perhaps it was their Lord Commander, bending Bellatorian directives to his own purpose. One way or another, *he* is the one carrying out the systematic attempts at our annihilation."

"No." Immediately, Rissa rose to her father's defense. "It couldn't be the Lord Commander. He's not the kind of man to . . ." At the Cat Man's suddenly intent look, Rissa's voice faded.

"And how can you be so sure? Do you know him?"

She shook her head, masking her rising agitation beneath an expressionless façade. "I-I met him when I was but a child," she hastened to reply, thinking a version of the truth her best defense, "but haven't seen him since. I remember him to be a kind and gentle man."

"Time can corrupt any of us." He paused, a troubled look in his eyes. "It hasn't passed kindly or gently for Morigan. This past cycle has changed him, hardened him . . ." Naren sighed. "It is *that* Morigan who treats you so harshly, who flares so quickly to anger, who lives for revenge. He has become a man who has lost all hope, forfeited all his dreams."

Rissa flung back the rapidly drying locks that had fallen

into her face. "But that's the only Morigan I know. And I don't know how to deal with him. Nor do I want to," she added vehemently.

"Morigan frightens you, doesn't he?"

She graced Naren with a withering look. "He's a Cat Man. He's dangerous and unpredictable. He'd frighten anyone."

"Yet he attracts you as well." At her look of dismay, the black-haired Cat Man smiled. "I'll tell you a secret, Rissa. I suspect he's equally frightened of—and attracted—to you."

It took a few seconds for Rissa to digest this newest bit of information. "No," she finally replied, fiercely shaking her head. "You're wrong, Naren. You see Morigan with the eyes of a friend. I see him with the eyes of a woman and enemy. He may lust after me, but that lust is tinged with hatred and loathing as well. If Morigan is in any conflict over me, it's whether or not he can force himself to mate with a woman whom he finds disgusting."

"He lost more than just his father and thousands of his people that autumn day the Bellatorians came to our forest lair," Naren murmured. "He lost his pregnant wife and two-year-old son. He lost the happy life he'd led. And the Cat Throne was thrust upon him at a time of gravest crisis. Since then, Morigan has taken nothing for himself. He has given everything he has to the salvation of his people. And to the hunger for vengeance that gnaws at him," he added, his eyes closing in despair.

Naren dragged in a ragged breath, then met Rissa's wide-eyed gaze once more. "I need your help, femina. I don't know what else to do for him, how to help him."

Somehow, Rissa found it extremely difficult to envision the big Cat Man as hurting or in need of anyone's help. If he were in pain, he hid it well behind a harsh, unyielding exterior. And, indeed, even if it were true, what did it matter to her?

No, even the barest consideration of attempting to help the Cat Lord, much less lowering the defenses she fought to maintain against him, was more than Rissa could handle.

He was her enemy, symbolized everything she hated most about her current plight, and was the one who held all the power over her. To help him now would serve no purpose but to grant him further advantage over her. And she didn't need that, didn't dare allow that to happen. Not if she ever wished to escape.

She shook her head. "No, I won't do it, Naren. I'm sorry he lost so much. I'm sorry such a tragedy has befallen your people. But I can't and won't get involved with Morigan. I am sorry, but I just won't."

Six

Morigan returned ten hours later, having sent Brandar in to rest while he stood guard at the mouth of the cave. Throughout the day, the weather had gradually changed, the wind commencing to blow and the temperature dropping until, by late afternoon, a sleeting rain pelted the ground and a gray fog rolled down from the mountains. In her thin garments, Rissa soon felt the chill. As the day wore on, even the addition of one of the Cat Men's blankets failed to cut the cold.

She refused to complain, however. Naren, in his weakened state, tolerated the temperature drop far worse than she. No matter how many blankets she piled atop him, he continued to shiver. Brandar, wrapped in a fur cloak, slept on, oblivious to his compatriot's plight.

Finally, Rissa could take it no longer. They needed a fire, and if she couldn't talk Morigan into going out to gather wood, she intended to get it herself.

Wrapping the blanket about her, she rose and strode down the tunnel to where the Cat Lord sat. He visibly tensed at her approach, but didn't turn around.

"What do you want?"

His deep voice, rising out of the gloom, gave her a moment's pause. There was no anger or irritation or disgust hovering there, only a flat, emotionless query. Had he finally resolved to distance himself from her, so nothing she said or did touched him again?

It didn't matter, one way or another, Rissa fiercely told herself. She was weary of the battling, of the pain, and the unnerving effect he had upon her. Better if both of them dealt with the other from a cool emotional distance.

"Naren. The cold." She forced her voice and words to mimic his reserved tone. "He suffers greatly from it. We need a fire."

"No. There'll be no fires of any kind. It's too dangerous."

"Dangerous?" In spite of her intentions to the contrary, exasperation threaded Rissa's voice. By the five moons, how she hated it when he slipped into his arbitrary, superior man and captor mode! "I've not seen or heard of anyone about all day. Why do you persist in being so—"

"There are Atroxes but a few kilometers away, camped for the night due to the bad weather. They'll smell the smoke and be on us before we'd have a chance to get Naren out of here."

His head turned, his eyes glittering. For the first time Rissa noted he had bathed. His face and body were free of grime; his hair fell soft and wavy to tumble down about his broad shoulders.

"We'd have to kill Naren and run for our lives," Morigan's words sliced through her wondering appraisal. "Is that what you want?"

Her lids slid shut. She exhaled a deep, frustrated breath. "No, you know that's not what I want. But I fear we'll lose him from the cold if we don't get him warm." Her eyes opened and she met his icy gaze. "I just don't know what else to do. And I don't want Naren to die."

He rose in a fluid motion of long, strong muscles to tower over her. "Neither do I, femina." He grasped Rissa's arm.

"Come. We've heavier clothing in our packs and fur cloaks. We anticipated the weather changing once we reached the mountains. It just changed a little sooner and lower in elevation than we'd planned."

She followed him back down the tunnel into the cave. In the light of the perpetual flame box, Morigan dragged over two large packs and began pulling out domare-hide tunics and breeches from the first of the packs. He tossed the smallest set over to her.

"Those are for you. That apparel of yours isn't suited for the climate we'll be going into or the roughness of the terrain ahead."

Rissa fingered the leather shirt. It was soft, tanned to a smooth, pliable texture that felt like serica cloth but was much thicker and sturdier. A pale beige in color, the tunic was long-sleeved and ample in length. Its neckline was scooped slightly, the front laced with leather thongs halfway down the front. A few bits of beadwork decorated the upper chest area, but other than that, the garment was simply made. The breeches were equally soft and pliable, fitted with a drawstring waist, and undecorated.

The garments were crude and Rissa had never worn animal skins, but it was too cold to quibble over the finer points of a gentlewoman's proper garb just now. She clutched them to herself and glanced up at Morigan. "Thank you. What about Naren's?"

"See to yourself. I'll take care of him."

"Fine. If you'll just give me a few moments of privacy . . ."

"Privacy?" He cocked a sardonic brow. "In here, with three Cat Men? That seems a bit unrealistic, femina."

"You . . . you could hold up my blanket to shield me," Rissa offered quickly, "and . . . and look the other way."

"Still playing that game, are you?" he growled. "I'd have thought after the spring, you'd have lost all your modesty around me."

Rissa bit back a stinging retort. Though Morigan's continued arrogance and dominating ways had stimulated her shameful behaviors at the spring, she couldn't blame him for his current opinion of her. What would anyone think of her after what she'd done?

She forced herself to meet his scornful gaze. "I doubt you'll believe this, but I've never done that kind of thing before. I've never even bared my body to a man's view, much less flaunted it like I did . . . did at the spring. And I'm not, nor never have been, an alley walker."

Morigan eyed her in cynical amusement. "Indeed? Then, why did you taunt me with your body? You took a real chance."

"Yes, I know," Rissa replied a bit unsteadily. "It was a stupid, foolish act, and I regret it deeply. But you made me so mad, made me feel so . . . so helpless, that I had to get back at you any way I could. My body seemed the only weapon I had left."

His eyes narrowed to smoldering slits. His mouth drew into a ruthless, forbidding line. "Weapons can be turned against you, femina. Don't ever forget that. And you'd be wise to cease your fight against me. I *am* the one in control here and intend to remain that way. But I'm not a cruel person, if you'll permit me the chance. Just don't ever flaunt yourself before me like that again. Understood?"

She swallowed hard. "Understood." *But don't fool yourself into imagining I'll ever accept your dominance over me, either,* Rissa silently added. *You may have won a skirmish in extracting an apology for what I did earlier, but you haven't*

*won the battle. I will leave you. I won't submit to being your
mate. And I'll never. ever, be your obedient slave.*

"Good." Morigan rose and motioned to her blanket. When
Rissa gazed blankly up at him, he reached down and pulled
the covering from her shoulders. "You asked for a shield
from the others while you changed. I'm giving it to you. Just
make it quick. Naren needs his warm clothes far more than
you."

As soon as Morigan lifted the blanket between them, Rissa
wasted no time in shrugging off her clothes and boots.
Though turning his head and averting his eyes was hardly
her idea of affording her privacy, she took what she could
get.

Morigan's point was well-taken, Rissa admitted as she
slipped into the doeskin-soft breeches and gathered and tied
them snugly at her waist. As much as she hated to admit it,
a continued false modesty around him made little sense. He'd
seen her body, knew her woman's secrets. He could take her
anytime he wished. Her brief nudity now wouldn't change a
thing. Morigan would do what he wished, when he wished to.

And, still, he had yet even to touch her in an untoward
manner, much less make any sexual overtures, she realized,
pulling the amply sized tunic over her head. His brief nuzzle
of her hand when she'd tried to slap him hardly counted as
any form of sexual trespass, even if the action had been unaccountably stimulating and exciting. No, in some strangely
comforting way, the big Cat Man possessed his own particular kind of morals.

"You can lower the blanket now." Rissa sat to pull on her
boots.

"I gathered as much." His gaze snared on the turcas stone
earrings and necklace she still wore. "Those seem rather
inappropriate with our form of clothing."

Rissa stiffened. Was he determined to take everything from her of her old life? She couldn't help the edge of defensiveness that crept into her voice. "My jewelry—and maidenhood—are all I have left. I won't willingly give either of them up."

Morigan scowled. "You're especially stubborn, even for a female. But keep your jewelry and maidenhood for a time more. It matters not to me. I but thought to assist in easing your transition in our lair. You, quite obviously, have other ideas and will pay the price for them."

He folded the blanket and handed it down to her. "In the meanwhile, you'd better keep this. The domare-hide garments are warm, but nothing will cut the chill of this cave indefinitely."

At his words, she noticed, as if for the first time, that Morigan was still clothed only in his loincloth and boots. How was it possible he'd borne the near freezing temperatures for so long without anything additional to cover him? He must be numb from the cold.

Further consideration of the dispute over her jewelry faded. He had, after all, given her what she wanted. "You should put on your own garments soon," Rissa forced out the observation, attempting to make amends. "Aren't you cold?"

"Yes, but I can bear it." A tinge of irritation still threaded his voice. "Naren comes first." He turned back to the packs and dug out another set of garments. When he rose again, Rissa was beside him.

"Yes, femina?" Morigan eyed her warily.

"Let me help you with Naren. Moving him will be difficult enough and, in this case, two pairs of hands are far better than one."

He studied her for a long moment. Rissa held her breath, fearing he'd refuse.

Then, Morigan nodded. "All right."

She couldn't quite hide her smile of relief. "Thank you."

"For what?"

"For trusting me. For being willing to work with me, even after all the fights and problems between us."

Green-gold eyes narrowed in a slight frown. "It's only because of Naren. I don't trust you any more than I ever have, which is not at all."

Rissa expelled an exasperated breath. "Has anyone ever told you that you can be the most irascible, prickly, and stand-offish of beings?"

"Not until I met you. *My* people tend to treat me with respect."

"Well, perhaps that's the problem. Power tends not only to corrupt, but to distance the wielder from reality as well. I'd say you're in dire need, from time to time, of someone to bring you back to earth."

"And you don't think Naren does a good enough job of that, do you?"

Rissa shrugged. "Oh, he tries. But he's a male, and some of your more irritating attributes are probably quite acceptable to him. I, on the other hand—"

"Let's save this most enlightening of conversations for another time, shall we?" he cut in with a long-suffering shake of his head. "Like perhaps until after we get Naren dressed and warm?"

She gave a small start, glanced over to where the injured Cat Man lay, and nodded. "Oh, yes. Of course." Not awaiting his response, Rissa strode over to Naren and knelt beside him. Ever so gently, she shook him awake.

His lids lifted. Gray eyes, cloudy with confusion, stared

up at her. "F-femina. What's wrong?" Naren paused to gather his scattered wits about him and, as he suddenly became aware of the acute cold, shivered. "Curse it all, but it's frigid in here!"

"That's why I woke you," Rissa explained with a smile. "Morigan and I are going to dress you in some warmer garb." She glanced over her shoulder at the tunic the Cat Lord held. Thankfully, it laced all the way down the front and would be easy to slip on Naren and still simplify caring for his wounds. "Perhaps if you unlace the front," she suggested to Morigan, "we can ease the tunic on without undue pain."

He nodded and, in the space of another few minutes, had the tunic open. Rissa scooted over to Naren's other side. Morigan handed her the tunic, then slid his hand and arm beneath the other Cat Man's shoulders and lifted. Rissa quickly pulled the tunic beneath Naren. A few minutes more and the tunic was on and laced loosely up the front.

The breeches were considerably more difficult, especially when Rissa insisted on averting her gaze for the entire process of pulling the breeches up past his knees to his waist. Morigan and Naren exchanged amused looks at her embarrassed attempts to respect Naren's modesty after his loincloth was discarded to ease the donning of his breeches, but said nothing. Belatedly, Morigan admitted Rissa's behavior was definitely not that of an alley walker or even a sexually experienced female.

Though the surge of guilt that flooded him at the realization was distinctly unappreciated, he nonetheless found the increasing evidence of her maidenhood a pleasing consideration. A consideration that shouldn't matter, one way or another, Morigan fiercely reminded himself. She could never be anything more to him than his mate and the breeder of his heirs. Yet, the fact she was most likely untouched by any man, and especially a Bellatorian, made the thought of coupling with her less disturbing. Whether Rissa realized it yet, she would be his, and his alone.

He watched her surreptitiously as she worked to settle Naren down once more and tuck the blankets and additional fur cloak Morigan had extracted from the second pack snugly around him. Her long blond hair, shining like silver in the flickering light of the perpetual flame box, fell like some luminous veil down her shoulders and back. Her slender body, outlined by the smooth sheen of the domare-hide clothing, was supple and pleasingly rounded. And her delicately shaped face, high cheekbones, and full, pink lips glowed with a soft radiance.

She was no Cat Woman. She was too softly formed, her eyes too round, her face too oval, and her looks and body more gently sculpted than the lithe, exotic, feline sensuality of their own kind. Yet, inexplicably, Morigan found her appealing.

And, just as inexplicably, found his attraction to her disturbing as well. Disturbing and disloyal. To desire a female of another species as much as—if not more than—his own kind seemed yet another blow to the already damaged self-esteem of the Cat People. Already, he dreaded the initial reaction of the Cat Women when they brought the Bellatorian females back to the lair. He knew, felt, their sense of failure at their seeming inability to conceive. The final insult would be the presence of alien females in the lair—and in the Cat Men's beds.

Though Morigan had taken care only to include the names of Cat Men without Cat Women mates in the initial lottery, if, in time, most of the Cat Women truly proved to be infertile, even their own mates would have to take alien females. That consideration, however, was more than Morigan cared to deal with at present. He had his hands full enough with this first group of Bellatorian females—and with Rissa, in particular.

It was past time he put forth an effort to ease her adjustment to him. Her friendship with Naren was more than evident, her comfort with and trust in him bordered on the unseemly. Rissa was *his* mate, not Naren's. No matter her feelings to the contrary, she must begin to act and appear that way.

Without the warmth of a fire tonight, it was imperative they all sleep close to one another. The early winter storm would keep the unsuspecting Atroxes in their own camp. As long as it snowed, there was no need for a guard. Brandar could share his body's warmth with Naren, and he would sleep with Rissa.

She wouldn't like it, that Morigan knew. She would protest vehemently. But, in the end, expediency would force her to acquiesce. He would at last place his scent on her, begin the process of claiming her for his own.

Squashing the surprising flare of anticipation that welled within him at the thought of holding Rissa in his arms, Morigan turned his efforts to digging out food for their evening meal. Once again it was simple fare, more meat sticks, journey bread, and dried fruit, supplemented by a round of domare milk cheese. Afterwards, he and Brandar talked for a time while Rissa tended to Naren.

As the evening burned on, Morigan found his irritation growing at her increasingly untoward relationship with his friend. It was bad enough she all but ignored him, but Brandar's raised brow and questioning glances began to grate on his nerves. Finally, Morigan had had enough. He rose, stalked over to Rissa, and offered his hand.

She glanced up in surprise. "What is it?"

"Time for bed. Come, femina."

There was something in the tone of his voice that warned her, even if she'd failed to note the dangerous glitter in his eyes. But Rissa caught it all. Morigan wanted something of her this night and was determined to get it.

Her throat dry, her heartbeat accelerating wildly, Rissa placed her hand in his and allowed him to pull her to her feet. She opened her mouth to ask Morigan what he wanted, then thought better of it. Knowing the course their interactions usually took, she was loath to get into an argument and add further to Naren's distress.

He'd developed a fever, and his wound, despite their care, had begun to fester. If he were to recover, Naren needed as much peace and quiet as he could get. She didn't dare risk upsetting him to the point he might feel compelled to come to her aid.

No, she must deal with whatever Morigan had planned for her this night herself. In the end, the real battle had always been between them. If only she had felt more his equal, she would have faced the undertaking with higher hopes. But it wasn't just his overwhelming strength and unusual Cat powers that intimidated her. As formidable as they were, she could still fight them and realize some tangible results for her efforts.

But the power Morigan held over her emotions was something else altogether. When he looked down at her, his green-gold eyes glinting dangerously from beneath dark, straight brows, it was all Rissa could do to overcome the strange, aching feeling that welled deep within her belly. He stirred her as no other man had done, in ways she was loath to examine or barely even admit to herself. Yet, though one part of her was unaccountably roused by the realization, another part could only feel revulsion for the humiliating desires.

Perhaps she hated him most for that. For making her fee
things for him that confused and disgusted her. He was a
alien, an animal, and he had taken her freedom from her. H
cared nothing for her own dreams and desires. All that mat
tered was that her body was of use to him and his people.

She should hate him. But she didn't.

That was the greatest shame of all. She was Bellatorian
Warrior's blood filled her, coursed through her body witl
each surging beat of her heart. And a Bellatorian would neve
permit anyone, especially some animalistic, savage alien spe
cies, to defeat him.

The journey to Agrica had heralded the onset of a nev
existence, new adventures, and the hope of at last finding
cause to devote all her energies to. She'd never envisioned
however, not in her most far flung dreams, that the journe
would also turn her life, her plans, and personal commit
ments, upside down. But it had. Now, Rissa desperatel
feared meeting Morigan, Lord of the Cat Men, would irrevo
cably change her. Change her into some person she'd other
wise never have become.

Yet, still, she meekly allowed him to lead her across th
cave to where a simple bed of fur cloaks and blankets wa
laid. No matter how she might inwardly rail against the pat
fate seemed to have set for her, tonight was beyond her powe
to change. If only he didn't—

"We'll sleep together tonight," Morigan's deep, husk
voice intruded on her tumultuous thoughts. "It'll be terribl
cold in here without a fire, and we both need to share th
heat of each other's body."

Warily she lifted her gaze. "Naren. Brandar. What abou
them?"

"They'll sleep beside each other for the same purpose."

Rissa licked her lips, slowly, carefully. "Naren. I woul

feel better sleeping next to him. If he wakes during the night in pain, I could be there to . . . to give him more of Zada's—"

"You are mine, femina. It wouldn't be acceptable for you to sleep with another male, however innocently. We don't normally share our mates."

A muscle ticked along his jaw. Something close to anger smoldered in his striking eyes. There were deeper issues than masculine pride and right of possession involved here, Rissa realized. She risked treading on Cat People customs and traditions in requesting to share even the simple warmth of her body with another Cat Man.

For all their apparently barbaric outward appearances, the Cat People seemed to possess their own code of conduct and morals. And monogamy appeared to be but one facet of that code. Rissa found that revelation strangely comforting.

Yet, still, the thought of sleeping next to Morigan frightened her. What if he decided to force himself on her? What if—

"We'll sleep together only for survival purposes," he said, answering her unspoken thoughts before she could even form them into words. "Despite what you may think of us, Cat People honor the act of mating. We don't couple in public, or even outside the safety of our lairs, if we can help it." Morigan's mouth twisted. "As difficult as this may be for you to believe, I *am* capable of controlling myself until we reach the lair. Besides, I've no desire to entertain Naren and Brandar this night at our expense."

He quirked a questioning brow. "Satisfied?"

Rissa swallowed hard. "I-I suppose I've no other choice but to take you at your word."

"No, I suppose you haven't." Morigan squatted beside the makeshift bed, flung back the fur cloak and blanket that served as their covering, and indicated that she climb in.

She eyed the bed for a moment more, then squared he
shoulders, flung back her head, and sank to her knees. "A
minute, if you please." Rissa pulled her long fall of hai
around to lie upon her chest. With quick, nimble fingers, she
wove the pale, gold-blond tresses into a single braid and fas
tened the end with a bit of leftover leathern thong.

"There, all done." She flung the thick braid back over he
shoulder and glanced up at Morigan.

The look in his eyes took her breath away. Grief, so raw
so deep, so haunting, burned but a moment, then was quickly
extinguished. He took Rissa's braid in his hand, sliding hi
fingers up and down the silken plaits. For a moment sus
pended in time Morigan held it, his fingers slowly clenching
until his knuckles went white. Then, he exhaled a long, shud
dering breath and gently released her hair.

Morigan dragged his gaze back up to Rissa's. At her intent
apprehensive look, he managed a bitter smile. "Your hai
When you braided it just now, you reminded me of m
wife . . ."

His wife. Slaughtered over a cycle ago. Rissa hesitated
unsure what she should admit to knowing. "Naren tol
me . . ."

"That I lost her in the massacre?" The stoic, inscrutabl
mask fell, shuttering his emotions and that brief glimpse he
allowed her of his inner self. "Naren talks too much. Now
get in bed. I've had about all I can take for one day."

Silently, she sat, pulled off her boots, and crawled beneat
the bedding. Rolling over onto her side, she faced the cav
wall. In the next moment Morigan was pulling off his ow
boots, lying down beside her, and settling the blanket an
fur over them. Then, with a firm grip about her waist, h
pulled her close.

She tensed. Even through the barrier of his domare-hid

clothing, Rissa could feel the hardness of his body, the heat of him. And, though he had bathed, she faintly caught his scent, musky, primal, and sense-stirring. Her throat went dry. Her pulse quickened.

Despair and excitement battled within her. Rissa's lids slid shut, and she released a long, tremulous breath. She would never be able to sleep tonight. Not with him beside her. Not with this intense awareness of him prickling through her.

"Relax, femina," Morigan's low command whispered down the side of her neck in a warm rush of air. "I mean you no harm. I just want to sleep. I swear it."

Rissa nodded, not daring to trust her own voice or reply. She forced her tautly strung frame to relax, or at least feign relaxation. There was nothing, however, she could do about the chaos of thoughts and sensations roiling through her head.

He lay there beside her, so close she could feel each breath he took, his hard chest rhythmically rising and falling against her. His muscular thighs pressed along the backs of her legs; his groin cupped the rounded fullness of her buttocks. It was too much, too intimate for a maiden unversed in the ways of men.

Frantically Rissa tried to think of something, anything, to distract herself from the panic rising in her. She tried to imagine home, the pristine stone houses and lush gardens, the five moons rising in the night sky, and the lavish banquets and extravagantly dressed people. Yet, time and again, the memory of Morigan's tormented eyes as he'd held her braid in his hand returned.

A sense of infinite sadness encompassed Rissa. His loss, and that of his people, was reality. Not her former empty, meaningless life of wealth and comfort. Strange, she mused, but everything seemed to pale in the harsh light of that realization. And nothing seemed as real—or as right— as lying here in this frigid cave, snug and warm in Morigan's arms.

Tears welled in her eyes. Rissa clenched them shut to staunch the unwanted moisture. She was going mad. That was all there was to it. The stress, the hardship, and the high emotions were all conspiring against her to drive her over the brink of insanity.

She should loathe Morigan, hate him, and fight him every step of the way. Instead, his private pain, a pain he fought so hard to keep hidden, touched her heart. And the same animal tendencies that initially revolted her, now stirred the deepest, most primitive part of her. She was drawn to him, emotionally and physically, by bonds so strong, so primal they alternately thrilled and terrified her.

Yet, it could never be. They were too different, had diametrically opposed goals and needs. And he was an alien species. She must never forget that. In the end, it *all* came down to that.

She didn't want to be assimilated into the Cat People. She didn't want to bear a half-breed child. She was Bellatorian. She must *never* forget that.

A small, frustrated breath escaped Rissa. It wasn't fair. Nothing in her life had prepared her for such a heart and conscience-wrenching experience. Yet, there was nothing left to her but face it—and find some honorable way through it all.

A strange lethargy stole into her limbs. Her mind moved more sluggishly, the thoughts coming with the greatest of efforts. She yawned, shifted against Morigan, and murmured sleepily.

He felt her relax, heard her breathing slow and deepen, and smiled grimly. Though he knew she'd fight him if he ever dared try to probe or control her mind again, Morigan had, by far more subtle means, managed to lull her into slumber. She'd been ready for it, wanted it, or he'd never have succeeded. For once, he'd won a battle against her.

A twinge of guilt plucked at him at having manipulated Rissa even in such an innocuous way, but her inner turmoil had been almost palpable. He'd never have been able to sleep until she did. Call it the strangest sort of self-preservation, but his own peace of mind was now inextricably entwined with hers.

The unsettling realization came upon Morigan gradually, snaking through him like the tenacious tendrils of the funis vine. Strong, inexorable, and unnerving. He didn't want to care how she felt, didn't want to know her needs and desires, and didn't dare allow her to touch his heart. Yet, she had.

Rissa moved again, mumbled sleepily to herself, then sighed contentedly. Gods, but she was so soft, so warm, molding her body to his as if it had always been meant that way! His heart beat faster, the blood surged through his body, hot and life-sustaining, pooling in his loins.

His sex swelled, thickened. Morigan bit back an anguished groan. He didn't need this, actually despised his response. It was torment of the cruelest kind.

Yet, still, the blood coursed down to fill his manhood, until he throbbed with each beat of his heart. Could she feel him, pressed so tightly as he was to her backside? Let her sleep, he prayed. He couldn't deal with her outrage now. Not now, not on top of the crazed whirl of emotions and needs already pounding through him.

He'd never imagined such a simple act as Rissa braiding her hair before bedtime could stir anew the painful memories he'd thought he'd buried of Winna. Never realized how much he'd missed his wife, or how deeply she'd filled his life and embedded herself into his heart. He'd never allowed himself to plumb the depths of his loss, never allowed himself to mourn her and his son. And, now . . . now, he feared to do it, feared what it would do to him after all this time.

Every minute of every waking hour had been filled with the desperate battle to survive. And, when he'd finally collapsed into sleep each night, his slumber had been as empty of dreams of Winna as he'd permitted his thoughts to be. Perhaps, even then, his mind had refused to permit his mourning. Perhaps that denial, vital though it might not be to his eventual healing, had been the only thing that had kept him going.

Morigan rested his chin on Rissa's shoulder. Once more he shuttered his heart, walling it with bands of impregnable resolve. He willed himself to relax, to ignore the soft, sweet pressure of her body against his, to sleep, and to cast aside the doubts and fears.

There was no other choice, not anymore. He and his people had survived, had thrived, because of the path he'd chosen. He dared not now take another, no matter how beguiling a certain Bellatorian female had become . . .

"Ah, he sleeps at last," Brandar breathed softly after a time, lying down beside Naren. "Things will go better between them now that he has finally bent her to his will and mingled his scent with hers. Strange how females always gentle once we place our scent upon them."

"I suppose so," Naren muttered. He pulled the fur cloak up about his shoulders.

"It was past time Morigan stake his claim to her," the other Cat Man rambled on. "She's a fiery one. There'd have been problems in the lair if he'd brought her back untamed."

And you think her tamed, do you? Naren silently asked. *On the contrary, Rissa is far from submitting her will to Morigan. But Morigan knows that. He's no fool.*

No, the only fool in this whole game of hearts is me, he
thought bitterly, his fever burning within him like tongues
of fire. *I chose Rissa for Morigan, all but forced her on him.
And now I find I regret that act, find I resent my best friend,
as well. Fool that I was, I gave him the female I now realize
I desire more than life itself.*

Seven

Morigan woke early the next morning to find himself flat on his back, and Rissa half-sprawled across an outstretched thigh in contented slumber. Her face nestled on his shoulder. One of her hands rested beneath his tunic that had inadvertently become unlaced during the night, her fingers entwined in his chest hair. Her tresses, most of them having curled free from her braid, lay fanned across his upper torso.

In her slumber, she'd symbolically claimed him as her own, from her uninhibited sleeping position to her long blond hair that had captured him in a web of spun gold. Her scent, flower-fresh and uniquely feminine, wafted up to Morigan. He inhaled deeply, filling his senses with her special fragrance, savoring it.

His arm curved about her, pressing her gently to him. Gods, but he'd forgotten how good a female could feel! She was soft, warm, and . . . he belatedly realized as she squirmed against him in her slumber, arousing him. With a muffled groan, Morigan fought to still his body's traitorous response. The effort was in vain.

He needed to get her off him, and quickly, before he either went mad or Rissa woke. Pressed as her thigh was against his groin, even her man-innocent body would recognize his arousal. And the last thing Morigan wanted was to have to deal with her indignation, or destroy the tenuous trust he'd managed to build in sleeping with her last night. But how to disengage Rissa without wakening her?

First, he must retrieve her hand from inside his tunic. That much was clear. He'd had enough of her claws when she was startled awake. Then, if he could just roll her gently off . . .

His hand closed over hers, captured her slender fingers in the curl of his, and pulled them free of his tunic. Lowering her arm to her side, Morigan grasped her firmly and—

"What do you think you're doing?"

His gaze slid down to hers. Furious brown eyes, flecked with gold, glared up at him. "I was just moving you off me. I didn't think you'd be particularly pleased if you woke up and found yourself situated so wantonly across my—"

"Wantonly!" She glanced down at herself, saw her leg nestled between his, her breasts pressed against his chest. With a muffled cry, Rissa flung herself up and off him. In the process, however, her knee slammed into Morigan's groin.

"Gods!" He shoved her away and rolled over onto his side, his knees drawing up protectively. For long minutes, he lay there, fighting to catch his breath as waves of agony washed over him.

"M-Morigan?" Rissa's voice pierced the mists of his torment. "What did I do? I-I'm sorry." Her hand reached out tentatively to clasp his shoulder.

"Don't!" he choked. "Just . . . don't touch . . . me!"

She jerked her hand back, hurt. Her glance swung across the cave, to find Brandar and Naren staring back at her. Sympathy for their injured comrade gleamed in their eyes.

"What did I do?" Rissa mouthed the question to Naren.

"You all but castrated him with your knee, Rissa," the Cat Man offered in explanation. "Have a care next time, will you? We'd like our lord to remain capable of fathering children."

Rissa flushed and glanced back at Morigan. He was beginning to calm, the look of excruciating pain ebbing from his face. "Oh."

Weakly he levered himself to one elbow, his brow damp with sweat. "Oh?" he rasped. "Is that all you have to say for yourself?"

"It was an accident!" Rissa cried. "And I already said I was sorry!"

"Every time you hurt me, it's an accident!" Morigan shoved himself to a sitting position. "I should've known better than ever to have imagined you soft and feminine!" With furious movements, he laced his tunic front closed, flung back his tangled mane from his face, and climbed to his feet. For an instant, he wobbled unsteadily over her. Then, with another low groan, the Cat Lord staggered across the cave.

"Where are you going?" she called after him. "You don't look all that well . . ."

"Well enough to get away from you while I'm able," he muttered hoarsely. Grabbing up the fur cloak that covered a smirking Naren and Brandar, Morigan stumbled down the tunnel.

Rissa shot Naren an imploring look. "What should I do? I didn't mean to hurt him, and I don't want him to go out into that cold just to avoid me."

Indecision warred in the Cat Man's gray eyes. Then, he sighed. "Go after him, femina. Make him listen and understand. Morigan will calm in time and accept the fact it was truly an accident. For all his flares of temper, he's a reasonable person."

"Thank you, Naren." Rissa tugged on her boots, then rose and flung their former bed cover of fur about her shoulders. Noting Morigan's boots still lying where he'd deposited them last night, she picked them up before heading down the tunnel.

He was sitting at the cave opening, huddled behind the large boulder that half-blocked the entrance from outside view. His fur cloak was tucked about him, his knees were drawn up beneath it, and his chin rested atop it all. At her approach, he shot her a thunderous look, then groaned.

"What do you want now?"

"I came to ask you to return to where it's warmer." She held out his boots. "And to bring you these."

Morigan eyed her for a long moment, then reached up and took the boots. "My thanks," he rasped as he pulled them on. "My feet were getting a bit frosty sitting out here."

"Will you come back into the cave?"

He scowled. "No, not just yet. I need time to calm." He glanced away. "My behavior in there wasn't the most dignified, nor the most appropriate."

Morigan was embarrassed by his outburst in front of his men, Rissa realized. Somehow, that tiny glimpse into his well-guarded inner self moved her as no apology—though it was there just the same—ever could. She sat down beside him, drawing her own knees up beneath her fur cloak to conserve her meager body heat.

At her action, he shot her a startled glance. "You shouldn't be out here. It's too cold."

"And what of you?" Rissa hunkered down in the thick fur until her nose and mouth were covered. The dense silky hairs tickled her face. "You'll get cold soon enough, too."

"I've suffered far worse."

His bitterly snarled words drew Rissa up short. There was a terrible history behind that statement, one she was afraid to pry deeper into. Suddenly, nothing mattered more than easing his pain, soothing the look of anguish that had flared, just now, in his eyes.

"Hold me," she whispered, scooting yet closer to him. "It's so cold, and I want to be warm."

"Rissa," Morigan began, a wary, uncertain look in his eyes. "I don't think—"

"Please, Morigan!"

With a soulful sigh, he lifted his cloak. "Come, femina."

Rissa slipped beneath his cloak to nestle in the warm, protective curve of his body. There was still so much that lay between them but, for this brief moment in time, it seemed right—and so very good—to be close to him.

It snowed heavily throughout the rest of the day. The land disappeared beneath a soft, gently undulating blanket of white. The unmarred beauty, however, only increased the danger of venturing outside and leaving betraying evidence of their presence. So, for the next two days, Rissa and the three Cat Men remained within the cave, save for the utmost of personal needs, and watched their food supplies dwindle to nothing.

By noon of the third day, the weather broke. The sun shone hot for the first time. The snow began to melt. Morigan, mightily weary of being cooped up in such close quarters with Rissa's increasingly disturbing presence, jumped at the excuse to go hunting.

"Brandar will stay here to guard you and Naren," he explained to her as he strapped his dagger to his waist. He wore only his domare-hide tunic, boots, and breeches, eschewing the fur cloak in the sudden warmth of the day. "I'll scout out the Atroxes to see if they remain nearby, then bring us back some fresh meat. If it's safe, we'll even cook the game over a fire."

"And if it isn't safe?" Rissa asked, dreading the reply.

Morigan shrugged. "We've eaten raw meat before. You can get used to anything, if you're hungry enough."

Rissa shuddered. "Well, *I* can't. I'd rather starve."

"And do you think I could permit you to do that, femina?" he asked softly. "I'm responsible for you now, for your safety and welfare. And for your continued health as well."

"You take too much upon yourself, Morigan," Rissa sniffed. "Save your energies for your people."

He stepped close. "But you forget, sweet femina, that you *are* one of my people now."

"Ah, yes," she muttered. "How *could* I forget? I must keep my body strong and healthy for childbearing." She shot him a mutinous look. "That *is* the point you were making, isn't it?"

"Partially." Morigan sighed and shook his head. "Will there never be peace between us, Rissa? You come willingly enough to bed with me now."

"You're warm, and that's all there is to it." Rissa averted her gaze, unable to face the piercing brilliance of his eyes, afraid he'd see the lies glimmering in her own eyes. "It's the only time each day I can count on easing the numbness in my hands and feet and feel warm for a while. Who wouldn't look forward to that, no matter whom it was with?"

"So that's all I am to you, then? A hairy bed warmer?"

At his tone of amused reproach, she glanced up. Rissa's lips tightened. Curse him. What did he want from her? Reassurance that she enjoyed sleeping next to him, or just some stroking of his male ego for the sake of the other two Cat Men? Well, she would never give him either. Never!

She gave him, instead, a shove. "Get on with you. You

play the role of hairy bed warmer quite well. Be content with that, for that's all you'll ever be to me. That and a provider of food," she added, "if you can manage to find us some game."

"And if I do bring back meat, will you swear to eat it raw to please me?"

"Please you?" Rissa gave a snort of disgust. "Truly, you ask far too much!"

He laughed, the sound rich and throaty, then turned and strode out of the cave. Brandar followed, intent on standing guard at the entrance until Morigan's return.

For a long moment Rissa stood there, shocked speechless by the Cat Lord's sudden outburst of merriment. Morigan laugh? Why, he'd rarely even smiled in all the past days. Whatever was the matter with him?

With a small frown furrowing her brow, she glanced questioningly at Naren. His scowl, which he quickly hid, gave her pause. "Naren, what's wrong?"

"Nothing. My wounds momentarily pained me, that's all." He made a big scene of shifting about on his pallet of blankets and furs, then gave the effort up in exasperation. "By the three moons, how I tire of lying here all the time!"

Rissa hurried over, knelt beside him, and felt his brow. "The fever has broken at last, and your wounds are finally clean and healing nicely. It won't be long before you can be up and about a bit more."

"It's all right, Rissa," the black-haired Cat Man said, taking her hand in his. Guilt surged through him at the jealousy he'd felt when watching Rissa and Morigan talk, seeing what appeared to be the first flickerings of warmth and affection flare between them, and at his pettish complaints to Rissa afterwards.

He'd be more than thankful when he could be up and about

again. He'd be ecstatic to get away from the constant sight of Rissa, her voice, her scent, and sweetly beguiling presence. It was the only way to ease his growing desire for her—and the resentment beginning to gnaw at him that she was Morigan's.

Naren smiled up at her, struggling to contain his inner turmoil. "I think the confinement of this cave is just getting to all of us, each in his own way. I'll be fine, just as soon as the others arrive and get me back to the lair."

"And what if they don't? Arrive, I mean?" Rissa didn't know whether to hope the rescue party made it to them or not, though, for Naren's sake, she knew she should. "How long do we dare remain here?"

"Not much longer, I'm afraid. And, though you've done wonders in aiding my healing, my strength won't be up to any strenuous mountain travel for at least another week."

"I'd say more like two weeks," Rissa corrected him grimly. "And that only if you continue to have a well-balanced diet. A diet that meat alone can't supply, no matter how much game Morigan and Brandar bring back."

"We Cat Men are a hardier lot than most other species. I'll be ready sooner than you think." His expression darkened. "I have to."

She remembered Morigan's admission that Naren might have to die if his infirmity ever endangered the rest of them. Anger—and a fierce determination—swelled within her. "I won't let him kill you, Naren. One way or another, we'll get you back to your lair."

He grinned. "You're starting to sound like you care about us. Are you, perhaps, beginning to accept your fate?"

The question drew Rissa up short. Warmth flooded her cheeks. "No." She vehemently shook her head. "I just care what happens to you, Naren. You've treated me kindly from the beginning. As for the rest, I can't so easily accept a fate I have no say in."

"And Morigan?" he prodded, choosing his next words with care. "Have you come to care for him as well?"

Rissa paused, her gaze narrowing. "And why do my feelings for him matter so much to you?"

Naren forced a nonchalant shrug. "I told you. I feel responsible for bringing you together." His scrutiny of her intensified. "Well, Rissa, do you?"

She licked her lips, hesitant, considering. Finally, Rissa sighed. "I can't tell you that, Naren. You're his friend. Whatever I say may be repeated to him."

"A dilemma I find myself increasingly at odds with. I'd like to think I was your friend as well."

A wild hope flared within her. Rissa averted her eyes, fearful she might betray her true intent. "A friend wouldn't force someone to stay where she didn't want to be."

Naren exhaled a long breath. "Another dilemma which pulls at me. One of even greater import than that of my friendship with you and Morigan. One that directly impacts on the survival of my people. And one," he emphasized slowly, "that must *always* take precedent."

"One female, more or less, wouldn't matter to your people!" Rissa cried, finally looking up. "I will die if you and Morigan compel me to remain at your lair! My spirit won't bear a forced confinement!"

"We hope, in time, that you and the other females will come to accept and love your new life with us. As we hope you'll all come to accept and love your Cat Men mates."

"I can never accept or love a man who takes away my freedom, however well-intentioned for the sake of his people it may be. There is something inherently wrong in that kind of relationship. At least for me, there is."

Naren shook his head, a quizzical look in his eyes. "You're a strange one, Rissa. For a Bellatorian, I mean. I'd thought only our own females were so headstrong and proud, but I was wrong. If the rest of the captured females are anything like you, we'll have our hands full."

"Females of most species are the same, I'd wager," Rissa observed, reluctantly facing the fact that her small, temporary advantage had been lost. "Why would you think we'd be any less proud or vigilant of our rights than you men would be? Though we may lack the physical strength to fight you for them, we've never lacked the heart or desire."

"We mean you no harm, Rissa," Naren countered softly. "We just have no other choice. What else would you have us do?"

There it was again, she thought. The question. And, the longer she was with the Cat Men and had the opportunity to get to know them, all the possible solutions, one by one, seemed to disappear. "I don't know," she finally replied. "I begin to think there isn't any answer that's fair to all. Someone, I fear, will suffer no matter what the Cat People do."

He stared up at her, an inexpressible sadness creeping into his eyes. "I'm afraid so, femina. And, though I greatly regret it, I fear you'll be one of those to—"

A low whistle cut him short. Naren shoved himself to his elbows, his glance swinging to the tunnel that led to the outside.

Rissa recognized the look and froze. "What? What's happening, Naren?"

"Brandar just signaled me. Someone's coming."

"Well, could it be Morigan?" she whispered.

"No. It's a group of five or six." He placed a finger against her lips. "Quiet, now. Atroxes have hearing nearly as acute as Cat Men."

She nodded silently. What if Atroxes *were* approaching? What if they knew there were Cat Men in here? With Naren weak and nearly helpless, there was only Brandar to protect them. She glanced around the cave, even as she remembered having seen Brandar take all three blasters with him as he followed Morigan out. Since her one chance at Naren's blaster, they were always careful to keep the weapons away from her.

But if Brandar needed help against the Atroxes, perhaps he just might trust her with a blaster. It was worth a try. As much as Rissa hated being the captive of the Cat Men, falling into the Atroxes' hands was an even worse fate. They were notoriously brutal to their captives, even if a ransom was involved. And the ones they chose to kill supposedly suffered horribly before they were finally permitted to die.

She leaned close to Naren. "I'm going to see if Brandar needs help. If there's to be a battle, I don't want to sit back here and helplessly await the outcome."

He eyed her for a long moment. "Then go, femina. I'd be there with you, if I could. It's your right to fight to protect yourself, as it would be for any of our females. Brandar won't refuse your offer, if he needs it."

Rissa took his hand for a brief instant, squeezed it, and smiled. "Thank you for that, and for everything you've done for me." Then, before Naren could reply, she rose to her feet and headed toward the tunnel.

The big, sandy-haired Cat Man was poised behind the rock near the cave's entrance, his blaster at the ready. As Rissa moved up beside him and knelt, he shot her a wary glance.

"What are you doing here, femina? Didn't Naren warn you of our unexpected visitors?"

"Yes." She scanned the terrain outside the cave. "I've come to help. Do you have any idea who our visitors might be?"

Brandar shook his head. "No, not yet. I thought I caught a sensation of movement out there, far away, several minutes ago, but nothing since then. Whoever they are, they're good."

"Morigan," she breathed, suddenly remembering him. "He's out there. What if they come upon him unawares?"

"Our lord is quite capable of taking care of himself. If I heard the strangers' approach, you can be certain he did."

"But what if he tries to attack them alone, divert them from finding us?" The consideration filled her with a cold fear. "He won't have a chance against a large group of Atroxes. And he doesn't even have a blaster this time!" She turned, gripping the Cat Man's arm in a fierce clasp. "You must go to him and bring him a blaster, Brandar. If you give me the other blaster, I can stay here and guard the cave until you both return."

He smiled wryly and shook his head. "I find your concern for Morigan most gratifying, as he will, if he makes it back safely. But my orders were to stay here and guard you and Naren. Morigan would never forgive me if I left you in danger."

"I'm not totally helpless, you know," Rissa muttered, embarrassed at so blatantly revealing her anxiety over the Cat Lord's welfare. All she needed was Morigan getting even more cocky when it came to her. She'd enough trouble dealing with him as it was. "I wouldn't betray you to the Atroxes."

"I never imagined you would, femina. You are Morigan's mate."

"I am not . . ." With a sigh of exasperation, Rissa let the worn-out protest die. What was the point, anyway? Morigan's followers would believe as he wished them to believe. In the end, all that mattered was that she escape. *That* would be the final and most telling rebuttal to their stubborn insistence that she was Morigan's property.

She released his arm. "Will you at least permit me to fight alongside you if it becomes necessary? Naren said it was my right to defend myself."

"If it becomes necessary, femina," was the Cat Man's reply before he once more settled into a vigilant silence.

Time dragged on. The minutes eased into a quarter hour, and then a half. Yet, try as she might, Rissa couldn't hear or see anything out of the ordinary. Nothing moved out there, not a bird in the sky, a stray breeze, or an unsuspecting animal.

The tension built, twisting her tautly strung nerves until she thought her sanity would shred. Fear, for all of them, vibrated through her. Yet, surprisingly enough, her fear for Morigan was greatest. If he suspected they were in danger, he'd step between the threat and them, sacrificing himself. Rissa knew that with a certainty deep and sure.

She wanted to scream out her frustration, her confusion, and her anger at her sense of helplessness to control the wild ride on which the Cat Lord was taking her emotions. A ride that, all the while, *he* embarked on only to fulfill a duty.

Shame, then self-disgust, filled her. Was she so desperate for love since her mother's death she'd stoop to grasp at the meager crumbs some alien Cat Man threw her way? Had she been so long deprived of a man's affection since her father had left her and her mother those many years ago, she'd settle now for any male's interest?

It seemed the only logical explanation for her strange and inappropriate attraction to Morigan. Yet, why hadn't she felt even more drawn to Naren, who treated her with far more respect and kindness than Morigan did? The questions roiled through Rissa's mind as the nerve-racking minutes passed, questions that maddeningly defied answers.

"Someone's coming," Brandar hissed, his voice so low Rissa almost thought she heard it in her head. She tensed, her nails digging into her palms. Then, several forms appeared from out of nowhere, five Cat Men and what could only be a Cat Woman. They carried a set of long poles, several packs, and blasters.

"Lisan," Brandar breathed in relief. He sprang up, grabbed the extra blasters and ran out of the cave.

Rissa climbed to her feet and watched as the two Cat Men embraced. Then, she turned and reentered the cave.

Naren glanced up. "It's Lisan and the others, isn't it?"

"Yes. They brought poles to make a litter for you and, hopefully, some additional food, if the size of the packs they carry is any indication."

He grinned. "Good. We'll have a feast tonight and head out for the lair on the morrow." He paused, noting Rissa's decided lack of enthusiasm. "What's wrong, femina? I thought you'd be happy to learn our visitors were Cat Men."

"I'm happy for you, Naren. But their arrival heralds the continued surety of my captivity. And once I get to your lair . . ."

"Femina, don't distress yourself." He propped himself on one elbow and offered her his other hand. "It'll be all right. I swear it. Come, sit by me until the others come in. Is Agna with them?"

"I suppose so," she replied, ignoring his outstretched hand. "There was a female with the men."

"She's a healer, you know. The only one in our lair." Naren lowered his hand. "You'll want to make friends with her. She can teach you a lot."

"I'm not particularly interested—" Footsteps echoing down the tunnel diverted Rissa from her glum response. She wheeled about and came face to face with an unfamiliar Cat Man.

He was tall and massively built, his hair reddish-brown and his eyes black. He appeared to be very hirsute of face and body, what little she could see of it beneath his own leathern garments. His mouth was thin and twisted into what seemed a permanent sneer. Rissa didn't like him.

As his glance slammed into hers, his black eyes widened momentarily. Then, he cocked a speculative brow and visually raked her from head to toe. "One of the Bellatorian females, I presume? A pretty morsel, for an alien."

"She's also Morigan's, Cradoc," Naren growled, not at all pleased by the leering look his compatriot had given Rissa. "Keep that in mind before you mire yourself even deeper in trouble."

"I'm quite aware of whose she is. His scent is all over her." Cradoc grinned. "For all his apparent reluctance to take a mate out of the first group of females captured, my cousin wasted no time in picking what I'd wager to be the best of the lot. I knew I should have come along on this mission."

"It wouldn't have mattered, one way or another. I chose Rissa for Morigan. You'd never have had a chance at her."

"Ever the loyal friend, eh, Naren?" the other Cat Man jeered. "I wonder where it'll get you in the end?"

"It doesn't have to get me anywhere," Naren snarled, struggling to push himself to a sitting position, "and I'll still be further ahead than you."

Rissa hurried to kneel beside Naren. "Lie down," she ordered crisply, pushing gently on his chest. "You'll break open your wounds if you aren't careful."

Naren shot the other Cat Man one last, seething look, then turned his attention to Rissa. "He was rude to you," he muttered. "I won't have anyone treating you unkindly."

"I thank you for your concern. Truly, I do." She began to unlace his tunic thongs. "Now, just lie back and let me look under that chest bandage and see if you—"

"No, let *me* see," a strange feminine voice intruded. "I'm the healer here, not you."

The Cat Woman knelt beside Rissa and all but shoved her aside. Rissa turned to eye her, not quite believing she'd actually been pushed. Agna was a lithe, graceful woman, about thirty-five cycles old, almond-eyed, with an exotically sculpted facial structure. Though not exactly pretty, the healer was still striking, with her pale-blue eyes and thick mane of lightly gray-streaked black hair.

When the other woman all but ignored her as she busied herself unlacing Naren's tunic, Rissa shot her a furious glance and opened her mouth to tell her exactly what she thought of her rude behavior. In that instant, Naren's hand closed around hers.

"Let Agna take care of me, femina," he said, a pleading look in his eyes. "You've all but worn yourself out in nursing me. Sit back and rest for a change."

"Very well," Rissa gritted, deciding on the spot she didn't like the Cat Woman, Agna, either. But she did as Naren requested, rising to stride across the cave to take her place on the bed she and Morigan shared. She couldn't help but feel resentful, however, at her treatment so far by these newest Cat People. Though the other three Cat Men kept a respectful distance, they, too, eyed her with less than a friendly mien. And Cradoc, whenever he thought Naren wasn't looking, visually stripped her.

Rissa shivered. Up until now, though the Cat Men had treated her a bit roughly at times, they'd never failed to demonstrate their acceptance of her standing as Morigan's new mate, rendering her a solicitous if wary respect. There were others, however, who obviously wouldn't be quite so kind or welcoming. Not to her, or the other women in her party.

Yet, she, of them all, possessed the potential to ease their way in the Cat People's lair. As Morigan's chosen mate, there was a certain power to be had—and used— for their benefit. Though Rissa had no intention of willingly mating with the Cat Lord, if and when they reached his lair, she would try to utilize everything else in her power to help the other Bellatorian captives.

Agna seemed to spend an interminable length of time examining Naren, cleansing his wounds and applying fresh bandages, but at last, she finished. She shot a cold look at Rissa over her shoulder. "You did passably well, for a Bellatorian. His wounds are healing."

Rissa took the grudging compliment for what it was. There was no point in going out of her way to antagonize the other woman. Just as long as Agna made even a minimal effort at civility . . .

"You're welcome," Rissa forced herself to reply.

Agna frowned. Climbing to her feet, she strode over to stand before Rissa. "So, you really are Morigan's mate, are you?"

Rissa stared up at her. "So I've been told."

The Cat Woman's eyes narrowed. "And you don't much care for it, do you?"

"Would you?" she challenged. "I don't know many women who'd particularly enjoy being abducted and informed they'll serve as breeders."

"No, I suppose not," Agna admitted, "but what Morigan chooses to do with you is none of my concern." She motioned to her. "Stand up."

At the imperious tone in the other woman's voice, Rissa stiffened. "Why?"

"I must examine you."

"Why?" This time, Rissa couldn't keep the rising anger from her voice.

"You look too small and frail to me. There's no sense in Morigan wasting his seed on you if you're too narrow-hipped to bear a Cat Child. Though all babes are of value to us, the heir to the throne is of the utmost import. And we don't need our future Lady, Bellatorian though she may be, dying in childbirth. Morigan's suffered enough without you failing him as well."

"You act as if all this is some honor you Cat People have bestowed upon me," Rissa cried, leaping to her feet. Her hands clenched at her sides as she advanced on the other woman. "Well, let me clarify a few things for you before any misunderstanding arises. I don't want and never asked—"

"Rissa," Naren called from behind Agna, "why not wait until Morigan returns to—"

"Let the femina speak," Cradoc interjected, a smug amusement tingeing his voice. "I'm very interested in hearing her opinion on being chosen Lady of our people. As are the other Cat Men here, I feel certain," he added, glancing at each of them.

"And I say no!" Naren roared, shoving himself, once more, to a sitting position. "She's Morigan's. She owes none of you an—"

"What's going on here?" a deep voice intruded from behind them.

Cradoc and Agna swung around as Naren, with a low groan of relief, fell back onto his pallet. With a dark brow arched in quiet inquiry, Morigan stood there at the mouth of the cave, holding three long-eared lepus in one hand.

"I ask again," he prodded softly when no one answered,

the expression in his eyes sharpening to a glittering awareness. "What's going on here?"

"Nothing more than my usual charm coming into play," Rissa hurried to offer, stepping around Agna to stroll casually over to Morigan.

There was no purpose served in becoming the center of a battle between Morigan and his followers in the first few minutes of their arrival, she decided. Besides, though Agna's motives in picking a fight with her were still unclear, Cradoc's weren't. He didn't want Morigan to have her and thought to stir discontent with his lord's choice by making her look bad. As much as she didn't want to be the Cat Lord's mate, Rissa was equally certain she wasn't going to allow Morigan to play into Cradoc's hands.

She glanced down at the lepus Morigan held. "A nice day for hunting, to be sure, but perhaps not quite successful enough, now that we have guests . . ." She lifted her gaze to meet his and smiled.

He stared back at her, finding an expression of innocent amusement curving her lips—and a warning not to pursue the current topic of conversation gleaming in her eyes. His well-practiced mask slid once more into place. "You really ought to work on your social skills, femina," Morigan drawled, deciding it best not to push the issue further. Or at least not in Rissa's presence where she could be dragged into it to her detriment. "Not all of my people will tolerate your charming ways as much as I."

"What are you talking about, Morigan?" Naren protested. "Rissa's not at fault here. She—"

"Here," Morigan said, handing Rissa the three lepus. "You'll be happy to know the Atroxes have left the area, and we can cook these tonight. Care to learn how to clean them?"

Gingerly, she accepted the dead animals, glancing down

at them with uncertainty. "I suppose so, if someone could help me."

"I'll help your lady, my Lord," Lisan offered eagerly. His bright blue eyes shone with a sincere intent.

Morigan smiled at last. "I'm sure Rissa would appreciate your assistance." He glanced toward the tunnel. "Why don't you take her down to the spring? It'll be easier to clean up there afterwards."

"Of course, my Lord." The young Cat Man turned to Rissa. "My Lady, if you'd prefer, I could carry the lepus until we reach the spring." He extended his hand to her. She readily surrendered the game.

"I'll leave you to your friends, then," she said, turning back to Morigan. "I'm sure you've much to discuss with them." With a quick smile of farewell, she headed down the tunnel, Lisan following in her wake.

"Indeed, I *will* have much to discuss," he muttered darkly, waiting until she was well out of earshot. Then, with a thunderous look clouding his brow, Morigan turned back to confront his compatriots.

Eight

"What, by the three moons, were you trying to do?" Morigan snarled, rounding on Cradoc. "Cause further dissent and turmoil among our people by dragging Rissa into it? I warn you, Cousin, don't start on her!"

The other Cat Man's lips curled in a derisive sneer. "If there's dissent and turmoil in the lair, it's only because some of us have come to doubt your ability to rule. The others have arrived with their Bellatorian females. Already, the lair is in an uproar."

He shook his head pityingly. "You dare bring enemy females into our midst, force them on our men, shaming our own females in the process, and then still have the audacity to act surprised that we're unhappy with you? Come, come, *Cousin,* surely you're not that naive."

Stirred once again by the longstanding animosity with his ambitious, manipulative first cousin, rage boiled up in Morigan. Gods, he didn't need Cradoc's opposition in times such as these—and especially not now, to compound his problems with Rissa and the other captive females. From the start, there'd been decided resistance to his plan to supplement their own breeding females with those of other humanoid species, and not just from the outraged Cat Women. Still, Morigan had hoped things would settle down in time and his people would accept the necessity of such an act.

But they wouldn't if Cradoc and his small faction of supporters continued to fan the flames of resistance and resentment. Though Morigan had tolerated his cousin's snide remarks and minor attempts at undermining him in the past, his growing, open opposition was beginning to wear thin. Things between them were fast drawing to a head. The solution to Cradoc was a simple if dangerous one, thanks to ancient laws on the right of challenge, but Morigan preferred not to allow events to lead to such dire consequences. He needed all the able-bodied Cat Men he had, and that included his cousin.

So, for the sake of peace in the lair, Morigan tempered his impulse to slap that insolent smile off Cradoc's face. "Naiveté had nothing to do with it," he replied calmly instead. "Reality drove my decision. The survival of our people is what matters, not issues of false pride and wounded egos. We must all make compromises and sacrifices. Perhaps this experiment of mine won't work out, but we had few options left. None of which," he added dryly, "I ever heard you offer in the Council of Elders."

Color crept up Cradoc's neck and face. "This isn't an issue so easily solved with a few alien females, Morigan! And, after viewing the other Bellatorian females, I see you took the comeliest one for yourself. Do you, perhaps, have an ulterior motive in your great and glorious plan? Do you, perhaps, no longer find our own females appealing?"

"You're a fool, Cradoc!" Naren snarled from his pallet. "I've never heard a more senseless accusation in my—"

"Cradoc knows he's losing the battle when he's forced to stoop to such despicable charges," Morigan cut in, a hard, ruthless light smoldering in his eyes. "I won't even dignify his questions with answers. But I warn you, Cradoc." He riveted his full attention once more on his cousin. "If you dare spread such cruel and hurtful lies in the lair, I'll bring you up on charges before the Council. And, in times such as these, the punishment could well be death."

"Afraid to fight me, are you, Morigan?"

The taunting reply caught the Cat Lord as he turned away. Morigan wheeled about. His eyes narrowed and a muscle ticked spasmodically in his suddenly clenched jaw.

"No, not at all, Cousin," he replied, his tone silky, dangerous. "But I also won't be goaded into a senseless battle that could only end in your death. Let it be, while you still have some control over your fate. You forget I have support for my plan from the entire Council. You go up against not only me, but them in this."

"She despises us," the auburn-haired Cat Man muttered. "She doesn't wish to be your mate or our Lady."

"No, Rissa doesn't," Morigan admitted, willing to offer Cradoc a small gesture of face-saving agreement. "But she will in time. As will all the captive females. We must be patient with them."

Cradoc gave a disparaging laugh. "Indeed? Well, time will tell, won't it?"

"Yes," the Cat Lord agreed. "I only ask you to give me that time. Can you do that?"

"I have little other choice, do I?" came the grudging, disgruntled reply. "At least, for now."

"No, I suppose you don't." Morigan gestured to the packs the other Cat Men had carried. "Did you bring additional food supplies? We're down to the three lepus I caught, and we'd relish some fruit and bread to supplement this evening's meal."

"There's cheese, journey bread, dried fruit and vegetables, and even a few sweet cakes," Agna hastened to offer. "With the lepus, we've all the ingredients for a hearty stew. If," she added snidely, "your mate would deign to make us one."

Morigan and Naren exchanged an amused glance.

"Rissa would be delighted to help you in the stew's preparation, Agna, but I'd prefer if you took charge of that. My new mate is rather," Morigan paused in his choice of words, "unschooled in the finer points of cooking."

The Cat Woman raised a mocking brow. "Indeed? She has a lot to learn then, or you'll soon be forced to beg at other cookfires for your meals, won't you?"

"I doubt it'll come to that."

Agna shrugged. "Well, one way or another, I'd say that was the least of your worries where that female's concerned. By far, the very least."

There was merit, unfortunately, in the healer's words, Morigan admitted glumly as he helped the others unpack and set out the ingredients for the lepus stew. Cradoc and the others had immediately noted and responded to Rissa's ripe sensuality. Morigan had felt the aura of sexual tension in the cave as soon as he'd walked in. The Cat Women in the lair would see it, as well, and not be happy with the reaction it stirred in their men. He was bringing Rissa into a potentially explosive situation, unclaimed as she yet was as his mate.

Though he'd already put his scent on her by sleeping with her the past few nights, precipitating the first step in the claiming process, only the actual act of mating would seal their initial commitment. And mate with her soon he must, or stir even further turmoil and conflict in the lair. Yet, another set of events Cradoc gladly would use to his advantage.

* * *

They left the next evening as dusk washed the plains and foothills in soft shades of mauve and violet. Brandar led out, scouting the way several hundred meters ahead, followed by Morigan and Rissa. The two litter bearers, carrying Naren, came next, Agna, Lisan, Cradoc, and the additional Cat Man bringing up the rear. The small band traveled through the night until the trail into the Serratus Mountains became too treacherous even for the Cat Men's surefooted agility and acute night vision. A few hours before dawn, they made camp in a rocky gorge.

The caves, little more than deep overhangs of rock, afforded only the barest of room. Morigan and Rissa took one of the smallest, Naren, Agna, and Lisan the next largest. Cradoc and the others made their beds about twenty meters away in the cave that provided the most space.

Rissa was exhausted and quickly fell into a deep slumber beside Morigan, not waking until midafternoon. She jerked awake, puzzled by the low drone that had penetrated her dreams. A hand, resting gently on her head, kept her anchored to a hard-muscled chest. The other hand held the rest of her to a tautly strung body.

"Morigan," she whispered in confusion, moving against him, "what's wrong? Let me go. I want to—"

"Hush, femina," came the softly couched reply. "Lie still and don't make a sound. There are skim crafts about."

"Skim crafts?" Confusion flooded Rissa. "But how is that possible? They're too far from Primasedes."

A callused hand covered her mouth. *I said be quiet,* hissed the mental command, as the droning of skim crafts grew louder.

She stilled then and nodded, while wild plans raced through her mind. Skim crafts. Bellatorians. However they had managed to extend their range of flight, all that really mattered was that they were here. Her father had discovered her capture and had sent out search parties. Surely, they were looking for her!

A sudden thought assailed her. Morigan. His psychic powers. She was fortunate he hadn't already discerned she was the Lord Commander's daughter. She must redouble her efforts to keep him from probing her mind. And make her escape as soon as possible.

But how was she to alert the Bellatorian search party, with her mouth covered and clasped so securely in Morigan's arms? Yet, somehow, someway, she must. It might be her only chance to escape. Above all, she *must* escape.

Briefly, the skim crafts appeared to circle overhead, then to sweep the length of the gorge. They'd see nothing, Rissa well knew. The Cat Men and Agna would cloak themselves into invisibility. She, shielded from outside view by Morigan's body, would be just as invisible.

Now was the time to alert the searchers, if ever there was one. Yet, the thought of bringing the Bellatorians down upon the Cat People gave her pause. Depending on how many soldiers flew overhead—soldiers who would be well-armed and possess the tactical advantage—the battle would, at best, be brutal and close-fought. At the worst, it could end in a slaughter.

Though Rissa didn't want her own countrymen to be killed, though she knew she desperately need to escape, she didn't wish for the Cat Men to be harmed, either. Naren, Brandar, and Lisan had become friends, each in his own way. And Morigan . . .

With a small sigh, the coiled tension eased from Rissa's body. She'd find some other way to escape that didn't endanger the Cat People in the process, and take her chances with

Morgan in the meanwhile. As deeply as she desired her freedom, she knew she could never buy it at their expense.

Morgan felt the turmoil leave Rissa's body, sensed her acquiescence to his demands. He smiled softly. It didn't take psychic abilities to know that Rissa had been contemplating betraying them to the Bellatorians, battled within herself, and finally decided against it.

He couldn't be certain what her final motives had been for her decision, refusing to probe her mind, but for now, it was enough she'd chosen for them. Someday, however, Morigan wanted more. He wanted her total loyalty and devotion; he wanted her lovingly committed to his people. And he wanted her to desire him as ardently, as fiercely as he desired her.

The drone of the skim crafts began to fade. Silence once more blanketed the mountains. The others stirred from their hiding places, muttered a few choice curses, and crawled out.

Morigan's hand slipped from Rissa's mouth. "My thanks."

"F-for what?"

"For not betraying us, or even attempting to do so. You could have given some warning, kicked a rock, rammed your knee into my groin again. You know as well as I the opportunity for escape that would have provided. But you did none of those things. Why?"

Morigan's warm breath caressed her cheek. A tremor of intense awareness rippled through Rissa. *Why?* She didn't know herself anymore. All Rissa could think about was the heady feel of him, his drugging, musky male scent, the hypnotically soothing thud of his heart beneath her ear.

Was this what it was supposed to be like, lying close to a man, his big body hot and hard against yours? Powerfully alive, throbbing with life, vitality, and a fierce determination?

It was so wonderful and yet, conversely, so terrifying. He could crush her, kill her with just one sweep of his clawed hand. He could so easily, as well, overpower her and force himself on her. Yet, it wasn't the tautly coiled strength of the man that frightened her. It was the emotional toll he took on her, every waking moment of the past nine days.

"Won't you answer me, femina?" Morigan prodded, dispelling her confusing jumble of thoughts.

She turned to glance up at him. "Why didn't I betray you?" Rissa licked her lips in careful deliberation. Should she tell him the truth? Well, at least a portion of it would do no harm.

"I'm not without conscience." She levered herself to one elbow to gain a bit of visual superiority over him. "Though you've totally disregarded my rights and disparaged the value I put on my life and personal freedom, I can't bring myself to do the same to you. You and I both know the Bellatorians possess weapons in their skim crafts that could have at least overpowered, if not annihilated you. Yet, as hard as it may be for you to believe this of a Bellatorian, I don't wish you, or any of your people, harm."

Morigan hesitated, inhaled a steadying breath, then fixed her with a piercing look. "Then, perhaps you might begin, as well, to find it in your heart to understand us better."

She quirked a puzzled brow. "Indeed? And how is that possible? I am a Bellatorian, after all."

"The Cat Women," Morigan muttered, ignoring her sarcasm. For an instant, he regretted even broaching the subject, feeling he verged on baring not only his soul, but the soul of his people. But he sensed, beneath Rissa's anger and resentment, a kindness and compassion that would stir to the Cat Women's plight.

"They won't be happy with your and the other Bellatorian

females' presence in our lair," he forced himself to continue. "They'll be jealous, angry, and hostile, I'm afraid."

"Like Agna?"

"Yes," he sighed, recalling the healer's decided frostiness to Rissa during the past two days, "like Agna."

Rissa sat up, her mouth setting into a stubborn line. "What do you expect from me? It's not my fault your women will resent me. I don't want to remain in your lair anymore than they want me there."

"I expect, no, I hope," Morigan quickly corrected himself, "that you, being a female, would understand and sympathize with other females' special pain. And, in the understanding, be willing to tolerate their hostility, for a time, without returning an equal measure of hostility."

"And what special pain might that be?" Rissa demanded tautly. "I know of your massacre. I deplore what happened. But it's not fair they should hate me for it."

"That's not the special pain I was speaking of." He shoved a hand through his mane. "It's more a matter of pride."

"Pride?"

He eyed her for a long moment, suddenly loath to reveal his females' secret shame. What if Rissa laughed at it, then resolved to use it against the Cat Women, to taunt and hurt them further? It was a weapon of inestimable potential.

But, somehow, Morigan sensed she'd never stoop to such a tactic, no matter how desperate she became. Even in the short time he'd known her, he'd never found her to be deliberately cruel. Rissa fought cleanly, kept her battles out in the open. Well, at least, those that didn't involve her emotions over him, he thought wryly. And those more intimate battles weren't any he cared to deal with right now.

"We've only fifty females left," Morigan began again. "Of those, only forty are of breedable age. Yet, though a cycle has passed since the massacre, only three have conceived and hope to bear Cat Children whom we pray will be delivered safely in the next few months. Our fear is that the others are permanently sterile." His mouth twisted bitterly. "Hence, our reason for hunting down additional humanoid females. Without them, we fear what is left of the Cat People will die out in just another generation or two."

"You can't be certain . . . it's too soon after just a cycle," Rissa breathed, horrified that, on top of everything else that had befallen the Cat People, they must now face this.

"No, we can't," Morigan agreed. "But I feared waiting much longer without doing anything. I may have been wrong in this, but I made the best decision I could."

Rissa stared up at him, moved by the terrible burdens he'd carried since the massacre. Though she hated what he'd done to her and the other women of her party, Rissa knew Morigan's first concern must always be for the welfare of his people. Perhaps, he'd been premature in deciding to abduct additional breeding females, yet she found she could no longer fault him for that.

She could, however, fault him for seeking his own people's welfare at her and the other Bellatorian women's expense. One species's needs didn't justify taking away the rights of another. She must remember that and not allow any emotional considerations to drag her into aiding and abetting his heinous act. In the end, she could never allow him to ignore her rights, or her personal freedom to choose the course her life should take.

"You *are* wrong in this," Rissa finally replied. "You are punishing innocent people for the wrongdoings of others. That can never be justified. But I, in turn, will not punish your innocent people."

The Cat Man smiled, unable to disguise a fleeting look of relief. "My thanks."

"And what do I gain for this?" Rissa inquired, knowing this might be her only opportunity to play upon his gratitude to obtain what she wanted. It was a hard, overtly manipulative ploy, but she was desperate. "What value do you place on your gratitude?"

Morigan's smile faded. "What do you want of me?"

"My freedom."

"It cannot be. Ask for something I *can* give you."

Her eyes narrowed. "Then, give your word not to mate with me."

He scowled; his lips tightened. "That cannot be, either. If not with me, you'll mate with some Cat Man in the lair. No matter the outcome, I'm committed to this course, femina. Choose again."

The old frustration flared anew. "Curse you, Morigan! Must you have it all? Must I always be the one to compromise?"

"And does your compromising mean you've given up your plans to escape?"

Rissa's mouth twisted. "What do you think?"

"I think," Morigan murmured huskily, stroking back the silken strands of hair that clung to her face, "with the proper encouragement, there's still a chance I can change your mind. An endeavor I find myself looking forward to, just as soon as we reach the lair."

"You're very sure of yourself," she retorted, angered by his arrogance and unsettled by his touch upon her face. She slapped his hand away. "It could well be your undoing."

"Perhaps." He smiled. "If any female can best me, I've no doubt you can, Rissa. And you're most certainly welcome to try." He shoved himself to a sitting position beneath the low overhang of rock. Patches of a fuzzy, red lichen covered the black-speckled gray walls. Sunlight streamed in from a crack in the rocks, warming the air.

There was something about his smile, a most feline and self-assured expression if ever Rissa had seen one, that angered her even further. "I'll do more than try, you cursedly smug and hopelessly misled specimen of the lowest form of manhood! I'll win. Best you give up while you still can—before your precious Cat's pride is ground down to defeat!"

How could she ever have imagined him wonderful? Rissa thought in outrage. How had she ever felt sorry for him and his plight? With those questions echoing mockingly in her mind, she crawled out from beneath the overhang and stomped away to check on Naren.

The Cat Lord watched her go, his smile slowly fading. Gods, what a she-cat he'd taken for his mate! She would indeed fight him every step of the way. Yet, the prize, Morigan now realized, might be well worth the effort. Well worth it, indeed.

When sunset threw the mountains once more into deepening shadows, they set out again. This time, however, Rissa's hands were loosely bound before her and her eyes were covered. They were within two days' journey of the secret lair, Morigan explained. For the lair's protection she—as had all the other captured women—had to be prevented from discovering the route. Though escape was all but impossible, the Cat Men intended to take no chances.

He kept her close to him the entire night, his arm clasped about her waist to guide her when the going was relatively smooth and carrying her in his arms when the trail became unstable or dangerous. Rissa hated the loss of her sight, seething against Morigan and silently damning him with every foul phrase she'd ever heard. And she knew, all along, the greatest humiliation was in being so helpless, so dependent upon him—and yet finding some perverse pleasure in it as well.

At dawn, they rested once more in a sheltered area. By sunset, they resumed the trek after a quick meal of more journey bread, meat sticks, fruit, and cheese. Yet, even for the meal, Morigan refused to allow Rissa to remove her blindfold and had permitted her to sleep without it only after he had carried her far enough into a cave to preclude her catching any glimpse of what lay outside. Rissa began to wish for the end of the journey, if only so that she could see again.

By midnight of the second day, they neared the lair. She sensed it by the sudden downward angle of their descent and the whispered, excited comments that grew louder with each passing moment. Then, soft cries and the sound of running feet came from below.

Anxious anticipation shivered through her. Rissa shifted restlessly in Morigan's arms. "Please," she murmured. "Let me down. Let me enter your lair with some bit of dignity. I am, after all, supposed to be your mate."

It was the first time Morigan had ever heard her admit to her new position in life. He knew she used it only to press her request, but it didn't matter. Rissa was right. The sooner she was seen and accepted as his mate, the better for all. He lowered her gently to the ground.

Unaccountably, his fingers trembled as he undid the cloth covering her eyes and the thongs that bound her hands. That her approval of him should matter so much, that he should wish so ardently to please her, unsettled him. He hadn't thought to allow any female to affect him so easily again.

"I give you this because I owe you much," he growled, attempting to hide the sudden swell of emotion that tightened his throat. "Forget not what you owe me, in return."

Somehow, his words stung. "I forget nothing," Rissa snapped.

His eyes glittered in the light of the three moons which were sinking, one by one, in the west. Grasping her by the arm, Morigan pulled her to him. "Follow my lead when we enter the lair. Though I'd hardly dare hope for a like expression of affection from you, try to contain your loathing if I must touch you or hold you close. It's imperative the other males think we're at least bonded, even if not yet mated. Do you understand, Rissa?"

For an instant, she was confused. Why was it so important the other Cat Men assume anything about them? Then, Morigan's words, that day he'd told her about the Cat Women, rushed back.

If not with me, you will mate with some Cat Man in the lair.

The full implications of Morigan's statement flooded her in one searing, horrible surge. Rissa's hand covered his where it lay upon her arm. Her nails gouged into his flesh. "And if I don't cooperate, what will you do? Give me to one of your Cat Men? Am I so disposable as a mate, then?"

Puzzlement furrowed his brow. "What are you talking about, femina?"

"You said before if you didn't take me as mate, you'd give me to another!"

Morigan searched his memory. Slowly, the realization of when he'd said those words and in what context filtered back. "You aren't disposable, Rissa," he softly replied. "I only meant I have first chance to win you as mate. If I fail, other Cat Men will then gain opportunity to claim you."

Nausea churned in Rissa's gut. To be passed around from Cat Man to Cat Man . . . "Y-you never explained that before."

He shrugged. "I had my reasons, however selfish they might have been." Morigan glanced down at her hand, still clenching his. "Could you perhaps sheathe your claws, femina? They begin to pain me."

She released him with a jerk, twisted her arm free, and stepped back. "Do you know how much I hate you?" she whispered hoarsely. "Do you know how angry you make me? And . . . and your customs! Gods, they grow more horrible, more disgusting with each passing day!"

"Dare I hope that means you prefer staying with me?" Morigan rubbed the scored marks Rissa had left on his hand. He grinned over at her. "Well, does it, femina?"

"No!" Rissa couldn't believe the cocky twist to his mouth or the smug look in his eyes. "I despise you! Do you hear me? Despise you!"

"Er," Lisan interrupted from behind them, clearly uncomfortable. "You and your lady, my Lord, are blocking the trail for the litter."

"And providing us with far too much entertainment as well," Naren offered cheerfully from atop the litter. "Perhaps another time, Morigan? At this moment, our people gather below. It might be best not to keep them waiting. Or," he pointedly added, "give them cause to wonder what's going on between you two up here."

"Fine," Morigan growled. "Far be it from me to inconvenience anyone!" He glared down at Rissa a moment more. Then, grasping her again by the arm, he all but dragged her down the trail that led to the lair.

Nine

It was like something out of a dream or drug-induced fantasy. There were eerie shadows and shapes of the jagged volcanic rocks, jutting out at grotesque angles from the sturdy sides of the mountain. The glittering, glassy bits of obsidian that speckled the duller, more porous lava-spewn rocks gleamed lustrous in the bright moonlight. The rough tread ran beneath Rissa's feet. Strange, that she hadn't realized its significance before.

Morigan had been right to blindfold her. There was only one part of the Serratus Mountains, if Rissa recalled correctly from her Agrican video tutor lessons, that was so heavily volcanic. It would explain his mention of hot springs, as well.

The Cat Lord had chosen wisely in selecting this rugged, if forbidding land. The soil, what little there was of it, was said to be rich and fertile; the terrain was a jumble of rocks and boulders where one could easily find shelter on short notice and where, most importantly of all, the Bellatorian scanning equipment would function poorly. Rissa couldn't recall the exact details, but it had to do with some sort of transmission interference from certain elements imbedded in the rock . . .

His choice of locations, however, also made her eventual escape all that more difficult. The trail leading down into the Cat People's lair lay in full view of any guards posted overhead. The journey back, thanks to Morigan's insistence that she be blindfolded, would be tricky without any exact idea of what direction they'd traveled. The volcanic area was most specific, but also covered the entire center of the mountain range. And, with the uneven terrain and towering stands of lava pillars crowding the trails, detection from overhead would be doubly hard. If any skim crafts ventured in here, they couldn't get low enough without danger of collision.

It was a sanctuary well-chosen—and a prison most secure. And, then, there were her most uniquely gifted jailers. Blessed with boundless stamina, the most acute hearing and night vision, and able to cloak their presence until the last moment, the Cat Men were formidable in every way. How could she ever hope to evade, much less outrun them, if she even managed to escape their lair?

Despair pricked at the edges of Rissa's confidence. Angrily, she shrugged the unpleasant feeling aside. There'd been only one other time in her life when she'd experienced such debilitating emotions—the first few months after her mother died. To mourn a loved one's passing was one thing. To allow herself to become mired in a lethargic, pitiful morass of helpless despair was quite another.

There was always some path past any challenge, she reminded herself with a fierce surge of resolve, no matter how impossible it might initially seem. She had to believe that. If not, there was nothing left her but submission. And that, for one such as she, was death.

As Rissa strode down the trail, she flung back her head and squared her shoulders. A fierce determination surged through her. She would *never* let the Cat People defeat her; she would *never* allow Morigan to turn her into some subservient, cowering little breeder. She was Bellatorian, and a Bellatorian never gave up.

Her renewed resolve faltered for a microsecond, however, when she caught the first glimpse of the crowd amassed below at the end of the trail. Though the night shaded their features and expressions from full view, Rissa couldn't help but be a bit overawed by her first meeting with the entire gathering of Cat People. Her pace slowed, faltered. She stared.

Morigan, walking beside her, his hand still clasping her arm, felt the hesitation flood Rissa even before she drew to a halt. Her sudden swell of apprehension washed over him. His hand released her arm to encircle her shoulders. He pulled her to him gently. "Courage, femina," he whispered, leaning over to brush his lips against her ear. "The first meeting is always the most difficult, the first impressions the most vital."

She shivered, but whether it was the result of the touch of his mouth or the truth of his words, Morigan didn't know. Rissa tilted her head toward him. A defiant light gleamed in her eyes.

"I'm not afraid. And you needn't hold me so closely." To add emphasis to her words, she squirmed in his clasp.

Morigan smiled, his strong, white teeth luminous in the dark. "Ah, but I do, femina. Remember what I said of a possible need to show possession. And first impressions—"

"Are the most vital," she finished for him irritably. "Fine. But keep those inquisitive fingers of yours in the proper place!"

He chuckled and stilled the hand that had, seemingly of its own accord, splayed to encompass the span of Rissa's upper arm and stroked perilously near the full swell of her breast. "My pardon. I presumed to liberties you've yet to grant me."

"Liberties I'll never grant!" she snapped back.

"Never is such a terminal word," he said, urging her back down the path. "It allows for no change of heart, no options."

"Exactly!"

There was no time for further discussion. They reached the end of the trail where the press of bodies awaiting them forced them to a halt. Five Cat Men, middle-aged and older, stood lined up, side by side, before the others.

Morigan's smile faded. "How have things fared since Cradoc and the others left?" He directed his question to the eldest Cat Man of the group.

"Better with each passing day," the old man replied. "The females," he added, glancing briefly at Rissa, "are well cared for and, as a whole, adapting well."

"It is done then." Morigan rendered him a formal half-bow. "Our mission is complete. I ask leave to reenter the lair."

The eldest Cat Man, his long mane shimmering silver in the moonlight, his face feline but furrowed with ageless strength, stepped forward. "We were lacking since you last left us, my Lord. We are complete once more." He bowed low from the waist in a slow, dignified movement, then straightened. "Welcome home."

As the final, ceremonial words of greeting fell from the old Cat Man's lips, a cheer sprang from the people gathered behind him. Morigan grinned, gave Rissa a joyous squeeze, and extended his hand to his silver-haired compatriot. "I'm glad to be back, Grandfather. More than you can imagine."

The two men clasped hand to elbow. Then, the elderly Cat Man's gaze swung to Rissa. He arched a brow in silent inquiry.

"Rissa, this is Ardan," Morigan said by way of introduction, "my father's father. He's my closest advisor and heads our Council of Elders." He turned back to the older Cat Man. "Grandfather, this is Rissa, my new mate."

Ardan's mouth quirked wryly. "Indeed? This is presuming, of course, she wins the final approval of the Council? The life mate of our lord is no decision to be made lightly, or without adherence to our ancient customs. Not even," he added, emphasizing the words, "in times such as these."

Morigan nodded in solemn agreement. "Of course. I think, however, once you and the rest of the Council have an opportunity to become acquainted with Rissa, you'll find her quite suitable. She's headstrong, but her heart is good and true. She'll bear me fine sons and daughters."

At his words, irritation rippled through Rissa. By the five moons, but they spoke about her as if she were nothing more than a prize equs being sold at auction. "Perhaps you'd like to examine my teeth as well?" she gritted, attempting to twist free of Morigan's possessive clasp. His grip only tightened. "Rumor has it a female's childbearing strength can be determined by the condition of her teeth."

Ardan's mouth opened in surprise, then clamped shut. His eyes narrowed. "Headstrong *and* impertinent, to be sure. Are you certain you need the extra aggravation, my Lord?"

Morigan's lips twitched. "She grows more tolerable with time."

"Will you two stop talking about me as if I'm not here?" Rissa hissed. "I am not some piece of—"

"No, you're not, femina," Morigan softly cut her off, smiling down at her. "I beg pardon for our lack of courtesy. It was just our joy at seeing each other again, and perhaps the wearying strain of the journey, that caused our sorry breach in manners."

He turned to his grandfather, his voice rising to reach the furthest limits of the crowd. "Rissa is entitled to all the respect due her position as my mate, until the Council decides otherwise. Though her blood and heritage are not our own, she, like all our captives, is now an equal member in our society. So it has been determined. So it must be."

The old Cat Man nodded his acquiescence. "And so it shall be." For the first time, he acknowledged Rissa's presence. "Are you weary, femina? Hungry?"

She met his cool, assessing gaze with an equally cool one of her own. "Weary mostly. Is there some place I might make a bed?"

Surprise flickered in Ardan's eyes. He shot Morigan a questioning glance.

The Cat Lord turned to Rissa. "You'll sleep in my lair. Come, femina. We'll go there now. The morrow is soon enough to be introduced to the rest of my people." He offered Ardan one final half bow. "By your leave, Grandfather?"

"It seems the wisest course," the old man replied. "Will you return to meet with the Council, once your mate is seen to?"

"Yes," Morigan said. Then, as if by some silent signal, Ardan and the other Elders moved aside. The Cat People standing behind them parted, opening up a corridor for Morigan and Rissa.

As they stepped out once more, Rissa scanned the crowd for sign of the other Bellatorian women, but saw none. Her overwhelming impression was one of feline faces, shaggy hair, and leathern clothing, mostly masculine in feature, interspersed with a few of more feminine mien. No matter the sex, though, suspicion, wariness, and overt curiosity tightened their expressions and glimmered in their eyes. Among the younger males there shone, as well, a hunger Rissa found most unnerving. Instinctively, she moved closer to Morigan, her arm curling about his waist.

He smiled, thoroughly enjoying the pressure of her soft young body against his. It was a small victory, Rissa's unconscious response to danger by turning to him for protection, but a victory nonetheless. In the ensuing days, he meant to become the integral link between her and his people. If he could manage to foster some semblance of dependence upon him, it might just be the key to her heart. And Morigan now knew he wanted the flaxen-haired Bellatorian no other way.

They strode through the crowd of Cat People, Morigan acknowledging their greetings with smiling nods and shouting promises to meet with several Cat Men on the morrow. At last, up ahead, he saw the soft glow of the entrance leading to his lair. In the doorway stood the form of an elderly female. His mother.

There were many obstacles for Rissa to overcome in her assimilation into the Cat People. Acceptance by his mother was only one of many. Though Sarna had gradually recovered from the trauma of the forest massacre, she was a fragile shadow of the powerful female she'd once been. It took very little to reduce her to a weeping wraith: one irritable word, a raised brow. If Rissa and his mother failed to become friends . . .

"My mother." Morigan gestured to the woman who awaited them as they turned at last toward his lair. "Her name is Sarna. She . . . she suffered greatly when she lost my father and my family in the forest massacre."

Rissa tilted her head to glance up at him. "I'm sorry for her."

"If you . . . if you could treat her gently," he forced himself to grit out the request, "I would be very grateful."

"Indeed?" She gave a small, mocking laugh. "There you go again, promising gratitude with no intent to fulfill any of it."

He stopped short and swung her around. A raw anguish burned in his eyes. "Curse it all, but I give what I can, Rissa. I'm sorry if it isn't enough for you, but it's all I can do."

And curse him, Rissa thought, inexplicably angry. She could deal with him with far more ease when he was arrogant and demanding. But now . . . She sighed. "Then do me one favor, Morigan."

"What's that?" Wariness tinged his words, hovered in his eyes.

"Don't promise what you can't—or won't—give." She twisted from his grip and headed for his lair. "I'm not totally without compassion or sensitivity for others," she tossed over her shoulder in high chagrin. "I wouldn't purposely be cruel to your mother just because she'd the misfortune to bear you!"

Relief—and a strange joy—flooded Morigan. Bless her for her kind heart! In spite of the personal battle that waged between them, in spite of her stubborn pride and headstrong ways, he liked knowing he could count on her innate goodness. Liked knowing she was a person of integrity and principles. He could almost forget she was Bellatorian.

Almost . . .

He quickened his pace to catch up with her. She shot him an exasperated glance. "No more promises I can't keep, femina. I swear."

She eyed him skeptically, then nodded. "Fine."

In the next instant, they were standing before Morigan's mother. She was a pleasant looking woman despite the feline set to her exotic, green-gold eyes and high cheekbones. Her hair was heavily streaked with gray, but still interspersed with dark auburn strands that lent soft color to her otherwise pale face. Careworn lines, however, rent the corners of her eyes and mouth, and her hands trembled slightly when she extended her arms to Morigan.

"Son, ah, my son," she murmured, in soft, chiding tones. "I was so worried for you when you didn't return with the others. You mustn't do that to me again."

Morigan smiled tenderly and stepped forward to take her in his arms. "We'd a slight delay. Naren decided to put himself between me and a blaster."

Sarna leaned back in consternation. "Is he . . . did he . . . ?"

"He's fine, Mother." Her son quickly soothed away her fears. "It'll be a few more weeks before he's back to his old tricks, but Naren will recover fully." His glance snared with Rissa's. "A large amount of Naren's good fortune must fall at this femina's feet."

Morigan turned her gently to face Rissa. "Mother, this is Rissa, my new mate. Rissa, this is my mother, Sarna."

Rissa smiled at the older woman. "I'm pleased to make your acquaintance, domina."

Sarna said nothing, only eyed her closely. Finally, she sighed and turned back to Morigan. "I saw the other females our men brought in, but I had hoped your mate would have been more . . . feline in features. It would have eased the lair's acceptance of her." She shook her head. "Now, it will be difficult. Very difficult, I fear."

"Nonetheless, I'm here," Rissa observed coolly, "and must be accepted for what I am." She extended her hand. "I hope we can at least be friends."

The old Cat Woman stepped back, as if fearful Rissa's touch might be harmful. "M-Morigan?" she quavered, gazing up at her son with wide, uncertain eyes.

He stroked her cheek and smiled. "It's all right, Mother. Rissa won't hurt you. And I'd like very much if you and she could become friends. I'll be very busy in the next few days and would appreciate it if you could take her under your care, show her the lair, and introduce her to the others." He leaned down to kiss her gently on the cheek. "Do you think you could do that for me, dear heart?"

Sarna swallowed hard, dared another glance at Rissa, and nodded. "For you, anything. You know that, Son."

"Then take Rissa's hand and greet her as a mother would her new daughter-in-law," he prodded softly. "Make her feel welcome here."

"As you wish, Son." The old woman turned back to Rissa. Ever so slowly, she extended her hand.

Rissa shot Morigan a questioning glance. He nodded, a look of entreaty burning in his eyes. She grasped the trembling hand of the elderly Cat Woman in hers, then covered it with her other hand.

"W-welcome to our lair, Daughter," Sarna said, her voice becoming stronger and more sure with each word she spoke. "You are alien to us, as we are to you, and there is much for both sides to overcome. But, if you are willing, I will do my best to aid you. I would do anything for my son. He is a brave, strong lad."

Her gaze lowered, taking in Rissa's body. "You look strong enough to bear him fine children." She looked up. "We need children. Many fine, strong children. Have you mated yet? Do you already carry his—"

"Mother." Morigan stepped forward to take her hand from Rissa's. "Time enough later to speak of grandchildren. Rissa has just arrived from a long journey and wishes to rest."

"Oh. Yes." Confusion momentarily clouded Sarna's eyes. "How thoughtless of me." She smiled over at Rissa. "On the morrow, we will talk more. And I will take you to meet the others."

She stood on tiptoe to kiss Morigan on the cheek. "Rest well yourself, Son. I am so happy to have you home."

"As am I to be here, Mother. Rest well."

With that, the old woman turned and headed across the cave to what appeared to be one of two rooms that led off at the other end. Rissa turned to Morigan and arched a questioning brow.

"She lives with me, femina. She has no one else."

There was something, some question in his eyes that unsettled her. "This is your lair. It's your right to ask your mother to stay with you," Rissa replied stiffly.

"It's now your lair as well." His green-gold eyes glowed from the shadows. "Have you any objections to her presence here?"

She shook her head. "I don't plan to stay long. You know that. Of course, I have no objections."

He bit back an impulse to dispute the logic of her continued plans to escape. There was no purpose served in further argument. Time would prove the fallacy of Rissa's words. "Then come." Morigan took her once more by the arm. "Let me show you my lair."

It wasn't at all what Rissa expected. The main stone chamber, of a round shape and moderately roomy size, was comfortably if simply furnished. Several perpetual light boxes illuminated the room, bathing everything in a soft, blue-violet glow. A square stone hearth sat in the middle of the room. Several smoked haunches of meat hung over it from a wheel-like apparatus suspended from the ceiling.

Off to one side was a long wooden table of rich red-brown robur wood, lovingly handrubbed to a smooth sheen. Six chairs of similar workmanship were stationed around it. Five books lay on the table; four more were stacked on one of the chairs. Two large, carved chests sat against a far wall along with various cooking pots, plates, and cups, some farming implements, and three blasters.

Rissa's gaze lingered briefly on the blasters, then discarded the thought. She'd already demonstrated—to the Cat Men as well as herself—she was incapable of using them to make good her escape.

Morigan followed Rissa's survey of the cave until it finally alighted once more on the books. Her eyes met his, full of wonder.

"You . . . you own books!"

His mouth quirked but he forced himself to answer in as solemn a manner as possible. "Yes, femina. Cat People only eschew technology that would bind us to a more frivolous, possession-oriented life. Knowledge, in any form, is not considered frivolous."

"But the ban," Rissa protested. "Since the loss of the Knowing Crystal, the Imperium has made possession of books a crime punishable by death!"

Morigan shrugged. "Hardly an additional concern to us, considering we already carry a death warrant on our heads. Rather unsettling to learn we're not quite the ignorant savages the tales make us out to be, isn't it?"

She started to deny his allegation, then gave it up as fruitless. It was more than obvious what she'd originally thought of him and his people. "Yes, it is," she admitted, looking him squarely in the eye. "I'm beginning to realize there are many misconceptions out there about the Cat People."

"Well, at least that's to your credit. You're more honest and open-minded than most."

"Am I?" Rissa walked over to the table and picked up the first volume on the top of the pile. "Hmmm. Maoten's *Ten*

Treatises on the Philosophy of the Ages. Very impressive."
Reverently, she laid down the ancient volume and took up
the next. "And Hesiona's *Secrets of the Crystal Makers,* not
to mention *The Eludian Proverbs, Moral Justice,* and
Tenorius's *Maxims."*

She glanced up, carefully wetting her lips. "Have you read
all these books, Morigan?"

He arched a dark brow. "Rather, didn't you mean to ask,
do I *know* how to read?"

"No, I didn't . . ." Rissa flushed. "Well, perhaps I did
mean that. Any fool can see you're not a stupid man, but
that doesn't presuppose an ability to read."

"My thanks for the compliment."

She bristled at his dry sarcasm. "I'm sorry if my question offended you. It's not as if you Cat People go out of
your way to share much of your culture with the rest of
the Imperium."

"No, we don't," Morigan admitted. "We're a proud and
independent people who have valued our ancient ways perhaps overmuch. Perhaps contributing to our own extinction."

"What do you mean?"

He shot her a hooded glance. "We eschewed the higher
technologies of the rest of the Imperium, as did most of
Agrica, choosing instead to keep to the simple ways of our
ancestors. Life was good; we never wanted, thanks to
Agrica's bounty. But we didn't progress, either." Morigan
shoved a hand through his mane and sighed. "And we, as a
people, have never learned to read or to begin recording our
learning or heritage in written form. Indeed, until my father
sent Naren and I to the only school on the planet at Primasedes, no Cat Man had ever been formally educated."

Rissa fingered the volume she still held in her hand. "So,
some of you do read. Are these books yours, then?"

"Yes. I carried every one of them out on my back after the massacre. Perhaps it was a frivolous gesture, considering how badly we needed each blanket and weapon and cooking utensil, but even then I knew the day would come when I would once again set my dreams into action." His mouth quirked bitterly. *"If* we survived long enough, at any rate."

She shouldn't ask, shouldn't delve any deeper into the man and his hopes and aspirations. She knew more about him already than she cared to know. Yet something compelled her, still, to ask. "What did you plan to do, Morigan? With the books?"

He shrugged. "What else? Teach my people to read, to write, to take a step forward into the future." The Cat Lord gestured toward the books. "I was teaching Winna to read. She was so eager, an excellent student, and as dedicated to the idea of education as I was. She was planning on setting up the school, one for the young and one for any adults who were interested. There was resistance among some, as there always is to new ideas, but my father was strongly behind our plans. He may have come late to the realization, but he was a man of vision."

"And, then, the massacre happened," Rissa finished for him, "and your wife, your plans, were destroyed."

"Yes," Morigan muttered, "destroyed. But anything, with the proper raw materials, can be rebuilt." His gaze narrowed on her. "And now, knowing Bellator's propensity for education, I have twelve females who can read, don't I? I have more teachers than I ever had before."

"You presume much in thinking we'll help you." She laid down the book. "You may be able to force us to mate, but coercing us to teach is another thing entirely. Once again, you are being arrogant and presumptuous."

A wry smile quirked Morigan's lips. "Perhaps I am,

femina, but these days presumption and arrogance are sometimes all that's left me. And one uses whatever is at one's
disposal."

Suddenly, Rissa couldn't bear the intensity of his gaze,
nor the resignation that hovered on his words and deepened
his voice. "Yes, I suppose anyone would do that." She
dragged her eyes back to the books. "None of this tragedy
might have come to pass, though, if your people hadn't been
so adamantly against progress. Bellator, instead, might have
thought to negotiate, to send—"

"It would've made no difference to Bellator! No difference at all!"

Rissa jerked her gaze back to his. Morigan's expression
had darkened ominously, like storm clouds on the horizon.

"On the contrary," he said bitterly, "it served Bellator's
purposes far too well to let everyone consider us backward
and savage. How better to justify our extinction?"

"That's not fair! Not all Bellatorians are that callous and
opportunistic. Sententians, for one, are peaceful, dedicated
to learning and the development of the psychic powers of
the—"

"Fautor Lindatees is no Sententian!" Morigan cut her off,
his voice cracking like a whiplash. "The spies I sent to Primasedes learned the truth of the massacre only a few months
after we'd fled to the Serratus Mountains. The Lord Commander purposely 'misinterpreted' a Bellatorian directive
suggesting 'judicious control' of any rebel elements on
Agrica. It seems Lindatees's interpretation of judicious control was annihilation, rather than negotiation and compromise."

"I can't believe he would purposely do such a thing!" She
wheeled around to face Morigan, her hands clenching the
tabletop behind her. "Fautor Lindatees is a good, fair man.
Those are lies, stirred, no doubt, by people jealous of him.

If you could just find some way to meet with him directly, I'm certain—"

The Cat Lord's features hardened into a mask of cynical incredulity. *"A good, fair man?"* Contempt—and a fury deep and all-consuming—exploded in his eyes, contorting Morigan's face into an expression of dreadful brutality. "Oh, I'll meet with him someday if it's the last thing I ever do," he snarled. "But it won't be to discuss politics. It'll be to slash out his heart with my bare hands!"

She'd never seen such virulent anger, such a soul-devouring need for revenge. It horrified and sickened her. Rissa paled. For an instant, the room swam wildly before her. Her knees buckled.

Then Morigan was there, gathering her up into his arms.

With a low moan, Rissa pushed at his chest, her eyes clenching shut. "Let me down. Please, I can't bear for you to touch me!"

"No." He crushed her to him, then turned and headed across the cave to the room that lay at the opposite end from his mother's sleeping chamber.

Ever so gently, Morigan laid her on a fur-strewn bed. Rissa's eyes snapped open. They were in a dimly lit, low-ceilinged room, large enough only for a generous bed, small wooden chest, and shallow alcove wherein sat a pitcher, basin of water, and drying cloths. She lifted herself to a sitting position and scooted back from him.

"Rissa, don't." An anguished regret burned in Morigan's eyes. "I forget myself sometimes and let my bitterness get the best of me."

"Bitterness?" Rissa echoed derisively. "You were *terrifying,* Morigan!"

"My words, those feelings, weren't directed at you."

"Yet you meant them, nonetheless, didn't you?"

The light in his striking eyes dimmed, flattened by a grim bleakness. "Yes, I meant them. Our dead cry out for retribution. The hunger for revenge burns in me like a fire that will not die." He paused, his glance softening. "But I don't want my need for revenge to come between us, femina. It has nothing to do with you and me."

Fiercely, she shook her head. "Oh, yes it does. As long as you harbor such hatred for one of my people, you harbor at least some remnants of that hatred for me." She buried her face in her hands. "Just go away. Leave me, please!"

Morigan stared down at Rissa, at a loss for what to say. He expelled a long, weary breath. "I'm capable of differentiating between friend and foe, Rissa. I don't hate you."

But you will, Morigan, she silently countered, *you will,* then quashed further thoughts of her true origins.

She blessed the instinct that had warned her not to reveal her identity to the other women who had traveled to Primasedes with her. Only Diona knew her secret. And Diona would never tell.

Rissa lifted her gaze. "It doesn't matter anyway, whether you hate me or not. We are enemies, Morigan. Too much pain and loss has come between us, though through no fault of our own, to ever bridge that chasm. It's a cruel reality, but reality nonetheless."

"Is it, femina?" He sat on the edge of the bed. "I used to think so, but I'm not so certain anymore." He extended his hand. "Come here, Rissa."

She eyed his outstretched hand with suspicion. Strange, she thought, she'd never noticed before how long and strong his fingers were. They were the hands of a man of learning, of creativity, and of gentleness. Not a warrior's. And, certainly, not those of a cold-blooded, vengeful killer.

But life didn't always lead one down the path one had

originally intended to follow. It certainly didn't seem to have done so for her. And it definitely hadn't for the Cat Lord.

Rissa shook her head. "No. I won't come to you. I don't want you touching me. Not now, or ever."

Pain, deep and searing, flared in Morigan's eyes, then was gone. "You may think so now . . . tonight . . . but we have time, femina. All the time in the world, now that I have you safe in my lair." He rose. "We're both weary from the journey. I have business that will keep me a time longer, but you must sleep."

"Yes." Rissa nodded her acquiescence, eager to be rid of him. "Yes, I need to sleep." When he remained standing there, she frowned, puzzled. "Well? What else do you want?"

"Do you intend to sleep in your boots and clothes?"

"What?" Startled Rissa glanced down at herself. She leaned over and dragged off her boots, tossing them onto the floor. "There, that's all I'll remove. I haven't any sleeping gown, and I refuse to sleep nude with you about."

His mouth quirked. "Too bad. That would've been a pretty sight."

She scowled.

Morigan turned, walked over to the small chest and lifted its lid. He removed a carefully folded piece of crimson cloth, hesitated, then turned and handed it to her.

Rissa took the garment. It was a woman's sleeping gown, made from the finest of serica cloth. "Whose was it?"

"Winna's. My mate's."

She tried to give it back to him. "I-I couldn't wear it. The memories . . . It wouldn't be right."

He inhaled a ragged breath. The familiar, shuttered look fell back in place. "No, she'd want you to be comfortable; she'd want to share this with you." He shoved the garment into Rissa's hands. "It's only a sleeping gown. It means noth-

ing to me. Please change into it. Your clothes are dirty, and
I can have them cleaned while you rest. On the morrow, I'll
have my mother take you to the communal bathing pool."

"As you wish." She accepted the gown, strangely unsettled
by his cold denial of any sentimentality regarding the garment. Rissa squashed the myriad of questions that suddenly
assailed her, telling herself Morigan's odd reaction was none
of her affair. "Could you at least leave for a few moments?
Until I change out of my clothes?"

He nodded. No flicker of emotion lit his eyes. "Call me
when you're ready." He turned and left the bedchamber.

The sleeping gown was silky sleek and fit her well, Rissa
noted as she slipped it over her head and smoothed it down
her body. Sleeveless, scooped low in front to reveal the full
swell of her breasts, it was a garment of subtle seduction.
An image of Morigan, naked and powerful, passionately
clasping a woman dressed in this sleeping gown to him,
flashed through Rissa's mind. She blushed and shoved the
disturbing image away.

Folding her clothes, Rissa turned to leave the bedchamber,
then hesitated. Her turcas stone necklace and earrings. There
seemed little point in wearing them to sleep anymore, no
matter how fiercely she'd refused to remove them since Morigan had first made comment about the jewelry.

Rissa hesitated, fearing he would see it as some sign she
was finally acquiescing to his will. Then she laughed. Morigan would learn, sooner or later, that he couldn't manipulate
her behavior—one way or another.

She slid the earrings off her ears and sprung the electronic
clasp of the necklace. Ever so carefully, Rissa placed them
beneath her pillow. Then, squaring her shoulders, she strode
down the short tunnel that led to the main chamber. "Mori-

gan?" she whispered when she saw him, not wishing to disturb his mother.

He wheeled about, flung his long brown mane back, and walked over to her. Rissa handed him her clothes. For a long, heated moment, his gaze captured hers, before dipping down the length of her body, then back up to linger on her breasts. "You flatter the gown, as did my Winna," he observed quietly. "I wish I could take you to bed, hold you in my arms, and mate with you."

Rissa's heart began a thunderous pounding. "But you can't. You have people waiting . . ."

"No, I can't," Morigan agreed, the sudden huskiness of his voice the only hint of the wild emotions roiling within him. "But, soon, Rissa. Very soon. I promise you. And that," he added, a resolute look in his eyes, "is one promise I fully intend to keep."

Ten

Rissa woke the next morning to a woman's soft voice, singing, the clatter of cook pots, and the grating sound of chairs sliding back and forth across the hard-packed dirt floor. Breakfast. Sarna already must be up and cooking breakfast.

A hot meal would be good, then a bath, Rissa thought in drowsy contentment, before embarking on a mission to see how all the other Bellatorian females were doing. She stretched leisurely, yawned hugely, then froze.

Morigan. He'd woken her briefly a few hours before dawn when he'd crawled into bed. So sleep-benumbed was she, Rissa had done little more than snuggle into him when he pulled her against his body, then dozed off.

But this was the morning, broad daylight from the sounds of activity in the main chamber, and there was only the flimsy barrier of a sleeping gown between her and nakedness. She recalled Morigan's words last night, promising to mate with her soon, and a shiver of dread rippled through her.

Gathering all her courage, Rissa opened her eyes. The bed was empty, the only sign he'd ever lain in it was the impression of his body left in the furs. She rolled over and scanned the room. Morigan wasn't there, either.

Relief filled her. With a sigh, Rissa rolled over onto her back. Thoughts, however, bombarded her, until the tension within her rose again. That the Cat Lord had left her a maiden one night more meant little. He intended to have her and would soon enough. Tonight even, perhaps. And there was nothing, absolutely nothing, she could do about it.

Fleetingly, she considered seeking out a knife from the household supplies in the other room. She could hide it beneath a pillow and threaten Morigan with it . . .

Rissa groaned and flipped over onto her stomach, burying her face in her arms. What a ludicrous thought—using some puny knife against a Cat Man. It hadn't protected her from him that first time. It wouldn't again. She was completely at his mercy.

Would he be gentle with her, or fly into one of those infamous, uncontrollable sexual frenzies? It wouldn't matter, Rissa decided. Either way, their mating would be against her will. Either way, it would be rape.

Tears of impotent rage welled in her eyes. It was so unfair, all of it. She'd never felt so frustrated, so helpless in her entire life. And the fact she found herself wildly attracted to Morigan didn't ease her distress one bit. Not one bit at all.

But that was one issue she certainly didn't want to dwell on. Not when even the slightest contemplation of him, lying naked beside her on this bed, filled her with such a curious ache deep in her belly. He was a magnificent animal, big, muscular, and most attractively furred. The brief loincloth he'd worn when she first met him left little to the imagination, even if that imagination was quite maidenly and unschooled in the ways of love.

As alien a species as he was, Rissa knew they could couple, that she was capable of carrying his child. Animalistic as his appearance was at first glance, he was still humanoid enough for her, after some opportunity to adjust to his feline looks, to find him attractive. Why not mate with him? Why not experience what it would be like to join with a Cat Man?

No one need ever know, once she escaped and returned to Primasedes. The contraceptive that old Zada had given her should be effective for at least another month. She wouldn't get pregnant, wouldn't have the shame of an unwanted Cat Child nine months from now. She could easily go on with her life, wed as her father intended, and no one would be the wiser.

Only she would know what few women ever knew, experience what many fantasized about but lacked the courage ever to seek out—a primal mating with a Cat Man. Why not give Morigan what he wanted? He desired her. She desired him. At least for a short time, they could enjoy each other, savor the depth and breadth of passion.

Yet, what would be left for either of them in the end? Morigan would fail to gain what he wanted most—an heir. She would have surrendered her principles and self-respect. She needed more from a man than lust.

She needed to give more as well. And that part of her, the part Rissa needed to share with the man she would eventually take as mate, was impossible to grant the Cat Man, Morigan.

Rissa shoved herself to a sitting position, tugging the fur coverlet up to clutch it in her hands. Her eyes squeezed shut, fighting against a sudden surge of tears. What had heretofore been a confusing jumble of emotions, now crystallized into the true reason Morigan frightened her so. It wasn't an issue of the physical differences between them. It wasn't the fact he'd abducted her, and carried her off with the intention of raping her and getting her with his child. It wasn't because he was her enemy, or that he hated her father and meant to see him dead.

In spite of it all, she still couldn't help but admire him—his courage, his single-minded devotion to his people, his sharp intelligence, and iron-willed self-control. But the same traits that drew her to him were also the same traits that sustained his bitter rancor against her father and Bellator, closing him off from allowing himself ever to love again.

In the course of seeking his vengeance and shutting out the gentler emotions of sorrow and love, Morigan would lose his soul. She feared that in him most of all. Perhaps some woman, wise to the world and life's deeper mysteries, could win him back. But she wasn't that woman. Not now, perhaps not ever. She'd other dreams, other goals. If she let herself love a man as driven by hatred as Morigan was, the bitter fires that would eventually consume him would consume her as well.

With a strangled sob, Rissa swiped away her tears and climbed down from the bed. The truth certainly didn't make things any easier, but it did clarify and strengthen her intent. At least now, she knew what she battled—and it wasn't a maiden's fear of her first mating, or her anger over the injustice of her capture. It wasn't her confusing attraction to him. It was the knowledge that Morigan, as long as he persisted in his dreams of vengeance, could never be the man for her. Such dark obsessions tended sooner or later to obliterate everything. Everything—especially love, tenderness and commitment.

Rissa removed the sleeping gown, folded it carefully, and placed it atop the chest. She dressed in the freshly cleaned clothes Morigan had so considerately returned, pulled on her boots, finger combed her hair, then straightened the furs on the bed. As she plumped the pillows, her glance snared on her jewelry.

Rissa retrieved the necklace and earrings, cupping the tangle of silvery metal and pale, blue-green stones in her hand.

Puzzlement wafted through her. Why did she feel so strongly about wearing her jewelry? Why did Morigan's request, no, demand, not to wear it anger her so? They were only trinkets, after all.

No, they *weren't* just trinkets, she realized. Her jewelry was a symbol—of her continued defiance of the Cat Lord's desire for her submission. It was a symbol of her personhood, her Bellatorian heritage, her right to choose how and where to live her life. And it was the only thing of any substance she'd left to cling to, to remind her this was just some horrible nightmare, a nightmare she would someday break free from.

Rissa clasped the earrings to her ears and refastened the necklace about her neck. For an instant more, she glanced down at the bed—Morigan's bed. Then, with a deep breath to fortify her for what lay ahead, she turned and marched out to see who was making all the racket in the next room.

Sarna was definitely trying to cook breakfast. The mess she'd managed to create in doing so, however, hardly seemed worth the effort. Even to Rissa's untutored eyes, a small bowl of singed porridge garnished with some rehydrated cerasa fruit, a cup of domare milk, and wedge of cheese didn't justify the five large, food-encrusted pottery bowls, overturned pitcher of milk, iron pot of burnt porridge still smoking over the hearth fire, and chairs scattered about the room.

But she withheld comment, gratefully accepting the old woman's cheerful offering. Rissa only wondered if Morigan had been there earlier to observe his mother's erratic behavior. She hoped not. Somehow, Rissa doubted Sarna had been this way before the massacre.

She pulled one of the chairs up to the table, fished a spoon out of the soaking tub of dirty dishes, scrubbed it off with a clean rag, then carried it back to the table and sat down to eat.

The porridge wasn't half bad, Rissa mused, when one poured on enough milk and added a generous serving of cerasa fruit and heavy dollop of apis honey to cover the slightly burnt flavor. Of course, she hadn't eaten since sunset of yesterday, either, which no doubt enhanced her lack of culinary discrimination.

"Care for more porridge, child?" Sarna asked, suddenly appearing over Rissa's left shoulder. "It's good to see a young female who knows how to eat well. There'll be no problem with your bearing of strong children."

At the reminder of her true purpose in the lair, Rissa's appetite fled. She laid down her spoon and forced a smile onto her face. "I think that's all I can manage, domina." She glanced around. "Shall we clean up, or do you and Morigan still need to eat?"

Sarna dismissed that query with an airy wave of her hand. "Morigan was gone before I woke. And I, well, I don't eat much of late." She smiled apologetically. "My appetite. It has never been the same since . . ." Her expression clouded and she quickly turned away.

Rissa rose from the table and hurried over to her. "Let me help you wash the dishes and straighten up in here, domina." She touched the old Cat Woman on the arm, afraid to presume any more intimate physical contact.

Sarna glanced at her and managed a wan little smile. Then, hesitating but an instant, she turned and gave Rissa a hug. "You're a kind child. Even for a Bellatorian."

"We're not all bloodthirsty killers, domina," Rissa said, awkwardly hugging her in return. "I haven't much to offer in comfort for your terrible loss, but if my companionship and assistance would help . . ."

Morigan's mother's expression brightened. "I would like that." She released her and strode over to the table. Once again filled with her earlier cheerfulness and energy, Sarna began gathering up the dirty dishes. "Fill that big pot over there from the vat of water," she told Rissa, indicating a large, covered wooden container that stood near the chests. "Then hang the pot over the fire to heat. We'll use it for wash water."

Rissa stared at her, startled by Sarna's sudden swings in mood, then did as requested. A laborious hour later the main chamber was neat. The pots and dishes were washed, dried, and put away, the chairs back in place, and the rest of the burnt porridge discarded.

Sarna glanced around, satisfaction gleaming in her eyes. "It's so good to have another female in the lair. The work goes so much more quickly—and pleasantly." She turned to Rissa. "Wouldn't you say, child?"

"Of course, domina." Rissa looked down at her rough, dry hands and split nails. Between the journey here and this morning's "work," her hands would never be the same. She'd an inkling, however, there were far easier ways to cook a meal. "Perhaps, when you've some extra time," she ventured carefully, "you could teach me how to cook. Morigan hasn't been pleased with my efforts so far."

Puzzlement furrowed Sarna's brow. "You can't cook, child? We must remedy that soon. My son has little patience with ignorance."

"He has little patience with much of anything at times," Rissa muttered under her breath, remembering the last twelve days. Then, recalling the horror Morigan had lived through in the past cycle, she immediately felt guilty. He'd reason, if any man did, to be a bit short of temper. And there were many other times when he could be so gentle, so kind, and so—

She brushed aside the memory of last night, when he'd offered her his wife's sleeping gown, of the heated look in his eyes when he'd first seen her in it. "Thank you, domina," she replied instead, her attention returning to Sarna. "Perhaps, we could begin my cooking lessons tonight?"

"No, not tonight. That meal is already being prepared by the other Cat Women." Morigan's mother smiled. "There will be a feast to welcome you to the lair this eve. There'll be dancing and singing and storytelling. Morigan commanded it, to honor his new mate."

The blood rushed from Rissa's face. "It wasn't necessary for Morigan to command such a thing for me. And I'm sure the other Cat Women have better things to do than cook some feast in my honor."

"Nonetheless, it shall be done." Sarna walked over, gathered up a small, wrapped bundle that lay on the table, then took Rissa by the arm and led her to the cave's opening. "You are our new lady. It is fitting you be honored, for it honors my son as well." The old woman paused at the doorway, a faraway look forming suddenly in her eyes. "He needs to be happy again," she mumbled vaguely. "He still holds so much pain within him, and he needs to let it go."

"Even I see that, domina," Rissa softly replied, knowing she spoke of Morigan. "Why is he so afraid to grieve?"

Sarna sighed. "He is Lord. He must be strong for all." She paused there a moment longer, then tugged once more on Rissa's arm. "Come, child."

Rissa shot her a questioning glance. "Where are we going?"

"To the hot springs." The old Cat Woman eyed her critically, her glance and mind once more sharp. "Your clothes may be clean enough, but you need a bath. It wouldn't do to shame Morigan tonight."

At mention of the hot springs, Rissa's expression brightened. "Oh, I'd love a bath, domina. Morigan's shame aside, I don't particularly like being dirty myself."

Sarna nodded in satisfaction. "I am pleased to hear it. One can't always be sure of the cleanliness habits of other species." She glanced at Rissa. "Afterwards, I'll take you on a tour of the lair and introduce you to some of our people. Morigan thought it best for you to begin your assimilation immediately."

Oh, he did, did he? Rissa thought tartly. Morigan was singularly overconfident when it came to his plans for her. But she bit back a stinging reply, knowing full well Sarna wasn't at fault here, and followed along. The battle, Rissa reminded herself for the hundredth time, was with the Cat Lord, not with his people.

"If possible, domina," she ventured carefully, thinking it as good a time as any to voice her request, "I'd like very much to see how my compatriots are doing. Could we perhaps meet with the other Bellatorian females today as well?"

Sarna laughed. "You will see them tonight at the feast, have no fear." At Rissa's crestfallen look, she patted her on the arm. "If there's time today, we can perhaps stop and speak with any we see about. Would that please you?"

"Yes, domina." Rissa smiled. "I'd like that very much."

They left the cave and stepped out into full sunshine. Rissa blinked several times to adjust to the intense brightness, then squinted up at the sun. Midmorning. She must have been more tired than she'd imagined to sleep so late. But then, considering the stress of the past days and the unbelievable comfort of Morigan's bed, her unusual lethargy shouldn't really surprise her.

The path from the cave led back down to the ground, then around some volcanic boulders, a small stand of trees, and along the side of the mountain. It was a beautiful, lush little valley. Surrounded on all sides by steep, mountain walls of glittering volcanic rock, it was sun-warmed and sheltered from the gusts of wind that surged high overhead, whipping the clouds into tattered shreds. Long and wide, the valley ran for what looked to be four or five thousand meters, then twisted along with the small stream that coursed down its length before both disappearing around a broad, gentle curve.

Stands of trees, many of which Rissa realized were fruit trees, dotted the area. Wild berry brambles grew in tangled profusion along the warm rock walls. There was no sign, however, of vegetable or grain crops or gardens.

The Cat People didn't dare reveal their presence in the valley by any outward signs of domestication, Rissa realized. The trees and berry bushes most likely grew wild here. No one would suspect anything upon seeing them. But as carnivorous as the Cat People seemed to be, they also obviously ate and required other foods. How did they acquire them?

"A question, domina," she said.

Sarna glanced over. "Yes, child?"

"How do your people find enough food to survive? You'd oats for the porridge, there had to be flour for the journey bread, and there was milk. But I see no fields of grain, no domare or other herd animals about."

The Cat Woman smiled. "We keep our herd animals penned in one of the larger caves, bringing them out to graze for several hours in the afternoon if our guards tell us it is safe. The fruit we gather from what grows wild in the valley.

"We grow a small portion of our vegetables and grains in some of our specially prepared caves," she said, pointing out several as they walked along, "the rest we trade furs for with the farming villages on the plains. We hope in time, though, if our attempts at adapting our perpetual light boxes to mimic sunlight more accurately are successful, to be able to grow all our grains and vegetables indoors."

"You Cat People amaze me," Rissa murmured. "I hadn't realized you'd the technology to do such things."

"Some we've always had, some we were forced to acquire. Traditionally, we are a nomadic people, living off the land, following the herds through most of the cycle, trading for what we couldn't acquire on our own." As if the memories were suddenly too much to bear, Sarna shook her head and lengthened her stride. "But enough of that. Here are the hot springs."

As they drew close to a small cave, the sound of churning water caught Rissa's attention. She exchanged a questioning glance with Sarna. The old woman nodded. "Please enter."

There were actually three springs inside, two in one huge, cavernous room in the first part of the cave, a smaller one farther down a short tunnel. "These are the communal bathing pools," Sarna explained, indicating the first two, where four Cat Women and several young girls bathed. "The one in the back is more private and reserved for mated couples." She smiled conspiratorially. "Perhaps you and Morigan would care to bathe there together some time?"

Rissa flushed. "Yes, perhaps we would." To change the subject, she pretended interest in the two pools that churned so invitingly before her. "Is this where I'm to bathe?"

The Cat Woman nodded. "Yes."

A sudden thought struck Rissa. "If the back pool is for mated couples, and there are women in here, where do the unmated men bathe?"

"Why, in here, as well." Surprise glimmered in Sarna's eyes. "That's why they're called communal pools."

"Are there then special times for the men and women to bathe separately?" Rissa asked, hoping, praying that this was so. "I see only females here now."

"No special hours. It just worked out that way this morning." Morigan's mother peered over at her. "Is this not Bellatorian custom? It's only a bath, after all, at least in the communal pools. That's why the private one in the back is only for mated couples." She chuckled. "And why only one couple is allowed in that area at a time."

She really didn't need to hear any more details, Rissa decided. "I-I suppose I'd better get on with my bath, before any males arrive. And, in answer to your question, no, communal bathing isn't the general custom on Bellator."

Sarna patted her on the hand. "Well, think nothing of it here. No one will take offense. There is a proper time and place for sexual interest, and such time is not at our communal bathing pools." She led Rissa around to where several crude, wooden benches sat against the cave's wall. Neatly folded piles of clothing and drying cloths lay stacked along them. "Put your things down here and disrobe. No one will disturb them."

Rissa hesitated for a moment, then quickly undressed, folded her own clothes into a tidy pile, and grabbed the cleansing sand and drying cloths Sarna offered from the bundle she'd brought along. With a surreptitious glance at the cave entrance to assure herself no Cat Men had just walked in, Rissa hurried over to the edge of the spring, across from where the other Cat Women and Children bathed. She laid down the drying cloth and container of cleansing sand, then lowered herself to the side of the pool and eased her way in.

Ignoring the spring's other occupants for the moment, Rissa surrendered herself to the sheer sensuality of the experience. By the five moons, but it felt heavenly, she thought as she slipped into the chest-deep water. The pool was warm, but pleasantly so, scented faintly of minerals. The water bubbled gently, churning to a light foam. A fine mist filled the air.

Rissa threw back her head, basking in the delicate spray showering her face. Then, something cool plopped on her nose. She opened her eyes. Overhead, the low, moss flower-covered ceiling dripped with moisture.

She could stay here forever, Rissa mused dreamily, swallowed up in this heated, secret little haven. She lay back, floating on the water. All the cares, all the heartache and frustration seemed to ebb away, gain a distance that lessened the frightening intensity of the past weeks. Then, she recalled Sarna's words, explaining the pools were communal.

Rissa jerked up. Her feet touched soft, velvety sand. As she headed back to the edge of the spring to retrieve the container of cleansing sand and complete her bath before any Cat Men might arrive, Sarna lowered herself into the water beside her.

"Come, child," she said, taking Rissa by the hand. "It's past time I begin the introductions."

"But my ba—," Rissa protested, then gave it up when she noted the determined set to the old Cat Woman's face. She sighed, and shoved her wet hair back from her face, preparing for the first formal meeting with women whose expressions boded little hope of a warm welcome.

"Come Mira, Leta, Anista, and Chondra." Sarna waved over the four Cat Women standing together. "Come and meet Morigan's new mate."

They were as reluctant to meet her as she was to meet them, Rissa realized. She managed a wan little smile, deciding someone had to make the first overtures of friendship. For her efforts, the expressions of three of the Cat Women only hardened. The other, a young, brown-haired woman of about twenty, very obviously in the last weeks of her pregnancy, smiled uncertainly.

Sarna caught up the smiling one's hand and pulled her over. "Mira, please, let me introduce you to Rissa." She placed the Cat Woman's hand in Rissa's. "Mira will be our first female to bear a Cat Child since . . ." Her voice momentarily faded. "Since the massacre," Sarna forced herself to finish. She smiled at Rissa. "As our lord's mate, you must attend her birthing and gift her with presents."

Rissa's eyes widened. "Oh. I'm afraid I've no experience whatsoever in birthing babies."

One of the other Cat Women, a striking beauty with long black hair, snickered loudly, but Sarna seemed oblivious to the sound. "Have no fear, child," she reassured her quickly. "Agna attends all birthings. As our Lady, you are present more for ceremony than whatever midwifery skills you may or may not possess."

Relief filled Rissa. Agna was hardly the most warm of companions, and their instant animosity hadn't cooled at all on the journey here, but for a birthing she'd tolerate her gladly. "In that case," she said, smiling warmly over at Mira, "I'd be honored if you'd have me."

Mira's gaze dipped. "My thanks for your generosity, my Lady. It is I who am honored." Her big brown eyes lifted, warming with admiration as she examined Rissa's earrings and necklace. "Those are so beautiful, my Lady. Is it turcas stone? I've heard of its rare colors, but never seen any, until now."

"Yes, they are turcas stone," Rissa replied. She fingered the necklace lovingly. "They are dear to me. My mother gifted me with this jewelry on my sixteenth birthing day."

"Sentimental value or not," the raven-haired Cat Woman

sniffed, moving to stand beside Mira, "it's in poor taste to flaunt it before females who have nothing of such extravagance! But then, what would one expect from a Bellatorian?"

Rissa flushed. Before she could reply, however, Sarna cut in. "For shame, Anista! Rissa is new to us here. Give her time to learn our ways. You are lacking in hospitality this day."

"Perhaps I am," Anista muttered, not looking at all contrite, "but her lack of sensitivity bodes poorly." She sent her other three companions a sly, smirking glance. "I'm finished with my bath. Are any of the rest of you ready to leave?"

Mira and the other two Cat Women exchanged hesitant looks, then nodded. Anista smiled thinly at Rissa. "We've work to do and cannot waste all day in sleeping late and bathing. Let me introduce my other two friends before we take our leave. This," she said, indicating the plump, brown-haired Cat Woman on her right, "is Chondra. This," she added, gesturing to the sandy-haired woman on the other side of Mira, "is Leta."

The two Cat Women smiled at Rissa and briefly dipped their heads. "My Lady," they replied in unison.

Sarna smiled broadly, seemingly unaware of the undercurrent of animosity emanating from Anista. "Good, good, that is much better. You see, child," she asked, turning back to Rissa, "now you have four new friends?"

Over the old Cat Woman's head, Rissa saw Anista once more smirk and glance slyly at her companions. Anger rose within her. For herself, she didn't care if these women ever came to like her. But for their disrespect to Sarna and her goodhearted intent to ease her way with them, well, that was beyond bearing.

"Perhaps, in time, domina," Rissa coolly said, locking gazes with the black-haired Cat Woman, "we'll come to an understanding, but only if I discover a greater depth of compassion in their hearts then I see now. Especially," she added fiercely, "for those older and perhaps more fragile than they."

Anista scowled and Mira went pale. Leta and Chondra's expressions remained blank. Then, with a toss of her long mane, Anista signaled for her friends to follow her. They headed across the spring to the opposite side, climbed out, dressed, and departed.

The young girls remained, playing in the water and laughing. Rissa watched them for a few minutes, then turned back to Sarna. The old woman was eyeing her intently. "You made no friends here today, did you, child?"

Sarna was no fool, Rissa realized, in her moments of lucidity. Yet the times of confusion and pain and her erratic behavior had apparently been enough to weaken her position of respect in the Cat lair, if Anista's and the other Cat Women's reactions to her were any indication. Did Morigan know? Rissa wondered, as overburdened as he must be with so many more pressing, immediate cares. And what good would it serve to tell him, save only to add to his pain and concerns?

No, Rissa resolved, as long as she remained in the lair, and with whatever power or influence she had as Morigan's mate, she would endeavor to rebuild Sarna's well-deserved position. Whether Anista and her cronies liked it or not, they would learn to honor their elders.

"No," she sighed, smiling over at Morigan's mother, "I suppose I didn't make a very good first impression with those women. But, though I'll try my best to be accepted here, I refuse to grovel for that same acceptance. I *am* Bellatorian. That fact will never change no matter how long I stay here. As I must learn to bridge the differences between us, so should they. They must meet me halfway, domina. Nothing else will ever work."

"I suppose you're right, child," Sarna said. "I was unrealistic to think this would go smoothly. Even the transition of your other females has been difficult, and will continue to be so for a while longer. And you, as our new Lady, will have an even worse time of it, I fear."

At mention of the other Bellatorian women who'd been captured, Rissa brightened. "There is one, Diona, who is a good friend of mine. Do you know where she may be?"

"Diona?" The old Cat Woman frowned. "I'm not certain, child. I don't know all of them very well yet." She smiled in apology. "I am sorry."

"It's all right, domina." Rissa smiled in return and patted her on the arm. "I'm sure your duties are many in this lair."

Sarna nodded self-importantly. "Ah, yes. Morigan depends greatly on me." She glanced around. "Well, it is past time we finished our bath and began your tour of the lair. Is there anything you'd like to see first?"

Rissa shook her head. "No, nothing . . ." She paused. "Yes, there is, after all. Naren. I'd like to visit him."

A graying auburn brow lifted in mild surprise. "Mated females don't usually visit the lairs of unmated males. It isn't considered proper."

The protest she wasn't mated and would visit whomever she wished formed on Rissa's lips. With the greatest of efforts, she bit it back. Unlike her son, Sarna wasn't trying to control her, just inform her of their customs. "I cared for Naren while he was ill," she carefully formed her next words. "He was kind to me. I can't help but see him as a friend. Isn't it considered proper for the Lady of the lair to visit the injured and infirm? To show concern for all would seem a most appropriate and kind act."

Sarna considered that for a moment. "Yes, it would seem so. And you won't be visiting him alone. I'll be there, as well as perhaps, Agna." She nodded. "I'll take you to him."

Ten minutes later, Morigan's mother led her from the hot springs and out into the valley. They turned back the way they'd come, past the wild berry brambles, fruit trees, and the trail to Morigan's lair, following the stream up the valley. There were many people about now, children running and playing, women hauling buckets of water from the stream to carry back to their lairs, and men gathered in groups, cleaning game they'd killed or laying out hides to scrape the fur and flesh away in preparation for tanning the leather.

"It seems a lot of work to go to for clothing," Rissa observed, noting the men's efforts.

"Yes, it does," Sarna agreed. "But we have little opportunity to range far and wide anymore, or trade for fabric clothing, and we have no coin at any rate. The farmers have always valued our furs and leather, though. There is none finer or longer lasting."

"No, I'd imagine not," Rissa said. Her gaze scanned the valley once more. Up ahead, several women worked around a huge iron pot suspended from a tripod of saplings. "What are they doing?"

"Making cleansing sand. Doesn't everyone make it in the autumn?"

Rissa smiled. "I've never made cleansing sand."

"Well, it's easy enough to make from animal fat, water, and lye. Later, we dry it and grind it into cleansing sand grains."

"Another laborious job."

"You don't like work, child?" Sarna's tone was mildly curious.

"No, it isn't that," Rissa hastened to reply. "I just never

realized how much effort went into so many of the things I take for granted. It would be . . . interesting . . . to learn more."

"Good." The Cat Woman nodded her head in satisfaction. "I was hoping you'd say that. It is expected, when she is not engaged in her more official duties, that the Lady of the lair involve herself in the seasonal tasks. Every able hand is needed if we are to survive."

"As you wish, domina," Rissa murmured, not wanting to appear difficult, though the thought of stripping hides and standing over a steaming pot of fermenting cleansing sand didn't overly excite her. She decided to change the subject. "Are we near Naren's lair yet?"

"Right here." Sarna pointed to a small cave. As Rissa stepped forward, intending to walk inside, the Cat Woman grabbed her arm, halting her. "No. It's best if I enter first, to make it appear I'm the one initiating the visit rather than you."

Rissa bit her lip, then nodded. "Thank you, domina." Clamping down on the temper that was beginning to flare at being constrained by what she viewed as repressive and outdated customs, she forced herself to follow Sarna inside. The interior was dimly lit, consisted of a single room complete with square hearth, a small table with two chairs, and a bed on which lay Naren, Agna bending over him.

At the sound of their entry, Agna turned. Her glance met Sarna's. She smiled in welcome. Then, as Rissa moved to the old Cat Woman's side, Agna's smile faded.

"What is she doing here?" the healer demanded. "You know it's not proper for a—"

"I brought her along with me. We were taking a tour of the lair, and Rissa expressed a desire to check on Naren's condition. Knowing she was responsible for his care and recovery until you arrived, Agna, I saw no harm in one visit."

"Well, no offense to you, domina," the other Cat Woman said, striding across the cave to block their way, "but *I* do."

Eleven

It was too much, Rissa thought, her patience at an end. From the very first Cat Woman she'd met, all of them, save for Sarna, had treated her with wariness or outright hostility. Though she understood their reaction to her, knowing what they'd suffered at Bellatorian hands, knowing she and the other captives were living representatives of that planet, she didn't understand their disloyalty to Morigan and his efforts to help his people in this. She herself had reason to sabotage the Cat Lord's plan. The Cat Women didn't.

"Proper or not," Rissa said, stepping up to Agna, her fists clenched at her sides, "I *will* see Naren. I'm Morigan's mate. As your new Lady, I hardly think you're in any position to order me around, Agna."

"Indeed?" the healer hissed softly. Her claws unsheathed. "Think again, Bellatorian."

Sarna glanced from one glaring woman to the other. "Rissa," she began uncertainly, "perhaps it would be best—"

"Let her by, Agna," Naren growled from behind them. "Rissa speaks true and well you know it. You've no authority to order her away. Only Morigan or the Elders possess that power."

Sheer, unmitigated hatred smoldered in the Cat Woman's eyes. "You make a grave error, Naren," she said, never breaking her gaze with an equally angry and uncowed Rissa, "in permitting the Bellatorian into your lair. Morigan, when he hears of it, won't be happy. He needs no further problems, and especially not from a male who claims to be his best friend."

"Morigan trusts me," the Cat Man muttered. "Have no doubt of that." He shoved himself to a sitting position. "You can go now, Agna. My thanks for the fresh bandages."

At his movement, the healer turned to glance down at him. She stood there an instant longer, her slender frame taut with anger. Then, she whirled around, grabbed up her bag of bandages and potions that lay on the table and, shooting Rissa a venomous look as she passed her, exited the cave.

Silence hung heavy in the chamber for several seconds, then Naren sighed. "She'll go straight to Morigan. Of that you can be sure, femina."

"I'm not afraid of her," Rissa snapped. "She'd no right to order me about. If I won't let Morigan do it, I certainly won't let her!"

"Oh dear. Oh dear," Sarna mumbled distractedly from behind her. "Perhaps I had best go after Agna. Talk some sense into her."

"There's no need, domina," Rissa tried to reassure the old Cat Woman as Sarna turned and began to amble toward the entrance. "You must not worry—"

It was too late. Sarna had disappeared from the cave. Rissa made a move to go after Morigan's mother when Naren's voice halted her. "Come, femina. Sarna will be back soon enough. Help me over to the table." He smiled. "The harm has been done. You might as well say what you came to say."

Rissa hesitated a moment more. Then, with a sigh, she walked over to Naren's bedside. Leaning down, she encircled his trim waist and helped him to stand. With slow, halting steps, they made their way to the table.

Once Naren was settled in his chair, Rissa took the opposite one. She smiled over at him. "It's good to see a friendly face again. There have been few of those this day."

The black-haired Cat Man frowned. "I was afraid of that. You and Sarna seem friendly enough, though."

"She's a kind old woman who doesn't seem to have a bit of meanness or cruelty in her." Rissa shot a quick glance over her shoulder. Sarna must still be outside.

A strong, callused hand settled over hers. She turned back to Naren. A look of concern gleamed in his gray eyes.

"Are you all right, femina?" His gaze narrowed. For an instant, she felt him probe her mind. "He has yet to mate with you, hasn't he?"

Rissa jerked her hand away. "Really, Naren, you presume too much! What's between Morigan and me is none of your concern."

"Ah, but it is, Rissa," he gently contradicted her. "For Cat People, it's a simple thing to discern who has mated with whom. And though Morigan's scent is on you and your clothes, the other unmated males will soon discover what I've already ascertained. Then the problems will begin."

"What problems?"

"Morigan has first chance to make you his mate. No one will dispute that. But if you two are found to be incompatible . . ." He paused.

"Well, what, Naren?" Rissa prodded in rising irritation. "Whatever does it matter, anyway?"

"It matters, Rissa," he solemnly informed her, "to a people on the verge of extinction. "You're a fertile female. We need children. But, even so, our laws forbid us to force a male on you for whom you have no desire."

"Then I don't have to mate with anyone, do I? No matter who tries to take me as mate?" Despite her best efforts, Rissa couldn't quite hide the sudden excitement that edged her voice.

Naren frowned. "No. You're too valuable to waste. You'll just be permitted to choose a more compatible mate from the rest of us, but you will choose one." A strange light flared in his eyes. "Is there, perhaps, some other male who has caught your favor?"

Rissa gave a disbelieving laugh. "In the one day since I've been here? Hardly!"

A dark flush crept up the Cat Man's face. "You spent time with several of us during the journey."

Whatever was the matter with Naren? Rissa thought, noting his sudden flare of anger. He seemed almost offended she hadn't found any other Cat Man attractive, almost as if—

"Naren, I didn't mean to imply I didn't find *you* attractive. It's just that . . . that I never looked at you that way. You're my friend."

His flush deepened. He found sudden fascination with some flaw in the tabletop. "Friendship can sometimes grow into love."

Rissa's thoughts raced. Naren? Was Naren saying what he seemed to be saying? Was he offering himself as her mate? It was too much to deal with, now, on top of everything else. She rose. "Perhaps it's best I be going."

He grabbed for her hand, captured it and pulled her back down. "Rissa, don't. Don't be offended." A look of intense entreaty burned in his eyes. "I just thought if you didn't want Morigan . . . we're friends and . . . and I thought . . ."

"That I'd feel more comfortable with you?" Rissa smiled softly. "Yes, we are friends, Naren. And yes, I do feel comfortable with you. But I don't know if I could ever feel . . . that way . . . about you."

"Not like you feel for Morigan, is that it, femina?" he snarled, angry again.

She paled and jerked her hand away. "I never said anything—"

"You didn't need to. I've seen how you two look at each other."

Confusion filled her. "Naren, please, don't be angry with me. I-I don't know what I want or feel anymore. But I do know I desperately need a friend, someone I can trust, whom I can talk to. If you turn from me . . . If I lose you, I don't know what I'll do!"

"I want you, Rissa." He leaned forward, his voice strained and husky. "I won't deny it. But I didn't mean to upset you. If you choose another, I won't turn from you. I'll always be your friend. That much I swear."

She pushed back her chair and walked around to stand behind him. She laid a hand on his shoulder. "Thank you, Naren. If you only knew how much that means to me."

He smiled, took her hand and turned his lips to it for a brief, tender kiss. "And I'm honored you cherish my friendship, Rissa. It gladdens my heart." He paused, pulling her hand down to hold it on his chest. "Nonetheless, you must heed my warning. You and Morigan must mate—and soon— or some of the other males will press their claim. The Council may then be forced to take you from Morigan."

Rissa's chin lifted to a stubborn tilt. "I won't be intimidated or coerced into mating with anyone against my will. Not even Morigan."

"The Council won't long tolerate your resistance," Naren warned. "There are ways, ways we aren't proud of, that can be used . . ."

"Gods!" Rissa's eyes clenched shut. "What am I to do? What am I to do?"

"Get away from Naren, to begin with," came a deep male voice, vibrating with cold fury. "Who *dared* permit you to visit him alone in his lair?"

Rissa's eyes snapped open. She wheeled around. There, in the doorway of the cave, his big body taut with anger, stood Morigan. "Come here, femina," he commanded. "Now!"

Her lips clamped shut over a sharp retort, her jaw tightening. Naren squeezed her hand, then released her. "Go to him, Rissa," he said, gazing up at her. "Don't fight him on this. Please!"

She shot Naren an agonized glance and swallowed hard. Then, like a woman going to her execution, Rissa turned and strode over to the Lord of the Cat People.

They walked in silence for a time, Morigan leading her down to the more deserted part of the valley, not pausing until they reached a grove of towering robur trees that grew beside the stream. There, in the many hued, leafy shade of the mightiest tree, he indicated that Rissa sit. She glared up at him, a defiant light in her eyes.

For an instant, an overwhelming impulse filled Morigan to grab Rissa and shake her, then turn her over his knee and beat her until she promised never again to disobey. The intensity of the emotion—and its inherent violence—startled him. He'd never lifted a hand to a female. Until he met Rissa, he'd rarely even raised his voice to one.

Morigan sighed, suddenly too weary for words—or for another fight with Rissa. He lowered himself to the ground and leaned against the gnarled trunk of the robur tree. "Please, Rissa. Sit," he said in a more neutral tone. "We need to talk."

"Talk?" she demanded tautly. "Funny, I thought my place was only to obey, without thought or question."

"I may have been overly harsh back there in Naren's lair, but your honor was in grave danger of being compromised. I hold Naren more at fault than you, though. What was he thinking, to allow you to remain alone in his lair with him after my mother left?"

"There was no danger, Morigan." Rissa sat down beside him. "I only went to see how he was doing. All we did was talk."

Morigan recalled how he'd found them, Naren in his chair, Rissa standing close behind him. Naren . . . holding her hand . . .

A very tender scene indeed.

His mood darkened, swinging wildly from anger, to torment, then uncertainty. "Perhaps, femina. And then again?" He dragged in an unsteady breath. "Do you desire Naren? Do you wish to take him as your mate instead . . . instead of me?"

"What?" Rissa threw up her hands and stared at him in disbelief. "By the five moons, are all you men alike? I've never seen a more insecure lot!"

"I cannot keep you against your will, Rissa, not within the lair."

"Yes, I know," she sighed. "Naren told me."

Morigan's eyes narrowed in suspicion. "Did he? Why? To convince you to leave me?"

Rissa turned, riveting the full intensity of her outrage on him. "That was hardly the purpose of our conversation. He's just concerned for me, wanted me to know my options, such as they are. And he told me more than you ever have!"

He rolled his eyes, then shoved his hand through his tousled mane. "Gods, but must you be so self-righteous about this? Perhaps I did withhold information but, knowing the attraction between us, can you blame me for wanting a chance at you myself? A chance, if you'll recall, *Naren* all but forced on me."

Her only reply was a glance of withering scorn.

Morgan sighed, exasperated. "The stricture against visiting unmated males isn't just an issue of trust, Rissa. It's ancient custom, the proper social behavior ordained between the sexes. A custom, in just the span of a day, you've managed to throw into total chaos!"

"Sounds to me as if it needed to be thrown into chaos, then reassembled and set forth in more reasonable terms." Rissa sniffed in disdain. "How ludicrous not to allow friends to visit each other!"

"I'll admit some of our laws are outdated, but there are good reasons for keeping unmated Cat People out of temptation's way. Especially now, when we must more carefully monitor any potential inbreeding."

"Well, that's now. What of your ancient reasons?"

"Must you question *everything?*"

Rissa graced him with an exaggerated look of innocence. "Why yes. I've always believed if some rule or law couldn't be explained satisfactorily, then it wasn't worth obeying."

"Did you now?" he muttered. "You must have been a joy as a child."

"Not always," she replied airily, "but then, my wild childhood escapades aren't the issue here, are they?"

"No." Morgan picked up a leafy branch that had fallen from the tree and began to pluck off the leaves. "You may have heard rumors of our, er, sexual prowess." He glanced up at her. "The tales are not without credence."

Rissa arched a slender brow. "Indeed? And exactly what tales are true? The part about your wildly uncontrollable sexual appetites, or your ability to seduce any female within fifty kilometers or that strange mating lust you Cat People seem to fall into every three cycles or so?"

Morigan scowled. "If you persist in that sarcastic tone, I'll just forget I ever offered to explain."

"Okay. Okay." Rissa held up a hand in truce. "I'm sorry. I guess this subject is beginning to make me a little uncomfortable, that's all."

His mouth twisted. "Afraid I'll talk myself into a lustful frenzy and force myself on you, femina?"

"Something like that."

The Cat Lord chuckled, then turned his attention back to the tree branch. "We're a deeply passionate, highly emotional people. It's the animal part of us. In many situations we've a tendency to react instinctively before our human, more logical side, can regain control. It can present problems, especially when it comes to the act of mating."

"In what ways, Morigan?"

"In unplanned pregnancies, in inbreeding—as I mentioned before—in the maintenance of order, right of inheritance, and determination of paternity." He looked over at her, his green-gold eyes intense, piercing. "Must I go on? We aren't savages, Rissa. We've the same problems as any society."

"But Bellator, which faces identical problems, doesn't repress its people in such a manner."

Morigan grew silent, his expression turning serious. "Bellator doesn't have uncontrollable mating urges to deal with when all its moons, one night about every three cycles, fall into perfect alignment."

Rissa's mouth went dry. Her heart began a wild beat beneath her breast. "What happens on that night, to make you fear it so?"

"It isn't so much a fear, as a shame," he forced himself to reply, his words slow and deliberate. "Though its consideration stirs great anticipation for the intense pleasure of the mating that occurs that night, conversely, that same knowledge remains a most uncomfortable reminder of our animalistic origins." He inhaled a deep breath and forged on. "That night of the triple moons, we Cat People mate like beasts, instinctively, unthinkingly."

Rissa's eyes widened in shock.

"We aren't proud of it, but have come to accept it as a part of our natures," Morigan hurried to explain, dreading the first glimmers of disgust and revulsion he felt certain would soon fill her, but compelled to tell her nonetheless. There was little hope for them if Rissa didn't know it all— and find some way to accept it. "It isn't something that can be changed or controlled at any rate. For a Cat Man—or Woman—who has come into full sexual maturity to deny him or herself on that night is fatal. The effort required to fight the urges quickly becomes excruciating, driving one to a terrible, pain-maddened death."

"I-I didn't know. How sad; how difficult it must be for you and your people," she whispered, her face pale, her voice tremulous. "When . . . when will it happen again . . . the three moons in alignment?"

"This time?" A muscle ticked along Morigan's jaw. "On the first day of our new cycle and the end of our short winter season."

"But that's less . . ." She mentally counted the weeks. "Less than a month away. What will you do? You haven't enough women for all your men!"

"A dilemma, to be sure."

"Only one of many, it seems."

For an instant he eyed her, not quite trusting the mildness

of her response. Rissa didn't seem at all repulsed. If anything, she sounded sympathetic. Ever so slowly, his mouth lifted in a crooked grin. "I suppose we could try to capture another two hundred or so females in the meantime. One for each and every Cat Man."

"You're mad!" she cried, once again outraged. "You shouldn't suggest something like that in jest. It's still a cruel and barbaric act."

"Survival frequently is cruel and barbaric, Rissa."

"Yes," she admitted, her gaze dropping, "I'm beginning to realize that."

Morigan laid down the tree branch and took Rissa's hand. He raised it to his lips.

At the unsettling touch of his mouth, Rissa went still. Her eyes lifted, snaring with his. Gods, but he felt so warm, so soft, so wonderful! She shouldn't enjoy it so much, shouldn't imagine what else he was capable of with those firm, sensual lips. Especially now, after what he'd just told her.

Animals. Morigan had admitted they were little more than animals—at least on that strange night of the triple moons. All the tales she'd ever heard were true. In fact, the real truth was far more shocking than even the most sordid rumors. And to think she'd railed against their restrictions on being in an unmated male's lair!

The recollection of that law stirred a final question in Rissa's mind. She withdrew her hand from his clasp and leaned away. At the sardonic quirk of Morigan's brow, Rissa smiled nervously. "You never finished your explanation of why the night of the three moons has impacted on your people's strictures against nonmated males and females being alone together."

His forehead furrowed momentarily. "What? Oh, yes, our customs. The Cat People frown on illegitimacy. We like knowing who the fathers of our children are. That night of the triple moon such controls are impossible to enforce. We give into our more animalistic impulses because we've no other choice. The rest of the time, however, we attempt to compensate, to exercise control, by strict adherence to our mating laws."

"Seems more like an extreme case of overreaction, to my way of thinking," Rissa observed dryly. "You cannot help what happens that one night. The rest of the time, though, your own abilities at self-control and prudent, moral behavior should be enough to govern you. Not some unreasonable and insulting laws."

"Perhaps," Morigan admitted. "Perhaps we do overreact. But, for all our animalistic tendencies, we don't like losing control for even one night. It's our deepest pain, a conflict within us that will never be resolved. Our laws and customs are but our way of coping with that special shame." Once more, he took her hand. "Those customs may not always suit you, Rissa, but we do the best we can. I only ask you to accept and respect them."

Once more, he lifted her hand to his face, this time rubbing her palm against his cheek. It felt strange, yet stimulating, she thought, the rasp of his beard-stubbled face against her flesh. Her fingers clenched and she tried to pull away. Morigan's grip tightened, but he allowed her to lower her hand.

"Can you, femina?" he prodded huskily. "Will you accept our laws?"

"I-I don't know." Gods, what was he doing to her? One moment he was the angry, domineering male. The next, he was baring his people's secrets to her. And the next? The next, he was seducing her!

She didn't know how to deal with him anymore. Before, it had been so simple, the battle lines clearly defined, the issues out in the open. Now, just as the stakes grew higher, the Cat Lord had changed tactics and become more subtle, more subversive. Or were they tactics at all? Was it, instead, his true nature finally breaking through as he began to lower his guard?

"What can be so hard about it, Rissa?" Morigan's deep voice pierced the cloud of her confusion. "I've explained as best I could why we do what we do. And you said yourself if some rule or law was explained satisfactorily, you'd obey it."

Exasperation exploded within her. "You needn't repeat my own words back to me, Morigan! I know what I said!"

"Then, what further obstacle remains?"

"Your laws apply to you because they're a part of your society, a society you choose to remain in. I, on the other hand, never chose to be here. I don't think it's fair for you to impose your laws on me, or expect me to obey them."

He opened his mouth, then clamped it shut. "Are we back to that again? By the three moons, Rissa, but you're the most maddening—"

"It will *always* come back to that, Morigan." *That and your terrible lust for revenge and fear of intimacy,* she silently added. "Why would you expect it to be otherwise? Would you submit, if you were in the same situation?"

"Well, if the female who wanted me was as pretty and well-rounded as you—"

"Morigan!"

He sobered. "Some of the females we captured are already settling in nicely. Your friend, for example."

"Diona?" Fear shot through Rissa. "What have you done to Diona?"

"Nothing." He scowled. "Truly, do you still imagine us so barbaric we would harm a female?"

"No, but there are ways to intimidate and frighten that can just as easily bend someone to your will."

Morigan sighed melodramatically. "Ah, if only I could discover which of those would finally work on you."

"Nothing will work on me," Rissa retorted. "Surely, you're smart enough to have figured that out by now. But you haven't answered my question. What has happened to Diona?"

"Your friend is quite safe and unharmed, femina," the Cat Man muttered. "I but tried to make the point that some of your compatriots have found their new mates quite pleasing. Diona is one of them."

Rissa shook her head. "No, not Diona. I can't believe she would ever submit."

"For her," Morigan gently offered, "I don't think it was so much a submission as a mutual attraction. She and Tavist seem surprisingly happy together. For such a short time together, I mean."

Suspicion narrowed her eyes. "And I think you hope to use Diona to manipulate me. Well, it won't work, Morigan!"

His expression shuttered. "See for yourself this eve at the feast then." Morigan climbed to his feet and extended his hand.

Rissa stared up at him. "What now?"

"I've squandered enough of this day's precious time trying to explain things to you," he growled. "I should've known better. Come," he said, reaching down to pull her to her feet. "It's past time I get you back to my mother."

"I'm a waste of time, am I? Then, pray, don't trouble yourself over me from here on out. That'll suit me just fine!"

"And me as well!" he snarled in return, dragging her back up the path to the main part of the valley. Morigan's frustration only grew, however, the longer they walked along. What was he to do with her? How was he ever to convince Rissa to accept her fate and take him as her mate?

Tonight. He intended to take her tonight. Somehow, some-way, he *must* carry through that first mating to bind Rissa to him. Later, they would have the luxury of working out some kind of affection between them.

He'd hoped she would have come to care for him by now. Thought the physical attraction that had so quickly, so heat-edly flared between them would grow, muting her more prin-cipled reasons for resistance. But now, there was no time left to overcome them. No time left—for either of them.

The low, melodious trill of flutes and the bright notes of some stringed instrument filled the night air, melding with the throbbing beat of drums. The sounds reached Rissa's ears long before she, Sarna, and Morigan reached the communal gathering place. The scent of roasting meat wafted to her as well, setting her nose to tingling and her mouth to watering. In spite of herself, an excited anticipation surged through her.

Though the night was cool, the decision had been made to have the feast out of doors. There would be few opportu-nities left, Morigan had informed her, before winter set in. And, above everything, the Cat People loved the freedom of the outdoors.

They entered the brightly lit area, sheltered on three sides by sheer rock walls guarded overhead by sentries. Off to the left, several cookfires burned, roasting whole carcasses of domare, as well as fowl and fish. Tables sat nearby, laden with loaves of brown bread, starchy tubers, fresh greens, fruit, and jugs of some dark, foaming beverage.

Rissa saw several of her compatriots, Diona among them,

standing together near the tables. Though Rissa had managed to speak briefly to a few of the captives during her tour of the lair earlier today, her serving maid had been nowhere to be found. She glanced up at Morigan. "My friend Diona." She gestured to the tables. "Could I go over and speak with her?"

He frowned and shook his head. "Not now. Later. First we must see to the welcome ceremony."

She accepted that, grateful he'd allowed her any opportunity at all to visit the other captives. But later, indeed, she meant to seek out Diona and hear the truth of her and the other women's plights. She couldn't believe they could be as content with their mates as Morigan and his mother would have her think. Surely, they were just cowed into obedience.

Her glance lifted to what lay ahead. In the middle of a seated circle of Cat People, a huge bonfire blazed. A crudely wrought stone throne stood at one end of the circle. On either side of the throne sat several wooden, high-backed chairs. Naren already awaited them there, seated two chairs down from what would be Morigan's right.

"You will sit between Naren and me," Morigan informed her as they drew near. "My mother will sit on my left."

Rissa glanced fleetingly at him. He looked magnificent tonight, garbed in a pale beige leathern tunic heavily decorated with fringe and bands of multicolored embroidery that swirled across the broad expanse of his chest. Pale beige leathern breeches stretched tautly around his heavily muscled legs, and soft, knee-high boots completed his dress. With his long mane of dark hair brushed back from his shoulders and the single aureum Cat's claw dangling at his throat, Morigan looked every bit the proud, powerful leader. And looked very attractive as well.

She quickly squelched that stimulating admission. "I'm

surprised you trust us so close together, after this morning. Have you talked with Naren since then?"

His jaw clenched, but his tone, when he finally replied, was measured and calm. "No, I haven't talked with him. I need time . . ." As if battling with some inner dilemma, Morigan paused. "Besides, to separate you and Naren now from your traditional positions beside my throne would only give rise to further gossip and speculation." He shot her a sharp glance. "None of us need that, do we, femina?"

No, none of them did, Rissa thought. Though she cared little for many of the Cat People's ridiculously constraining laws, both Morigan and Naren did. And, even as her determination to escape grew, she knew she'd never force a confrontation between the two men. It wouldn't be right to destroy their lifelong friendship over a woman neither of them could ever have. There wasn't much else she could leave them, but she would try at least to leave them friends.

"I won't cause problems tonight," Rissa replied, "if that's what you're asking. I'm not a total social boor, you know."

His gaze riveted on his throne. "I'll look forward to that."

She scowled, contemplated a scathing comeback, then gave it up as pointless. Instead, Rissa graced Naren with a quick smile as she drew up beside him and took her seat. After helping his mother to her chair, Morigan came to stand before his throne.

For a long, fire lit moment, he gazed out on the mass of people gathered there. A myriad of loving faces, from young to old, stared back at him, attentive and expectant. He smiled.

"We've had little occasion to dance and sing and feast in the past cycle, and even less of a reason," Morigan's strong, rich voice carried to the farthest reaches of the crowd. "But time—and our lives—must journey on. Decisions, hard ones, have had to be made, if we are ever again to prosper as a people. Bringing Rissa and the other women here was one of those decisions."

Morigan turned to her and offered his hand. Their gazes met. Burning there beneath the firm purpose, Rissa saw his silent entreaty. She rose and walked over to him, taking his hand.

An instant longer, Morigan's eyes locked with hers. A confused mix of wariness and proud possession gleamed there. Then, as if remembering himself, the old, shuttered look slid back in place.

He pulled her close, then turned to his people. "Rissa is my mate. She is now your Lady. Welcome her. Help her. Teach her. For my sake; for us all." The Cat Lord grinned. "Now, let the gifts be brought forth."

Rissa glanced up at him. "Gifts?"

"Of course, femina. Yet another one of our strange customs. We welcome guests with gifts and, as our new Lady, you are doubly entitled to some show of appreciation."

Guilt surged through her. "But Morigan, I haven't accepted, nor want this . . . honor . . . as your mate. It seems hypocritical to go so far as to take your people's gifts. They have so little as it is."

He impaled her with a green-gold stare. "We also believe to give is to receive, Rissa. Please accept the tokens my people offer. To do otherwise would be deeply to offend them."

"As you wish," Rissa sighed her acquiescence. "I've never wished anything ill for your people."

"I know that, femina," Morigan rasped, his gaze dark and disturbingly sensual. "I think I've always known that about you."

She couldn't bear the piercing intensity of his stare, nor the heated emotions his glance stirred. Suddenly, Rissa could hardly endure even standing this close to him. He was too potent, too virile, too overwhelming.

Two Cat Women approached. Gratefully, Rissa turned to acknowledge their presence. Morigan did as well.

"This is Mira," he said by way of introduction, gesturing to the pregnant Cat Woman.

Rissa smiled. "We've already met."

He arched a dark brow. "Indeed?" He motioned Mira forward. "Come, femina. What have you brought for our new Lady?"

The brown-haired woman stepped up and extended a small, leather-wrapped package. "It isn't much," Mira began shyly, "but I thought your lady might like something for her hair."

Rissa accepted the gift and glanced questioningly at Morigan.

"Open it, femina."

With the utmost care, she unwrapped the parcel. It was a long-toothed wooden comb, its handle carved into intricate swirls that surrounded an impressionistic cat head. The work was masterfully done, the wood oiled to a rich, deep red hue.

She glanced up at Mira. "My thanks. It is beautiful." Rissa grinned. "And I most definitely need something to tame this mass of hair."

Mira smiled. "I am honored my humble gift pleases you, my Lady."

Morigan gestured to the other Cat Woman, who walked up to stand beside Mira. He shot Rissa a questioning glance. "Do you know this female, as well?"

Rissa shook her head. "No, my Lord."

At her title of respect, surprise flickered in Morigan's eyes. His mouth quirked briefly. "This is Joshi. She is our head seamstress."

"Joshi." Rissa inclined her head. "I'm pleased to make your acquaintance."

"And I, you, my Lady." The tall, thin Cat Woman offered her a larger wrapped package. "I hope this meets with your approval."

Rissa accepted the parcel and just as carefully unwrapped it. A long-sleeved over tunic and skirt of thick, warm lana cloth lay within. She fingered the rich green fabric. It would serve her well in the cold mountain weather.

"It's beautiful, as well as practical, Joshi," Rissa murmured. "And the stitching is flawless. You truly deserve your title as head seamstress."

Joshi's expression remained stoic, but a spark of pleasure flared in her eyes. "I am honored you see it so, my Lady."

"And I, too, have a gift, femina."

Rissa turned to Morigan. She flushed. "Truly, there was no need . . ."

He signaled over a Cat Man who bore a furry bundle. Morigan took it from him and unfurled it. The bundle became a long, hooded, phoca fur cloak. "To keep you warm in the winter to come." He laid it over her shoulders. "The evening is cool enough to wear it even now, wouldn't you say?"

She couldn't meet his gaze. She couldn't even think, with his hands lingering so strongly, so possessively on her shoulders. "Yes, indeed it is." Summoning all the strength within her, Rissa lifted her eyes to meet his. "My thanks, as well, for your wonderful gift."

He smiled down at her. "I'm pleased you like it. I want you to be happy here, femina. I want . . ." He paused, as if wishing to say something more, then murmured softly, "later."

A ripple of intense awareness, of delicious anticipation, coursed through Rissa. Before she could question him further, however, he released her and turned back to the crowd. "Let the feast begin!" Morigan shouted.

And, with jubilant agreement, the Cat People did just that. Morigan led Rissa back to her chair. "It's yet another of our customs for the males to serve the females at these feasts. I'll return shortly with your and my mother's food." He cocked a brow. "Any special requests?"

Unnerved by his nearness and what had transpired between them just a few seconds ago, Rissa could hardly think, much less find appetite. "No, anything will do, thank you."

He eyed her, hesitating as if he wished to say more. Then, with a shrug of his powerful shoulders, Morigan turned and strode away.

She watched until he disappeared into the crowd. A few Cat Women standing nearby, Anista among them, stared pointedly from Morigan to Rissa, then put their heads together and laughed. Cradoc strolled over to them, shot Rissa a heated, assessing look, and joined in the women's conversation. A conversation, Rissa well knew, of which she was the topic.

Clutching the phoca fur cape about her, she turned back to her chair.

"Don't let them get to you, femina," Naren said.

As she draped the cloak across the back of her chair, she glanced over at him. "It's to be expected." Rissa took her seat. "Despite the ceremony of gifts, I'm well aware most don't want me here." She hesitated. "There were more than a few Cat Women who entertained hopes of becoming Morigan's mate, weren't there?"

Naren chuckled. "More than a few." His gaze sharpened. "What did he say to you, after he took you away today?"

"Morigan? He tried to explain your customs, why I shouldn't be visiting you."

A smile twitched at the corner of Naren's mouth. "And do you now accept the reasons for our customs?"

"I understand better why *you* accept them. But they're still unfair. You Cat People would do well to temper them with a little more common sense."

"Yes, perhaps, we would." Naren paused. "He wasn't happy with you, then, was he?"

Her chin tilted a defiant notch. She glanced away. "No."

Naren expelled a long, weary breath. "Rissa, when will you cease this battle of wills? Principles are one thing, but the true wisdom lies in knowing when the battle is lost and salvaging what you can. Whether you realize it or not, femina, you have a lot you can salvage."

"And will you, too, determine the course of my life for me?" Rissa turned, exasperation filling her. "True friends accept each other for what they are and don't try to change one another."

"A true friend, as well," he countered, "has the courage and caring to tell the other the truth. Morigan has offered you his affection, his protection, and considerable power as his mate. For all his tormenting conflicts and cares, he's a good male. He's the mate for you, Rissa. The longer I see you two together, the stronger that realization becomes."

She laughed softly. "And what a change this is, to hear those words from you. Truly, Naren, you confuse me almost as much as Morigan does!"

He flushed. "It's truth, nonetheless, femina. I thought long and hard about you and me and Morigan after we parted this morn. As much as I still want you, I know it can never be. You are Morigan's, were destined to be his mate. Don't you see that, Rissa? You came to him at a time when he needed you most."

"And what of my needs? Why must it all be for Morigan?"

"I think," Naren replied, "your needs will be met as well. You just have yet to open your eyes and see what is here for you."

"There's nothing here for me. Do you hear me? Nothing! And I don't wish to speak further about it!" Hurt by what she saw as Naren's sudden realliance with Morigan, Rissa twisted in her chair, turning her back to him. Her glance settled on Sarna, who was happily engaged nearby in conversation with several other Cat Women.

The old woman noted Rissa's gaze. She smiled and motioned her over. "Come, child. Allow me to introduce you to more of our people."

For once, Rissa rose and approached the others without hesitation. Anything was better than dealing with Naren just now. He was Morigan's friend, not hers. The sooner she accepted that, the better. Better for them all.

The introductions were made, the greetings formal but cool. After a time of small talk, the Cat Women politely excused themselves. Loathe to return to her chair and Naren's vicinity just yet, Rissa glanced about the gathering in the hope of seeking out some of the other Bellatorian women. As she did, a hand settled on her shoulder.

"I see you made it here safely," a familiar feminine voice observed dryly, "and managed to snare the most handsome and powerful Cat Man in the bargain."

Rissa wheeled about. "Diona!" She flung her arms about her serving maid and hugged her tightly. "I'm so happy to have found you at last." Rissa leaned back, studying her intently. "Are you all right? Is your Cat Man kind to you?"

Diona smiled and shook her head. "Well, he treats me more gently than you, squeezing me so I can hardly draw in a breath."

"Oh." Rissa released her and stepped back, embarrassed. "I'm sorry. I didn't mean—"

"Hush," Diona soothed, patting her cheek. "I'm honored you cared so much for my welfare to express such happiness at seeing me again. I'm touched."

Rissa eyed her uncertainly. "I don't know what came over me. The stress of the past weeks, I suppose. It's been difficult . . ."

The other woman was immediately solicitous. She looked around, then pulled Rissa several meters away, out of close earshot of any potential eavesdroppers. "What happened, Rissa? Did he discover who your father is?"

"Hush, Diona!" her mistress hissed, glancing about apprehensively. Cat People milled around them in happy celebration, but none seemed to pay them heed. "No one knows, and I intend to keep it that way."

Diona grinned. "Your secret's safe with me. The Cat Lord will find out sooner or later, though. The prudent thing would be to tell him first."

"No." Vehemently, Rissa shook her head. "That would be the worst thing to do. There's no telling what Morigan would do if he knew . . ."

"Why?" Her friend's gaze narrowed. "Has the Cat Lord harmed you in any way? Did he force himself on you? If he dared, I swear I'll—"

"No, no, Diona," Rissa hurried to calm her fears. "Morigan hasn't laid a hand on me. In *any* way."

"Indeed?" Diona's glance turned speculative, assessing, sweeping down the length of Rissa's body. "Are you telling me he has yet to mate with you?"

"Diona, please," Rissa murmured, flushing hotly. "Not so loud. It's no one's business but Morigan's and mine."

"But he must mate with you. That's why the Cat Men took us."

"Not if I can help it," her mistress muttered. "I'm no man's chattel."

Diona laughed. "Well, from the looks of him, I'd gladly volunteer to be his chattel—and anything else he wanted."

"Diona!"

The serving maid shrugged, not at all abashed. "Are you blind, Rissa? The man is magnificent! I couldn't have chosen a finer specimen for you if I'd tried. Though I find my sweet Tavist a *most* satisfying mate, I would swoon from delight if your Morigan turned a favorable eye on me. And *you* have him. Talk about good fortune!"

"Good fortune! Not while he's so insistent upon . . ." Noting the suddenly overawed expression on Diona's face, Rissa turned to follow her gaze. Morigan, three wooden platters of food in his hands, was striding back to his throne. Rissa grabbed Diona's arm, wrenching her attention back to her.

"I must return to him," she explained to the startled woman. "We'll talk more later. Just tell me one thing before I go. Are you truly happy here, with this Tavist as your mate?"

"Yes," Diona breathed, a warm, contented smile playing about her lips. "He's a good man, and the most virile of lovers." She giggled. "He's quite eager to learn from me, too. The first time we mated, he—"

"Never mind," Rissa cut her off, not quite ready for a detailed report of their lovemaking. "Another time, perhaps." She gave Diona a quick hug and, turning, fled after Morigan.

Gods, she thought as she hurried back to her chair, would the woman never cease to embarrass her? She must make certain never to introduce her to the Cat Lord. Diona's matchmaking attempts, if she did, would only cause additional difficulties between her and Morigan. Additional difficulties she most certainly didn't need.

He awaited her before his throne, his hands laden with the platters of food. Rissa accepted his offering, took her seat, and silently ate, refusing to look at or speak with either man she sat beside. Morigan eyed her with open curiosity, but refrained from forcing the conversation.

After the meal, the music quickened to a livelier pace. Several Cat Women rose and began to sway sensually before the bonfire. One by one, additional women joined them until twenty moved in unison to what was obviously a traditional dance. As the tempo accelerated so did their steps, skillfully swirling and twirling them about. Their tunic dresses, some of softly sheened leather, others of sturdy, brightly hued lana cloth, fluttered and shimmered in the flickering firelight.

The drums throbbed, the beat pounding and primal. The music, like some coquettish girl, teased and frolicked, then turned sultry and seductive, plucking at emotions and stirring passions. Around the circle, feet began to stomp and hands to clap in exultant, ardent rhythm. An aura of expectation and rising jubilation filled the air.

Rissa, caught up in the growing excitement, joined in, tapping her feet and clapping her hands. A soft smile played about her lips. Then, before she could react, much less protest, Morigan pulled her from her chair and into the circle.

His arms ensnared her waist, clutching her tightly to him. Rissa reared back. "What are you—?"

"Hold onto my arms," he commanded tautly. "Dance with me. It's custom the Lord and his Lady participate in the flame dance. Dance with me, Rissa."

"I-I don't know how!"

"But I do. Trust me. I'll lead you, teach you."

And then, there was no time left for doubt or protest. Morigan whirled her around, weaving in and out among the other dancers, his steps agile and sure. Caught in his powerful clasp, Rissa could do little more than struggle to keep up with him, to move her feet swiftly enough just to maintain her balance. Her breath came erratically, but whether it was from the exertion or the nearness of him, she didn't know.

Heat flared between them. His gaze, searing, mesmerizing, captured hers. A spark ignited, flickered momentarily before catching fire to roar into a blazing conflagration.

She was lost, tumbling into the depths of his eyes, plunging into his very soul. Then, everything stilled, quieted. There was nothing but them, the torrid press of their bodies, the rise and fall of ragged breathing, the scent of passion, and hungering need. And still they danced, but the movements flowed effortlessly now, attuned as they were one to the other.

The music rose around them, consuming them in a wild, pulsating rhythm. Their spirits soared, breaking free from the bonds of earth to leap into the heavens where, once again, they came together. Came together, deep within their souls, to join in a silken haze of erotic perceptions and desires.

A mass of sensations built, rioted within Rissa. Her awareness of Morigan intensified, grew. An awareness of his body hardening, his sex filling, thickening to press against her belly. Of his eyes glowing, burning. Of his sweat, sheening his brow.

Then, he pulled her hard up against him, lifting her from the ground, twirling her round and round. Dizziness engulfed Rissa. Her nails dug into his arms. Her eyes clenched shut. Yet, still, the strange new wave of pleasure burgeoned within her.

She shook her head, pushing back against him, fighting it, fearing it. Her mouth opened in silent, agonized protest.

Then, the music stopped.

Morigan stood there for a long moment, Rissa still suspended in his arms, his heart pounding, his breath raw and unsteady. Gradually, sounds of people laughing, talking, walking about filtered into his heightened consciousness. Morigan flushed and lowered Rissa to the ground. "My thanks for the dance," he muttered, suddenly unable to meet her gaze.

"Y-yes," she replied, equally uncomfortable in the aftermath of what had just transpired. They'd all but mated, dancing together. She knew it and knew, as well, Morigan knew it.

As if her heated realization had sparked a similar response within him, he jerked his head around. A fierce determination tightened his features. He swung her back up into his arms.

She grabbed frantically for his neck. "Wh-what are you doing?" Rissa cried as Morigan strode off out of the enclosure, leaving the festivities behind.

"Taking you back to my lair," he growled, his tone brooking no argument or protest. "The games are over, femina. It's past time I make you my mate in every sense of the word. And, after our dance, you know it now as surely as I!"

Twelve

He carried her into the darkened night, into the cool autumn air and blanketing silence; the sights and sounds of the revelry faded until they seemed but a distant memory. Reality was now, within the possessive clasp of Morigan's powerful arms, pressed tightly to his hard, warm body.

His passing was effortless, silent save for the slight rasp of his breath and strong beat of his heart. His profile, when Rissa finally dared look up at him, was solid as granite, firm with determination.

A determination to mate with her this night, she realized with a ripple of fear. The moment she'd long dreaded and, conversely, anticipated, had arrived. The decisive battle of battles was upon them.

Her hands curled into fists where she clasped him about his neck. Her head lowered to rest upon his shoulder. A crazed mixture of awful, ardent longing warred with her deeper principles. Gods, what was she to do? *What was she to do?*

Then, Morigan was climbing the short trail that led to his lair, entering the cave, carrying her over to—

"Please!" Rissa jerked back, shoving against him. "Don't! Put me down. Please!"

He halted, hesitated but a moment, then lowered her gently to the ground. His hold about her, however, didn't loosen.

"It's meant to be, femina." Morigan's eyes gleamed with an eerie, smoldering light. "You only prolong the inevitable."

She struggled with the strange lethargy that engulfed her, standing so close to him, his primitive male essence entwining about her, warm, seductive, and sense-stirring . . . Her eyes clenched shut. It was his mind powers working on her again!

With a painful wrench, Rissa mentally shoved him back. "Perhaps I do," she gritted out the words, "but I ask for . . . some time . . . to accept it, nonetheless." She dared another glance at his strangely burning eyes. "Will you give me that time?"

Morigan stared down at her, his expression tormented, as if he fought his own inner battle. Finally, he shrugged and released her. "A few minutes more won't change what must be." He gestured to a small side table standing against the wall. On it sat a small, pottery flask and several cups. "Have a cup of uva wine with me. It'll help calm your fears."

Rissa nodded slowly. "Yes, perhaps a cup of wine would help." She watched him head over to the small table, then turned and walked to the dining table. With shaking hands, Rissa pulled out a chair and sat. Her lids slid shut. Her hands clenched before her.

A reprieve. Morigan had given her a reprieve. Gods, if only the wine would work, would calm her fears and lull her into a state of uncaring submissiveness! She almost wished the decision would be taken from her. Almost . . .

Behind her, as tense and conflicted as Rissa, Morigan unstopped the flask of uva wine, poured out his cup, then, setting down the flask, slipped a small vial of cloudy white liquid from beneath the waistband of his breeches. For a long, indecisive moment, he held it in his hands, torn between duty and honor.

It was the lust inducer Agna had given him earlier in the day, once his mind had been made to mate with Rissa this night. It would make the flaxen-haired Bellatorian wild with need for him and the consequent mating easy and highly pleasurable. It solved all his problems.

All, save one.

He would have Rissa this night without struggle or force but, in the morning, he would face the repercussions of what he'd done. And Morigan knew Rissa well enough to realize she'd never forgive him for it. To take away her freedom and deny her choice was anathema to the proud, headstrong beauty. She would hate him for this night, he feared, to her dying day.

Yet, if he didn't mate with Rissa and seal their joining, the other males had the right to petition the Council for a chance at her. And they would, very soon now, if he didn't make her his. There'd been talk aplenty this very eve during the feast, other unmated males covertly eyeing Rissa and speculating as to their own chances with her. Cradoc, curse his dark, conniving soul, had been the primary instigator of the discussions, circulating through the crowd with a flagrant openness that even Morigan, beset with a myriad of his people pressing their congratulations upon him, couldn't miss.

No, there was no other choice. Rissa would mate, sooner or later, with one of the Cat Men. Morigan wanted that man to be him.

He'd originally intended, if his Cat's psychic sensual powers failed, to use a lust inducer on whomever he'd taken as mate. That had been the plan, for them all if necessary, to ease the captive females' acceptance of their fate. A lust inducer could safely be used for several weeks without untoward side effects, surely long enough, when coupled with kindness and consideration, to win any of the females over. He was just following through on the original plan.

Yet, why did it disturb him so, to use it now on Rissa? In the end, what mattered was his people, their survival. He must *always* remember that. Always.

With a rough jerk, Morigan unstopped the vial and poured its contents into Rissa's cup. Next, he filled the cup with uva wine and swirled the rich crimson liquid about to mix the lust inducer. Fortunately, the drug was tasteless and odorless. Rissa would never suspect until it was too late.

He picked up the flask, both cups, and turned. With a resolute squaring of his shoulders, Morigan strode back to the table. As he drew to a halt beside her, Rissa looked up at him, her glance nervous and uncertain.

Morigan forced a smile. "Here, drink this down. A few cups of uva wine will do wonders."

Rissa's lips quirked briefly. "Trying to get me drunk, are you?"

He sat down across from her. "I'd have preferred a more willing response from you, but if the wine will ease this first time . . ."

She picked up her cup, eyed it for the space of Morigan's inhaled breath, then downed its contents. She shoved the empty cup over to him. "More, please."

Her action startled him. Silently, Morigan refilled her cup. Then, setting down the flask, he picked up his own cup and sipped sparingly from it. He wanted no alcohol dulling this night's experience for him.

As if finding some strange fascination in its swirling depths, this time Rissa played with the contents of her cup. Morigan watched her, gauging her mood. It was too soon to take her to bed, but if he could stimulate her own natural desires for him before the lust inducer began to work, she might later imagine it all a result of her own feelings. Gods, if it could only happen so!

"I'm afraid," she finally murmured, her words so soft that, for an instant, Morigan was uncertain if he'd heard or just imagined them. Then, Rissa glanced up. An anxious uncertainty gleamed in her eyes. "I don't want this, at least not now."

"How can you be so sure what you really want," Morigan asked gently, "until you know what it is you're deciding upon? A mating, when both people desire it, is one of the most satisfying and pleasurable—"

"But I want more than just a physical easing," Rissa cried, her hand clenching about her cup. "I want . . ." She paused, then shook her head and sighed. "Ah, what does it matter? My desires have never been the concern here."

Morigan reached across the table and grasped her wrist. "They *do* matter, Rissa. I swear it! If you would only compromise on this one issue, become my mate in every way, you would see that. My people come first. They must. I'm their lord. But after them . . ." His voice faded and he glanced away.

"After them, what, Morigan?"

He dragged his gaze back to hers. "After them, there's you, Rissa. I never thought to feel this way. I thought my heart had shattered into a million irretrievable pieces after Winna died. And I never dreamed it possible to care so strongly for a Bellatorian. But I do."

Rissa sat there, stunned, struggling to fathom the implications of his words. Morigan felt strongly for her? After his people, she was foremost in his heart? A curious, soaring joy filled her. Fiercely, Rissa squelched it. "In the end," she forced herself to reply, "whatever affection you might feel for me is still inadequate. It'll never be enough for me."

Morigan's eyes narrowed to slits, the irises darkening to black in the flickering, perpetual light. "Why?" he demanded tautly. "Because I'm a Cat Man and not good enough for you?"

Her eyes widened in bewilderment. Rissa shook her head, vehemently. "No. I might have thought that at first, but not now. Not after being with you, seeing you and your people . . ." She sighed. "No, Morigan. Perhaps, I should still be repulsed, being Bellatorian and your enemy, but I'm not."

"Then what, Rissa?" His hand tightened about hers. "What still stands between us?"

A flush of warmth flooded her body. Her skin tingled. Rissa hesitated, wondering how Morigan's touch could now set her body afire. Then, with a focus of will, she brushed the strange sensations aside. "We've gone over all this before. Your laws, your determination to take away my freedom of choice. I want the freedom to choose my own mate, not have him forced on me. I want the freedom to choose the life I will lead, not have it predetermined for me. I want the freedom to come and go as I please, not be walled up in some heavily guarded valley where I must ask permission to leave. *That* is what still stands between us, Morigan."

"And if I gave you permission to leave, would you come back to me?"

"I wouldn't know until I left, would I?"

He released her and leaned back, a bleak look in his eyes. "It's a dead issue, at any rate. I'm as bound by our laws as are any of my people. The decision has been made for you and the other females. It must stand."

Her skin prickled, tingled with sensation. A warm ache flared low in Rissa's belly. She shifted in her chair, willing the curious feelings to abate. This time, they didn't. Her glance lifted. Morigan stared back at her, his gaze strangely intent, almost predatory. Whatever was the matter with him all of a sudden? Indeed, what was the matter with her?

She struggled to regain her train of thought. It slipped away, caught up in the surging tide of heated memories, of rising needs, of unrequited hunger that cried out for sustenance . . .

"Then . . . then, my decision must stand as well," Rissa muttered, angry and unsettled by the riot of sensations rampaging through her. "I . . . I cannot give myself to a man who, ultimately, puts greater importance on his own needs than mine."

"They aren't *my* needs, femina," he growled, his expression gone taut and waiting. "They're my people's. Why do you persist in confusing the two?"

Gods, what was he saying? she thought, her mind in a muddle. Didn't he know she wanted him? Couldn't think of anything but him, of his taking her to his bed, stripping her naked, and mating with her? Why did he persist in talking? Why was he tormenting her so?

Her fingers clenched, closing around her cup. Wine. That's what she needed. Just a bit more wine to soothe her suddenly parched throat, to ease the fine tremors rippling through her body, and to still the crazed surge of lust that had all but taken hold of her.

Rissa lifted the cup to her lips, then paused. Lust. Lust inducers. Had Morigan . . . had he plied her with one of those hideous drugs in the hope of encouraging her response to him this night? But how? When?

Her glance dropped to the cup. The wine. He'd put it in her wine.

With a horrified cry, Rissa flung down the cup. Uva wine spilled everywhere, staining the table in an ever widening circle of crimson. Angry, accusing eyes lifted to his.

"You drugged me, didn't you?" she hissed furiously, leaning across the table, her hands in fists, her face an agonized mask of despair and disbelief, shaking and shuddering with her rampaging desires. "You didn't care how you had me, just as long as you had me!" Rissa flung herself back in her chair, torn between her anger and the wild sensations roiling within her. Sensations that were inexorably taking over her mind and body.

She threw back her head, her eyes clenched shut. A miserable sense of her own helplessness filled her. "Gods, I can't believe I ever thought you honorable or good! How could you do this to me?" Her eyes snapped open, passion-glazed yet tear-filled. "I hate you, Morigan! I'll never forgive you for this!"

He rose and walked around the table. "I know, Rissa. I know." Reaching down, he grasped her by the shoulders and pulled her to her feet. "I only hope that, someday, you'll find it in your heart to understand. Then, perhaps, you *will* finally forgive me."

"No," she sobbed, the tears coursing now down her cheeks. She hated them, hated her weakness, but could do nothing to control either. "I won't . . . I can't . . ." Her hands grasped his arms, sliding up and down their muscled length in a fevered caress. "Ah, Gods, I don't want this. My body . . ." Sobs wracked her slender frame. "Look at me . . . I-I'm not myself . . . I can't stop—"

With a superhuman effort, Rissa wrenched free of Morigan's loose hold. She backed away unsteadily, her arms clasped protectively about her, weeping uncontrollably.

Agony flared in the Cat Man's soul. "Rissa, femina." He followed her. "Gods, don't do this to yourself . . . to me!"

She stumbled, fell, sprawling on the dirt floor. Morigan

We've got your authors!

If you seek out the latest historical romances by today's bestselling authors, our new reader's service, KENSINGTON CHOICE, is the club for you.

KENSINGTON CHOICE is the only club where you can find authors like Janelle Taylor, Shannon Drake, Rosanne Bittner, Sylvie Sommerfield, Penelope Neri and Phoebe Conn all in one place...

...and the only service that will deliver their romances direct to your home as soon as they are published—even before they reach the bookstores.

KENSINGTON CHOICE is also the only service that will give you a substantial guaranteed discount off the publisher's prices on every one of those romances.

That's right: Every month, the Editors at Zebra and Pinnacle select four of the newest novels by our bestselling authors and rush them straight to you, usually *before they reach the bookstores.* The publisher's prices for these romances range from $4.99 to $5.99—but they are always yours for the guaranteed low price of just *$3.95!*

That means you'll always save over $1.00...often as much as *$2.00*...off the publisher's prices on every new novel you get from KENSINGTON CHOICE!

All books are sent on a 10-day free examination basis, and there is no minimum number of books to buy. (A postage and handling charge of $1.50 is added to each shipment.)

As your introduction to the convenience and value of this new service, we invite you to accept

4 BOOKS FREE

The 4 books, worth up to $23.96, are our welcoming gift. You pay only $1 to help cover postage and handling.

To start your subscription to KENSINGTON CHOICE and receive your introductory package of 4 FREE romances, detach and mail the postpaid card at right *today.*

We have 4 FREE BOOKS for you
as your introduction to
KENSINGTON CHOICE
To get your FREE BOOKS, worth
up to $23.96, mail the card below.

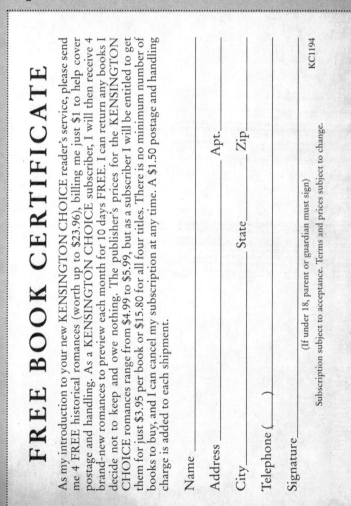

FREE BOOK CERTIFICATE

As my introduction to your new KENSINGTON CHOICE reader's service, please send me 4 FREE historical romances (worth up to $23.96), billing me just $1 to help cover postage and handling. As a KENSINGTON CHOICE subscriber, I will then receive 4 brand-new romances to preview each month for 10 days FREE. I can return any books I decide not to keep and owe nothing. The publisher's prices for the KENSINGTON CHOICE romances range from $4.99 to $5.99, but as a subscriber I will be entitled to get them for just $3.95 per book or $15.80 for all four titles. There is no minimum number of books to buy, and I can cancel my subscription at any time. A $1.50 postage and handling charge is added to each shipment.

KC1194

Name _____

Address _____ Apt. _____

City _____ State _____ Zip _____

Telephone ( ) _____

Signature _____
(If under 18, parent or guardian must sign)

Subscription subject to acceptance. Terms and prices subject to change.

We have
4
FREE
Historical
Romances
for you!

(worth up
to $23.96!)

Details inside!

reached out for her. Rissa scooted away, her movements frantic, wild. "No! Stay away! Ah, Gods, stay away!"

"Rissa, don't!" He flung himself down beside her, pulling her struggling body into his arms. "Gods, I didn't mean for it to frighten you, to turn you against me. I just wanted—" He dragged in a shuddering breath. "I just didn't want to have to force you."

"Don't do this," she whimpered, even as she pressed her body into his, even as her hands stroked his back, his buttocks in a heated frenzy, even as she squirmed against him. "I-I beg you, Morigan. *I beg you!*"

At her impassioned plea, Morigan thought the heart would tear from his chest. He clasped Rissa to him, fighting against the surge of terrible frustration and despair that flooded him. Gods, what was he to do? In a few seconds, Rissa would lose the last of her former restraint, would know only the burgeoning fire in her groin and wantonly, unthinkingly, seek out its relief. In a few seconds more, she would be his.

But he didn't want her this way. Didn't want the tortured memories of her desperate entreaty ringing in his ears for the rest of his days. And knew, no matter how strong his sense of duty ran, he couldn't do this to Rissa.

"Hush, sweet one," he soothed, kissing her forehead, her tear-streaked cheek. "I won't . . . take you. Not now, not drugged. I swear it."

"M-Morigan!" she sighed, the last bit of conscious resistance draining from her.

Then, a battle of a different kind began. As she writhed against him, murmuring in tormented pleasure, her little needing sounds all but driving him over the edge of his own control, Morigan lifted Rissa into his arms and carried her into his bedchamber. Gently, tenderly, he laid her down on

the bed and removed her boots, then sat beside her and pulled
off his own. Slipping his leather tunic off, he tossed it aside.

She came to him then, crawling into his lap, fumbling at
the lacings of her own tunic, attempting to tug it off as well.
Morigan stilled her hands. "No, femina. It's best if you leave
it on."

"Nooo," Rissa moaned, pressing against him, rubbing her
sweetly rounded bottom against his groin. "I want to lie naked with you. I want to feel your body next to mine."

"Soon, femina," he whispered and, ever so gently, caught
her eager hands and pulled them away from him. He rolled
over with her and pressed her down upon the bed, anchoring
her hands above her. "Soon, sweet one, but first, sleep. Sleep
and all will be better when you wake."

"Nooo," Rissa moaned again, arching her body into his.
"I don't want to sleep. I want you, Morigan. Mate with me,
touch me. Please!"

Gods, he thought in an agony of barely restrained desire,
how was he ever to make it through the next few hours?
Agna had told him the lust inducer's effects generally lasted
two to three hours, building to a peak within a half hour then
leveling off for another hour or two before gradually declin-
ing. If Rissa had another few hours of torment to go, so
indeed did he. But his torment was well-deserved. Rissa's
wasn't.

As time passed and Morigan fought to contain her, Rissa
begged, pleaded, sobbed, and raged. She called him every
foul name he'd ever heard, and a few more he hadn't. Then,
in the next moment, as she moved seductively beneath him,
she would purr and cajole and speak all manner of sweetly
enticing things. Morigan thought he'd go mad from his need,
that the blood pounding in his throbbing, tautly swollen sex
would finally burst through a vessel, and he'd die.

Time ceased to lose its meaning as he held Rissa from him, crooning to her, soothing her, and battling, all the while, against his own anguished desires. And, finally, she cried herself into an unrequited slumber, falling limply against him to sleep in his arms. She'd be sore from her ferocious struggles in the morning, Morigan told himself as he brushed aside her tousled, sweat-damp hair and kissed her tenderly on the forehead. Sore and very, very angry. But at least she'd still be a maiden.

Somehow, the realization was a poor consolation. This night had solved nothing between them. It had, instead, set into motion events that might well have long-term consequences. Consequences that might lose him the woman he now realized he loved.

Rissa woke from a fitful slumber, feeling sluggish and not at all refreshed. She propped open one eye and glanced grumpily around. Morigan's bedchamber. Too bad.

In her dreams, she'd been back in her luxurious bed on Bellator, snuggling deep into plump bed cushions and a fluffy down comforter. In the next room, Diona was drawing a warm mineral bath and laying out thick, soft drying cloths. It had promised to be a beautiful day.

Instead, she was in a dark cave, the captive of a handsome but arrogant Cat Man. Rissa stretched languidly. Surely a fate worse than—

Overextended muscles protested, sending twinges of pain shooting through limbs not used to such sensations. Whatever was the matter with her? She'd done nothing yesterday or last evening to warrant—

Rissa froze. Images of Morigan and the wine, of the effects of the lust inducer, flashed across her mind. Frantically, she searched her memory. The last thing she remembered was begging Morigan not to mate with her.

With a low moan, she rolled over—and came face to face with the sleeping Cat Man. His feline features, relaxed in unguarded slumber, had lost their perpetually harsh edge. He looked peaceful, almost boyish, with a lock of his dark mane falling across his face and dangling in one eye.

Unconsciously, Rissa reached out to brush it aside, then halted her hand in midair, as she noted his bare chest and the fur coverlet pulled up to his waist. Was he totally naked beneath the covers? Had he indeed taken advantage of her drug-induced passion?

She glanced down at herself. She wore the sleeping gown he'd given her. Someone, Morigan most likely, had undressed her and put it on her. But had that occurred before or after they'd mated?

Anger and a deep sense of betrayal flooded her. Rissa rolled onto her back, choking back a moan of despair. She flung an arm across her eyes. How could he? *How could he?*

"Nothing happened, Rissa. Nothing."

With a jerk of surprise, Rissa sat bolt upright. Morigan lay there on his side, watching her. In her movement, she inadvertently knocked the furs askew. A naked male hip peeked above the covers, shielding his lower abdomen with the barest of modesty. His glance followed hers down his torso, then lifted. The merest glimmer of a smile played about his firm, sensual lips.

"Yes, I'm naked beneath the furs," he calmly answered the question burning in her eyes. "And, yes, I put you in your sleeping gown last night. But nothing happened."

"Indeed?" Rissa scooted away from him. "Your state of undress belies that, as does my garb. I don't recall asking for nor needing your assistance in determining my sleeping attire."

Morigan's mouth quirked. "Oh, you definitely needed and wanted my assistance last night—and your choice of sleeping attire was far less modest than the gown I put you in. In fact, you pleaded most nicely for me to strip you naked and mate with you. Unfortunately, for the both of us, I chose not to take you up on your offer."

Rissa scowled. "And why is that? You *were* the one who put a lust inducer in my wine, weren't you?"

He exhaled a weary breath. "I changed my mind."

"Why? Why did you change your mind?"

A broad shoulder lifted in a negligent shrug. "Does it matter? Content yourself with the fact that your precious maidenhood is still intact. At least for a time longer, at any rate."

"And what does that mean?" Rissa demanded, flushing furiously.

"You must mate with some Cat Man in the lair. That much is a foregone conclusion. And I can assure you most of the others won't hesitate to use a lust inducer on you, and then gladly take advantage of your passionate response."

"No doubt," she sniffed. "I ask again. Why didn't you?"

"Rissa," Morigan growled, irritation twisting his features, "don't press. It doesn't matter anyway. You obviously don't wish to be my mate. I won't force my loathsome advances on you again. This very day I'll offer you the opportunity to consider some of our other unmated males." He arched a sardonic brow. "Perhaps you'd like to reconsider Naren?"

"Curse you!" Rissa grabbed a pillow and threw it at him.

With the most minimal of efforts, Morigan deflected the feeble missile. He shoved himself to a sitting position, the furs settling in his lap. "What do you want from me, femina?

Will nothing I do ever please you? I just offered to allow you to take another mate, one of *your* choosing, and still, you're not satisfied."

"I-I don't want another mate," Rissa cried, suddenly terrified at the prospect of leaving Morigan. "I'd rather stay with you!"

Morigan went still. "Why? Why do you want to stay with me?"

She bowed her head, her tousled hair tumbling to shield her face. "I don't know why," she mumbled. "I just know I do."

"Rissa, you can't hope to keep your maidenhood if you stay with me. I spared you last night because I found I couldn't take you drugged, that I wanted you fully aware of who was mating with you and why. And I wanted you to want me, when we finally mated. But if last night didn't convince you of the seriousness of my intent, I don't know what will."

"Oh, you convinced me all right," she replied grimly. "That cursed lust inducer you gave me most graphically made the point."

"Then, if you want to stay with me, when *will* you mate with me?"

Rissa paled. Her mind raced. There was no time left for her, and she'd yet to find opportunity to examine the valley for signs of possible escape routes. She knew now she must submit to Morigan, or be forced to take another. But she needed more time!

She lifted her head, a desperate plan filling her. "When I reach my fertile time. I'll mate with you then. It seems pointless to do so until you can get me with child, wouldn't you say? That *is* my real purpose, is it not?"

Morigan frowned with frustrated annoyance. "We mate

for other reasons as well. For the mutual pleasure of the act, for the intimacy, the sharing."

"Well, if I must mate with you, I'd prefer to keep it to the real purpose you intended me for."

"Rissa, you try my patience." His hands clenched in the coverlet. "When is your next fertile time?"

Longer than you think, she silently answered him. "In normal circumstances," Rissa replied instead, "but a week or so." She shrugged a slender shoulder. "But who knows now, considering the stress you've put me through of late."

"Rissa!"

"I don't know, Morigan!" she cried. "You ask for guarantees on something governed by nature. What do you expect me to do?"

"Fine." He shoved a hand through his mane in exasperation. "I'll know when it happens, though. You won't be able to hide it from me."

"Then you'll wait?" Rissa couldn't believe her good fortune. "You won't touch me until then?"

"No, I won't touch you until then," he muttered, "but I want something from you in return."

Her eyes narrowed in suspicion. "What do you want?"

Morigan's jaw set with implacable determination. He leaned over and took her by the arm, pulling her close. "Your word that, when your fertile time arrives, you'll come to me willingly, without protest or battle, and never fight me on this again. That you'll be my mate in all things, bear my children, and obey me."

"Obey you?" Outrage filled Rissa. She attempted to jerk away, but Morigan's strength held her to him. "Are you mad? You ask too much!"

"As do you, in demanding I wait," he calmly countered. "You've no idea what you ask of me, or the conflict it'll cause in the lair. You place a high price on yourself, femina. A high price, indeed. It's only fair I gain an equal measure in the bargain."

When she didn't answer, Morigan gave her a small shake. "Well, Rissa? Have the stakes of your little game finally gotten too high? If so, we could always go back to something simpler like, perhaps, you agreeing to forego your extended waiting period and mating with me right now?"

"No," she whispered, fury blazing in her eyes. "I accept the terms as they are. Obedience it'll be, if and when the time comes."

"Oh, it'll come," he chuckled grimly. "One way or another it *will* come. I swear it."

But only if I fail to find a way out of here, Rissa silently countered. *And, if there's a way out, I swear I'll find it.*

A resolute determination filled her. She met Morigan's heated gaze with an equally fiery one of her own. He challenged her, daring her to back down before it was too late. But it was already too late. It had been too late from the first moment they'd met. And, one way or another, Rissa vowed, she, too, planned on keeping her word.

Rissa spent the next three hours helping Sarna and a large group of Cat Women and teen-age girls extract a sugarlike substance from the root of the wild bacula bush. It was a tedious process, pounding the root between two stones to flatten it, then setting it out to dry in the sun for several days until the root shriveled into brittle strands. Later, when a sweetener was needed for baking or beverages, the crisp root could then be easily crumbled into a fine powder and added to the food.

When that task was finally over, Rissa rose, arched her

back to ease the tension of the hours spent hunched over working at the roots, and glanced at Sarna. "If you've no objections, domina, I'd like time for a short stroll before helping prepare the noon meal."

The old Cat Woman nodded. "Come, I'll walk you to the entrance." As they paused at the cave opening, she took one look outside, noted the gray sky with its wind-whipped clouds and shook her head. "Perhaps it would be best if you stayed inside today, child. The weather appears to be taking a turn for the worse."

Rissa smiled. "It doesn't matter. In fact, a brisk walk in the cold air would do me good. So much has happened of late. I desperately need some time alone to clear my mind."

Sarna cocked her head, a concerned look in her eyes. "Are you certain, child? Sometimes a sympathetic ear is better than being alone with one's cares."

"My thanks, domina," Rissa said, "but not this time."

"Is it Morigan? I see a continued tension between you. He is my son, but if he's not the mate for you, you have the right—"

"We are working things out, domina. I just . . . need time."

"Good. Good," Sarna replied happily. "You're a good child and will make Morigan a fine mate. I would hate to lose you as a daughter." She paused, as if some idea had just struck her. "Wait here a moment, child." She disappeared back into the cave.

Minutes later, Sarna returned with her cloak. "Put it on, child. You'll need it against the cold."

"But you need it," Rissa protested.

"Me?" Morigan's mother laughed. "I'm not leaving this warm cave and fire until you return. Of that you can be certain." She shooed her away. "Now, go for your walk. If you tarry here much longer, we'll both miss our midday meal."

At the old woman's thoughtfulness, gratitude swelled in Rissa. She accepted the cloak, flung it over her shoulders, then turned and hurried down the valley.

As she walked along a pang of guilt plucked at Rissa, knowing full well all her actions here were but a deception. She did indeed care for the tormented old woman, wanted to help her find stability and happiness again, and wanted, as well, not to hurt Morigan. Yet, there seemed little else she could do—not if she ever hoped to salvage what remained of her independence and self-respect.

Strange, she mused, in light of the Cat People's plight, how suddenly self-serving her own desires seemed. Especially since she'd come to know Morigan, Sarna, and Naren, learned of their hopes, their fears, and their own special kind of humanity.

She could stay, Rissa realized, and help these people in so many ways, if only Morigan would let her. But she didn't know if he would, or could, constrained as even he was by their archaic laws. Still, she could stay, become his mate and bear his children. In some small way, that, too, would help the Cat People.

Diona's words filtered back, from that day in the merchants' caravan just before the Cat Men attacked. *And isn't being the mate of a fine, handsome man and bearing him strong, healthy children enough of a calling for any woman?*

It must seem so to many, Rissa had replied, *but still I suspect there must be more. Should be more.*

The awful truth of her words hammered at Rissa, bruising her mind, her heart, and her emotions. Yet, still, the reality remained the same. Even then, she'd known she needed more than just a mate and children. Even then . . .

Outside, the Cat People's lair, she could do much more for them. She could speak to her father and convince him of the injustice of the Bellatorian persecution against them. She, with her now more intimate knowledge of the Cat People and their ways, could serve as an intermediary and ease the animosity. She knew Morigan, knew how to deal with him. And, as Fautor Lindatees's daughter, she'd have influence with the Lord Commander as well. It was the perfect solution . . . if only she could escape.

The wind whistled down from the mountains, bringing with it the frigid reminder of the need for haste. The cloak had indeed been a wise idea, Rissa thought, pulling it more tightly about her. It was a chilly, bleak day; the rapidly dipping temperatures heralded snow before nightfall. Winter would fast be upon them. She must find some way out of the mountains soon, or all her plans, all her hopes, would be for naught.

"R-Rissa!" The panting voice carried down the valley to where Rissa walked, her concentration now totally focused on making her surreptitious scan of the mountainside for a possible escape route appear but a late morning stroll.

Rissa threw a quick glance over her shoulder. It was Diona. She halted, awaiting her friend with an eager smile.

"Wh-where are you going?" the other woman gasped, finally drawing up before her. "It's freezing out here!"

"I needed some time to gather my thoughts."

Diona shivered and flipped up the hood of her own cloak that had apparently fallen back in her chase after Rissa. "Well, I hope you've gathered your thoughts sufficiently. There's trouble afoot."

Rissa frowned. "What trouble? Is it with one of our women."

"More with one of the Cat Men," her serving maid muttered grimly.

Unease spiraled within Rissa. "Indeed? In what way?"

"That girl, Hali? The pretty one who was so shy and anxious all the time? She was given to that red-haired Cat Man who captured us."

"Ah, him," Rissa wryly replied, recalling him and his net. "The gentle one."

"Exactly," Diona agreed, nodding vigorously. "He's been beating Hali every night to make her mate with him. We need to stop him, Rissa, before he kills her!"

"How do you know this?"

"How else? Hali told me."

Rissa hesitated but an instant more, her brow furrowing in thought, then wheeled about and strode back the way she'd come.

"Rissa! Wait!" Diona called after her. "Where are you going?"

"Where else?" she tossed over her shoulder as her pace quickened into a run. "To talk with Hali!"

Thirteen

Diona led Rissa to a small cave that lay at the outskirts of the most densely populated part of the valley. There, she paused.

"This is Hali and her mate's lair." Diona eyed Rissa uncertainly. "I'm not sure it would be such a good idea to barge right in, though. Try calling for her. That's how I got her to come out last time."

"This is hardly the time suddenly to turn timid." Rissa walked a few meters into the tunnel leading into the cave and halted. Diona pulled up behind her. "Hali? Hali, are you there?" Rissa called. "It's Rissa from the merchants' caravan. May I come in to visit?"

There was no reply. Rissa turned to Diona. "Well, either no one's about or Hali isn't answering."

"What shall we do now?"

Rissa considered that for a moment. "You keep watch outside and call me if someone approaches. I'm going in to make certain Hali isn't hiding in the cave."

"Rissa, the Cat People seem to guard the privacy of their individual lairs highly. Hali's mate won't be happy to find you inside, nosing around."

"It's a chance I'm willing to take, Diona. Morigan told me no Cat Man can harm or force his mate. If that's true, I intend to see what he'll do about this." She gave Diona's arm a quick squeeze. "Now, no more of it. The longer we linger here, the greater our chance of drawing notice."

Before Diona could protest further, Rissa wheeled around and headed down the tunnel. It was dimly lit inside, the perpetual flame torches turned low. Perhaps to hide the clutter and filth, she thought disgustedly, as she entered the small cave itself and noted the interior.

Uneaten, rotting food sat on the table. A cup was overturned, stuck to the gooey remnants of uva wine spilled on the tabletop. Unwashed pots soaked in a tub of grease-congealed water. A chair lay overturned; a pile of bedding was stuffed in one corner. The air was heavy, musty, and reeked of decaying things.

Rissa choked back a swell of nausea. The living conditions in here were deplorable. If for nothing else than sanitary principles, Morigan must be told. She turned to leave when a small moan caught her ear. Rissa glanced back at the pile of bedding in the corner. Something moved, shifted, then went still.

The hairs stood up on the back of Rissa's neck. She swallowed hard. "H-Hali? Is that you, Hali?"

The pile of furs moaned again, choking back a strangled sob. "G-go away!"

Rissa ran over to her, knelt, and pulled away the furs. A filthy, tousled-haired face peered up at her, a face horribly bruised and swollen. She brushed the grime-matted hair from the girl's cheeks, for girl she still was at just seventeen cycles.

"Hali, Hali," Rissa murmured, "how did this happen? And why didn't you ask for help?"

"H-help?" Hali whimpered, tried to pull away from Rissa's touch, and grimaced in pain. "Who would help me here? The Cat Men are all savages. And their women hate us. Limos said I was his now and no one would stop him, much less care, even if he needed to beat me into submission."

"Well, he lies!" Rissa slid her hands up and down the girl's arms, then her legs, searching for any broken bones. Hali cried out and jerked away. "Is anything broken?" Rissa asked, ceasing her examination.

"N-no," Hali sobbed. "I-I just hurt so badly. And I'm so hungry and thirsty. I get nothing to eat or drink all day. Limos takes away all the food that's fit to eat and the clean water and won't give me any until he returns each evening. Then, he makes . . . he makes me do horrible things to please him before he'll let me eat or drink." The girl grasped Rissa by the arm. "I'm so tired. I just want to die."

"Hush, sweet one," Rissa soothed. Ever so gently she pried Hali's clutching fingers from her arm. "No one will hurt you again. I swear it!" She rose.

"Wh-where are you going?" Hali quavered. "Don't leave me! Please!"

"Just for a short while longer," Rissa said. "I need help taking you away from here. But I'll be back very soon. I swear." Before the girl could reply, Rissa turned and fled the dank, dark cave.

Diona awaited her at the entrance. "Didn't I tell you it was bad?" she asked when she saw the look of horror burning in Rissa's eyes.

"Yes, you did. How did you find out about Hali? It seems Limos never lets her leave his lair."

"Some of the other women who knew Hali began to ask about her when they noticed they never saw her about. We all watched then and, when none of us ever saw her, we began to worry. It was simple enough for me to get Tavist to inquire whose lair she was in. Then, this morning, I sought her out."

"That was brave of you, Diona. If that foul-hearted Limos had returned . . ."

The serving woman shrugged. "Well, I could've said the same for you a few minutes ago. What do we do now?"

"You'll stay here and keep watch. I don't want Limos returning and harming Hali before I get back with Morigan."

Diona's eyes widened. "You plan to bring the Cat Lord here? What if Limos returns in the meantime?"

"All the better," Rissa muttered. "I'd like nothing better than to hear him explain himself to Morigan."

"So, you think he'll punish Limos?"

"I know he will!"

Diona eyed her closely. "You think a lot of him, don't you?"

Rissa paused in her thoughts, momentarily confused. "Who?"

"Morigan, of course."

She considered that briefly. "Yes, I suppose I do. He has never been anything but a kind, reasonable man." Rissa grinned. "Well, unless driven to the limits of his tolerance, which I seem to do quite frequently."

"But he's never raised a hand to you, has he? Or forced himself on you?"

"No," Rissa admitted, "he never has." She stood there a moment longer, marveling at her good fortune in having a mate like Morigan, then wrenched herself back to the moment at hand. "I must go, Diona. I'll be back soon. Take care."

"Have no fear for me," the serving maid laughingly called after her. "I can handle Limos if he dares show his vicious hide around here in the meanwhile."

Rissa grinned, her fleet limbs already carrying her back down the valley. Gone were her earlier plans to seek out an escape route. Gone were her doubts, her concerns over ever finding purpose in a life here.

All she thought or cared about was Hali. Her desires were secondary now. Later, she would pick up the threads of her own needs. Later . . .

"No, I disagree, Cradoc," Morigan said, his irritation growing with each passing minute at his cousin's stubborn insistence that the night guard detail be lightened to half its usual strength. "The Bellatorians are constantly developing new technologies to aid in their apprehension of us. And, now, in the wake of our abduction of their females, I've no doubt their efforts will redouble. From all reports, Bellatorians seem as fiercely possessive of their females as we are of our own."

"And I say you keep the males so exhausted with guard detail and the hunting and other tasks in order to prevent them from seeing you for the ineffectual leader you truly are!" Cradoc angrily countered. "A people so busy all they can do is work and sleep haven't the time, much less the energy, to gather together and talk, do they?"

"Or listen to you spread malicious gossip and untruths," Naren, sitting nearby with Lisan and Agna, interjected dryly. "That's the truth of it, isn't it, Cradoc? The Cat People are too busy laboring to survive to waste time on malcontents like you."

The dark auburn-haired Cat Man shot Naren a seething glance. "At least I haven't wasted my time slavering after Morigan's mate!" he snapped. "Not that Morigan would notice," Cradoc turned back to the Cat Lord, sensing a new battle he could more easily win. "He's so passion-besotted with a female who has yet to mate with him, I fear she could do anything, demand what she would, and he'd fall over himself giving it to her. There's talk aplenty already that the yellow-haired Bellatorian need only waggle her bottom and Morigan would make a fool of himself striving to please her."

Morigan's jaw went taut with rage. "Rissa isn't the issue here. I see your game for what it is, Cradoc. You but attempt to use any and every weapon at your disposal to undermine me. And I grow weary of it."

His cousin laughed. "Do you deny you've yet to mate with her?"

Naren half-rose from his chair before Agna pulled him back. "What's between Morigan and Rissa is none of your concern, Cradoc! Stay out of it and let them resolve their problems in their own time."

"But that cannot be, can it, Morigan?" Cradoc demanded softly, never breaking glance with the Cat Lord. "Your 'own time' will soon be in direct violation of our laws. And there are at least fifty or sixty unmated Cat Men who think it's past time you step aside and give the Bellatorian up."

"You included, perhaps?" Morigan silkily inquired. His fists clenched at his sides.

The other Cat Man smirked. "Why not? I need a mate as much as any male."

"And would you perhaps like the Cat Throne to go with her, do you think?"

Cradoc shrugged. "That, too, would suit me just fine. Care to call upon your right of challenge, Morigan? If you managed to kill me, at least one threat to your mate and throne would be gone."

"You flatter yourself, Cousin," Morigan snarled. "I see you as no challenge—to anything. You're not fit to rule, and Rissa would never choose you as her mate. Of that I'm certain."

"Are you now?" Cradoc chuckled grimly. "I wouldn't be so sure of that. But, then, what can one expect from a male so hot for a female he refuses to—"

"Morigan!"

At the sound of his name, the Cat Lord turned. Rissa ran down the valley toward him, her long blond hair whipping out behind her, her cloak flapping wildly in the wind. "Morigan, I . . . I need your help!"

He awaited her, his lips tightening in annoyance. By the three moons, of all the times for Rissa to appear with what was quite evidently some request for him! He walked forward to meet her. "What is it, femina?" he asked, containing his irritation with only the greatest of efforts. "We're in conference, and I can't—"

"H-Hali," Rissa panted. "Her mate . . . Limos. He's beating her, starving her into submission! You must . . . come . . . and take her away from him!"

Morigan scowled. "Whatever are you talking about? I've told you before no Cat Man is permitted—"

"Limos has beaten Hali!" Rissa grabbed his arm and attempted to tug him along. "Come with me. Please. I'll show you."

Behind him, he heard Cradoc snicker, "What did I say? He's so hot for her he'll let her drag him about wherever she pleases."

At that, something exploded in Morigan. He wheeled around. "Enough, Cradoc! Our meeting is over!"

He motioned for the healer to join him. "Agna, to me." Then, Morigan turned back to Rissa. "I'll come with you, femina, but this had better be something of import. If this Hali lied or is using some injury to cast blame on Limos, it'll go badly for her. Things are strained enough in the lair right now over you females not to add further turmoil with lies and deceit."

"Is that what you think of us, of me?" Rissa cried in outrage. "That I would purposely cause trouble among your people and try to bring an innocent Cat Man to punishment?"

"You've made it more than apparent you wish to leave here," Morigan drawled. "And desperation can fuel many a foul plot."

Her mouth twisted in disgust. "Come and see for yourself. And then tell me of my foul plot!"

With that, Rissa turned and headed back the way she had come, her head held high, her stride stiff with indignation.

Agna drew up beside Morigan and smirked. "What did I tell you? She's trouble, make no mistake."

"Don't start," her lord muttered in disgust. "I don't need *your* harping on top of Cradoc's." Then, expelling a weary breath, he followed after Rissa.

Diona awaited them outside Limos's cave, her glance turning nervous and uncertain when Morigan and Agna drew up before her and Rissa. "I'm honored you could come, my Lord. We need your help—"

"Where is the female?" Morigan demanded tautly, interrupting her. "I wish to see her."

"Inside, of course," Rissa muttered. She shot him a furious glance, then turned and strode down the tunnel leading to Limos's cave.

As he stepped into the tunnel to follow Rissa, Morigan was instantly assailed with a strong stench of rot and unwashed bodies. Revulsion filled him. Even if Hali had refused to perform her womanly tasks, there was no excuse for Limos to allow things to reach this state of filth. He glanced at Agna. She, too, was surprised and revolted.

They found Rissa kneeling beside a small figure huddled in a pile of rags in one corner of the cave. Morigan motioned to Agna. "Turn up the perpetual flame torches."

As Morigan knelt beside Rissa, the light in the cave gradually brightened. The girl buried in the rags pulled back when she saw him.

"Nooo," she whimpered. "Don't touch me!" She grabbed for Rissa's hand. "Don't let him hurt me. Please, Rissa!"

Rissa covered Hali's hand with her own. "He won't hurt you, sweet one. This is Morigan, the Lord of the Cat People and my mate. He's a good and kind man." She brushed back the grimy, dark blond hair from the girl's face. "Let him look at you."

Hali turned her fearful gaze to Morigan. "He beat me, my Lord. I didn't want to mate with him, and he beat me, then still forced himself on me. I-I didn't know what to do. I'd never been . . . been with a man before."

Ever so gently, the Cat Lord took the girl's chin in his hand. He turned her face to one side to better examine it, then to the other. "Be damned," Morigan swore. "Does the rest of your body look like this?"

A big tear rolled down Hali's face, leaving a track of white through the dirt and grime. "I-I think so. I hurt so badly I've not wanted to look."

Morigan wheeled about. "Agna, come here, please. I wish for you to examine the girl. I'll await you outside."

With that, he rose and strode from the cave. Rissa stared after him, debating whether to follow, when Hali squeezed her hand. "Stay with me, Rissa," the girl pleaded. "I-I'm afraid of her."

Agna went rigid. "She's a healer," Rissa hastened to say. "Her name is Agna, and she won't hurt you. That's not her way."

The Cat Woman glanced over at her, her expression shuttered and her mouth tight. "That's right, femina," Agna soothed, turning back to Hali. "I wish you no harm. But I cannot help you if I don't know the full extent of your injuries." She began to unlace the girl's leathern tunic. "Here, first let's get this off. It won't take very long, and then we'll take you away from here."

Agna was capable of great gentleness, Rissa thought as she watched the Cat Woman skillfully and quickly undress and examine Hali's poor, bruised body, then redress her. As great as the mutual animosity was between them, there was no denying the innate goodness and intelligence of the woman. If only there were some way to dispel their hostility. But her arrival in the lair symbolized, far more overtly than the other captive females', the Cat Women's personal failure in this time of great difficulty and need.

There was so much healing needed in the Cats' Lair, so much still to be done. The longer she was with them, the greater the realization filled Rissa of the weight of responsibility Morigan bore. How could he go on? Yet, being the man he was, how could he not?

She rose. "I'll fetch Morigan now. I don't think Hali can walk very well on her own."

"Yes, that would be wise, I think," the healer agreed. "We'll take her to my lair for a time."

Rissa turned and left the cave. Diona waited at the entrance, but Morigan had moved further away to take his seat on a pile of nearby boulders. Briefly Rissa watched him, his one leg drawn up, his arms resting on his knee, and a bleak, bitter expression on his face. She almost regretted drawing him into this unpleasant situation.

She walked over to him. Though his position altered subtly, evidence he was aware of her, Morigan didn't turn to acknowledge Rissa. "Agna is finished with her examination and wants to take Hali to her lair," she finally said. "We'll need help with the girl, though."

"Was her body bruised as well?"

His voice was flat, emotionless, but Rissa heard, nonetheless, the edge of pain that hovered on his words. She nodded. "Yes. I don't think even Agna could deny what happened after examining her."

He shot her a tormented, angry look. "Agna's not heartless nor cruel, Rissa. Most of us aren't."

She sat beside him, so close their thighs brushed. "I know that, Morigan. I know this is an exception."

"Yes. It most definitely is."

"What will you do about it?"

The Cat Lord expelled a long breath. "Limos will be sent before the Council. They'll determine his punishment. At the very least, Hali will be taken from him and given to another male."

"She's so young," Rissa murmured. "And after this terrible first experience . . ."

"Will you help her? I don't want this to mar her for the rest of her days. I want her to be happy here, Rissa."

He turned, his anguish-darkened eyes meeting hers. Something swelled in Rissa, rising until it lodged in her throat, making it all but impossible to swallow. Hot tears burned her eyes.

Morigan needed her, wanted her help. He truly cared about the welfare of his people, and that now included the females he and his men had captured. He was a leader beset with some of the most difficult and painful decisions anyone had to face, yet his fierce pride frequently precluded his asking for help. Still, in spite of it all, he'd asked her.

Why Morigan had turned to her, when he rarely seemed

to do so with his own people, was a source of wonderment to Rissa. It also made her own decision to escape all that harder. "I'll do what I can, Morigan," Rissa forced herself to reply. "None of this would've happened to Hali, though, if you hadn't taken her from the life she was meant for."

His expression hardened. "None of this would've *had* to happen, if your people hadn't attacked our lair and slaughtered my people! We didn't start this, Rissa. Don't ever forget that!"

He slid down off the boulder and stood. Without a backward glance, Morigan strode off to the cave. Rissa sat there a moment longer. Gods, how was she to deal with him? He was such a bitter, emotionally erratic man. She hadn't helped things, though, by her constant reminders of the new problems he'd set into motion with his capture of her and the other Bellatorian women. Why did she keep pricking at him about it?

Because it was still inherently wrong, she realized, no matter how desperate the Cat People were. And not once had he ever admitted to it. Not once had he ever offered to let her or any of the other women go. He would not, could not, it seemed, relinquish his need to always be in control, of himself and others. He must *always* be in control—even in his bitter hatred. And until he could finally let that need go, she would always be less than him, never his equal.

Rissa rose and followed Morigan back to the cave, filled with sadness for a man who'd so few options left him—and even less of a chance to regain some semblance of whatever happiness he'd ever possessed.

The Council of Elders convened that evening, with Morigan presiding as Lord of the Cat People. Naren, as his second-in-command, was there as well. Cradoc, who, as Morigan's closest kin next to his grandfather, also sat on the Council, was the only one who protested Limos's punishment, claiming no alien female was of more import than one of their own. Ardan, as head of the Elders, quickly squelched that claim, stating when the Council agreed to captive mates, they, too, became one with the Cat People.

After that, it was a quick and simple thing to take Hali from Limos, sentence him to a cycle without the right to have another mate, and require he not only formally apologize to Hali, but serve at her beck and call for the next month. Limos was most unhappy with his punishment and accepted it grudgingly, before stalking out of the Council chambers with Cradoc at his side.

"Cradoc has just won another ally," Naren muttered as he and Morigan finally left the cavernous room that served as both communal meeting place and Council chambers. "And there are several more Cat Men who have already decided you are unfairly siding with the Bellatorian females over our people."

"No doubt aided by Rissa's influence over me," Morigan growled as they walked down the valley back to Naren's lair. The black-haired Cat Man was improving rapidly, but still needed assistance with any extended exercise. Wishing an opportunity to speak with him, Morigan had offered to accompany his friend this night.

"You need to stake your claim to her," Naren said. "It would end much of the speculation and rumors."

Morigan scowled. "I know that. And I will, in my own good time."

"Are you certain she wants you?"

The Cat Lord halted and wheeled about. "She wants me.

She's just not happy relinquishing her principles, or with the thought of submitting to me."

"And, indeed, why should she be?" Naren asked. "Rissa's the female she is because of her pride and courage and principles. What makes you think she'll ever submit?"

"She gave me her word."

Naren chuckled. "Well, knowing Rissa, that's a considerable concession."

"I offered to let her choose another mate. She wanted to stay with me."

"I'm happy for you, Morigan."

"Are you, Naren? Do you truly wish me well with her?"

Gray eyes narrowed, measuring him. "I won't lie to you. I care for Rissa," his friend finally replied. "I'd like her for my own. But she's yours, has always been. I'm content with that."

"But if something should happen, and she chose to leave me . . ."

"Then, I'd vie with the other males to have her." Naren grinned. "I'm not *that* big of a fool."

Pain slashed through Morigan. His expression hardened. "If something should happen to me, keep her from Cradoc. He's not the male for her. He'd break that wonderful spirit of hers."

Naren's mouth tightened. "You know I will. I swear it." He motioned for Morigan to set out with him again. "You foresee a right of challenge in the future, do you?"

"Cradoc's pushing for it. He sees it as his only chance to gain the Cat Throne. And he wants it badly enough to risk his life." Morigan sighed. "It's only a matter of time, I'm afraid."

"You're a match for him, if any Cat Man in the lair is."

Morigan tossed Naren an amused glance. "Funny, I'd have rather thought you were the match of Cradoc, not I."

"Well, now that you mention it . . ."

Both men laughed. For the next few minutes, they walked along in companionable silence, savoring the brisk night air, the sharp bits of starlight glimmering overhead, and the heavy silence that blanketed the valley.

"He'll try and use the Bellatorian women as a wedge between you and the others," Naren finally said. "And Rissa most especially."

"I was thinking the same thing," Morigan admitted ruefully. "Though the onset of winter has perhaps muted the Lord Commander's response to our abduction of the females, I'm certain his retribution won't be long in coming. I sent out Brandar to spy on Primasedes. The more we learn of Lindatees's plans for us, the better prepared we can be."

"And, in the meanwhile, you've your hands full with problems at home. Problems that will only be compounded when the Lord Commander resumes his search for us. Cradoc will be certain to use that as yet another example of your poor judgment in bringing the females to the lair."

Morigan chuckled wryly. "And you thought I'd trouble enough just with Rissa!"

"Both are equally difficult. At least the problems with Rissa, though, bear some hope of eventually being solved. *If* we can keep her out of Cradoc's manipulative clutches."

The Cat Lord frowned. "Yes. I think it best, for the time being, that she not be allowed to go out unattended for any reason."

"I wish you good fortune with that," his friend said. "From all I can gather, she especially doesn't take kindly to orders from you."

Morigan glanced at him. "That's why I thought *you* might broach it to her."

"Me?" Naren gave a hollow laugh. "And whatever makes you think my influence would be greater than yours?"

"You're her friend, Naren. I'm . . . well, I don't think Rissa looks upon me as a friend."

"Would you care to trade positions?"

The Cat Lord chuckled. "There are times I must admit to being tempted, but no, I suppose not."

They drew up before Naren's lair. "You managed that walk fairly well," Morigan observed. "Another week or so and you should be back to full strength."

"Yes, that I should." Naren paused, recalling he'd yet to give his friend an answer to his request. "I'll speak to Rissa on the morrow."

Morigan clasped his arm in farewell. "My thanks. I need all the help I can get with her."

"Yes, you do, my friend. I think, though, she'll be well worth the effort." Naren released his clasp on Morigan's arm and stepped back.

The Cat Lord watched his friend turn and enter his lair. He stood there for a moment more, then wheeled about and strode off into the night.

"Rissa," Agna said the next morning as she placed warm poultices of crushed bacula leaves on Hali's bruises, "would you please take that bucket and bring me some fresh water from the stream? I need it to boil more bacula leaves."

Rissa glanced up from the new tunic she was attempting to sew for Hali. Though the girl desperately needed another set of clothes, there was beginning to be great doubt if the tunic Rissa was working on would be wearable, much less even fit.

Sewing had never been one of her particular interests, though her mother had tried many times to teach the skill to her, for creative reasons if not necessarily for the ability to make her own clothes. With a grateful sigh, Rissa set her sewing down. For a change, the healer's demands were a welcome respite.

She rose, flung her fur cloak over her shoulders, and fastened it, then picked up the wooden bucket Agna had pointed to on the table. "I'd be glad to fetch water. I'll be back in a few minutes."

Agna shot her a hooded look, then turned back to Hali. "Take your time," she said.

It had snowed late last night; a light layer of white still lingered this morning, dusting everything in sparkling, sun-kissed brilliance. The air was frosty and Rissa entertained herself as she walked along exhaling puffs of her breath that billowed briefly before dissipating. The frozen grass crunched underfoot, the trees rattled their skeletal branches with each passing breeze, and the birds, what few remained, sang. The valley seemed a glorious, fairy-tale kingdom.

A thin layer of ice covered the stream but, underneath, it ran as swiftly as ever. Rissa used the bucket to crack the ice and make a hole big enough through which to dip the bucket. The water was frigid, numbing her fingers. She filled the bucket as full as she could, then stepped back from the stream's edge, set down the bucket, and shoved her hands beneath her fur cloak.

"Need someone to warm you, do you, femina?" a deep male voice came from behind her.

Rissa wheeled around. Cradoc stood but a few meters

away, grinning down at her. She didn't like the look in his eyes. "What do you want?"

He feigned an expression of hurt. "I came down to offer my assistance with that heavy bucket, and all you can do is act as if I've just climbed out from beneath some stone. For shame, femina. I'm Morigan's cousin, after all."

"Well, I need no help, thank you." She grabbed the bucket and tried to walk around him. Cradoc neatly sidestepped to stand once more in her path. Rissa glared up at him. "You're in my way. Please move."

He grasped her by the arms, sliding one hand down until he pried the bucket from her fingers and tossed it aside. "You're a very pretty femina. I've had a deep curiosity about how your lips would taste from almost the first moment I saw you. And I think I tire of waiting for you to come to me of your own accord."

"Are you mad?" Rissa squirmed in his clasp. "I'm Morigan's. He'll kill you if you dare—"

"He can try," Cradoc snarled. "And that's exactly what I want him to do." His hands caressed her arms. "But first, I intend to have a little of his mate."

In a lightning swift move, the Cat Man swooped down on Rissa, encircling her in the iron clasp of his arms, imprisoning her so she couldn't move. Then, with a feral smile, Cradoc lowered his head—and took Rissa in a brutal, punishing kiss.

She fought him, pushing, beating, and clawing at him, but Cradoc's strength was too much for her. He squeezed her to him, until Rissa couldn't draw in a breath. Panic engulfed her. He was suffocating her!

The sky grayed, the world about her dimmed. She went limp in his arms. Then, from some place far away, Rissa heard voices, male voices, edged with anger and heavy with disapproval.

"Is this how you repay Morigan's trust in you, Cradoc?" Ardan's deep, sonorous voice pierced Rissa's waning consciousness. "Sneaking off to some clandestine meeting with his mate?"

"Clandestine it might have been, but I wasn't alone in my eagerness to meet here," Cradoc snarled. "I didn't drag Morigan's mate down here unwillingly."

"Perhaps not. You didn't plan for us to happen by, either, but we did. Agna invited us to see for ourselves the extent of her young patient's injuries this morn and, in the process, we came upon you two," Ardan drawled. "Strange how these kinds of things can never be kept secret for very long. Now, step away from her, I say. It sickens me to see you together."

Cradoc loosened his grip on Rissa. Blessed air, sharp and cold and life-giving, rushed into her lungs. She groaned, dragged in several deep breaths, then shoved away from her captor with a ferocious rage. He released her, and the backward momentum nearly sent her sprawling.

For a long moment Rissa stood there, swaying, fighting to clear her head and vision. Then, she saw it all. Agna, Ardan, and two other of the Elders, standing there on the path leading down to the stream, shock and disbelief in their eyes. Eyes staring down at her with as much accusation as they did at Cradoc.

"No." Rissa shook her head, denying what she knew to be in their minds. "I didn't . . . not with Cradoc. Ah, Gods, not with Cradoc!"

"I sent you off for a bucket of water," Agna hissed in disgust, a strangely triumphant light gleaming in her eyes. "I thought I could trust you out of my sight for a few minutes.

But instead," she said, curling her lip, "you run to Cradoc's arms. You're despicable!"

"Curse you, Agna!" Frustration, and a sense of a trap closing about her, filled Rissa. "I did nothing! Nothing!"

"Spare us your protests, femina." Morigan's grandfather stepped forward. "This isn't the time nor place for such discussions. Save it for later."

"Later?" Rissa blinked in surprise, suddenly wary. "Why? What's happening later?"

"A Council of Elders," Ardan replied. A look of deep sadness gleamed in his eyes. "It's past time, I fear, a decision be made as to your fitness to remain Morigan's mate."

Fourteen

"Curse them! Curse them all!" Rissa raged at Naren who, noting the procession back to Morigan's lair, quickly joined Rissa and Sarna there after the Elders had departed. "From the start they've been waiting for some excuse to find fault with me and prove Morigan wrong. And I'm certain Cradoc was in league with them!"

"Perhaps it *was* all some carefully orchestrated scheme," the Cat Man agreed, "but I think, rather, it was Cradoc's idea, with perhaps some outside help."

"Outside help?"

"Who were you with just before all this happened?"

Rissa frowned. "Agna. But she just sent me out for a bucket of water."

"Gods!" Naren shook his head in frustrated despair. "I should've gotten to you sooner, warned you to be careful."

"What's wrong, Naren? Surely Agna wouldn't do such a . . ." Rissa's voice faded. The healer's longstanding animosity might well have motivated her to conspire with Cradoc.

"Yes, she would and most likely did, femina," the Cat Man muttered. "Doesn't it seem all too convenient that Cradoc happened by just at the time she sent you out for water?"

Her mind raced. "And . . . and that Agna had invited the Elders down to see how Hali was doing this morn. Is it possible? Could Agna and Cradoc be in league against Morigan?"

"Cradoc definitely seeks Morigan's dethronement and will stop at nothing to destroy him. Agna, on the other hand, seems more intent on destroying you."

Sarna ambled over with a pot of herbal tea. "Oh dear," she murmured as she busied herself pouring out three cups. "I don't understand any of this. Cradoc is Morigan's cousin and Agna, our healer. Why would they wish my son harm?"

Rissa and Naren exchanged glances.

"Surely, it's all a misunderstanding, domina." Rissa took the cup of tea Sarna offered and sipped carefully. "It's delicious." She smiled reassuringly up at the old woman.

Naren took his cup and, after checking its temperature, emptied it in one swallow. He set down the cup. "I must speak with Morigan."

Rissa put down her own cup. "Let me go with you."

"No. It wouldn't look good if the others saw you in my company right now. I'll talk with Morigan first, then send him back here to you." He paused. "Have a care with him when he returns. He won't be happy."

"Will he believe me, Naren?" Rissa asked, suddenly overcome with apprehension. "Gods, I don't want to be the cause of additional problems to him! I don't!"

Naren smiled. "And I thought you were as against his decision to take captive females as some of my own people obviously are."

"Well, I still am on principle, mind you," Rissa sighed, "but I also know Morigan truly believes he's doing the right thing for the Cat People. Ah, Gods!" She threw up her hands in frustration. "I don't know whose side I'm on anymore. I just know I don't want to hurt him, if I can possibly help it."

"He'll be glad to hear that."

Rissa's eyes narrowed in suspicion. "It doesn't mean anything more than that, Naren. Don't you dare lead him to believe otherwise."

The big Cat Man shoved back his chair and extended his hand. "Come, femina." He glanced briefly at Sarna. "Walk with me to the entrance."

Rissa took his hand, rose, and followed him.

When they paused at the cave opening, Naren turned and cradled her chin in his callused palm. "Why?" he asked softly, his striking gray eyes searching her face. "Why would letting Morigan know how you truly feel about him be such a terrible thing? What are you still afraid of, Rissa?"

She wrenched her face free, unable to meet his gaze. "I'm not afraid of anything. Just let it be, Naren."

"You must make some decision about yourself and Morigan soon, femina," he warned. "This issue with Cradoc won't go away. He has finally, I fear, managed to bring things to a head."

Hearing the deep concern in Naren's voice, Rissa glanced back at him. "What has been brought to a head?"

"The conflict between Cradoc and Morigan." He shoved a hand unsteadily through his thick, black mane. "Morigan's honor has been impugned by Cradoc's insinuations that you and he are lovers. There are few ways to regain that honor, save through the right of challenge."

Presentiment wove its chilling tendrils about Rissa's heart. "And what does this right of challenge entail?"

"Another one of our ancient and perhaps outdated traditions," Naren sighed. "Though the Cat Throne is inherited, it can be taken away from the heir through the right of challenge. If another Cat Man challenges the Cat Lord to battle, and the Cat Lord accepts and is consequently defeated, the challenger becomes the new Lord. He wins not only the throne, but the former Cat Lord's lair, possessions, and mate as well."

"How cruel," Rissa murmured.

"It's but a matter of practicality. The former Cat Lord is dead, at any rate."

She paled. "What do you mean?"

"The right of challenge is a battle to the death, femina."

"That . . . that's barbaric!" The first wisps of rising panic engulfed her. "And archaic! No one settles disputes like that anymore!"

"We do."

"Oh, Gods." Rissa stepped back from Naren. "Morigan. He's a powerful man, a brave warrior. Surely, he'll prevail."

Naren stared down at her, a stricken look creeping into his eyes. Stark fear rushed in to swallow her panic. "Naren," Rissa cried, then lowered her voice when she noticed Sarna's quick, worried glance over at them. "Naren, what's wrong?"

"Morigan *is* powerful and a brave warrior, but Cradoc is better, our very best, to be exact. It's very likely Cradoc will kill him."

"No. Gods, no!" Rissa gripped Naren by the arms, her fingers gouging into his taut, leather-covered muscles. "This is all my fault, isn't it? If I'd supported Morigan, if I'd mated with him—"

He twisted from her grasp. Grasping her by the shoulders, he gave her a gentle shake. "Stop it, femina. It's not your fault. You're a pawn between them. This confrontation was only a matter of time. We all knew that. If not for Morigan's admirable restraint, they'd have clashed long ago."

"What can I do, Naren?" She searched his face. "I can't just stand by and—"

"There's nothing you can do, Rissa," he gently silenced her. "Our laws dictate the course from here on out."

"And I say, curse your laws!" she cried, not caring any-more if Sarna overheard. "They're cruel; they're stupid. They're worse than unfair if they permit someone of Cradoc's mettle to challenge and perhaps defeat a man like Morigan. Surely, you see that?"

Naren released her and stepped back, anguish burning in his eyes. "You may well be right, femina. But there's nothing I can do about it. Nothing any of us can do." He turned then and strode away, leaving Rissa to stand there, feeling as if he'd ripped her heart asunder.

She remained for a time, until the frigid wind whistling down from the mountains wrenched her back to reality. Then, with a shuddering sigh, Rissa turned and walked back into Morigan's lair.

The soft murmur of voices woke Rissa. She lay buried in cozy warmth beneath the furs, hovering between the seduc-tive lure of sleep and the strange compulsion to drag herself to full wakefulness. Something heavy, ominous hung over her drowsy consciousness, and she reached for it, but rec-ognition nimbly eluded her.

The voices grew in clarity. It was Sarna, Rissa realized, talking with—

Morigan!

Morigan. The right of challenge.

For an instant longer she hesitated, torn between the urge to hide from the harsh reality and snuggle back into the depths of his big, warm bed and the need to see him, talk with him. She'd waited for Morigan to return all day and well into the night, before exhaustion finally claimed her.

As the hours passed, her anxiety had grown, until she'd restlessly paced the confines of his lair and drove Sarna to the edge of distraction. But nothing helped, as she well knew it wouldn't. Nothing would help, save seeing and speaking with Morigan. And, now, he'd finally returned.

Rissa flipped back the furs, bit back a gasp at the rush of cold air that assailed her, then shoved herself out of bed. Pulling on her boots and flinging her fur cloak over her bed gown, she resolutely headed down the short tunnel to the main chamber. Though she dreaded the meeting with him, she desperately needed to know what had transpired this day. There was no way to help him until she knew exactly what they were up against.

Sarna saw her before Morigan, who sat at the table, his back turned to her, his shoulders hunched in exhaustion. The old woman took one look at Rissa's face, then nodded silently and slipped across the room and into her own bed-chamber. Rissa stood there, suddenly afraid to approach Morigan.

"Come here, femina." He turned slightly to glance over his shoulder. "There's no sense in prolonging this. Come sit with me."

She forced herself to move toward him, her cloak clutched about her, and walked around the table to take the opposite chair. His glance was bleary; deep lines of frustration furrowed his brow and both sides of his mouth. His dark, lush mane was disheveled. Yet, it was the despairing slump to his shoulders that filled Rissa with the greatest concern.

"Morigan, I . . ." Her voice faded. Tears flooded her eyes and spilled down her cheeks. "Gods!" she muttered, embarrassed. "I *hate* to cry!"

His mouth twisted wryly. He leaned across the table to wipe her tears away with a gentle, but unsteady touch. "Dare I hope some of that was shed for me?"

For an instant, Rissa was speechless. Then anger surged

in to burn away the tears. She jerked back from him and slammed her fist on the table. "Of course it was, you big, rock-headed son of a—"

He covered her hand with his. "I'm deeply flattered."

She wrenched her hand away, her anger blazing into fury. "Curse you, Morigan. Don't toy with me. Not at a time like this!"

Morigan cocked his head. "And what would you have me do? Break down and weep my heart out?"

"At least it would be honest!"

"Perhaps," he sighed, "but that's not my way. Nor will it ever be. I need, rather, to marshal all my strength and confidence about me, not squander it bemoaning my fate. The decision has been made, and I must see it through."

"You've agreed to meet Cradoc in that cursed right of challenge, haven't you?"

His expression hardened. "Yes. It was the only way to keep the Council from taking you from me this very day."

A wild hope flared within her breast. Perhaps there was still some way to save him. "And if they had, would you still have had to fight Cradoc?"

He started, stared at her, then firmly shook his head. "Do you think I could've stood by and let you go, Rissa, most likely right to Cradoc?" Morigan paused, his glance sharpening. "Unless you truly wish to be his mate?"

Her lips curled in disgust. "Never. I didn't plan to meet with Cradoc down by the stream. I swear it! But if giving myself to Cradoc now would turn this battle aside . . ."

"No!" Fury blazed in Morigan's eyes. "Don't even think it! I'll not have you sacrificing yourself for me. That would be the final humiliation."

Rissa grasped Morigan's wrist. His warmth, his vitality, the essence of him, shot through her with all the force of some lightning bolt. Gods, even now, in this time of greatest peril, she was still so intensely aware of—and so linked to—him.

The knowledge tore through her, twisting her heart into a tight, anguished little knot. She would never be free of him, no matter what happened, no matter if he died or she finally escaped. He was all she'd ever wanted, needed.

And now, thanks to her stubborn pride and foolish fears, she well may have sent him to his death.

Rissa's fingers clenched in the taut sinews and muscles of his lower arm. "I don't offer this to humiliate you, Morigan. I offer it to try and repair the damage already done. It's my fault, in so many ways, but I never meant for this to happen." She lowered her eyes and dragged in an unsteady breath. "And I never betrayed you to Cradoc. You do believe me, don't you, Morigan? I don't care what the others think, but if you imagined I went to him willingly . . ."

Ever so slowly, Rissa lifted her gaze to his.

He studied her in thoughtful silence, the tension growing until Rissa thought she would scream. "Yes, I believe you, femina," he finally replied, his voice deep and rich and tender. "That's why the right of challenge was my only recourse. And, in the end, the only one the Elders could allow me."

"What do you mean?"

"A Council was called. Ardan demanded I give you up and end the matter right then and there."

She released his arm and leaned back. "He's never liked me, from the first moment we met." Rissa sighed. "What did the others say?"

"My grandfather's affections, understandably, lie first with his grandson," Morigan offered gently. "He sought only to avoid the final confrontation between Cradoc and me. The other Elders, save for Naren and Cradoc, were willing to go along with Ardan's plan."

Rissa frowned in puzzlement. "Then how did you prevail?"

Morigan shrugged, a bitter smile playing about his lips. "I convinced them it would do no good. They all knew Cradoc wouldn't stop because he was once more thwarted. He's been chipping away at me since I assumed the Cat Throne, watching for the first sign of weakness." The Cat Lord averted his gaze. "He finally found it."

Rissa's heart began a staccato rhythm beneath her breast. Her mouth went dry and her palms grew clammy. "What was it, Morigan?"

He turned his head and impaled her with his green-gold stare. "Haven't you figured it out yet, Rissa? It's you. You're my one weakness. I can endure Cradoc's insults, his petty attempts to discredit me, and his constant opposition in Council. But I cannot bear him touching you or hurting you to get to me. And I will not tolerate his efforts to dishonor you. He has finally gone too far."

She rose and, walking around the table, knelt beside him. Her small hands settled on his leather-clad thigh. At her touch, he flinched, the muscles in his leg bunching, tightening. He inhaled a ragged breath. "Rissa . . ."

"I don't care for my honor. I don't care if he touches or hurts me," she whispered achingly. "I only care you don't fight Cradoc. Naren said . . . Naren said he's a very dangerous foe . . . That you might not best him in mortal combat." Once more, Rissa blinked back tears. "I don't want you to die, Morigan. Especially not for my sake."

His eyes brimmed with emotion. He leaned down and pulled Rissa up to him, turning her gently to draw her onto his lap. His arms encircled her. "And if not for you, sweet femina, than for whom?"

"For your people, Morigan," Rissa breathed. "That and only that is worth your life."

"Yes," he sighed, the sound one of utter despair. "That *is* truly worth the sacrifice of my life. But you're well worth it, too. Don't distress yourself, sweet one." He tenderly wiped away the single tear that welled to trickle down her cheek. "Sooner or later Cradoc would've found some way to bring things to a head. It was just a matter of time."

"Is-is there nothing I-I can do?" Rissa sobbed, assailed with the most bitterly poignant mix of happiness and sorrow. "I can't stand by and watch him ki—"

"Hush, sweet femina." Morigan gathered her close and stood, cradling her in his arms. "I don't want you there, at any rate. What will be, will be. Now, let's go to bed. The night draws on, and I must meet Cradoc at dawn."

Go to bed. The night draws on.

The words plucked at Rissa, sending the first surges of freshened hope thrumming through her. Morigan's honor wouldn't permit him to give her to Cradoc to save himself. But if giving herself to Morigan, becoming his mate in the fullest sense of the word would save him . . . Surely, he'd not spurn that offer.

She clasped her arms about his neck and lay her head upon his breast. Morigan's heart, so strong, so steady, thudded through his thick chest wall against her ear. His body, warm with life, fragrant with the potent man scent of him, encompassed her.

"Yes," Rissa whispered. "Let's go to bed." She gazed up at him and smiled. "It's past time you made me yours."

Morigan stiffened. He glanced down at her, his gaze narrowed. "You wish to mate with me now, do you?"

"Yes." She flushed and looked away, suddenly embarrassed by her boldness.

"Why, Rissa? Why now, after all this time of fighting me? After I already agreed to wait until your fertile time?"

"It's my fault all this has happened." She forced herself to meet his smoky, jade green gaze. "If I'd lain with you sooner, Cradoc could never have used such a ploy to force you into this battle. If we mate this night, you can go back to the Council in the morning and—"

"No, femina." Morigan lowered her to the ground and pulled her arms from about his neck. He shoved her away. "It's far too late for that. I won't have you out of pity or a misguided sense of self-sacrifice. I won't have you because you think I'm the lesser of two evils. And lying with you tonight would change nothing at any rate. My honor, as well as yours, has been sullied. Nothing short of the right of challenge will redeem it."

She stared up at him in horrified disbelief. "And that's why you think I offered myself to you? Because I feel sorry for you? Because I'd rather have you than Cradoc and think this is the only way to save myself from him? Gods, Morigan, but you can sometimes be the most prideful and stupid of men!"

His face went dark with anger. "Can I? Strange, but I could've sworn it was *your* pride and foolishness that kept us apart all this time, not mine. I wanted you almost from the first moment I saw you. Gods, I *did* want you from the first moment I saw you, as hard as that truth was for me to face. And as equally hard for me to face was the fact that I wanted you—a Bellatorian, my enemy—to want me."

Morigan stepped back from her, his expression ravaged, his mouth grim. "But I won't take you tonight. I'd never truly know, if I lived *or* died, the reason you chose this night of all nights to mate with me. There would always be the doubt; I'd always secretly wonder as to your true motives.

I'm not sure *you* even know your true motives! But I do know there wouldn't be any honor in it for either of us. And I've little enough honor left as it is."

"Morigan, I—" Rissa lifted a hand to touch him, but he shot her a look of warning and stepped yet further away. "Don't go," she cried. "Don't leave me like this. Let me explain."

"No. You've said too much as it is, femina." The mask fell, slamming shut on all emotion, all expression. "Leave it be. If, on the morrow, I live, we can perhaps begin again. And if I don't . . . well, I suppose it really won't matter anymore, will it?"

With that, Morigan turned and strode out of his lair, never hesitating, never once looking back, even when Rissa cried out his name.

"Wake up! Wake up you lazy female!"

Rissa groaned and buried her head in the pillows. "Go away. T-too early . . ."

"No, it's not," came the irritated feminine voice. "Not unless you want to lose the only chance you'll ever have to escape."

"Wh-what?" Rissa jerked upright, furiously blinking the sleep away. Agna stood there, a grim set to her mouth.

"Almost everyone has gone to the meeting place to watch Morigan and Cradoc battle for the Cat Throne," the healer said. "The valley is guarded by a minimal force. If you still wish to leave us, I'll help you get away."

Rissa brushed the tousled hair from her eyes. "Why? Why now, Agna?" she demanded, immediately suspicious. "Why would you suddenly wish to help me?"

"Because no matter who wins this day, you'll continue to

cause problems. Problems we don't need." The Cat Woman paused to eye her critically. "Now, make up your mind, and make it quickly. I'll wait in the main chamber while you dress."

She disappeared down the tunnel before Rissa could respond. For a moment more, Rissa sat there, the full implications of Agna's words and what the dawning of this day had set into motion swelling within her. Morigan and Cradoc. They battled for the Cat Throne.

What time was it? she thought in panic. Were they fighting even now?

Morigan had said her presence wouldn't change what would happen. She knew, as well, after last night, her appearance at the right of challenge would lend him little comfort. He didn't want her there. No one did.

Far better to seize this unexpected opportunity Agna offered. Far better to be far away when the battle was done. If Cradoc won, she didn't care to be here when he came to gloat over her. If Morigan won, she didn't know if she could face him.

Besides, her original plan still held. She could help him and his people far better back at her father's side. No matter the depth of their feelings for each other, however confused and tumultuous they might be, it was still best they parted.

Rissa jumped out of bed and began hurriedly to dress, donning her warm, green lana cloth over-tunic and long skirt, then pulling on her boots. She splashed water on her face to clear the lingering cobwebs of sleep, then ran her wooden comb through her hair to free the tangles.

Her turcas jewelry caught her glance, lying where she'd put it beside the wash basin. After the briefest hesitation, Rissa donned the earrings and necklace. Her warm, phoca fur cloak lay where she'd folded it, atop Morigan's wife's clothes chest. Rissa grabbed it up and strode from the bed-chamber.

Agna wheeled about when she entered the main room. Her glance swept Rissa from head to toe. She smirked. "I see my offer has been accepted." She picked up a bulging backpack and held it out to Rissa. "Here. There are provisions for a week's journey, plus two blankets, a stunner, and your dagger."

Rissa took it from her. "How far will you lead me from the lair before you leave me?"

Agna shrugged. "Far enough for you to get your bearings. The way back to the plains is southwest. If you plot the course of the sun during the day, you should have no trouble." She gestured to her. "Are you ready?"

An instant's hesitation, no more, then Rissa nodded. "Yes. Let's go."

She followed Agna out of the lair, not daring a backward glance. With each step she took, however, the sense of her betrayal and desertion of Morigan pounded through her. No matter the harsh words spoken last night, he fought for her honor and the welfare of his people, while she turned her back and slunk away, too cowardly to stand by him or see it through to the end, however horrible it might ultimately be.

And if he died, he would die never knowing she loved him.

The backpack dropped from Rissa's suddenly nerveless fingers. She halted.

Agna turned and shot her an exasperated glance. "Whatever is the matter now?"

"Where?" Rissa whispered. "Where are Morigan and Cradoc?"

"What does it matter?" the Cat Woman snapped. "We've other matters to—"

A shout rose, carried down the valley on a gusting breeze.

A sound of primal excitement, of blood lust stirred to a frenzy by the sight of two men locked in a battle to the death. Rissa turned.

"Morigan . . ." she whispered.

Before Agna could utter another word, Rissa bolted down the valley, her love, her fear, lending her a swiftness that even the healer, watching her, wondered at. The wind, rising to whip and whistle through the twisting confines of the valley, tore at her cloak, tugging at the heavy fur until it weighed on her and slowed her forward progress. With a small cry of frustration, Rissa unfastened the cloak and let it go. Nothing must keep her from Morigan. She *must* reach him before it was too late.

The Cat People crowding at the entrance of the large, communal meeting cave were densely packed. Faces loomed before her, familiar yet still strangely foreign and out of focus. Faces, tormented, confused, as if struggling to fathom the events that now played out before them.

Panic consumed Rissa when her initial attempts to get through were thwarted. Something inside her snapped. She clawed; she struck out; she screamed. "Gods, let me through! Let me see Morigan!"

And miraculously they turned, looked back, recognized her, and moved aside. Her lungs burning, the tears streaming down her cheeks, her hair and eyes wild with her fear, Rissa stumbled through the people, not caring that their looks told her they thought her gone mad, not caring about anything save reaching Morigan.

Then, she was there, at the front of the large circle of Cat People who encompassed the ring where Morigan and Cradoc fought. Naren . . . Sarna . . . Ardan . . . and the other Elders. As if in slow motion, all turned toward her, their expressions shocked, then horrified.

Their mouths moved, forming words, phrases. Rissa couldn't hear them. A roaring encompassed her, drowning out all sound but the crazed beat of her heart—and the raw, ragged, agonized breathing of the two combatants.

She spun around, seeking Morigan. He faced Cradoc, claws bared, the most feral, terrible expression on his face, clothed in nothing but his loincloth. His chest and arms were viciously slashed, the blood coursing down his hair-roughened torso and legs to soak into the hard-packed dirt floor. The right side of his face was horribly bruised, swelling and purpling rapidly. His chest heaved, his muscles strained, and a heavy sweat glistened on the powerful planes of his body.

Cradoc was equally slashed and bloody, but it was evident even to Rissa's untrained eye he was slowly wearing Morigan down. Yet, still the Cat Lord fought on, even as Cradoc repeatedly inflicted agonizing wounds upon him, one after another. He would battle until the last drop of blood drained from his body, Rissa realized, the knowledge filling her with a soul-wrenching anguish. He'd never give up, until his heart burst within his chest or ceased to beat.

She glanced around the circle, visually beseeching anyone—everyone—to help him. But none would, or could. They were bound by the finest yet most indestructible of bonds—their sacred laws. Only they could break free, if they wished it, yet, though some struggled even then, fear of the consequences, of the unknown held them still. The old ways called strongly; the threat of change in a world gone crazed and fraught with danger and death appeared bewildering, terrifying. They hovered between the past and the future, and none seemed able to take the first step to bridge the chasm.

In that instant of vivid, shattering realization, a rage flared, grew within Rissa, compelling her to do what none other dared.

"Stop it!" she screamed and flung herself into the ring. "Stop this senseless brutality!" Before any could react, much less restrain her, Rissa sprinted across the expanse of blood-soaked ground and threw herself into Morigan's arms.

He staggered backward in surprise. His unsheathed claws raked her arm before he could retract them. Then, his arms were around her, pulling her hard up against him. His blood, warm and wet, soaked into her gown.

"G-Gods, Rissa!" Morigan gasped. "What are you doing?"

A snarl rose from behind her. She whirled around, intentionally placing herself between Cradoc and Morigan. The expression on the auburn-haired Cat Man's face chilled her soul. His look of hatred, of thwarted rage, was the most horrible thing Rissa had ever seen. And, as he lunged at her, she knew he meant to kill her.

In the next instant, she was shoved aside. Morigan leaped past her. The sickening thud of two hard bodies slamming into each other filled the air. Breaths expelled in agonized grunts. The metallic tang of fresh blood flooded her nostrils. Rissa caught her breath, suddenly afraid she'd retch.

She staggered forward, struggling past the dizzying mists. She must stop them. She must . . .

Strong arms pulled her back, dragging her away from the two bloodied men now wrestling in merciless combat on the ground.

"No!" Rissa cried. "Let me go! Stop this! Would you have him kill your lord, the man who has sacrificed everything for you?"

"Hush, femina," Naren's voice raggedly rasped against her ear. "There's nothing you can do. It's the law."

"Curse your laws!" she sobbed. "Laws that sanction the death of a brave and noble leader are laws that must be changed! If you don't, you condemn yourselves to certain destruction. You won't need the Bellatorians to finish what they began a cycle ago: you'll do it to yourselves!" Rissa twisted and fought against Naren. "Ah, Gods, why are you punishing Morigan for this? If you truly think me at fault, punish me, but not Morigan. Gods, not Morigan!"

"Rissa, femina," Naren soothed, imprisoning her in his arms. "You only make matters worse. And you shame Morigan in the process."

She jerked about to glare up at him. "And I say you shame yourself, and all the rest of you, too!" she shouted, twisting to take in the circle of people. "Shame on all of you, for your cowardice in failing to change what you know to be wrong. Shame on you, for your unwillingness to adapt to what must be. You are blind—all of you—and you'll kill Morigan because of it. Ah, Gods. Ah, G-Gods . . ."

Suddenly, the fight drained from her. There was nothing more for her to give or say. Rissa slumped against Naren, sobbing as if her heart would break.

Naren pulled her to him, went still, then inhaled a fortifying breath. Rissa in his arms, he swung around to the Elders. "She's right," he roared, his strong, sure voice carrying to the farthest reaches of the crowd. "She alone has had the vision and courage to question and condemn what we refuse to face. End this now, I beg of you. Before Morigan dies and with him dies the heart and final hope for our people!"

"Yes!" Agna cried, elbowing her way to the front of the crowd. A wild, fierce light gleamed in her eyes. "The Bellatorian is right. End this now!"

Bedlam reigned, people shoving, jockeying for position, eyes wide, mouths agape. Voices spoke out, uncertain but, for once, questioning, challenging.

"It isn't right!"

"What good's a law that kills a Lord like Morigan?"

"The law's outdated. Repeal it!"

"Past time we move on. Stop the challenge!"

Like a freshened breeze in a room long closed and stagnant, the murmuring flowed about the chamber. Eyes brightened with hope, heads lifted, and Cat People looked each other squarely in the eye. Almost to a man, they turned, their glances settling on the Council of Elders.

A hush settled over the gathering. Ardan stepped forward. He motioned to the two Cat Men still fighting in the ring. "End the challenge. It no longer serves us. End it now!"

Six young, burly Cat Men sprang into the ring. In the space of a few seconds, they had Morigan and Cradoc wrenched apart and dragged away from each other. Cradoc fought wildly, attempting to break free, snarling oaths and crazed threats. Morigan, winded and nearly at the end of his strength, sagged back against the men who held him. The light of battle, however, still blazed in his eyes.

His grandfather walked over to him. Their gazes locked. "It is past time, I think," Ardan said, "to rethink some of our laws. Your mate is right. We not only shame ourselves, but threaten our very existence in senselessly adhering to traditions that no longer serve our needs. As we did in resisting change, when some of us refused to accept the Bellatorian females you brought into our lair. We have all been fools, my Lord. Fools who nearly destroyed you in the process."

With a superhuman effort, Morigan shrugged off the support of the men who held him. He took a step forward to stand free and proud. Though the blood poured from his wounds, though the breath shuddered from him, and he shook from the strain, he flung back his shoulders and lifted his head. "If this is the will of the people, so be it. There's still the issue of Cradoc, however. He'll continue to fight me, no matter how our laws change."

"What would you have us do with him?"

Morigan turned to eye his cousin. "There's too much to be considered just now. Imprison him until the Council, as a whole, can meet and decide his fate." His knees buckled then. If not for the swift response of the three Cat Men who stood behind him, Morigan would have fallen.

Agna rushed forward. "Carry him, quickly now, back to his lair." She turned to Lisan, who stood nearby. "Run to my lair and bring my box of healing supplies."

Her gaze followed the Cat Men who carried Morigan away, then swung back to lock with Rissa's. Something flickered in the healer's eyes, regret, shame, and a hope for understanding and forgiveness. "Will you come with me, my Lady? I think your lord would wish for you to be at his side."

Rissa glanced up at Naren. He released her. She turned to Agna. "Yes, I'll come and gladly," she softly replied. "I, too, wish to be with him . . . with all my heart."

Fifteen

"Lay him on the table," Agna ordered. "No, wait a moment. Place a blanket beneath him and fetch a pillow for his head. And Sarna," she said, turning to Morigan's mother, "would you stoke the fire and place a pot of water on to boil? We'll need hot water as well as a hot fire soon enough."

Rissa stood aside as the Cat Men lowered Morigan onto the table. Then, as the others stepped back, she hurried over to stand opposite Agna and took Morigan's hand. He turned to her.

"You're a brave little she-cat, aren't you?" he whispered, his strength all but gone. He grimaced as Agna pressed a folded cloth over his most copiously bleeding wound, a vicious gash down the length of his right arm.

"I couldn't stand by and let Cradoc kill you." Rissa squeezed his hand. "Look at me, Morigan. Talk with me. It'll help distract you from what Agna must do."

"Y-you think so, eh?" he gasped and turned to see what the healer was doing.

"No," Rissa firmly reiterated, her fingers clenching about his jaw to hold his head in place. "Look at me."

He relented. "Yes, femina."

A fierce love for him welled in her heart. He looked brutalized, his face battered, his body slashed and bleeding. Yet, not once did he complain or cry out in his pain. Like some animal, Rissa realized, suffering it all in silence. She knelt beside him and kissed him on the cheek.

He smiled, then closed his eyes. Lisan rushed in with Agna's box of healing supplies in his hand. The healer swiftly extracted several jars, a long, thick metal rod with a wooden handle, and a roll of bandages and some fluffy compresses. She laid them out on one of the chairs, then handed the metal rod to Naren. "Heat it in the fire."

Rissa glanced up, her eyes huge. "What do you intend to do, Agna?"

"What else?" the Cat Woman replied briskly. "Cauterize Morigan's wounds."

"But . . . but that's barbaric!" Rissa protested. "No one uses such archaic methods anymore!"

Agna shot her an exasperated glance. "It's all we have. Would you prefer I let him bleed to death?"

"No, of course not. But first give Morigan a narcotic. Anything." Rissa choked back a sob. "I-I just don't want him to suffer."

A hand squeezed hers. She glanced down. "It's all right, femina. There's not enough time for a narcotic to take effect at any rate. If you'll stay with me, I can bear the pain."

"But can I?" she whispered. "I don't know if I'll have the strength."

"We'll do it together."

His striking eyes held hers and, from somewhere in their mesmerizing depths, Rissa found the courage to go on. "Yes," she murmured. "Together."

Naren approached with the rod, red hot and glowing. Agna took it from him and walked over to Morigan. "It's time, my Lord."

Morigan never took his eyes off Rissa's face. "Get on with it, then."

The rod touched him, again and again, searing his raw, bleeding wounds. He hissed in agony, jerked, and went rigid, but never once cried out. As Agna relentlessly reapplied the cautery, the scent of scorched flesh filled the air. Finally, Morigan lapsed into unconsciousness. Rissa stayed by him, holding his hand, stroking his face, and murmuring soothing words.

"It's over," Agna said at last. She handed the rod back to Naren. "Now, we'll clean him up and apply the healing powder, then bandage him." She glanced at Rissa, who still knelt beside Morigan. "Why don't you go lie down? You look nearly as pale as he does."

Rissa roused herself and shook her head. "No, I want to stay with Morigan. Besides, I'd like to learn how to care for him, if you'd teach me."

The healer eyed her impassively, then sighed her acquiescence. "If you wish. Some of this will be unpleasant. There's ruined flesh I must cut away."

Rissa swallowed hard. "If you deem it necessary for Morigan's recovery, then I'll learn to do it."

Agna nodded. She scanned the room. "There's no further need of your assistance," she said, glancing around at the Cat Men. "You may return to your other duties."

Naren stepped forward. "I'd like to stay for a time, to make sure Morigan is all right."

"He's as well as can be expected," Agna snapped, "and his condition won't change much in the next several hours. I've more than enough help with Sarna and Rissa here. Get on with you, I say!"

"Fine." Naren held up his hands and backed away. "You will send for me if Morigan's condition worsens or he asks for me, though, won't you?"

"Yes, of course." The healer turned away to dig in her box,

extracting a sharp little knife. "Now, my Lady, let me show you what flesh is good and what needs to be discarded," she said, effectively dismissing Naren.

Rissa shot the Cat Man a reassuring little smile, then directed her attention back to Agna. A few minutes later, they were alone in the lair, save for Sarna, worrying over the pot of steaming water, and an unconscious Morigan.

"Males," Agna muttered, as she skillfully sliced away the dead flesh. "Always standing about and getting in the way, yet, when you offer to let them do anything, they nearly keel over themselves. I can't abide them about for long."

"Have you never had a mate, then, Agna?"

The healer's head snapped up. "What did you say?"

Rissa flushed, realizing she'd touched on a nerve. "I only meant, you sound as if you don't like men."

"Oh, I like them well enough when it comes to mating," Agna said. "I had a mate—and children—until the Bellatorians killed them all. I just don't like them in the way of my healing."

"I'm sorry, Agna," Rissa murmured. "About your family, I mean," she hurried to add when she noted a look of wariness flare in the Cat Woman's eyes. "I didn't know. It explains a lot about your, er, unfriendliness to me."

Agna gave a bitter laugh. "Does it now? Well, I almost succeeded in destroying Morigan in my single-minded intent to see you gone. I was a fool—a fool Cradoc easily used."

"So, Naren was right. You did conspire with Cradoc to have me caught with him when the Elders happened by."

"Yes." The Cat Woman flushed. "I never imagined Morigan would go so far as to fight Cradoc over you. He must care for you deeply to have done so."

It was Rissa's turn to flush. "He said I was his weakness, a weakness Cradoc would never cease using against him."

Tears stung her eyes. "Oh, Agna, Morigan almost died because of me!"

"No, my Lady," the healer corrected her firmly. "Morigan almost died because of his people's foolishness, not because of you." She hesitated, as if considering her next words. "I'd never intended for Morigan to be dragged into Cradocs' and my scheme. But Cradoc had always had other plans. When I saw what my deceit had wrought, I was so angry, I irrationally placed the blame on you. I intended to do more than just lead you from the lair this morn. I intended on killing you, once I got you far enough away. I hated you that much."

The woman's eyes filled with tears. "I'm glad I never had the chance."

Rissa managed a rueful smile. "I think I would've deserved it, if I'd turned my back on Morigan." She shuddered. "By the five moons, to think I almost left him to die at Cradoc's hands!"

"Well," Agna said, returning her attention to Morigan's wounds, "neither of us had the chance to make the worst mistake of our lives. We're both fortunate."

Wonder and a deep sense of her good fortune filled Rissa. "Yes, indeed we are."

They moved Morigan to his bed a few hours later, once Agna had finished with his wounds and bandaged him. Naren, Lisan, and several other Cat Men were once more summoned to carry their lord from the main chamber to his bed, then again sent away. When the still unconscious Cat Man was settled, Agna gathered up her tools and potions.

"I would like to check on some of my other patients," she said, turning to Rissa, "if you feel comfortable staying with

Morigan. Mira is due to deliver soon and isn't feeling well. I know, though, Sarna won't be of any real help . . ."

"She's more lucid than most of you give her credit for."

Agna shrugged. "Perhaps she is. None of us have had much time to spare for her since the massacre. And especially not Morigan. Perhaps all Sarna really needs is someone to talk with, and guide her back from her terrible loss." The healer smiled. "You're good for her, my Lady. As you are for Morigan."

"I hope so, Agna. I would like to be of some real use here."

"Would you, now?" Agna laughed. "Well, I'll just see what I can do about that." She picked up her box and turned to go.

Rissa halted her with an outstretched hand.

The healer arched a dark brow. "Yes?"

"Do you think it possible for us ever to become friends?"

Pale blue, almond-shaped eyes briefly considered Rissa. "After all that's happened, all I've tried to do to you, are you certain you'd want me as a friend?"

"You're a woman of strongly held convictions. I like that in a person."

Agna chuckled. "As do I, my Lady. I think a friendship between us is a very strong possibility."

"Good." Rissa smiled. "I'd like that very much." She followed the healer to the entrance. "Give my best wishes to Mira, will you, Agna?"

"But of course, my Lady," the Cat Woman replied before heading down the trail from Morigan's lair.

Rissa watched her until she disappeared across the snow-covered valley. As she turned back to the cave, a low "my Lady?" caught her ear. Rissa glanced over her shoulder. Lisan stood at the bottom of the trail, an uncertain and decidedly embarrassed look on his face. She gestured for him to come up.

The blond young Cat Man hurried to her. The wind whipped about them, showering them with fat snowflakes. Rissa shivered and wrapped her arms about her. "What is it, Lisan?"

"The girl, Hali. I would ask a favor . . ." His voice faded and he glanced away.

"Yes, what about Hali?" Rissa only hoped she wasn't going to have to drag the reason for his surprising visit out of him. It was turning very cold.

"How does she fare?"

Puzzlement crept into Rissa's voice. "Well enough. She is walking now and able to help Agna with some of the chores. Why do you ask?"

Lisan turned a striking shade of crimson. "She'll soon need to choose a new mate. I find her most . . . attractive." He shot her a mortified glance.

"Do you now?" Amusement filled Rissa. Lisan was interested in the girl. She considered such a mating. Yes, he would be perfect for her. In fact, Rissa couldn't think of another Cat Man who would care for and love Hali like Lisan would. "And what do you wish of me?"

"A chance to speak with her, allow her to get to know me." He frowned. "But she's so afraid of us now I thought if I could visit her someday with you, perhaps she'd be less fearful. Hali needs a chance to learn not all Cat Men are like Limos."

"Yes, she does indeed," Rissa agreed. "I visit her every day about midmorning. If Morigan is doing well enough tomorrow, I'll go to see her then. Meet me here, and you may accompany me."

"Thank you, my Lady." Lisan began to back away, smiling

widely. "I only want a chance with her. I'd never force myself on her. I swear it."

"I know that." She made a shooing motion toward him. "Now, get on with you. It's freezing out here, and I must get back inside."

His blue eyes widened in horror. "Oh, yes. Please, forgive my thoughtlessness. I didn't think . . ."

Rissa laughed and ducked inside. Strange how things could change from one day to the next. Lisan was now asking for her help as matchmaker. Agna's opinion of her had markedly changed. And she now knew she'd fallen in love with Morigan.

She shook her head, both amused and surprised by it all. Perhaps there was indeed a place for her here—if only she could find some way to heal Morigan's ravaged, embittered heart.

The next four days, Morigan did little but sleep, save for the times Agna woke him to tend his wounds or Rissa forced a bowlful of soup down his throat. Though his extended lethargy worried Rissa, the healer assured her it was the normal healing process of Cat People. He was but rebuilding and storing reserves of energy. The change in him, when it finally came, would be all that more sudden and impressive because of it.

On the fifth day, Agna's words came to fruition. Rissa woke early to find him gone. Fear surged through her. She leaped from bed, expecting to find him unconscious on the floor, but he wasn't there. Heedless of her sleep-tousled hair or bare feet, Rissa flung on her green tunic and skirt and rushed from the bedchamber.

Morigan was seated at the table, fully dressed, enjoying a

bowl of Sarna's overcooked porridge. He glanced up when she ran in, quirked a brow, then resumed his meal. "Hungry, are you?" he inquired mildly. "I've never seen a person in such a hurry for breakfast before."

"What, by the five moons, are you doing out of bed?" Rissa stalked over to stand beside him. Her hands fisted in righteous indignation on her hips. "Your wounds aren't—"

"They're all but healed," he replied around a mouthful of porridge. "Care to have a look at them, do you?"

"As a matter of fact, yes!"

Morigan exchanged an amused glance with his mother. "I see she needs yet another lesson in the amazing powers of the Cat People."

"Oh, I do, do I?" Rissa snapped. "And I assume you're just the person to teach me?"

He shot her a feral smile. "As a matter of fact. And quite up to it, too." Morigan laid down his spoon. "I need a bath. Care to accompany me to the hot springs? It'll be the perfect opportunity for you to examine my wounds."

Rissa hesitated, suddenly wary. "Well, perhaps it would be better if I waited here . . ."

"You'll have a very long wait, femina. After my bath, I intend on calling a Council to decide Cradoc's fate. I may not be back until this evening."

"This evening?" Rissa's mouth fell open in amazement. "You can't be serious. By the time you finish your bath, I'd wager you won't even be able to make it back to your lair without help."

"Then more the reason for you to accompany me. If I truly have overestimated my abilities, you'll want to be there to see to my welfare, not to mention berate me soundly for my foolishness."

"Well, since you put it that way . . ." She scowled. Curse

him. Morigan had neatly trapped her. Besides, she really did want to keep a close eye on him, convinced his sudden surge of energy was nothing more than a male's natural arrogance and inaccurate assessment of his abilities.

Sarna laughed and ambled over. "I think he has you there, child. Go, comb your hair and let Morigan finish his porridge." Her glance lowered to Rissa's feet, peeking out from beneath her hem. "And put on your boots before you take a chill. It's freezing outside and, as warm as the fire keeps the cave, it does little for the floor."

Rissa eyed Morigan a moment more, then turned and hurried back to their bedchamber. By the time she returned, her hair combed and braided down her back, her boots on, and cloak about her shoulders, Morigan was done with his meal and awaited her at the entrance. He, too, wore a thick phoca fur cloak and carried a large leather bag.

"The bathing supplies," he explained, noting her glance at the bag. "Mother put it together for us."

"I've no intention of bathing today," Rissa hastened to inform him. "I'm coming along to keep an eye on you."

A broad shoulder shrugged negligently. "Suit yourself, femina." He lifted the thick leather panel covering the entrance. "After you, my Lady."

She shot him a withering look and strode past, into a world of swirling white. Rissa gasped at the cold, drew in a sharp breath, and instantly regretted it. The air was frosty and made her chest ache. Morigan moved to stand beside her, grasped her arm, and started forward. She lowered her head against the frigid blast of wind and trudged on.

The winter must be terrible up here in the mountains, she thought, a challenge to anyone to survive. Yet, the Cat People had managed not only to survive but to turn the hidden valley into a home. The courage and dogged perseverance this settlement had required, however, was mind-boggling. It had taken a very special leader to guide the Cat People through it all. A very special leader named Morigan.

Despite the cold, the wind, the bleakness, and whirling snow, Rissa felt content, happy to be with Morigan. She'd almost lost him. She'd never realized how empty her heart and life would've been without him. Naren had indeed chosen well in picking his lord for her mate. Chosen well indeed . . .

They reached the hot springs cavern, the first hint of its nearness the blast of warm air that engulfed her as Morigan lifted back the thick leather door covering. Gratefully, Rissa stepped inside. It seemed steamier than usual, as the pools' heat rose to condense in the cooler air that crept in from the outside. The sound of voices and splashing water alerted Rissa to the springs' other occupants even before she could make out their forms in the heavy mist shrouding the cavern.

As they neared the first pool, nubile feminine figures glided by. The women called out to Morigan before diving into the water, inviting him to join them. He chuckled and continued on.

Jealousy vibrated through Rissa. She didn't like the idea of any of the Cat Women bathing near Morigan, much less seeing him naked. She could well imagine the hot, covetous looks they'd send him. She'd seen them often enough as it was in the nine days she'd been here.

"Are both pools in use?" Rissa asked. "This one seems rather crowded."

"Does it? Well, no matter. I'd hoped the pool for the mated couples was free, and it is. We'll use that one."

Her glance lifted to where the tunnel to the private pool lay. A mist-muted light gleamed from the open doorway. Rissa slid to a halt. "Well, on second thought, perhaps the public pools aren't all that crowded. And I'm sure you'd like the opportunity to speak with some of your people."

"No, not this time." He gently pulled her forward. "I'd like the chance to bathe in private. Hopefully, with you."

"Er, no. No thank you." She shook her head. "I already told you I didn't plan to bathe. I'm only here to help you."

As he led her down the short tunnel leading to the private hot springs, Morigan sighed. "Will you at least promise to help me undress and wash my back? Though, thanks to Agna's healing powder, my wounds are nearly healed, my body is still bruised and sore. A little assistance would be greatly appreciated."

"I-I don't know if that would be . . ." Rissa hesitated, torn between the impulse to help Morigan and the embarrassment of assisting him to undress. She'd seen him all but naked when he'd worn his brief loincloth. There was little more about his body to know. And he *was* her mate, even if she'd yet to join with him.

There was indeed nothing wrong in what they did. Yet, still, the thought of finally seeing Morigan naked, of being in the same room with him while he was in such a state of undress, was most unnerving. And most stimulating as well.

The smaller cavern was open, its interior lit softly by hidden perpetual lights. Rissa paused at the entrance. The small pool in the center of the room churned noisily, the agitated water foaming and bubbling up to throw a silvery mist into the air. The scent of minerals was strong, but not unpleasant. Moss flowers grew along the sides of the cavern and even more densely in thick, lush patches of emerald green and lavender-pink about the pool edges. Sheltered deep in the mountain, the setting was warm and cozy, a little haven shut off from the outside world.

Rissa could understand why this particular pool had been

selected for the private use of the mated couples. It was the perfect spot for a romantic seduction. But, surely, Morigan didn't intend it for such a purpose. Not in his current condition, at any rate.

A strong hand slid down her arm to take her elbow, impelling her forward. Morigan led her inside, then turned, closed the wooden door and slid a long piece of wood in place to secure it. Rissa arched a brow.

"I thought perhaps the privacy of a bolted door might ease any hesitations you have about bathing." He grinned. "I know I don't particularly want to be disturbed."

Her eyes narrowed. "What game do you play, Morigan?"

"Nothing you don't wish to play, femina. Though you offered differently not so long ago, I gave my word to wait until your fertile time. I'll stand by it."

"I came only to help with your bath."

He shrugged. "Then that's all you'll do." He moved to a wooden bench next to the wall and, laying the bag on the floor beside him, sat. "Would you help me with my boots?" he asked, gesturing to them.

Rissa walked over and knelt before him. Without comment, she tugged off his boots and set them aside.

Morigan unlaced his tunic and slid it off his shoulders. He folded it and laid it on the bench. Bandages still swathed his torso. He turned to his side, where the strips of cloth were tied, and began painfully to fumble with the knots.

After watching his unsuccessful attempts, Rissa rose and sat beside him. "Here, let me help." Her nimble fingers soon had the knots untied and the bandages removed.

Save for slightly reddened, scabbed over slashes on his chest, abdomen, and arms, Morigan looked nearly healed. Rissa shook her head in wonder. "You Cat People truly do possess some amazing powers."

"It's mainly thanks to Agna's healing powder, and the fact my wounds didn't fester. That's the difference between my more rapid recovery and Naren's. Besides the fact," he added dryly, glancing down at himself, "Cat claws leave wounds that heal a lot faster than blaster burns."

Once more, his gaze met Rissa's. "Will you help me with my breeches?"

The question took her by surprise. "If you wish." A sudden thought struck her. Rissa flushed. "You do wear a loincloth beneath your breeches, don't you?"

Morigan's mouth quirked. "No. What would be the point?"

Rissa's flush deepened. "Well, modesty for one thing."

A rich chuckle rumbled in the Cat Lord's chest. "And must I now be modest around you, femina?"

She didn't reply, only lowered her eyes.

He took her chin, gently, in the callused expanse of his palm. "Rissa." He lifted her gaze to his. "You're my mate. My nakedness is no danger to you."

"Isn't it, Morigan?"

A frown furrowed his broad, proud brow. "You know I won't force you. What danger is there?"

"N-none." She jerked her chin away. "None at all. I was just being foolish."

"No, not foolish, sweet one," the sound of his deep voice rippled softly, sensuously, down her spine, "just wary of your feelings . . . and what they call you to."

Rissa's head snapped up. "Indeed? And what exactly do my feelings call me to, all-wise and all-knowing Cat Man?"

A lazy grin flashed across his features. Morigan stood and began to unfasten his breeches. "A mating with me, sooner or later." He spread open the waistband, revealing a flat, hard belly and tangle of dark body hair. "Now, I think the time has passed for talk. I need a bath."

As Rissa stared up at him in shock, Morigan slipped his leathern breeches off and let them fall to his knees. She caught a glimpse of lean, rock-hard legs covered with a generous sprinkling of hair, smooth flanks and, at the juncture of his thighs, a dense nest of dark hair and a huge—

Quickly, she averted her gaze.

Noting the maidenly blush and lowered head, Morigan smiled. He sat and bent to pull off his breeches. In the process, he twisted to one side. The effort sent bruised abdominal muscles screaming in protest.

Morigan winced, inadvertently drawing in a sharp breath. A nauseating dizziness roiled through him. He leaned back, suddenly clammy and panting. His eyes slid shut.

"Here, let me help." Rissa's hand touched Morigan on the chest, pushing him back to rest against the rock wall. She finished tugging his breeches free.

He forced open one eye. Her back was now turned. "Wh-what are you doing?"

"Folding your breeches." She laid them atop his tunic, paused, squared her shoulders, and turned. Her gaze, however, never left his face. "And you said you were ready for this!"

Morigan didn't like the censure he heard in her voice. "I never said I was totally healed," he grumbled. "If I hadn't bent and twisted, I would've been fine."

"Exactly what you'll have to do to wash yourself, too. Are you certain you don't want to give up this idea and go back to the lair?"

"I need a bath, Rissa. And I *want* a bath, as well. I've been five days without one and can't bear my scent." He shoved himself back to a sitting position and stood, swaying only for an instant. "I'll be all right."

"Yes, I'm quite certain of that," Rissa muttered. "Wait a moment."

Morigan arched a dark brow and turned to glance back at her. "What exactly did you have in . . ." His voice faded. She had already pulled off one boot and was tugging on the other. A minute later, her tunic was off. At the sight of her lush, white breasts tipped with soft pink nipples, a warm heat flooded him. It was Morigan's turn to avert his gaze.

Her long, leathern skirt came next, falling to the ground with a soft, soughing sound. He swallowed hard. Without even seeing her, he recalled how she'd looked naked before. His sex swelled.

Turning, Morigan busied himself digging through the leather bag to extract two drying cloths and a container of cleansing sand. Then, the cloths held discreetly before him, he strode over to the edge of the heated pool, laid the cleansing supplies on the pool's stone edge, and lowered himself gingerly into the water.

Only then, shielded by the water, did Morigan dare glance up at Rissa. She stood there, a bemused look on her face, completely and unashamedly naked. "Well, obviously you decided to help with my bath," he growled, suddenly wary of her. "Don't stand there and catch a chill. Come into the water."

She smiled, one of those infuriatingly mysterious female kinds of smiles, and walked over. Sitting down at the edge of the spring, Rissa, instead of immediately jumping in, pulled her braid around and began to unfasten it. Long, silky strands of pale-gold unfurled from the braid to flutter down about her shoulders.

The seductive picture she made, a picture perhaps not as

unpremeditated as she might wish him to believe, Morigan thought sourly, sent hot blood pounding through his groin. His semiflaccid organ flared to its full, jutting height.

He bit back a groan and sank beneath the water. For a brief instant, Morigan sought respite from the taunting perfection of Rissa's young body, his earlier plan for a bath fast becoming one of the sorriest decisions of his life. The water swirled around him, pulsating with a life of its own, warm, soothing, and healing. He luxuriated in it, determined to stay in its surging depths for as long as his breath—

Something snared in his hair and tugged—hard—on the long strands. With a furious curse, Morigan rose to break the surface. "By the th-three moons, wh-what do you think you're d-doing?" he sputtered, flinging his sodden mane from his face.

She graced him with an innocent stare. "Well, so much for gratitude."

"Gratitude?"

"You stayed under so long, I feared you were drowning. I but sought to pull you up, thinking your strength not equal to the task."

Morigan raked a hand through his hair in aggravation. "I wished to savor the water for a moment, nothing more. There were too many distractions . . ." His glance snared on Rissa's breasts, half-covered by the water. Plump and moisture-sheened, they presented a delectable sight.

Once more, Morigan bit back a curse. He strode around Rissa to where the container of cleansing sand lay. Grabbing it, he twisted off its lid and whirled about. "Here, you said you wanted to help with my bath. It's past time we began."

She smiled and silently accepted the container. "Where would you like me to begin, my Lord?"

Morigan scowled. He could name one special place where

he'd like her hands around him, but knew he risked offending her if he named it. "My hair," he rasped instead. "If you would wash my hair . . ."

"As you wish." Rissa scooped out a large handful of the cleansing sand into one palm, added some water, and mixed it into a rich lather. "Turn around, if you will."

He hesitated but an instant longer, then did as she asked. She moved to stand behind him. "Kneel, if you would, my Lord. The water's not so deep here, and you're too tall for me to reach your hair otherwise."

Morigan sank to his knees. "Much better," she murmured, her soap-slick fingers slipping through his thick mane. She began a gentle kneading motion, thoroughly working her way over every millimeter of his scalp. His skin tingled, grew warm. Slowly, a delicious sense of calm and relaxation permeated him.

Gods, Morigan thought, but he'd never felt so good! "This is wonderful," he breathed. "If I'd known you possessed such a talent . . ."

"Hush," Rissa whispered huskily. "Don't say anything. Just enjoy it."

Yes, enjoy it, he told himself. Enjoy whatever she allowed herself to give, and not dare let himself want more. He had given his word, knew he must go slowly with her. If only his body didn't have other plans and desires!

He threw back his head and yielded to the firm pressure of Rissa's fingers, kneading, rubbing, and massaging his taut scalp, sending currents of delight rippling through him. He sighed, leaning against her.

Something hard, peaked, brushed his head. Her breasts. Morigan stiffened, afraid Rissa would draw away, but she didn't. Instead, to steady him, she pressed even more firmly against him. Her woman's mound nestled in the curve of his back. He thought he'd go mad.

"Lean on me," she said, her voice, low and throaty. "Let the anger, the bitterness, the hatred go. Trust me; need me. I swear I won't let harm come to you."

Strange, he thought from his dreamy haze, but her words, so applicable to their current situation in the pool, seemed to possess yet another, deeper meaning as well. As if . . . as if she were asking—

"Down you go," Rissa said, firmly pressing on his shoulders. "Time to rinse your hair."

Obediently, Morigan sank beneath the water, felt her gentle fingers stroke through his mane, shaking the suds away. And, then, she was pulling on his hair again, tugging him back to the surface. He turned, flinging back his dripping mane, and smiled up at her.

She grinned, then laughed.

"What?" he demanded, suddenly all wary male and fragile masculine pride. "What's so funny?"

"Oh, nothing," Rissa giggled. "For a moment there, you just looked like a drowned Arborian hopping rat. They're quite shaggy, you know and—"

"Yes, I can well imagine," Morigan said. "My thanks for the most complimentary comparison."

"Don't get indignant on me." She reached down to stroke the side of his face. "In all honesty, I found you quite endearing."

"Did you now?" he growled, suddenly, the predatory male sensing a softening in his female's defenses. He might not savor the pleasures of joining with Rissa this day, but Morigan would content himself with but a simple kiss or—dare he hope for it?—a brief clasp of naked, water-slick bodies. "I never considered myself particularly 'endearing,'" he said, moving closer, "but if it would win me a kiss, I'd gladly be anything you wish."

An impish light danced in Rissa's eyes. "A kiss? And that would satisfy you, would it?"

"Yes. It would have to, wouldn't it?"

Her eyes narrowed, and she cocked her head, as if considering that question. "In all truth, I cannot say. I've never been kissed by a man, at least not by any man save my father, and that was years ago. But yes, I believe I would like you to kiss me, Morigan."

Dimly, he realized he knew very little about Rissa's family and background, save she'd obviously lived a life of great wealth and ease. And then, as Morigan rose and closed the distance between them, as his upper abdomen brushed Rissa's jutting breasts, there was no time for further consideration of such petty concerns. A jolt of sensual awareness shot through him. For a fleeting moment, he forgot himself.

"Then, kiss you, I will." His arm encircled her, pulling her close. His throbbing erection pressed against her belly. His head lowered, until his mouth hovered but a warm breath from hers. "But be forewarned. This won't be some chaste little brush of lips or some lad's unskilled first attempt."

At the heady feel of him, at the anticipation of his mouth on hers, excitement thrummed through Rissa. "Indeed? Are you warning or bragging?"

"Neither. I'm just telling you how it'll be. How it has always been between us."

She gazed up at him, her eyes smoldering, hungry. "And how has it always been, Morigan? How?"

"Like this."

Before she could even draw breath into her suddenly constricted chest, he closed the final distance between them. His mouth settled over hers, hot, insistent, and wild—and so exquisitely, so deliciously sweet.

Rissa gasped. In her moment of unguarded surprise, Morigan plunged his tongue into her, questing, teasing, supping greedily of her mouth and lips and tongue. Her hands, clutching his upper arms, clenched, gouging into tautly drawn skin and bulging muscle. She tried to push away, both horrified and inexplicably drawn, but he held her fast.

Then Morigan groaned, low in his throat, the sound one of unfettered pleasure and anguished need. Something within Rissa shattered. All she knew was an overwhelming, an uncontrollable urge to press into him, to feel his hot hardness against her, to taste the sweetness of his mouth, his tongue. He was a confection, a precious nectar, a soul-sustaining, delightsome ambrosia. Rissa thought she'd never get enough.

With a soft, strangled cry she surrendered to the sweet, secret pleasure that was Morigan. Morigan, her mate, her love. Rissa clung to his massive shoulders, reveling in the rasp of his crisp body hair against her silky, highly sensitized flesh, mating her tongue with his in a fierce, passionate dance.

Shuddering in delight, Morigan responded, his ardor building to explosive heights, his body's needs, so long denied, blazing forth in an uncontrollable, mind-searing conflagration. He must have her, he thought through a passion-clouded haze.

Now.

Then he remembered, or perhaps that tiny voice, all that remained of his cursed conscience, managed to pierce the raging passion and fire and hunger. He'd asked but for a simple kiss and had vowed to deny himself until she came into her fertility. And, though he'd roused Rissa to the point of an almost equally senseless need, he still owed her what he'd promised.

A fierce tremor wracked his powerful frame. Morgan released Rissa, his hands moving from around her to grasp her arms. He shoved her back. "I think that kiss was sufficient," he said savagely. *"More* than sufficient, if the truth be known."

Rissa blinked, her tawny brown eyes clouding with confusion. "I-I didn't want to stop. Why *did* you stop, Morgan?"

He gave a harsh laugh. "Gods, femina! Isn't that obvious? I all but lost control just kissing you! We came to bathe, and bathe we will. Now, finish your bath," he ordered, his voice gruffer than he wished it to be, motioning to the container of cleansing sand sitting on the bank. He couldn't control, however, the trembling of his hands. "We'd better leave before things really get out of control."

"And why is that, Morgan?" Rissa silkily inquired. "I was just beginning to enjoy 'things.' "

He stared down at her, dumbfounded at her seeming naiveté. "Why? Why?" he demanded incredulously. "Gods, even for a maiden you can be singularly—" He inhaled a ragged breath. "Because," Morgan began again, his voice raw but calmer, "if we tarry here much longer, I fear I'll mate with you whether you want it or not!"

Rissa stepped up to him. Her hands settled upon his chest, boldly rubbing his thick pectoral muscles. Impudent fingers circled his flat male nipples. "And what is there to fear in that," she whispered, "if both of us want it? This *is* what this pool is meant for, isn't it?"

Morgan's heart skipped a beat, then commenced a wild pounding. "What are you saying, Rissa?"

"I am saying, you poor, befuddled man," she patiently explained, "that I've changed my mind. You brought me here intent on seducing me if you could. We both knew that from the start. And I've just decided to take you up on your most attractive offer."

Sixteen

Morigan studied her in thoughtful silence. As the seconds passed, Rissa thought she'd scream from the tension. Had she said something to offend? Had she been too forward?

Whatever was the matter with him? He acted as if he wanted her. Had she done irreparable damage to their relationship, that night before the right of challenge? Her thoughts whirled in a confused maelstrom of shame, anger, and frustration. She was no good at this seductive game. Ah, curse him! Curse all men!

Rissa backed away, flushing crimson. "I see I've overstepped myself in so boldly propositioning you. I didn't realize you liked the game only to be yours."

In a blur of movement, Morigan grabbed Rissa and pulled her to him. "No, that wasn't it at all, femina." His teeth flashed white in a lazy smile. "I was just wondering what your motive was this time. Pity, perhaps, at my debilitated condition? Concern that no female would want me now, as horribly scarred as I am?"

Her mouth quirked wryly. "Well, now that you mention it, you are rather pitiful looking, standing there all wet and waterlogged. And I'm certain no Cat Woman would have you anymore."

"Indeed, and why's that?"

A knowing woman's smile played about her lips. "Because

you're mine, Morigan. And you're the only one in this entire lair who hasn't realized it."

Something flickered in his striking eyes. "Then you *do* make this offer because you desire me?"

Rissa laughed, unaccountably touched by his surprising flare of vulnerability. "Of course, Morigan. Wasn't that obvious after the kiss we just shared? I only thought you were displeased with—"

He laid a finger upon her lips. "Hush, sweet one. There's no need to explain further. I'm more than happy to serve you and your needs in any way I can."

"B-but . . ." Rissa pulled back. "I don't know what my needs are, save that I like how you kiss me and how your body feels pressed against mine. And that," she blushed again and dropped her gaze, "I find you most pleasing and no longer fear the thought of mating with you." She lifted her gaze to lock resolutely with his. "I want you in every way a man and woman can know each other."

Morigan's lips twitched with laughter. His hands moved to settle on her waist. Ever so gently, he pulled her up and out of the water.

Rissa's eyes widened in bewilderment. "Wh-what are you doing?"

"Your legs." His voice lowered to a deep velvet whisper. "Wrap your legs around my waist."

"Oh, I couldn't do that," she murmured, shaking her head emphatically. "We're naked. I would touch . . . you . . ."

"Exactly, sweet one." His glance raked over her, her lithe young body moisture-slick and nubile, the pouting nipples so full, so succulent, so close to his hungry mouth. "You said you liked how our bodies felt together, that you wanted to know me in every way you could. There's no harm in this, only pleasure." Morigan smiled up at her, every bit the virile, confident, seductive male. "You do trust me, don't you?"

She nodded, unable to meet his gaze. "Yes," she whispered achingly. "I trust you, Morigan."

"Then come to me, femina." He lowered her back into the water and pulled her to him. "Hold me tight within the sweet prison of your legs. Press your breasts to my lips, and I promise I'll give you such pleasure as you've never known."

An image, of a hard, hungry mouth suckling her breasts, flooded Rissa's mind. Of Morigan's dark head bent over her white flesh, his lips worshiping, caressing her. She knew it for the shared psychic link it was. Knew it for the conjured vision in his own mind.

Yet, this time, Rissa accepted it eagerly. There was so much to learn, and this was but her first lesson, a lesson she wished to surrender to wholeheartedly and without reserve. As wholeheartedly as she wished to give herself to the exotically handsome Cat Man who held her so tenderly in his arms, the man who had stolen her heart with his courage, his selfless devotion to his people, his kindness, and his gentle patience toward her.

"Y-yes," she whispered. "Oh, yes, Morigan!"

His hands cupped her buttocks, clenching in the soft flesh for an instant before grasping Rissa and lifting her to him. She spread her legs, wrapping her silken limbs around his powerful, potent male body. The first touch of his manhood took Rissa's breath away.

His thick erection pressed like some stiff, deadly weapon between them. A weapon, velvet-sheathed as it was, capable of piercing her maidenhead and burying itself deep within her. A weapon that, no matter how lovingly he attempted to wield it, would put an end to the last vestiges of her youth and lead her, wounded but fulfilled, into womanhood.

In the same crazily sense-laden moment, Rissa both feared and desired him. Yet, one look into Morigan's tormented green-gold eyes sealed her fate. She would give him whatever he wished if only she could soothe his anguish forever—and make him happy once again.

"R-Rissa," he moaned, his hands drifting over her back in a slow, restless caress, moving her yet closer and closer to his heated length. "Don't ever leave me. I couldn't bear it if I lost you!"

"We'll make it work, my love," she breathed. "I know we will."

With an anguished groan, Morigan lowered his head to nuzzle her breasts. "Gods, but you smell so good! Like . . . like the sweet scent of these delicate moss flowers. Like sunlight on the mountain after a storm."

She giggled. "I never knew you to be a poet, my Lord, on top of all your other talents."

He smiled. "I do, indeed, have many talents. Tell me how well you like this, sweet one." Then, before Rissa could reply or utter protest, he took one pale nipple into his mouth and suckled it gently. Fire shot through her. She threw back her head, arching into him.

"M-Morigan!" Rissa whimpered. "Ah, what are you doing—"

"Don't you like it?" he growled, withdrawing to trace moist little circles about her suddenly turgid nipple. "Do you want me to stop?"

"S-stop?" Frantically, Rissa tried to clear her mind, to sort through the tangle of sensations and emotions bombarding her. "No . . . please . . . don't stop. I just don't understand . . ."

"What your body is capable of? Ah, but you will before we're done."

She smiled tremulously. "Yes."

One hand slipped across Rissa's buttocks to anchor her to him and, with his other hand, Morgan captured the side of her face. His expression was one of the most ineffable, loving things Rissa had ever seen. She thought her heart would burst with happiness. Then his mouth moved, taking hers in a fierce, passionate kiss.

Wildly, she stroked his back, her nails gouging into the bulge of moisture-dampened muscle and sinew. She pressed him close, greedy for the feel of him, needing contact with every delicious bit of his hard male body, and yet wanting still more. Wanting, craving . . . something . . . Something she instinctively knew only Morgan could give her.

Her hands traced a path down his back to grasp his taut male buttocks. At her touch, he clenched the powerful muscles and shuddered. His response only excited her more. She ran her nails beneath his buttocks to stroke his huge sac and the base of his stiffly throbbing erection.

Morgan sucked in a ragged breath. His eyes clenched shut. "R-Rissa! Gods, don't!"

"Why, my love?" she purred. "Don't you like it?"

"Curse you!" he gasped, capturing her hands, his eyes wild and passion-glazed. "You drive me to the very brink of my control!"

"And what will it take to drive you past it?" She pulled one hand free and lowered her gaze, her fingers toying with the Cat's claw nestled in his dense swirl of chest hair.

In response to her huskily couched query, Morgan loosened his hold to swing Rissa up into his arms. "You push too hard and too fast for your own good, femina," he snarled, his face contorting with the fierce effort it took to contain his release. "But you'll have what you wish of me—and now!"

He reached the side of the pool and laid her on a thick mound of moss flowers. The pressure of her body crushed the delicate lavender-pink blooms, releasing a fragrantly sweet scent. He climbed from the water, a dripping god of slick, sleek muscle and hair-roughened flesh, and moved to kneel beside her. Then, there was nothing else but Morigan, the feel of his strong hands on her, grasping her waist, lifting her to her knees, and turning her to face away from him, then the delicious rasp of his hair-whorled groin and stiff erection against her buttocks.

His fingers slid into her moist woman's cleft, thrust into her sheath. His touch, delving deeply into heretofore forbidden places, sent crazed little shivers shooting through Rissa. She arched her back to him, knowing only that the action would grant him greater access and that she wanted it with every fiber of her being. And, as he thrust his fingers repeatedly in and out of her, Rissa began an instinctive thrusting of her own.

"Yes, that's it, sweet one," his deep voice grated raw and ragged in her ear. "That's how your body will respond when I take you. Ah, Gods, but you're so wet, so hot for me!"

"M-Morigan!" Rissa cried, unable to bear the exquisite torment a moment longer. She was on fire, her body, her mind, her soul. "Take me. Now! I beg you!"

He shoved her down, until she leaned on her forearms. "You're mine. You've always been mine!" he groaned in hoarse triumph. "Mine, Rissa. Always and forever!"

In a swift, fevered action, Morigan grasped her hips with one hand and his manhood with the other. His glans, dark red and swollen, flared as it neared Rissa's lush white buttocks. For an instant, Morigan feared he'd spill his seed before he entered her.

Rissa, he told himself over and over. Rissa was what mattered, not his selfish desires. With trembling hand, he stroked his flesh against her. She whimpered, arching once more to him. He caught a glimpse of her moist, plump woman's flesh. The sight was finally enough to drive him over the edge.

In a swift, expert thrust, Morigan guided himself into her, driving his sex past the slight resistance of her maidenhead, impaling himself to his full length. Rissa cried out, stiffened, and went still. He leaned over her, pressing his body atop her back and buttocks, forcing himself to await the relaxation of her suddenly abused muscles.

His hands slipped around, one cupping a full, firm breast to knead the highly sensitized nipple, the other sliding down to find the secret button of flesh between Rissa's legs. She shivered when he touched her there and moaned, spreading her legs to give him greater access. And, as he gradually worked the tender bud to a swollen, raised nubbin, Rissa forgot the pain of her penetration. She began, once more, to move in sharp, rhythmic little jerks.

Morigan rode her, fighting, straining to his utmost ability to contain his release. Agony burgeoned within him. His abdominal muscles clenched and twisted. His body broke out in a sweat. He groaned, panted, cursed.

And finally, blessedly, Rissa came. The delicious sensations between her legs grew, building within her until they engulfed her in a mist of dark, heated passion. A passion that, finally, could no longer be contained.

She cried out sharply, her body racked with ecstatic spasms, spasms that gripped her in a maddened, fiery, primitive release. Everything tingled, felt on fire—her woman's sheath, her breasts, and nipples, her skin. Never. Never, had she imagined it could be like this!

As Morigan quickened his pace, driving into her now more roughly and deeply, Rissa's cries subsided to moans, then little whimpers. He braced one hand beside her to bear his weight and grasped her about her hips with the other. Bit by agonizing bit, his control shredded, exploding violently, ecstatically.

Morigan cried out, the sound savage and primal. Exquisite shudders racked his body. He arched into Rissa hard, froze for an instant, then thrust into her again and again. And all the while, in the depths of his passion he held her to him, never once relinquishing his hold, needing her there with him in his moment of release, needing her to complete his pleasure as he needed her to complete his life.

Gradually, the last vestiges of strength drained from him. His body still joined with hers, Morigan pulled Rissa down with him to lie on the fragrant bed of moss flowers, scooting her sweet woman's body back into the protective, possessive clasp of his arms.

There was nothing more to be said or experienced. He'd found his heaven and fulfillment in the arms of a brave, loving, and beautiful woman. A woman who was finally his mate—in every way.

She slept beside him in intimate abandon, snuggling close in the warm haven of his arms. Morigan held her tightly to him, too happy, too thrilled to find his own repose. They lay there for a time, warmed by the spring's heated mist until, finally, Morigan leaned over and kissed Rissa awake.

"Come, sweet one," he whispered, his voice rich and mellow against her ear. "Time for us to leave."

Rissa stirred, arching into him when he brushed his lips down the silken length of her neck and shoulder. "Just a while longer," she murmured sleepily. "It feels so good, lying here beside you."

"Then we'll do it again—this very night." Morigan turned Rissa to face him. His gaze, soft as a caress, brushed over her. "But it's past time I took you back to our lair and saw to my duties. The Council awaits me."

She frowned, remembering the purpose of the Council meeting. "What will you do with Cradoc?"

Morigan shrugged. "That's up to the Council."

"He won't change," she muttered, "no matter how you punish him. As much as I hate to say it, the Cat People would be safer if he were dead."

He smiled wryly and shoved himself to a sitting position. "You aren't worrying about one specific Cat Man above all, are you?"

She levered herself to an elbow. "Of course, I am! Cradoc won't be content until he's Cat Lord and you're dead. You must convince the Council of that, Morigan!"

"I'll do my best, femina." He pulled her up with him as he rose. His glance raked her naked form and his jaw hardened. Morigan turned, walked over to where the drying cloths lay and picked one up. Returning to Rissa's side, he wrapped it about her.

"I'm not cold." She gazed up at him in puzzlement.

"That's not why I covered you."

She cocked her head, bemused, then a smile of understanding lifted her lips. "Oh. And if I dropped this cloth right now, could you be persuaded to stay?"

"No." Morigan chuckled at her fledgling efforts at seduction. "Staying would only make things worse. You're tender from our first mating. You need time to heal. I won't mate with you again for the next seven days. It's the law."

"The law?" Rissa bit back another scathing opinion of the Cat People's laws. "How dare they intrude into the bedchamber with laws?"

His big hands settled on her shoulders. "Our females are precious to us. We wish no harm to befall them. It was hard enough hurting you in order to pierce your maidenhead, femina. I wish never to cause you pain in our mating again."

She took his hand in hers. "I have no regrets, Morigan. And I'm not so fragile that I can't bear a few days of discomfort." She lowered her head to kiss his big hand. "I wouldn't want to miss even one night of pleasure with you, no matter the price."

"And did I say there would be no pleasure?"

Rissa jerked her gaze back to his. "I don't understand."

"Mating isn't the only way to experience a deep and satisfying pleasure." He smiled wolfishly. "And your lessons have just begun."

She didn't know whether to flush or hug him for joy. A moment's consideration more and Rissa decided on the hug. After all, his lessons so far had never failed to please. And she certainly had no reason to begin doubting him now.

"By the five moons! I'm so glad my time of restriction will soon be over!" Rissa exclaimed five days later, as she sat beside the flickering hearth fire in Diona's lair. Hali was there as well, and all three women were busily engaged in sewing new tunics. Outside, a fierce winter storm ravaged the valley. Inside, however, they were snug and warm.

Rissa blushed, suddenly embarrassed by her outburst, when both pairs of eyes riveted on her. "Though Morigan has pleasured me in what must be every manner imaginable save for the actual joining of our bodies," she hurried to explain, "I confess to a longing for a true mating with all my heart!"

"Do you indeed?" came her maid servant's dry query.

"My, my, how my proud, defiant mistress has changed. You haven't stopped raving about Morigan in some form or another since you arrived here today. You're not perhaps in love with our handsome Cat Lord, are you?"

"And what if I am?" Rissa lifted the finger she'd just stabbed with her sewing needle to her mouth, her sudden realization where her unguarded talk was leading filling her with a belated caution. "It's no one's business but my own. And I'll thank the both of you to keep it to yourselves!"

Diona shot Hali a conspiratorial look. The girl blushed and lowered her gaze. "And who would we tell, at any rate?"

"Your Tavist, for one," Rissa readily supplied. "And, then, he'd go running to Morigan and tell him all."

"What's the harm in Morigan knowing you love him?"

"Nothing, I suppose, when I'm ready for him to know. But he's been so busy of late out hunting for game with the others, not to mention dealing with Cradoc's renewed attempts at undermining him. Ah, curse the Council for freeing Cradoc with nothing more than a stern warning! How can they be so blind?"

"Cradoc is a crafty one," Diona observed grimly. "He garbs all his acts against Morigan in the guise of well-meaning concern for the Cat People. And, though the harsh demands of winter will likely mute most of his subversive activity, he can well afford to bide his time. Further problems are sure to arise to use against Morigan."

Hali rose and walked over to stoke the hearth fire. Diona cast her a surreptitious glance, then scooted closer to Rissa. "Have you told him about your father yet?" she asked in a whisper.

Rissa paled. "No," she whispered back.

"Why not? The knowledge would be a terrible weapon in

Cradoc's hands, if he were ever to find out. Morigan must know, if he's to have time to prepare a defense."

"I-I'm afraid to tell him." Rissa bit her lip and looked away. "Our . . . relationship . . . is still so new. And his anger at Bellator—at my father—burns so close to the surface. I need more time . . . before I dare tell him."

Diona covered her hand with one of hers. "Have a care how long you wait. You risk even greater harm—both to Morigan and your love—by withholding this. Remember that, when the fear gives you pause."

Rissa lifted her gaze to lock with her friend's. "I will, Diona. I promise. The time must be right. That's all."

Hali walked up and pulled over her stool to join the other women. Diona smiled at her, then released Rissa's hand and leaned back. "I was just trying to convince Rissa here to tell Morigan she loves him. What do you think, Hali?"

The girl flushed. "I-I know nothing of such things. She should do what she feels best."

Rissa busied herself with her sewing, not daring to lift her gaze to Diona's for fear of laughing at her friend's skillful change in the course of the conversation. "My thanks, Hali, for your confidence in my ability to handle this in my own time and way. Besides, Morigan has said nothing to me of love, so I see no point—"

"Ah, I understand now," Diona chuckled. "You're afraid he'll think he has won, that he's now your lord and master."

"Lord and master, indeed!" Rissa scowled. "Perhaps, it would be better if we changed this subject as well."

Diona shrugged. "Have it your way. What do you think of the Cat Men's mating techniques?"

"Wh-what?"

"Their preference for the animal position—mating with

us from behind," her friend explained. "Tavist told me that's the way they always do it."

Rissa eyed her warily, not certain where this particular topic was leading. "Yes, and what of it?"

Her maid servant laughed. "Do you, like the Cat Men, think that's the only way to mate?"

"Well," Hali ventured, back in the conversation and suddenly embarrassed, "isn't it?"

"Yes, isn't it?" Rissa chimed in.

"No, most definitely not." A self-satisfied little smile stole across Diona's face. "And I must say Tavist was quite pleasantly surprised when I finally convinced him to let me take charge. When it comes to mating, Cat Men are wonderfully open to new experiences."

"Are they now?" Intrigued, Rissa laid down her needle. To teach the supremely experienced Morigan something new in the mating bed was far too tempting, even if it did require she wheedle the information out of her sly friend. "Are you planning on sharing some of your expertise with us, or do you just enjoy teasing?"

"Oh, I don't want to hear," Hali immediately protested. "I never want another Cat Man to touch me, much less mate with me!"

Rissa exchanged a frowning glance with Diona. Even the careful introduction of Hali to Lisan and his subsequent, well-chaperoned visits, had failed to ease the girl's fear of the Cat Men. The damage done by Limos had been great. Rissa had begun to wonder if it could ever be repaired. But Lisan, despite his less than friendly reception each time he visited Hali, seemed determined to continue. Because of that, Rissa would continue to help his cause, just as long as Hali appeared able to tolerate it.

"Well, don't listen if it offends you so," Diona said, laying down her own sewing. She again leaned close to Rissa and took her hand. "I'll tell you all," she whispered conspiratorially, "if you promise to let me know how your lessons go."

"Diona, what happens between Morigan and me is—"

"I don't want details, silly one," her friend hurried to assure her. "I just want to know if it worked, that's all. It would be wonderful to teach these proud Cat Men a thing or two, especially when it comes to mating. They think they're the supreme masters of it, you know."

"Well, aren't they?" Rissa asked. "I can't imagine finding more pleasure than I do in Morigan's arms."

Diona grinned. "Yes, they're quite masterful, to be sure. But it doesn't serve our purposes to let them think they're always in control. We women have our special talents as well. And the unexpected, you can be sure, brings the men back time and again."

"Then, tell me all," Rissa begged, leaning forward in eager anticipation. "I would dearly love to ruffle a bit of Morigan's eternally self-assured facade. Especially," she giggled, "when it comes to our lovemaking."

That night, as Rissa helped Sarna prepare the evening meal, the discussion turned, once again, to the impending end of Rissa and Morigan's time of mating restriction. Though it embarrassed Rissa that Morigan's mother not only knew they'd finally mated, but also when the restriction ended, the elderly Cat Woman seemed to take it all in stride. In fact, she seemed quite pleased and full of helpful, womanly advice.

"Morigan is bound, as are all our males, to the fulfillment of all your needs," Sarna happily rambled on. "If there is something that displeases you or fails to meet your fullest satisfaction about his mating techniques, you must not hesitate to tell him. He would be deeply offended if you kept such vital information from him. And it would lessen his own pleasure, as well." The old woman smiled up at her. "It is the psychic link, you know. We mate with the mind as well as the body."

"Er, yes," Rissa mumbled, grateful for the task of setting the table in order to avoid Sarna's piercing scrutiny. "My thanks for all your help in understanding your people's . . . er, mating practices."

"It is my duty, child. A strong life mating is the best foundation for parenthood." She began to count on her fingers. "Hmm, the babe should be born about early summer or so." Sarna glanced over at Rissa. "Ah, how I long for a sweet grandbabe! It will be such a blessing for us all."

"There's no guarantee I conceived that first time we mated," Rissa hurried to protest, "or will anytime soon."

"Cat Men are unfailingly potent, child," Sarna assured her. "And, though our own females have experienced difficulties of late, there is no reason for *your* fertility to be in question. Why, several of your own women are pregnant even as we speak."

Rissa frowned in puzzlement. "But how can you know that? Not quite a full month has passed since we were captured. It's too soon . . ."

"Not for Cat People. Just as our males can sense the fertile time of their mates, they also know when their seed takes root in their mate's womb. Morigan will know when you are with child."

Guilt flooded Rissa. She turned and hurried over to the fire to stir the pot of vegetable soup simmering there. Gods, was there no end to the deceitful games she must play with Morigan? Not only had she withheld the truth about her background and parentage, but she also had yet to tell him about her infertility, thanks to the contraceptive Zada had given her.

The contraceptive effect would cease in another two weeks, if not less, she consoled herself. That issue could most likely be ignored. Morigan needn't ever know. But the truth about her father . . .

Recalling Diona's words of warning earlier in the day, Rissa shivered. How would she ever be able to tell him about her father?

It wasn't Morigan's reaction to the revelation that worried her—at least not in the sense of some physical response of his that might endanger her life. No, it was the fear he might turn from her, that his bitterness against her father was so great it would overshadow everything else. And it was also the fear of what the other Cat People—and the Council of Elders and Cradoc, in particular—might do with the information.

As Lord of his people Morigan would, at the very least, feel obligated to share the information with the Council. And, as Lord, he would also be obligated to abide by the Council's decisions—even if, in the end because of who her father was, the Council decided against their life mating.

Perhaps she was worrying needlessly, but Rissa didn't think so. It was one thing for the Cat People to accept her, a Bellatorian, as their lord's mate. It was an entirely different matter for them to accept the daughter of the man who had ordered their slaughter.

"Child, will you stir the soup until it turns to mush?"

Sarna's voice, edged with concern, intruded into Rissa's anguished thoughts. She glanced up. The old Cat Woman stood at her side. Rissa flushed and pulled the spoon from the pot. "I-I'm sorry, domina. My thoughts were elsewhere."

"Here, dish me up some soup." Morigan's mother handed her a thick pottery bowl. "I've a wish to retire early this night."

Rissa accepted the bowl. "But I was hoping to share the meal with you and Morigan."

"Not tonight, child." Sarna smiled down at her. "This is a special time for you and my son. You should be alone. There will be time enough for me once the foundation of your life mating is strong."

Alone with Morigan. And alone, as well, with my guilt, my doubts, and fears, Rissa thought morosely as she ladled out a generous helping of the savory soup. Then, mired in an ever deepening morass of indecision and dread, she rose and joined Sarna at the table.

Tonight was indeed a special time—as all the nights since their first mating had been—one she anticipated with great longing and excitement. Yet, conversely, the thought of it also filled her with a sharp, searing pain. Tonight could only serve to deepen her and Morigan's relationship as they once more joined hearts and minds, if not bodies. But, in the end, the same deepening would only serve to heighten the inevitable pain—when she finally found the courage to tell him who she really was.

Seventeen

Two days later, Morigan stalked back to his lair in a raging snow storm, through the all-consuming darkness and howling wind, his thoughts elsewhere, his spirit deeply troubled. Too much. There was just too much, one more overwhelming problem heaped upon his shoulders after another.

Brandar had returned but a few hours ago, through the snow and cold and nearly impassable mountains, to report a stunning revelation. One of the captured females possessed a political significance that could well mean the Cat People's salvation. Or, conversely, serve as the ultimate revenge against the Lord Commander.

In their attempt to gain breeding females and set into motion their renewed war against the Bellatorian presence on Agrica, it seemed their hunting party had inadvertently captured the only child of Fautor Lindatees. A child he now offered a substantial ransom for—in the form of amnesty for the Cat People. The war between them would be over, the remaining Cat People free to return to their former way of life with no danger of further retribution, if only they returned Lindatees's daughter.

But two questions remained. Which of the females was Lindatees's daughter and should they return her?

A part of Morigan—the part seething with a barely contained rage against the Lord Commander—wanted to keep the daughter here, to punish Lindatees in the only way he could. It was poor revenge—one female in payment for the lives of thousands—but at present it was all the power he possessed over the Lord Commander. Murdering her and sending her lifeless body back to Lindatees had never been an option. The Cat People didn't kill innocent, helpless beings.

A pressing dilemma, to be sure, Morigan thought, one that must be solved soon. Until he could devise a plan, however, he had sworn Brandar to silence. Naren was the only other Cat Man who knew. Tomorrow was soon enough for the Council to be told.

Tonight, he needed time to sort through this new and disturbing information. Tonight, he needed to determine how to discover the identity of the female who had kept her secret so carefully hidden. A secret that must be exposed without stirring anew the barely subdued animosity against the Bellatorian females.

By the three moons! Morigan cursed as he plowed through the ever deepening snow and gusting winds. Just when it appeared, after Rissa's brave defense of his life against Cradoc and the Council, that his people were finally coming to accept the captive females, this had to happen. They would never tolerate Fautor Lindatees's daughter in their midst. Gods, *he* couldn't even stomach the idea!

Rissa. He would get Rissa to help him search out Lindatees's daughter. She cared for him and for his people. That much had been made abundantly clear in the passing weeks—and especially, since she'd come willingly into his arms at the pool. She would understand the delicacy of his problem and would help him.

A passing doubt, if Rissa could herself be Lindatees's daughter, snaked through him. She was from a higher social class than most of the other females, intelligent, and unabashedly outspoken in her opinions. But, surely, she would have told him. If not when he first captured her to protect herself from what she then saw as his loathsome advances, then later, after they'd mated. Surely, then, Rissa would've wanted all secrets between them revealed.

He considered briefly probing her mind one more time as he climbed the path up to his lair, then fiercely shoved the thought aside. It wasn't Rissa. It *had* to be one of the other females.

Morigan found her in his bedchamber, folding clean clothes that she'd washed earlier in the day. Before she even suspected his presence, he had his hands on her shoulders and was turning her around.

"Morigan!" With a husky laugh Rissa was in his arms, her hands twined about his neck.

"Did I frighten you, sweet one?" He savored the soft curves pressed so warmly to him. If only he could block out all the problems, even if but for a short time, in her arms!

"You know you did," she pouted teasingly. "At every opportunity, you use your Cat powers and always to *my* disadvantage. It's not fair."

"And what of your own, special female powers?" he growled. "Do you deny their use is unfair?"

She leaned back and frowned, apparently considering his question. "I think fairness has nothing to do with it," Rissa finally replied. "It's more a matter of self-defense."

"Against what? Me?"

"But, of course, you silly man." Rissa laughed. "You don't imagine I could ever be some simpering love slave, obedient to your every wish or whim, do you?"

A slow, lazy smile crept across his face. "Never. I'd never imagine such a ludicrous thing. Nor," he added, with a dry chuckle, "would I want you any way other than how you are. A strange concept, desiring a female who's defiant, sharp-tongued, and proud, but one I find, nonetheless, strangely appealing. As long as you don't make a habit of such behaviors," he hastened to add when he saw a mischievous light twinkle in her tawny brown eyes.

"Oh, I won't, my Lord." Rissa smiled in turn. "There's no need, just as long as *you* remember *your* place."

"Which is?"

"My love slave obedient to *my* every wish or whim." A slender blond brow arched in query. "You haven't forgotten what day this is, have you? My time of restriction is over."

He threw back his head and roared, the cares that had followed him through the wind and snow finally fading in the rising heat of the past minutes with the fiery Rissa. "By the three moons, but you've quickly become the seductive little she-cat." With an effort, Morgan forced himself to sober. "No, I haven't forgotten, femina. But first, if you think you can contain your eagerness for a short while longer, I've a wish for some of that stew I smelled cooking over the fire. That and a time to speak with you about a new problem that has arisen."

Rissa cocked her head, concern flaring in her eyes. "A problem? Is it Cradoc again?"

"No." Taking her arm, Morgan led her from the bedchamber. "It isn't Cradoc." He glanced around when they reentered the main room. "Where's Mother?"

"As always of late, she ate her meal earlier and went to bed." Rissa smiled. "She wished to give us some time alone, considering . . ."

A warm light smoldered in his eyes. "You've done so much for my mother. In just the few weeks you've been here with us, your kindness and concern for her have helped bring her out of her shell far more than any of our efforts the past cycle have. I can't thank you enough."

Rissa flushed. "She was ready, that's all. Anyone could've helped her."

Morigan released her arm to cup her face between the callused expanse of his two, big hands. "No, you're wrong, Rissa. Only you could've done it. Just as you've thawed that block of ice that was once my heart." His lips brushed hers. "You're all the mate I could ever wish for."

A hunger, to feel his mouth settle over hers in a hard, hungry, fulfilling kiss and to press against him in naked abandon, flooded Rissa. Instead, she forced herself to set her selfish desires aside and push away from him. He said nothing, only stared down at her with a quizzical look.

"Your . . . your supper." She turned to grab a bowl and hurry over to the pot. "You said you were hungry."

Behind her Morigan chuckled, a deep, rich sound that prickled warmly down Rissa's spine. He pulled out a chair. There was something about the harsh scrape of wood against hard-packed earth that filled her with a fierce, soulful sense of contentment. This was as it was meant to be, she thought, as she bent to ladle up a bowlful of thick, flavorful stew. Snug and warm in their lair, a fearsome winter storm blowing outside, with the eager anticipation to come of a night spent in passion and love in each other's arms.

She returned to the table, offered Morigan the stew and a spoon, then lowered her gaze, suddenly shy with him and her newly discovered emotions. Seemingly unaware of anything but the mouth-watering meal placed before him, Morigan dug into the stew. Rissa busied herself in pouring him a cup of uva wine and adding several thick slices of brown bread to a wooden platter, which he hungrily accepted to wolf down along with his stew.

It was enough to sit there at the table across from Morigan and watch him, she mused dreamily. Everything he did, be it eating a meal or taking command of some problem, was done in the same confident, forceful manner. As was even his mating . . .

"What are you thinking, femina?" Morigan paused with his cup of wine halfway to his lips. "You seem suddenly elsewhere."

Rissa started. "What?" She blushed. "Oh, it was nothing. I was just thinking how pleasant it is, being here with you, watching you eat."

His mouth quirked. "Watching me eat, eh? A most entertaining experience, to be sure." He swiped at his mouth with the back of his hand. "Have I some food on my face, perhaps?"

She laughed, softly, tenderly and leaned over to flick a crumb of bread from the corner of his mouth. "Only that. Your table manners are impeccable, my Lord."

"That's reassuring." Morigan laid down his cup, his expression turning solemn. "I mentioned a problem I need your help with. It concerns one of the other Bellatorian females."

Puzzlement wrinkled her brow. "I would help you if I can. You know that, my Lord."

A bleak look flattened the usual self-confident gleam in his green-gold eyes. "There's one among you who hides her identity. I must know who she is, but I don't wish for her secret to become common knowledge." He reached over and took Rissa's hand. "It would only cause unnecessary pain and turmoil again."

"I understand. I, too, wish for peace and acceptance among us all. Tell me what it is you wish me to do."

He inhaled a deep breath. "When we captured you and the others, we unknowingly captured the daughter of the

Lord Commander. He knows we have her and has offered a ransom for her return. I must know who she is."

Ice spread through Rissa, moving up her body to encase her heart in a prison of cold. Her hands went numb; her chest constricted. For a terrifying moment, the room swirled dizzingly before her. Then Morigan's grip on her hand tightened painfully, pulling her back.

"Rissa. Femina," he whispered hoarsely. "What's wrong?"

She shook her head, a head that suddenly throbbed with the effort to keep herself from fainting, to maintain some semblance of normalcy in a world gone spinning out of control. "N-nothing. Nothing's wrong. Your . . . news . . . just surprised me." She forced herself to meet his searching gaze. "Do you know who the female might be?"

"No," he sighed. "That's why I need your help. I thought you might have some idea or could at least quietly find out for me."

"And what will you do to her, once you find her?"

He scowled. "I don't know. Unfortunately, the decision isn't just mine. The Council will be brought in on this."

"The ransom. What did the Lord Commander offer?"

"Amnesty for my people." His jaw went taut, hard as stone. "If we dare trust his word."

Rissa choked down the lump that had risen in her throat. "A powerful incentive for the return of his daughter. One you cannot turn from lightly."

Morigan shoved a hand through his mane, setting the strands as awry as his tumultuous mood. He averted his gaze. "No, I certainly can't."

"What if she doesn't want to go? What if she has decided to make her life with the Cat People? What if she loves her mate, and he, her?"

He turned back to Rissa, riveting her with an anguished

look. "In light of the greater needs of our people, none of that may matter." He shook his head. "I just . . . don't know."

"But you're the Cat Lord!" Rissa cried. "If you don't make some decision on this before you go to the Council, you *know* what they'll decide. None of them really seemed happy with our presence in the lair. They'll gladly send Lindatees's daughter back!"

"I suppose not if the female already carried her mate's child." Morigan picked up his cup of wine, toying with it briefly before tossing the remainder of its contents down his throat. "A Cat Child might be a strong incentive to consider keeping her here."

Like the dead, dried leaves clinging to the skeletal autumn trees, Rissa felt her options blown, one by one, away. A child. A child growing within her body would've been her only chance to convince the Council to let her stay.

A child. Morigan's child. But she'd taken Zada's contraceptive and was now infertile. Her own ploy to thwart the Cat Lord had, in the end, been turned against her!

It was too much. Too much to bear. No sooner than she'd found love and a purpose to fulfill her life, it was taken from her. The thought of returning to her father, to the safe, comfortable, and now unattractive life of a Bellatorian gentlewoman, no longer filled her with longing. She wanted to stay here, with Morigan, with Sarna and Naren and Agna and Diona. She wanted—

"Ah, Gods!" Rissa buried her face in her hands. "What have I done? Ah, what have I done?"

A chair scraped back. In the next instant, Morigan was beside her, pulling her to stand before him. She forced her tear-filled gaze to meet his. A wary, narrow look gleamed in his eyes.

"What are you saying, Rissa? Are you . . ." He paled, his

eyes widening in rising disbelief and horror. *"Gods, tell me you aren't Lindatees's daughter!"*

She tried to turn away, but he grasped her chin in an unrelenting grip and forced her to face him. The tears spilled over and streamed down her cheeks. "And w-would my lie ch-change what is?" she sobbed. "What would you have me d-do, lay this instead on one of the o-other women?"

His mouth drew into a ruthless, forbidding line, "No," he ground out the word. "I'd have you finally tell me the truth—once and for all."

Rissa wrenched her face away. "Then hear it, once and for all. My name is Rissa Lindatees. I am Fautor Lindatees's daughter. The man you hate above everything else in life."

Morigan sucked in a ragged breath. "Gods, Rissa! Why didn't you tell me? Did you think me such a monster I would've hurt you to avenge my people?"

"No. No," she whispered. "Well, perhaps at first, but not for a long while now. But I wanted to escape, and I knew you'd lock me away before you'd let that happen, if you knew who my father was. And then, later, as we became . . . closer, I was afraid to tell you because I thought you'd turn from me." She lifted glistening eyes. "I thought if only we'd a little more time . . ."

"And, now, there's no time left, is there, femina?" Morigan's hands fell to his sides. His big body trembled with the effort to contain his anger and pain and frustration. "You've hidden the truth from me and, in doing so, destroyed what little advantage I may have ever had to remedy this problem."

Morigan wheeled about and strode over to stand before the fire, his broad, leather-clad back turned from her. For long, anguished moments, Rissa watched him, filled with a sense of despairing, utter helplessness. To hurt him, to cause him pain and problems, had seemingly been her fate since the first moment they'd met. Perhaps it was best this had happened, before she managed finally to destroy him.

Rissa walked over to stand beside Morigan, wanting, needing, to touch him, but didn't. "I'm sorry for all the trouble I've caused you. I would at least like to make this as easy for you as I can. What would you have me do?"

He drew in a shuddering breath, his chest seesawing with the effort it took to control himself. Then he turned to her. His face was white, withdrawn, sealed off in his grief. "I don't know, Rissa," Morigan softly said. "I'm out of answers. What do you want to do?"

Anger, inexplicably, surged through her. Curse him! Why must the answers come from her? He was the one with all the power. He was the one who would decide if she stayed or went. She opened her mouth to tell him so, when something in his eyes gave her pause.

It was a look of haunted hunger, of barely leashed anguish, of walls not well-fortified, revealing teetering inner defenses. Defenses that she, with but a few, well-placed and heartless words, could send crumbling down. Her reply, Rissa realized, would determine what course he took in this cruelly timed dilemma. And would determine perhaps, as well, whether he shut the doors to his heart once more—or left them open.

This time she owed Morigan the truth, all of it, no matter how he accepted it, no matter if it angered him so badly he finally turned from her. Only then could he be fully armed to do battle. Only then could he have any hope of victory.

"I want to stay with you, Morigan." She faced him proudly, all the love in her heart shining in her eyes. "I want to be your mate, bear your children, help you with your people. I no longer want to go back to my father or the life I once had. *You* are my life now."

A wild hope sprang to his eyes. He took a step toward

her. She lifted a hand. "There is one thing more. No matter how hard you try, you cannot get me with child for another week or two. When I was at Zada's, I begged her for a contraceptive, and she gave it to me."

Shock blazed in Morigan's eyes, then gradual realization. "Gods, Rissa. Have you managed finally to close off every avenue of hope for us?" He groaned. "I should've guessed. Your fertile time is past due. I just never thought Zada would betray me . . ."

"It was only a temporary thing," Rissa rushed to defend the old healer. "I was so afraid of you then, so intent on escaping and dreading the possibility of bearing your child, of being your breeder. It was the only chance I had for some control over my body. Zada understood. She gave me a contraceptive to protect me, to buy me a little time, that's all."

"Yet, if she hadn't, you might already be carrying my child. And I might have had some reason to justify keeping you here." The Cat Lord's shoulders sagged. His head lowered until his dark mane cascaded about his face. "I don't want you to go, Rissa, but I've nothing left with which to fight for you. You've taken everything from me."

"No, not everything!" Rissa grasped his face in her hands, smoothing back the long locks, lifting his gaze to hers. "We're life mates. We're joined now, body and mind and heart. Surely, that will mean something to the Council. Surely, that will touch them!"

Morigan smiled wanly, then turned his face to kiss her palm. "Perhaps, femina. Perhaps." He took her hands and clasped them between his. "One way or another, there's nothing more to be done about it this night. Come, I'm weary. Come to bed and hold me."

A smile trembled on her lips. "I'd like that very much, my love. Tonight . . . and for the rest of our lives."

He nodded. "Tonight—and always." Morgan turned and led her down the tunnel to their bedchamber. Behind them, the winter storm howled out its lament. As it swept through the mountains, its mournful cry echoed off rock and earth, a mocking reflection, Rissa realized, of the anguished emotions beating within two hearts. Two hearts that had finally found love—only now to risk losing it.

"Please, Morigan," Rissa pleaded the next morning. The storm had abated but the day was shrouded in a dim, fog-laden haze. "Please let me go with you to stand before the Council."

He shrugged into his thick, phoca fur cloak and fastened it closed before turning to her. Naren, who waited just inside the doorway, caught his pointed glance. He lifted the leather skin and stepped outside.

Morigan took Rissa by the shoulders. "No, femina," he softly reiterated his earlier decision. "Your presence on such a delicate occasion would only inflame feelings all the more. Our personal concerns are greatly outweighed by the larger risk to my people if you aren't returned. This must be handled very carefully if we're to have any hope of success."

"I realize that, Morigan, but I am your lady," she protested. "As such, I should think my desires would count in this lair. It certainly seemed to have made an impression when you fought Cradoc."

"And in most cases it does, and will." Morigan ran his finger down the side of her face, his touch tender, loving. "But not this time. This issue is too fraught with old pains and memories, with barely buried vengeances. I can plead the cause of our life mating, the affection between us, without your presence. And, as much as I hate to say it, my need for you will hold greater weight with the Council than yours for me."

"I'm certain it will." She took his big hand in hers and kissed it fervently. "Then, go, Morigan. Go and fight for us. And know I am there in spirit, if not in body."

"I'll remember, femina." He paused a moment longer then turned and, lifting the flap, exited the cave.

Naren awaited him. His brow arched in query. "She took it well then?"

Morigan nodded. "Better than I'd hoped. She didn't like staying behind, though, you can be sure." He strode out, Naren at his side. "The situation, nonetheless, is grave. Though I tried to pretend otherwise with Rissa, this time, I fear there's nothing I can say that will sway the Council."

"Amnesty is a powerful incentive," his friend agreed, "if we dare trust the Lord Commander. One female, even if she *is* your mate, is hardly worth risking a treasure like that."

"I know," Morigan muttered bleakly. "But, Gods, Naren, to lose Rissa now that I've finally won her! I don't know what I'll do if I have to give her up!"

"You'll do what the rest of us have done. You'll go on. What other choice is there?"

"I'm sick to death of never having choices!" Morigan's hand clenched, knuckle-white, in the folds of his cloak where he held it closed against the frigid winds. "You know how I felt about taking a new mate so soon after Winna's death, and especially a Bellatorian, but I did my duty. And, now, when I've finally come to love her . . ."

"We'll fight, the two of us, for your right to keep Rissa. Somehow, we'll make the Council see."

As he walked along, Morigan's jaw set in implacable determination. "Yes, that we will, my friend. Lindatees won't honor his offer. I know it. The man isn't to be trusted. And

I won't lose Rissa in some futile attempt to win the Lord Commander's goodwill. The man is our direst enemy. We must never forget that."

"Have a care how you press your cause," Naren cautioned, bending his head against the bitter winds. "Though your desire for vengeance against Lindatees is justified, as is your mistrust of him, it can be misconstrued as stronger than your concern for our people. And, coupled with your affection for Rissa . . ."

Morigan drew up before the cave housing the Council chambers and turned to his second-in-command. "I know the pitfalls that lie ahead, my friend. All I ask is that you stand by me."

Naren clasped his shoulder for a brief moment, a fierce resolve gleaming in his eyes. "We've endured much together in the past. We'll endure much in the future. But no matter what happens, we'll always do so together. This I swear."

A big hand settled over his. "I feared once Rissa might be the wedge that finally drove us apart. I could see you desired her. For a time, I feared she desired you as well." Morigan's voice cracked, went rusty with emotion. "I don't deserve either of you."

"You're wrong, my friend," Naren growled, his own voice gone taut. "Even a fool such as I couldn't miss the fact you and Rissa were right for each other." He managed a lopsided grin. "Why do you think I chose her for you in the first place?"

"To torment me?" Morigan asked wryly, releasing his compatriot's hand. "To prevent me from having even a moment's peace of mind? To send me plummeting into the depths of madness as I strove to understand Rissa?"

Naren's grin widened. "Perhaps. But, perhaps, most of all, to shake you out of that emotionless prison you'd encased your heart in. And to force that heart of yours to beat anew with hope and happiness and love." He cocked his head and, letting go of Morigan's shoulder, stepped back. "It's working, isn't it?"

"Yes, it's working all too well," his lord agreed, his mouth twisting grimly. Then, squaring his shoulders, Morigan gestured for Naren to proceed him into the cave.

The Council listened with raised brows and pale countenances to Brandar's tale. Then, after some succinct questions to clarify a few points, Ardan, as eldest and head of the Council, dismissed the Cat Man. Once Brandar was gone, he turned to Morigan.

"We must discover the identity of the female as soon as possible. No time can be lost—"

"I already know the female's identity," his grandson brusquely cut him off, rising. "But that's hardly the issue. The Council needs to decide what to do about Lindatees's offer."

Ardan frowned. "Isn't that obvious? One female to ensure the safety of our people is more than a fair price. We'll give the Lord Commander what he wants."

Morigan and Naren exchanged glances. "And I say," the Cat Lord began again, "Lindatees isn't to be trusted. We waste a precious breeding female for naught if we give her over to him."

"I agree with Morigan," Naren said, standing. "Why lose even one female to play into Lindatees's hands? He'll take his daughter back, laugh at our foolish desperation, and immediately return to his war against us."

"Or, he might well see our offer as an overture of peace," the elderly Cat Man countered, "as a sign of our willingness to work with him, compromise." Ardan cocked a speculative brow. "There's more here than just suspicion of the Lord Commander's true intentions, isn't there?" His gaze swung to Morigan. "Exactly who *is* the female, my Lord?"

Morigan's features twisted fleetingly in a mask of anguish. He turned to his grandfather. "Rissa. Rissa is Lindatees's daughter."

The old Cat Man's eyes widened, comprehension, then concern darkening them. "I see," he replied softly. "That complicates things, doesn't it? Complicates, but changes naught. It seems we have no choice but to return her to her father." Ardan glanced about at the other Council members. "Have any of you comment to offer?"

The rest of the Council was unanimously in favor of Ardan's decision that Rissa be taken back to Primasedes to ensure the Lord Commander's offer of amnesty. Ardan turned back to Morigan. "Have you anything else to say on this matter before we take a formal vote?"

Despair welled in Morigan, bitter, acrid, soul-searing. Then, anger rushed in, setting his gut to churning and his heart to pounding. He rose, his hands clenched at his sides. A fierce indignation—at the injustice, the unfairness of it all—flooded him.

"Rissa's my life mate," he ground out the words. "I love her. She loves me. And, almost more importantly, I need her. She fills me with joy. She challenges me, compels me to delve deeper into my motives and decisions. She presses me to be an even better man—and leader." Morigan's fisted hand rose to press against his chest. "And, yet, you can sit there and callously decide to send her away with barely a few minutes' deliberation. With barely a second thought, you toss my pleas aside, then turn to the cold-blooded act of voting on something that, though it means little to you, means everything to me!"

"You are Lord," Ardan's stoic words pierced the mists of Morigan's torment. "If it requires the sacrifice of everything you hold dear for the sake of our people, you must give it. You were raised to know your sacred duty; it is pointless to rail against it now. *Especially* now and for a Bellatorian female, no less, no matter how desirable you find her. There will be other females. There won't be many other chances as good as this to save our people."

Morigan clamped down on a bitter retort. His grandfather spoke true. He did know his duty and had known the probable outcome of this Council even before it had convened. He was just so weary, so tired of compromising, of constantly having to put his own needs and happiness aside. They would pick him clean with their demands someday, he thought despairingly, until he was nothing more than an outward shell, his insides gutted, his emotions dried and shriveled, a useless husk of a man.

Had his father ever felt thusly? Was this all that was ultimately left for any ruler? He didn't think so. It was only the times that had forced him into such an untenable position. It was Lindatees—curse his vicious, heartless soul—who had brought him to this. The man had taken his first mate from him. He would now take Rissa as well.

Rissa. Ah, Gods, he would lose Rissa!

"Vote, then," Morigan snarled, wanting it over, done with before he shamed himself before them all. He steeled his features into an expressionless mask. His pain was his own. He wouldn't expose his heart, nor wallow in further and pointless self-pity. "But you—all of you—are wrong about Lindatees. You'll see that in time. Mark my words well."

Compassion gleamed in Ardan's eyes. "That may be, my

Lord, but we have no other choice. It is a chance worth taking." He turned to glance down the row of other Elders. "Who wishes for the female to be sent back to her father?"

Ten hands lifted. Ardan's expression never altered. "And who wishes to keep the female in the lair?"

Only Morigan's and Naren's hands raised this time. The elderly Cat Man sighed. "The vote is ten to two, my Lord. The female must be returned to the Lord Commander."

"When?" Morigan demanded hoarsely.

Ardan considered the question for a moment. "As soon as possible. When the storm clears and the passes through the mountains open. You may choose the man to escort her back. It would not be wise or kind to either of you, if you were to take her back yourself."

As if struck by a blow, Morigan shuddered with each word that fell from his grandfather's lips. Rissa, gone in perhaps a few more days. Taken away by another, never to be seen again.

"Naren will take Rissa," he forced himself to reply, shooting the other man a questioning glance that was immediately answered with a nod. "She'll at least return with a friend at her side."

"So be it," Ardan said. "See to the preparations for the journey." He paused, eyeing his grandson intently. "Is there more you wish to say, my Lord?"

Morigan's jaw hardened. "There seems no point, does there?"

"No, I suppose not. This meeting is now at an end."

As was the fragile hope of a new life, a new beginning with the woman he loved, Morigan thought in bitter, searing despair. Why had he thought it could ever be any other way? With that, the Lord of the Cat People turned on his heel and stalked from the Council chambers.

Eighteen

Rissa waited all day, knowing, as the hours ticked by, things hadn't gone well in the Council meeting. It was the only explanation for Morigan's extended absence. He couldn't find the courage to face her.

That realization hurt as much as the growing knowledge she would soon be leaving him. While he selfishly chose to deal with his pain alone, he left her to burn with hers. To burn with the uncertainty, with the dread gnawing in her gut like wildfire, and with a deep, hollow grief nothing could ever hope to fill. Nothing, save Morigan at her side, cradling her in the warm, protective haven of his arms, whispering reassurances that somehow, someway, they'd always be together.

A gray haze settled over the valley as morn eased into afternoon, then early evening. The temperatures plummeted once more and a bone-aching cold filled the air. Rissa stoked the hearth fire incessantly to keep it at a roaring blaze. By twilight, the wood supply had diminished to a small pile of twigs and tinder. Dreading venturing out into the frigid night but knowing there wasn't any other choice with Morigan still gone, Rissa finally rose and donned her fur cloak.

Sarna, snuggled up next to the fire and working on another tunic, glanced over. Wood smoke and heat from the fire cast a shimmering haze between them. "Where are you going, child?"

Rissa gestured to the scanty wood pile. "We need more fuel. Tonight will be unbearable if we don't keep the fire going."

The old Cat Woman frowned. "Morigan should be back any time now. Let him bring in wood."

"It'll take both of us, at any rate," Rissa said, smiling, "to bring in enough wood for the night. Besides, I'm tired of being cooped up in here all day. A bit of exercise outdoors will do me good."

"Yes, I suppose so." Sarna laid down her sewing, a look of confusion clouding her eyes. "I don't understand what's taking Morigan so long. No Council meeting has ever gone on all day. And he's never been this late, especially with the evening meal waiting."

Rissa knew exactly why the Cat Lord hadn't returned, but chose not to elaborate. Sarna didn't know about Brandar's return or of the real reason for the Council meeting today. And Rissa didn't have the heart to tell her. Let her son, the brave and all-powerful Cat Lord, tell her. *If* he ever again had the courage to face either one of them.

"He'll return soon, I'm sure, domina." Rissa paused at the leather door covering to pull her hood up over her head. "And, in the meanwhile, I'll keep us nice and warm with more wood."

Before Morigan's mother could reply, Rissa lifted the door flap and stepped outside. Immediately, a raw wind engulfed her, swirling her cloak about her, penetrating to probe at tender flesh with icy fingers. Rissa shivered and pulled the heavy fur more closely to her, lowering her head against the frigid blasts of air to slog on down the trail that led from their lair.

The wood had been but an excuse to escape the heavy sense of doom and hopelessness pervading the little cave, that rose around her to press down upon her spirit, threatening to snuff out all the joy she'd ever experienced here. Morigan had already deserted her, if not in body, then in heart and mind.

Before, she would've attributed that fear to a woman's hysterical imaginings. But not now. Now, she knew the truth of it with a surety sprung from some place outside her. Perhaps, it was the psychic link that had grown between them, but Rissa *felt* Morigan drawing back to spare his own heart.

The communal wood pile, hidden from overhead view in a thick stand of trees, was only a short walk from Morigan's cave. Rissa hurried over to it, loaded as many of the split logs of pungent sempervivus wood as she could into her arms, then fought her way back through the wind and cold. A half hour later and several trips more, however, did little to diminish Rissa's anguish or increase the height of the wood pile. Sarna seemed to be adding fuel to the fire as fast as Rissa brought it back.

There was nothing to be done save continuing to carry in wood. Once again, Rissa headed out into the biting wind. As she walked along, a light flurry of crystalline flakes scattered before her, rising to cling to her face, a face gone numb from the frigid temperatures. Just a few trips more, Rissa thought wearily. Just a few trips more before she must stop to warm herself by the fire.

But not yet, she fiercely commanded herself, struggling out of the heavy exhaustion that had suddenly consumed her as she stooped once more to gather wood. The pain in her heart was still too fresh, too raw. And the dark, glacial night, swallowing her in its maw of blackness and anonymity, was kin to her mood. Alone, cold, bereft. It almost felt good to be so numb, to no longer feel her hands and feet. Soon, if she were lucky, that lack of all sensation would creep through her body to encompass her. Then, at last, she could return to the lair and warm herself—

A big hand ensnared her arm and jerked her to her feet. Startled, Rissa whirled around, slipped, then went down on one knee. The armload of wood flew into the air.

"Little fool!" Morigan snarled, pulling her back to her feet. "Are you intent on killing yourself out here in the cold? This is no time for you to be outside!"

Rissa twisted from his grasp. "And what do you care?" she cried through lips gone stiff and awkward. "You left me all day without a word, knowing I'd be eating my heart out with worry waiting to hear what the Council had decided, and never once thought to return." Tears, held firmly in check until now, welled and coursed down her cheeks, freezing as they fell. "Leave me to my work. I'll not have your mother going cold because her son hides away, too much a coward to face me."

With a savage curse, Morigan jerked her to him. "If being a coward isn't wanting to hurt you, not wanting to see the pain my words would cause, then call me a coward. And call me a coward, as well, because I needed time to deal with my own pain, somehow to find the strength to do a thing every fiber of my being cries out against." He inhaled a shuddering breath. "But I won't let you kill yourself in the process. I'm not worth it, Rissa. No male is."

He swung her up into his arms and wheeled around, hugging her close as if he feared ever letting her go. It was small comfort to Rissa, however. Whether he'd truly wanted to or not, Morigan had chosen his people over her. And that choice would finally force them apart.

Exhaustion engulfed her. Suddenly, too weary to fight

him, too cold, too empty for emotions of any kind, Rissa laid her head upon his chest and allowed him to carry her back to the lair. Nothing mattered anymore. Nothing . . .

Sarna gave a small cry when Morigan entered with Rissa. "Ah, by the three moons, what has happened?" She hurried over to her son's side. "Is Rissa all right?"

"She's but over-chilled, Mother," he soothed, carrying Rissa to the chair placed by the fire. "Make us some hot tea. We've both a need for something warm in our bellies." He threw his cloak aside, pulled off Rissa's frost-encrusted cloak, then lowered her to the chair. Squatting before her, Morigan tugged off her stiff, wet boots.

Sarna hurried over with blankets, handed them to her son, then turned to the task of putting on the pot of water to boil. After setting out two pottery cups, spoons and crushed herbal tea leaves, the old woman paused to eye Rissa and Morigan closely. "Is there anything else you need, Son?"

Morigan glanced up, his expression taut, grim. "No, Mother."

"Then, I'll be off to bed." Compassion gleamed in her eyes. "Call me, though, if you need for anything."

Gratitude flared briefly in the depths of Morigan's tormented eyes. "Thank you, Mother." He turned to Rissa. She stared back at him, her expression cold, wary. He took her small feet and lifted them to rest upon his thighs, kneading the chilled flesh with gentle care. "Your feet. Do you know how close you came to frostbite?"

"I don't care. I didn't feel anything." She closed her eyes. "I don't think I ever want to feel anything again."

Morigan lifted his tunic and, one by one, pulled her feet to lie against his tautly muscled belly. At the touch of his hair-roughened body, Rissa jerked back in alarm. Her eyes snapped open. "Wh-what are you doing?"

"Warming your feet in the fastest and safest way I know how," he replied matter-of-factly, holding her feet in place by sheer dint of greater strength.

"Well," Rissa muttered, stirred to action by indignation and the first glimmers of anger, "I don't want or need your help. Let me go!"

"You don't know what you want or need at this moment," Morigan growled in return, refusing to release her feet. "Now, hold still and stop gouging your toes into my belly!"

She went rigid. "Fine. Just get it over with then. You always get what you want in the end anyway."

"Do I?" He smiled bitterly. "I suppose I usually do, at least when it comes to getting what I want for my people. But when it comes to my own desires . . ." Morigan let the sentence, and its accompanying thought, die. What was the point in bemoaning what couldn't be changed? Better to cease his impotent railings against a fate gone suddenly cruel and accept what must be. Better for him *and* Rissa.

"The Council voted to send you back to your father," he forced himself to answer Rissa's unspoken question. "Naren will take you to him just as soon as the weather breaks and the mountains are once more passable."

She gave a harsh laugh. "And that can't come soon enough for you, can it, Morigan?"

He flinched. "The decision is made. There's no point prolonging the inevitable."

Rissa's eyes widened in disbelief. "Is that all you have to say? After all we've been to each other? All we've shared? *No point in prolonging the inevitable?*"

She pulled first one, then the other foot away. Her hands clenched in the fabric of her gown to keep from striking out at him, from raking his face with her nails. A fierce tremor racked her body. And she waited, waited for some word, some small bit of encouragement, of hope, to fall from Morigan's lips.

Waited in vain.

"It's the end of us, then, is it? Well, so be it." She rose. "You haven't any heart left to fight for me, do you? You never really did. It has always been bound up in saving your people, and whatever's left is devoted to fanning the fires of your hatred for Bellator. I'm only surprised you'd so willingly give me back to curry favor with my father. A strange form of vengeance, to my way of thinking."

Rissa gazed down at Morigan, searching wildly for any sign of emotion her words might have stirred. There was none. His old mask was firmly back in place, the expression in his eyes flat, his mouth set in implacable determination.

I've lost him.

The realization sent a shard of agony arrowing to the depths of her soul. *I was never the woman for him, if there even exists a woman who can ever truly thaw that block of ice he calls a heart.*

Inexplicably, the knowledge didn't anger her. It filled Rissa, instead, with a deep anguish and compassion. He deserved better from life. He always had.

"I-I'm tired," she said finally. "I don't want to sleep next to you, though. I'll ask Sarna if I can—"

"Take the bed," Morigan gritted. "I'll sleep out here tonight and for however long it takes until the weather breaks and you can leave. There's no purpose served in continuing to force my presence on you."

"No, I suppose there isn't." With a proud tilt of her chin, Rissa turned and strode away.

Morigan watched her go, wanting, needing to call her back with each step she took. But he didn't. From somewhere in the depths of his being, he found the strength to let Rissa walk away, to allow her to think he didn't care for her anymore or want her—desperately so—to stay. A small kindness, to be sure, with an act that appeared just the opposite. It was all he'd left to give her.

Hatred was an easier emotion to bear than pain. It fueled one's heart and body, rather than draining it with endless doubts and a heart-rending emptiness. He'd learned that lesson well in the past cycle of struggling to survive and to fight on for the sake of his people. And now, as his last act of love for Rissa, he must teach her the same lesson. He must let her imagine him callous and shallow; he must stir her anger and frustration with him until it consumed any tender emotions that might yet dwell in her heart.

Love, Morigan thought glumly as he flung his fur cloak about him and headed back outside to bring in more wood. A strange, twisted thing it could be, when to show the greatest affection for another was to turn them from you.

Late that night, Anista came for Rissa. Mira was in labor, and Agna had sent for Morigan's lady to attend the birth. Morigan hesitated, knowing Rissa might not be in the most charitable of moods when it came to him, then let Anista in. Excusing himself, he walked back to their bedchamber, frantically considering how best to present the request for the Lady of the lair's traditional presence at a birthing. Nothing especially eloquent came to him.

Rissa was asleep in the big, fur-strewn bed, her long hair a shimmering veil about her. Morigan's chest constricted painfully. It was too much to bear, seeing her lying there.

She was where she was meant to be, in his bed. She was his mate, a warm, vibrant, loving female. He longed to lie down beside her, pull her soft curves into him and join with her. And, in the act, cast aside, if only for a short while, the horror that had finally captured them and threatened to tear them apart.

But it wasn't meant to be. Not this night and perhaps not ever again. In the meanwhile, there were more pressing matters at hand. Like Mira's childbirth.

He sat on the edge of the bed and gently shook Rissa awake. She came to consciousness by degrees, smiling contentedly, then stretching like a cat, languorously, sensuously. The furs fell back to reveal the rounded fullness of her breasts beneath the thin sleeping gown, her slender arms, and narrow waist.

Morigan bit back a savage curse and grasped Rissa by the shoulder. "Wake up, femina," he gruffly commanded. "Agna has need of your presence."

She turned toward him, blinked drowsily. "Agna?" she murmured. "What's wrong?" Then, as if suddenly remembering what had so recently transpired between them, Rissa drew back. A cold, shuttered look flattened her gaze.

Morigan sighed and rose. "Mira's in labor. Agna requests your presence."

"As Lady of the Cat People?" Rissa demanded mockingly. "But, surely, I hold no such position after today? Surely, no one would value my presence at a Cat Child's birthing?"

He shoved a hand raggedly through his mane. "Rissa, please. Don't start. All I know is Agna asked for you."

"Well, I'm quite certain her request was only for ceremonial reasons. You can explain to her why my presence now would be most inappropriate." With that, Rissa rolled over and turned her back to him, pulling up the furs to cover her.

For a long, seething moment, Morigan stood there, so frustrated yet so helpless he could do nothing, think of nothing. Then, with an unsteady breath, he turned and strode out of the bedchamber. Anista glanced up as he approached, surprise lifting her slender brows.

"She refuses to come. She doesn't feel she's truly wanted at the birthing."

"Oh, she doesn't, does she?" the Cat Woman demanded. "And since when has that stopped her from barging in where she's not wanted?" Anista headed across the cave toward Morigan's bedchamber. "Well, this is one time she's going, whether she wants to or not!"

Morigan made a move to go after the Cat Woman, then halted. He turned back to the fire, instead, and added more wood. Perhaps another female appealing to Rissa might work where his attempts had failed. And, if not, what did it matter anyway? The Council had all but rejected Rissa as his lady, in making the decision they had today. What purpose was served in pretending otherwise? Let Rissa have whatever peace she desired in the few days left her in the lair.

Anista, however, had no such kindly intent. She stormed into the bedchamber, reached over, and flung the furs off Rissa. "Get up! Mira's in terrible pain and begging for you. You won her trust—not that you deserve it with this childish display—and now, you must pay the price. You're coming with me if I have to drag you there!"

Rissa wheeled around and sat up. "Mira? Mira asked for me?"

"Yes," the Cat Woman snapped irritably. "Didn't I just say that? Now, are you coming or do I—"

"How is she?" Rissa demanded as she swung out of bed and began to dress. "Is her labor going badly?"

"No worse than any first birthing," Anista admitted grudgingly. "But the girl's terrified and seems to think things will go better if you're there."

Rissa pulled on her boots, tied back her hair, and motioned

for Anista to lead the way out of the room. "Well, I can do little more than hold her hand, but if she wants me I'll go to her."

"But not because it's your duty or Morigan asked you to?" Anista asked with a wry twist of her lips.

"No, not after today." Rissa flushed hotly at the Cat Woman's knowing look. "Now, come on."

The two women reentered the main room. Morigan glanced up from the chair he'd pulled over to the fire, lowering his long legs from their position propped on the hearth ledge. He stood. "So, you decided to go after all?" His glance locked with Rissa's.

"Yes." She flung her cloak about her shoulders and stalked over to the leather door hanging. "Don't wait up."

Anista snickered. Morigan shot her a furious look. She quickly gathered her own cloak about her and followed Rissa out the door.

The trek to Mira's lair was silent. The wind had finally subsided, and the night lay still and quiet about them. The three moons, two in perfect alignment, the third drawing near, shimmered in the ebony sky. Booted feet crunched on the crisp snow. Breath vapor swirled around them in the frigid air. The night was pristine, magical, and yet, all Rissa could think of was the sight of Morigan standing there in his lair as she'd left him, magnificent, proud, and heartbreakingly distant. Distant, walled off from her, from his emotions, from his own wants and needs.

It was all he had left, she realized sadly. The final escape from pain, from facing a life that had dealt so cruelly with him of late. She couldn't fault him. He did the best he could. He just shut out her and any hope of happiness in the process.

"You're kind to go to Mira," Anista said, intruding finally on Rissa's glum musings. "You owe her—us—nothing anymore, and yet, you still . . ." She paused. "I may have been too harsh with you when you first arrived. I began to realize that after your defense of Morigan. You care for him, and for our people as well."

Rissa sighed. "My thanks for that, Anista. It comes too late to do me any good, but I appreciate your honesty nonetheless."

"It needed to be said," the Cat Woman muttered gruffly as they drew up before a small cave. "To have done less would've been dishonorable."

She motioned for Rissa to enter, then followed after. The lair was brightly lit and warm. Mira's mate, a tall, thin Cat Man, paced in one corner. Across the room, Agna worked over the writhing form of the young Cat Woman. Rissa nodded briefly to the Cat Man, then squared her shoulders and walked over to stand beside Agna.

"What would you have me do?"

The healer glanced up in surprise, then smiled grimly. "If you would, pull up a stool by Mira's head and comfort her." She handed Rissa a damp cloth. "And wipe her face to keep her cool."

Rissa did as requested and was soon sitting beside the young Cat Woman. A fierce contraction had just passed. Mira slumped in relief, grasping for Rissa's hand.

"Th-thank you for c-coming, my Lady," she whispered. "I-I wanted you here to welcome my babe into the world, as all our Ladies have done in the past." She smiled. "Now, I can birth my babe in peace."

"I am here, Mira," Rissa soothed as another contraction began to ripple through the young mother. "I am here for you, for as long as it takes."

Mira's body arched in the bed, her face contorting with the intensity of the pain. Her mouth opened in soundless agony. Rissa clasped the girl's hand in both of hers and held on, attempting, with all the mental effort she was capable of, to lend support. Finally, Mira collapsed in exhaustion. Rissa gently wiped the sweat from the young woman's brow, then shot Agna a questioning glance.

"A hard labor, but she's progressing well," the healer answered her silent question. "It'll be dawn before the babe comes, though."

"No matter," Rissa said. "I couldn't have gotten back to sleep at any rate."

"I was sorry to hear the Council's ruling," Agna replied simply. "I think, this time, they've made the wrong decision."

Rissa smiled wanly. "Thank you for saying that."

Mira groaned beside her. "A-ah, it c-comes again." Her grip tightened on Rissa's hand. "H-hold me, my Lady. H-help me!"

The contraction gripped her in an excruciating vise. Mira screamed, went rigid, arching once more from her bed. Rissa stroked the hair from her sweat-damp face and murmured soothingly. Finally, the contraction passed.

On and on through the night, Mira labored. It took all of Rissa, Agna, and Anista's combined efforts to keep the girl in control, to get her to push when the time came and not to lapse into hysteria as the contractions began incessantly to pound her exhausted young body.

Rissa, who'd never seen a birthing, was horrified at the pain and blood and noise. As the hellish night wore on, she mentally thanked Zada over and over for the contraceptive. Not even for Morigan, even if things had gone differently, would she ever wish to bear a child. Nothing was worth such agony. Nothing.

And then, as dawn streaked the mountain sky in the softest

shades of amber and rose, Mira's babe was born. She was a large, squalling child who immediately began to suckle greedily when put to her mother's breast. While Agna tidied mother and babe, Anista put on a pot of water for tea. Rissa, totally overwhelmed, simply sat there and stared down at the pair in amazement. Even the hot cup of herbal tea Anista eventually pressed into her hand did little to recall her back to reality.

"Send for Morigan," Agna finally said to the proud if somewhat baffled father. At the Cat Lord's name, Rissa's head jerked up. Her hand clenched about her cup.

"He must present the babe to our people," Agna gently explained. "There'll be songs, gifts, and celebration. It's tradition."

Gifts. Vaguely, Rissa recalled Sarna's words that day at the hot springs, when she'd first informed her of her duties as Morigan's mate. She was supposed to give Mira a birthing gift.

Impulsively, Rissa reached up and pulled off the turcas stone jewelry she'd forgotten to remove last night. Mira had been the one to admire the jewelry that day at the springs. She had also been the first Cat Woman, aside from Morigan's mother, to offer her friendship.

"Here," Rissa said, pressing the earrings and necklace into the young woman's hand. "I wish to give you this in honor of your childbirth."

Mira's eyes grew wide. "Oh, but I couldn't, my Lady. They're precious to you. They were from your mother."

"And I give them to you, to pass down someday to your own daughter." Rissa smiled. "Truly, I want you to have them. There's no one I'd rather give this jewelry to than you, Mira."

"My thanks, my Lady," was the girl's embarrassed reply.

She clasped the turcas stones in her hand and pressed them tightly to her chest, tears of gratitude trickling from her eyes.

Rissa rose, brushed out the wrinkles from her tunic dress, and smiled down at Mira. "It's time for me to go now. I'm happy I could be here for you."

"My thanks, my Lady," the girl whispered, then wearily closed her eyes. The babe sucked noisily at her mother's breast.

With a soft, wondering smile, Rissa leaned down to stroke the child's downy soft cheek. The babe grimaced at the interruption, then resumed her nursing. Rissa grinned.

"That's what makes it all worth it," Agna said. "That, and the joy one brings to one's mate in bearing him a child. A new life is always precious, and doubly so for us just now. Once more, you've been here when we needed you."

Rissa straightened, deeply moved by the tender scene and Agna's words. "I'll leave now, before Morigan arrives. I don't want—"

"You must stay, my Lady," the healer was quick to interject. "It is you who holds the babe while our lord presents it to the people. That, too, is tradition."

"No." Rissa firmly shook her head. "To stand at Morigan's side and pretend to be what I'm not would be a travesty of all your people hold dear. I won't do that."

"And would you shame Mira and her mate by refusing to honor their babe's birthing?"

"I didn't mean . . ." Rissa frowned. "Would I shame them by refusing, Agna? Tell me true."

"Yes, my Lady. And shame Morigan as well." She smiled wryly. "Of course, I imagine that particular contemplation hardly gives you pause right now, does it?"

Rissa's lips tightened. "You know it doesn't. But I won't embarrass Morigan at Mira's expense, either." She sighed and glanced down at herself. Her skirt and the lower part of her tunic was bloodstained and wrinkled. "I hardly look presentable myself."

"No matter." Agna rose and walked behind Rissa to finger comb her hair into some semblance of order. "As our males proudly wear the blood of their slain enemies, we females are just as quick to flaunt the blood shed of childbirth. We, too, have bravely fought and won."

"Only women bring life into the world," Rissa wonderingly added, "not take it."

Agna grinned. "You understand the mystery, the victory then, every time a female gives birth. There is *nothing* more noble, more honorable, or courageous, is there?"

A sense of unity, of oneness with the Cat Women and every other woman who'd ever lived, filled Rissa. She understood at last why Mira had risked such pain, even to the endangerment of her life, to bear her child. And knew, as well, that someday, with some man whom she loved greater than life itself, she, too, would do the same.

But not with Morigan. As much as she still loved and wanted him, such a life was never to be theirs.

Tears, held so precariously at bay since her meeting last night with Morigan, spilled over and down Rissa's cheeks. Agna, standing behind her, deftly braiding her hair, sensed rather than saw Rissa's sudden surge of sorrow. "Not this morn, my Lady," she whispered. "This is no time for tears, but a time for great joy. A child is born, the first of many, we hope, to enrich our race. Be happy for us. Be happy for Morigan. It was his courage, his insight, and sacrifices, that brought us to this. He's a great Lord . . . perhaps one of our greatest."

"Yes, he is," Rissa softly replied, as the leather door covering lifted and Morigan paused there. The rising sun shone behind him, casting his face in shadow, but outlining his big, powerful form in a nimbus of glowing light. He looked impossibly virile, the embodiment of a man in his prime, a proud, wild animal. And leader of an equally proud, wild race of people.

He'd hurt her; he'd turned from her. But he was still a man to be reckoned with, a man to be respected. And, if only for a brief moment in time, she'd been his mate. She would never forget him, no matter how long she lived. And never forgive him, either, for not being the man she needed.

Marveling at the wide contrast in her emotions when it came to Morigan, Rissa squared her shoulders, lifted her chin, and walked over to join him.

Five days later, Agna stopped by early as Rissa and Naren were finishing the last preparations for their journey back to Primasedes. The healer awkwardly hugged Rissa, then pressed several packages of healing powder and salves into her hands. "For the journey," she explained. Then, she smiled. "Naren tends to be a bit accident-prone."

"Only when Morigan *tends* to get in the way of blasters," the black-haired Cat Man, stuffing the final items into their backpacks, protested. "Otherwise, I'm quite capable of taking care of myself. And Rissa," he added pointedly.

Agna laughed. "Just be certain you do. You'll never hear the end of it from me if she suffers even one scratch." She turned back to Rissa, her expression now solemn. "Don't forget us here. And if there's anything you can do to plead our cause with your father . . ."

"You know I will, Agna." Rissa choked back a sudden, hot surge of tears. Not today, she silently vowed. She'd not cry today no matter what happened. She wouldn't give Morigan the satisfaction of seeing her pain. "Perhaps . . . someday . . . we'll meet again."

"Yes, someday," the healer repeated.

Naren straightened and slung the heavier of the two packs over his shoulder. "Time to go, femina." He handed her the other backpack, then shouldered his blaster.

"A moment more," a feminine voice spoke from behind them. Rissa turned, to find Sarna standing there, a parcel in her hand. "Here, this is for you. To replace the turcas stone jewelry you gave Mira. It's not nearly as fine, but I've always thought there was a certain beauty in the obsidian stone nonetheless."

"Thank you, domina." Rissa accepted the small package. With fingers gone suddenly unsteady, she carefully unwrapped the gift. A pair of silvery argentum earrings, cunningly fashioned into Cat's claws that cradled smoothly polished chips of obsidian, gleamed back at her. Rissa lifted her gaze to Sarna. "Th-they're beautiful. I'll wear them with pride."

"And remember us, when you do," the old Cat Woman added hopefully. "Here, let me help you put them on." She took the earrings and slipped them into Rissa's ears. "Yes, they look quite fine next to your lovely hair."

Rissa touched the jewelry. "Do they? I think I've never had anything so special. My thanks again for your kindness. I didn't know any of the Cat People possessed such skill with metal."

"Morigan made them for you. He always possessed a talent for such things and used to enjoy the craft, especially during the long winter evenings. He ceased his work, though, after the massacre. Until now, he has never made another piece of jewelry."

"Oh . . . I didn't know," Rissa whispered, going pale, yet

touched by this aspect of a complex man revealed in the gift his mother offered. Bittersweet pain, then a wild surge of anger, flooded her.

An impulse, to tear the earrings off and fling them to the ground, assailed her. Her barely contained anguish and frustration boiled up to encompass Rissa in an unthinking rage. How dare Morigan, after all he'd done, attempt to appease her now with a pair of earrings? Gods, how could he be so cruel, so heartless? How could he hurt her so?

"It was all he could give you, child." Sarna's compassionate gaze spoke, louder than words, of her deep awareness of Rissa's torment. "He wished for you to have something of him when you were gone. I don't think he wanted you to forget him."

"D-did he tell you this?"

Sarna smiled sadly. "No, but Morigan wouldn't. You know that as well as I. He has learned to hide his deeper emotions." She sighed. "You were good for my son, child. You were a good mate. I grieve losing you, for myself, for our people and, most of all, for Morigan."

From some place deep within her, Rissa summoned forth a self-control, a courage she'd never known she possessed. She gave Sarna a heartfelt hug, then stepped back from the old Cat Woman. "And I grieve as well, domina, but, in the end, it changes nothing. Fare you well." Rissa turned to Naren. "Please, Naren, let us go. My heart is ready to break."

He nodded, then bowed briefly to Sarna. "Domina. Fare you well until my return."

Tears streamed down Morigan's mother's face. "Fare you well, the both of you. Fare you well."

Rissa followed Naren from the cave, fighting to hold back the tears. "Help me, Naren," she choked. "I don't want to cry."

"And why not cry?" he growled angrily. "Why not show the Council the extent of the pain they've caused, not only to you, but to those of us who have come to love you? Why should they be the only ones who escape unscathed?"

She shot him a quick, startled glance. His jaw worked, a muscle twitched, and his own eyes looked unnaturally bright. "Leave it be, Naren," Rissa whispered. "Don't make it any worse. I can't bear much more."

"As you wish, my Lady." His glance lifted to where a small gathering of females stood. Bellatorian females, as well as Anista and Mira, holding her babe in her arms. "Be brave, though. There are more farewells to be said."

Rissa glanced up. She smiled. "It seems I leave a few friends behind. That's good to know."

As they approached, Diona broke from the crowd and ran up. Sobbing as if her heart would break, the serving maid clasped Rissa to her. "Ah, Rissa," she wept. "What am I to do; what are any of us to do without you here? How could Morigan be so cruel? We need you far more than your father ever will!"

"Hush, Diona." Rissa stroked her friend's hair. "I can do more for the Cat People at my father's side than I could ever do here. You must believe that. It'll give you comfort, just as it does me."

"I hate him," Diona sniffled. "I hate Morigan for doing this!"

"It wasn't his decision, sweet one," Rissa patiently explained. "The Council wished to send me away, not Morigan."

"If he'd loved you like he should have, he could've still done something. I know he could!"

Rissa managed a wan little smile. "Perhaps. But it doesn't matter anymore. He must live with his choice, as must we all." She kissed Diona on the forehead. "Take care of the other women, especially Hali. She's so fragile. I fear for her."

Diona smiled through her tears. "She's been seeing Lisan more often of late, Agna tells me. And, sometimes, she doesn't even demand the healer's presence when Lisan visits. He's so good with her, so patient. I think he just might succeed."

"Good. I'm glad to hear that. The Cat Men's success with our women is heartening. I'll share that with my father as well." Rissa disengaged herself from Diona's clasp and walked over to speak with the other women briefly. Then, she turned back to her friend for a quick hug and farewell kiss before joining Naren once more.

They headed down the valley to the trail leading up into the mountains. Cat People were out and about on the sun-bedazzled morn, the air crisp and cool, the ice-tipped snow sparkling like clear gemstones in the sunlight. Some smiled and waved goodbye to Rissa; others eyed her narrowly or avoided her gaze altogether. She'd won many to her side, she realized, but there were still many in the lair who opposed her presence and that of the other Bellatorian women. Even with her gone, Morigan's battles weren't over.

And there was still Cradoc, she thought with a shudder, noting his triumphant smile as she and Naren made their way past him and several other Cat Men standing down by the frozen stream, their heads together in some sort of discussion. Plotting against Morigan, most likely, Rissa thought. But there was nothing more she could do about it. She'd saved Morigan from Cradoc once. He must now manage alone.

But that was his choice, she reminded herself. She would most likely never know what became of Morigan, or if Cradoc ultimately succeeded against him. Soon, all that had transpired here would be behind her—the pain, the joy, the love she'd once shared with Morigan. All she'd have would be memories.

Up ahead, a small gathering of Cat Men awaited them at the base of the trail leading out of the valley. Morigan stood at its head, with Ardan beside him, and the other Elders behind them. Rissa shot Naren an uncertain glance. "Why? What purpose does this serve?"

"Morigan insisted on saying his farewells," the big Cat Man muttered. "Ardan felt a formal meeting, in the presence of the Elders, was far safer than some private encounter. The old man knows how close Morigan hangs on the edge of rebelling against the Council."

"Does he, now?" Rissa laughed bitterly. "And whatever for? Certainly, not because of me?"

"You're wrong, femina," Naren said. "This is tearing his heart out."

"He has no heart. He doesn't dare let himself feel anything."

"I'd say, rather, you won't let yourself admit he has a heart and can still let you go." Naren glanced at Rissa, noted the set, implacable look to her features, and sighed. "You're both hurting and hiding that hurt behind a wall of anger. Your pride won't let you approach Morigan, and his need to maintain control has shut him off from you. Gods, but I've never seen a more tempestuous pair of lovers!"

"I don't love Morigan!" Even as she said it, she knew she teetered on the brink of her control, her pain, her need for Morigan, a seething, burgeoning tumult within her.

"And you lie."

"Curse you, Naren!" Rissa cried, halting to face him. "Curse all of you and your crazy sense of honor and cruel laws! And your Council and its formal farewell be damned!

I won't talk to Morigan or any of them. I won't play this stupid, senseless game a moment longer!"

He took her by the arm. "Rissa, don't—"

"*You* talk to them! *You* say our farewells!" She wrenched free of his grip. "I'll await you on the trail."

With that she strode off, leaving Naren standing there. He shot Morigan a frustrated glance, then set out after Rissa who stalked straight toward the trail and the Cat Men standing before it. She'd walk right through them without halting, he realized, if he didn't stop her in time. And the Elders wouldn't like that at all.

Naren slowed his stride. Suddenly, he no longer cared what the Elders would think. Let them all be damned. Let them be scandalized by Rissa's behavior. They deserved it, everyone of them. Everyone, but Morigan . . .

Rissa's resolve wavered as she approached the Cat Men. Morigan stood directly in her way, and the look in his eyes boded poorly for her. He'd read her intent. He wasn't moving. At the realization, something shattered inside her. Gods, couldn't he at least spare her this final humiliation? Couldn't he just let her pass?

She tried to go around him, but he was, as always, too quick for her. Rissa tried again, swerving to pass on his other side. Once more, Morigan was there.

"Rissa," he said huskily, his expression bleak, anguished. "Stop. Let me speak with you."

"No. No." She shook her head fiercely. "It's past time for talk. Just let me go."

He grabbed her by the arms, halting her. His gaze snared, fleetingly, on her earrings. A tender warmth flared in his eyes, then was quickly extinguished. "I'll let you go because I have to," he ground out the words. "But before I do, I want you to know, I want you to believe with every fiber of your being, that I don't let you go willingly. Gods," he groaned, "never, ever, willingly."

"Morigan," his grandfather said behind him, "that's enough. Say your farewells and let the female pass. No purpose is served—"

"I'll say what I want and how I want it!" Morigan snarled savagely. "You and the other Elders have taken everything else from me. You have my obedience to the Council's decision. But you *will not* keep me from saying farewell to Rissa in whatever manner I wish!"

His arm encircled her and he half-led, half-dragged her a short distance away. Then, one arm still containing her, Morigan took Rissa's chin in his other hand and lifted her gaze to his. Tears sparkled in her eyes, but her jaw was set in an expression of remote indifference.

Morigan clamped down on a sad smile. This was the Rissa he knew and loved. Defiant little she-cat to the end, proud and fearless. Fighting her pain as valiantly as he.

"I won't have you leaving here thinking I don't care, thinking I callously cast you aside," he forced the words past a constricted throat. "Thinking I don't love you."

Her eyes widened and she swallowed convulsively. "Love me? No, I don't believe that. I don't believe you love me. You're too afraid to open yourself to love. You're still too tied to the horrors of the massacre, too terrified of relinquishing the anger and need for revenge for fear there'll be nothing left to keep you going if you do. This offer from my father, this decision of the Council, was but the excuse you needed to run away."

She jerked her chin from his grasp. "At least have the honesty to admit it, Morigan. At least have the courage to face the fact your people were—and have always been—the pretense you've needed to keep from confronting your own emotions. There's never been any time for yourself, has there? And, deep inside you, you like it that way; you've allowed it to happen. It's safer, more honorable, more manly to bury your pain and loss than to cry your heart out and work through it all. It's more courageous to pledge undying revenge against my father, than to admit he took so much from you that he ripped your heart out and crushed it underfoot."

"And what good would any of that do—for me *or* my people?" Morigan demanded tautly. "I needed to go on, to survive, to lead."

"But you also needed to heal," Rissa whispered achingly. "To face the fears, the weakness, the pain within you. You can never be whole until you do."

He stepped back from her, his countenance dark, thunderous. "I've all I need, all I want. I thought you, too, could be a part of that, but I see now I was wrong. You ask too much. You don't understand."

Frustration flooded Rissa. "I understand all too well, Morigan. All too well. And I pity you."

Surprise flashed in his eyes, then anger. "I don't want your pity," he snarled. "I don't need anyone's pity! I am what I am, and I survive!"

"But you aren't all the man you could be because of it," Rissa softly replied. "And not the man for me. Now, let me pass, Morigan. Our farewells have been given, though perhaps not quite as you envisioned them. There's nothing more to be said."

"Go then. Leave!" The Cat Lord stepped aside and motioned her on with a vicious stab of his hand. "Go back to your father. Back to the shallow, futile little life you always dreamed of. You've never been woman enough for me. *Never!*"

Rissa flinched, then faced him squarely. "Perhaps not, but I'll never forget the loving, the times I shared in your arms. And I'll remember you and hope someday life smiles on you again. I truly will, Morigan."

She walked around him then and headed up the trail, the Elders parting for her as she did. She never looked back, never once faltered in her resolute stride. There was no point. They'd said hurtful, albeit honestly felt, things to each other this day. There was an end, at last, to all the past week's unspoken thoughts and feelings.

There was nothing more to be said, nothing more to be done. Nothing, save return to the home where she really belonged.

Nineteen

Naren halted her a half hour out of the valley. "Rissa, there's something I—"

"There's nothing more to say," she snapped, her control frayed to its limits. "Just let it be, Naren. Please."

"I didn't intend to force any discussion or argument." He drew up beside her. In his hand was a long piece of cloth. "It's just past time to wear the blindfold."

She eyed the cloth in disbelief. "You can't mean to lead me through these mountains with my eyes covered? Haven't I proven my loyalty to your people? Must I now, on top of everything else, be insulted as well?"

"This is no insult, femina." Naren looked exceedingly uncomfortable. "I swear it. The blindfold is meant to protect you as well as us."

"I'd never betray the location of your lair. Never!" Rissa stepped back, her hands clenched at her sides. "No matter how Morigan and I parted, no matter how bitter I feel toward your Council, I'd never, ever, endanger the lives of innocent people!"

"But the Bellatorians are known to have ways of extracting information out of even the most unwilling subjects." He offered her the blindfold. "I'd not like to have to force this on you, femina. Please don't make me do that."

"My father would never . . ." She let the protestation die.

She didn't really know what her father would or wouldn't do. She didn't really know anything about him and, after the weeks spent with the Cat People, she was no longer even certain of his innocence in ordering their massacre. Rissa took the blindfold from Naren. "As you wish. I'll do whatever it takes to protect your people."

A tender look flared in his eyes. "I know that, femina. I think I saw that, and all your other wonderful possibilities, from the first moment we met. I'm just so sorry things didn't work out. Losing you is our loss, and a sad one it is." He walked over. "Would you like some help with that?" He indicated the blindfold.

Rissa smiled. It was impossible to stay mad at Naren for long. "Yes, please. And don't you dare let me fall in all this snow, with my eyes covered. I'm depending on you, Naren."

He took the cloth and turned her around. "I'll defend you with my life," his deep voice rumbled from behind her as he lifted the blindfold to cover her eyes. "Not only for Morigan and our friendship, but for myself. You're precious to me, femina. More than you could ever know."

As he spoke, there was the merest catch in the dark register of his voice. It sent a pang of regret, of compassion spiraling through Rissa. Though he'd stepped aside in deference to Morigan, Naren still cared deeply for her.

Bittersweet sadness welled within her. Two good, brave men cared for her, one tormented, with a heart well-guarded, the other open and honest and kind. And she could have neither of them.

Rissa turned when Naren finished tying the blindfold. She reached out, awkwardly, and found his hand. Lifting it to her face, she pressed a kiss to his palm. "And you're precious to me, sweet Naren. I've never had such a friend as you."

"But even with what has come between you and Morigan . . ."

She lowered his hand and released it, the old pain and frustration filling her. "It doesn't matter anymore. That's over. Forever."

Naren slipped his arm about her waist and urged her forward. "Perhaps," he said with a resigned sigh, "but such things don't easily die. Especially not a love such as yours."

The going became arduous as the snow, drifted into deep piles by the wind, worsened. With Rissa's eyes covered, she was an awkward partner. If not for Naren's great strength and sharp reflexes, she would have slipped and fallen numerous times. As it was, their progress was slow. Camp that night was made in a lonely cave high in the mountains.

The next morning dawned bright and cold. At Naren's request, Rissa donned her blindfold even before leaving the cave. The journey was just as arduous as the previous day. By nightfall Rissa was exhausted. After a Spartan meal of journey bread and meat sticks, she promptly fell asleep.

The third day the trail angled downward. They descended from the higher elevations and headed toward the foothills. Though thick, gray clouds lowered over the mountains they'd left behind, boding ominously of yet another winter storm, Rissa's mood improved nonetheless. Despite her lack of sight, they made good time. Naren decided to make camp early, and they were snugly ensconced before a crackling fire just as the first rays of sunset swept the land.

A long-eared lepus cooked on a spit over the fire, courtesy of Naren's quick response when the animal leapt from its hiding place alongside the trail. The aroma of roasting meat filled the air, making Rissa's mouth water. She leaned back with a cup of herbal tea she'd just brewed and sighed in contentment. They were safe, warm, and would reach Zada's hut by tomorrow. Her pleasures were few, but Rissa did look forward to seeing the old healer again.

"What will you do?" Naren sliced off a generous portion of the crispy skinned lepus a short while later and handed it to Rissa. "When you get back to Primasedes, I mean?"

She paused to take a bite of the perfectly cooked meat and wipe the juices from her mouth. Briefly, she considered his question. "I'd originally intended to find some place of influence at my father's side, to aid him in the peaceful and successful colonization of Agrica." Her lips quirked wryly. "I was also meant to wed one of his young officers with hopes of a promising political career."

"And now?" Naren prodded as he hacked off a haunch of lepus for himself. "Are your goals the same?"

"To aid in bringing peace to Agrica?" Rissa took a sip of her hot tea. "Yes, but in a more humane way than has been attempted in the past. I want also to plead your people's cause with my father. Bellator's in no danger from the Cat People and must stop its senseless vendetta against them."

"Have a care for how you go about that particular cause, femina. A stand for us may not be popular in Primasedes right now." He smiled grimly. "Remember, we did attack that merchants' caravan, loot it, kill Bellatorian soldiers, and abduct twelve females. No matter our reasons, Bellator won't view our actions favorably."

Rissa frowned. "No, they won't. I'll just have to be as tactful and diplomatic as I can."

Naren chuckled softly.

"What's so funny?" Her eyes narrowed, immediately suspicious.

"You, talking about being tactful and diplomatic. That's never been your strong suit."

"Well, it most certainly can be," Rissa replied indignantly, "when I'm dealing with reasonable people and laws!" She stopped, then flushed. "By the five moons, I didn't mean to insult . . ."

The Cat Man threw back his head and laughed. "Yes, you did indeed mean to insult us and our laws. You've made it clear time and again you think us archaic in many ways. And *I* think you were a breath of fresh air and exactly what we needed. But," he added, his expression turning solemn, "your forthrightness offended many. As it will with your own kind, I'm sure."

"So, what are you saying, Naren?" Rissa laid down her piece of lepus and stared at him, an intent look in her eyes. "How should I act when I get back to Primasedes? I want so much to be successful at something."

"Your father, perhaps, will imagine your most successful role as mate to that young officer," Naren ventured carefully. "What then, Rissa?"

She went pale. Tears flooded her eyes. "Ah, Gods, Naren! The thought of lying with another man fills me with horror. I don't want anyone but . . ." Her head fell, her hair tumbling about her face.

"But Morigan?"

Tawny brown eyes lifted. "He's all I've ever wanted. How can I ever feel the same about another man?"

Naren smiled. "You will in time, femina. You must just give it time. And convince your father to be patient with you while you do."

A distant look clouded her eyes. "I wonder what he'll think, when he hears I've been mate to a Cat Man?"

"I don't know, femina." He studied his piece of lepus as if it had suddenly acquired a life of its own. "My advice would be to tread carefully in that area, too, until you can ascertain his mood." His head lifted to lock gazes with her.

"There are many of your kind, I'd wager, who'd not only find what you did disgusting and shameful, but condemn you for it as well. We're considered little more than animalistic savages, you know."

"Yes, I know." Rissa smiled. "I used to think the same until I came to know your people. It seems only fair, does it not, that the task of changing that false perception now falls to me? Who else would have greater influence with the Lord Commander of Agrica than his daughter?"

Naren took another bite of his meat. "I hope you're right, femina. Not only for our sake, but for yours as well."

They finished the meal in thoughtful silence, cleaned up, and talked for a while longer. Their discussions, however, were overlaid by a thoughtful poignancy. Naren had spoken true, Rissa realized. Her return to her own kind didn't necessarily promise to be a smooth or easy transition.

Too much had transpired in the past weeks. She'd grown from a girl to a woman, had taken a mate, and experienced love, had faced fear and hardship and had prevailed. In the process, she'd had all her preconceived ideas and aspirations turned upside down. She wasn't the girl her father might still be expecting. Neither was her world the same, viewed as it would now be through different, more experienced eyes.

All too soon, Rissa realized with a small twinge of fear as she finally lay down for the night, she'd be thrust back into a life she was no longer quite so familiar with or well-prepared for. A life she no longer so fervently desired. But there were few options. Whether he wished to or not, Morigan had sent her away. She'd nowhere else to go . . .

In the middle of the night, Naren woke her. Rissa jerked awake. When she noted it was still dark outside, she blinked in confusion. The coals of the fire glowed red in the blackness, shedding a meager light on the form of the big Cat Man who loomed over her.

"Naren," she whispered. "What's wrong?"

He pulled her to a sitting position, his clasp tight, urgent. "We've visitors."

Terror rippled down Rissa's spine. From the grim tone of Naren's voice, it was evident their visitors weren't friends. "Who?" she demanded, leaning close to him. "Do you know who they are?"

"Yes," he growled, shoving himself to his feet. For an instant longer, he stared down at her, his eyes, in the dim light, smoldering with rage.

Rissa's mouth went dry. "Naren?"

"They're Cat Men, femina," he ground out the reply. "Cat Men."

"You're picking at your food again," Sarna observed mildly, the afternoon after Rissa's departure. She eyed her son from across the table of their midday meal.

Morigan continued to stab distractedly at a slice of roast domare. "I'm not hungry."

"Well, you're a strong man." His mother resumed her meal. "A day or two of poor appetite won't do much harm."

Anger flared in Morigan. Would his own mother expect him to cast the memory and pain of losing Rissa aside, just like all the rest, in but a day or two? His hand clenched around his fork.

Sarna noted her son's reaction. Her gaze flew guiltily to his face. "I am sorry. I didn't mean to imply you should so quickly and easily forget Rissa. I, too, mourn her absence. Our lair seems so . . . so empty, so joyless, without her. I was just trying to make conversation." Her voice broke. "I-I cannot bear the silence. I miss her so!"

Morigan laid down his fork, shoved his plate aside, and reached over to take her hand. "As do I, Mother. As do I. But the decision has been made, Rissa sent away. There's no purpose served in wallowing in self-pity."

"That is what makes you such a fine leader," Sarna softly said. "There is none other as fit to rule as you."

Morigan gave a snort of disgust. "You flatter me, Mother. Naren would be a fine leader. Lisan shows future potential as well. I'm not indispensable."

"No one is indispensable, Son. But you are of the Blood; you represent our continuity, our heritage, at a time when we desperately need a link with the past and a hope for the future."

"Fine words, Mother, but of little comfort." He glanced down, his jaw taut.

"There's been little comfort for you for a long while now, hasn't there? Save what Rissa brought you."

He lifted his tortured gaze. "Before she left, I told Rissa I loved her. She didn't believe me. She said I was too afraid to open myself to love and too frightened to let go of my need for anger and vengeance. She said the Council's decision and the needs of my people were just an excuse to run away from my emotions."

"And what did you say to that?"

"What could I say? I denied it, of course."

"And now? Do you still deny it, my son?"

Morigan stared back at her, momentarily at a loss for words. How did she know? How could she guess the doubts that had assailed him since parting with Rissa? He'd thought he'd walled off his anguish and his misgivings from everyone, too proud to let them see or sense his suffering.

But she was his mother. No matter how hard he tried to spare her, he could never seem to hide his pain or deeper emotions from her. Had that failure, in the end, only prolonged Sarna's own recovery, added to her pain?

"Yes," she answered his unspoken question. "Your pain has always been mine, a pain you would allow neither of us to face. Then, when Rissa arrived she brought you happiness; she forced you to face your terrible anguish. And, because she did, I, too, began to heal."

Sarna rose, walked around the table and took Morigan into her arms. She pulled him close, pressing his head against her breast as she had so long ago when he was a child. "Ah, my son," she murmured sadly. "I don't want to go back to that dark time. I don't want you to, either."

With a groan, Morigan clutched his mother to him. "I won't let all I've worked so hard, sacrificed so much for, go to waste. That, in the end, though we've lost her, will be Rissa's legacy to us."

"And what of your mourning for Winna, Calder, and your unborn babe? For your father?"

He pulled back, his features gone hard. "I've mourned them the best I can. There's no time for more. That's behind me now, just as further regret for Rissa must—"

A shout came from outside their lair. Morigan frowned, then shoved back his chair and rose. He strode over to the leather door covering and lifted it. A frigid blast of air swirled in. He looked outside. Lisan stood there.

"May I enter, my Lord?" the young Cat Man asked. "I've disturbing news, news for your ears alone."

Morigan cocked a wary brow. "Indeed? Wait a moment. It's better if we talk outside."

He lowered the door flap, strode over to where his fur cloak lay, and swung it over his shoulders. Sarna glanced up.

"Lisan and I are going for a walk," Morigan explained. "I'll be back shortly."

His mother nodded. She rose and began clearing off the plates. "As you wish."

Morigan eyed her for a moment longer, then strode back across the cave to the door. Lifting the flap, he slipped outside.

Lisan awaited him, a troubled look in his eyes. Morigan motioned for the other Cat Man to join him as they headed down the trail. They walked in silence until they reached the stream.

The day was clear but cold, shadows from the mountain peaks fingering through the valley as the winter-bleached sun slid past its zenith and headed into the west. Few were about. Finally, Morigan halted. "What news have you, Lisan?"

"I heard comment this morn no one had seen Cradoc or Limos about. I thought that strange, as there were no hunting parties sent out of late. So strange I decided quietly to search the valley."

"And?"

Lisan squarely met his gaze. "They aren't here. Their spoor, along with two other Cat Men's, leads out of the valley and into the mountains. Following Naren and Rissa's trail."

Morigan's mouth went grim. "Are you certain? That trail's the most common one out of the valley."

"I followed it for several hours, my Lord, to be sure. Cradoc's tracks never deviated from Naren's."

Fear snaked through the Cat Lord, then a cold fury. Curse Cradoc. It would be so like him to plot something like this. Though he'd sent her away, his cousin knew how much Rissa meant to him. Everyone did. And Naren . . . Naren was his best friend. What cruel and devious evil did Cradoc plot against him now?

Morigan's hands fisted in his cloak. "How old? How old is Cradoc's trail?"

"About eight hours by now, my Lord," Lisan said, glancing up at the sun. "I'd wager he left with Limos and the others just before dawn."

Four Cat Men out after Naren and Rissa. Something exploded in Morigan, shattering the fragile remnants of his control. Gods, no matter Naren's battle prowess and strength, he wouldn't have a chance against four of his kind. Especially, not with Cradoc involved. And Rissa . . .

His mind made up, Morigan clasped Lisan by the shoulders. "Gather a party of five Cat Men and the necessary weapons and supplies. Lead them out after Cradoc's trail. You know what must be done if you come upon them, don't you?"

Lisan smiled, but the look never reached his eyes. "Yes, my Lord. I know. And what of you? What will you do?"

"I?" The Cat Lord's voice vibrated with cold fury. "I, too, am going after Cradoc. This time we'll settle what's between us—once and for all."

The blood froze in Rissa's veins. "Cat Men? Then why would you think—"

"It's Cradoc and Limos and two others," Naren savagely cut her off. "And they haven't followed us to wish us well or offer safe escort to Primasedes. You can be certain of that, femina."

"Then why? What purpose would be served coming after us?"

"For one, I'd wager Cradoc means to avenge himself on Morigan. Limos and the others," he shrugged, "most likely follow Cradoc. Nothing good will come of this, though."

She recalled seeing Cradoc and several other Cat Men in discussion that morn she'd left the valley. Even then, he'd made her shudder, her instincts telling her he plotted against Morigan. But, now, to discover she—and Naren—had been the target of Cradoc's plans all along . . .

"What can we do? There are four to your one, but we've a blaster. Tell me what you need from me and I'll do it."

He smiled grimly down at her. "There's nothing we can do but wait and see what they want. We've a blaster, but they may just as easily have one or two of their own. To attempt an escape would make us easy targets. Whether we like it or not, we're trapped here."

Rissa swallowed hard. "I'm afraid, Naren. What if they mean to harm you?"

He stroked her cheek, the action exquisitely tender. "I was rather more concerned with your welfare, femina. I hardly think Cradoc followed us all the way through these mountains just to get back at me. He knows your value. He knows that even though Morigan was forced to send you back, if he harms you, he strikes a blow Morigan may never recover from. And, then, there's the issue of your father . . ." Naren shook his head. "It could be one or both of these things. He won't succeed, though, not as long as I live."

Fear leapt in Rissa, constricting her throat and sending her heart to hammering. "No, Naren." She grasped his face between her hands and forced him to look at her. "If it's me Cradoc wants, give me to him. We buy time the longer we keep alive, buy a chance at escape, at rescue. But if you force things to a battle . . ." She choked back a sob. "I don't want you risking your life for me!"

Naren smiled softly. "And if not for you, sweet femina, for whom?" Ever so gently, he pulled her hands from his face and clasped them in his. "Morigan placed his trust in me to protect you when he chose me to take you home. I cannot turn from that trust. And I'll be dead before Cradoc or any of his minions lay one finger on you." He picked up the blaster and rose. "I'll keep guard until Cradoc makes his move."

An irrational anger coursed through her. How could Naren imagine she could sit here quietly while he took guard? She wanted to scream instead, to grab the blaster, and rush out into the night, firing wildly. Anything but sit here and wait in helpless passivity.

A voice, shouting Naren's name, pierced the tumult in Rissa's mind.

"What do you want, Cradoc?" Naren scooted over to take refuge behind an outcropping of rock just inside the cave entrance.

"Give us the female, and we'll spare your life!" came the reply. "She cannot go back to Primasedes. She knows too much about us. Lindatees will use her against our people."

"And what will you do with Rissa if I give her over to you?"

"You know the answer as well as I. The female must die! No one need know she never reached Primasedes. Join with me against Morigan. He's made a debacle of this whole incident. With you at my side, I'm sure to bring him down!"

"And condemn our people to certain disaster with you as Cat Lord? You're mad, Cradoc, if you think I'll ever let that happen!" Naren let go a searing blast of fire. "And just to reassure you we're not unarmed, here's a taste of my blaster's warmth."

"It'll do you no good, Naren." Cradoc laughed, his voice echoing eerily in the silent night. "We've blasters as well. You set one foot out of that cave and we'll finish you off."

"Then, it's a stalemate, isn't it?"

"Only for a time," came the snarling reply. "Only for a time."

With a sigh, Naren sank down behind the outcropping and set his blaster aside. His glance met Rissa's. "Still interested in giving yourself over to him?"

She clasped her arms about her and shivered. "No."

His gaze softened. "Go to sleep, femina. There's not much else to be done right now at any rate. I'll stand guard. They may be my own kind, but they'll not get past me."

Rissa shook her head. "I-I couldn't sleep."

"Then just rest. I've no further time to spare for talk. I need all my senses about me to stay alert against them." He turned back to scan the cloud-shrouded night.

Silently, she stared at him, then sighed and lay back on her bed. Naren was right. There was no more to be said. He was up against the most formidable of foes—other Cat Men. He needed no further distractions from her.

She closed her eyes, her mind awhirl, and faced alone her own private horrors of the night. A night that could well be her last on Agrica, her final night of life.

Ah, Morgan, Rissa cried out to him with an anguished, aching heart. *I'm so sorry . . . for my last, cruel words to you . . . for all the pain and frustration I gave you. Would that you'd never known me, though I cannot say the same for having known you.*

The memories, of his mouth, hot and man-hungry upon hers, of his big, hard, powerful body, his beautiful eyes, his passionate nature, and tender loving, filled her with a sweet, special joy. She'd lived deeply and fully in the weeks she'd been with him and his people. She'd known love, fulfillment, a sense of purpose. She'd suffered, but she'd also triumphed. It was enough. It had to be . . .

Smoke, acrid, and choking, woke her. Rissa shoved herself

up on one elbow and glanced frantically around. Through the smoke billowing into the cave, she saw Naren, crouched before the entrance.

"N-Naren!" Rissa cried. "What's happening?"

He shot her a despairing look and crawled over. "They mean to smoke us out, femina, or suffocate us. Either way, they bring this little stalemate to a close."

"I don't want to die in here," she whispered. "I want to fight them!"

Naren smiled, the warmth in his eyes belying the hard set of his jaw. "I thought you might. Here's my plan. I'll leap out of the cave, scattering the pile of brush that burns in our way. You come out an instant later with the blaster. It'll be time enough for me to draw their fire. Use the blaster to rake everything in your path. Don't hesitate, even if I get in your way. You'll only get one chance, femina."

Rissa nodded, her lips set in grim determination. "I'll do my best."

"I know you will. You've always had the heart of a warrior. Now, come. It's time."

The smoke swirled into the cave, smothering and blinding. Naren gripped her hand in his for a fleeting moment more, squeezed it, then tugged her forward. At the entrance, he released her. "Fare well, femina," he whispered hoarsely. "If we don't meet again in this life, may we do so sometime, somewhere in the vast, spiritual cosmos of space."

Then, Naren was gone. With a roar of pure, animalistic rage he sprang from the cave, diving straight for the thick pile of flaming brush a few meters away. A terrible shout of exultation went up from the Cat Men awaiting them. Naren made contact with the brush, scattered it in a shower of spark and fire, then rolled over and flipped agilely to his feet.

Rissa saw little more. Her heart thundering, she ran from

the cave, firing her blaster. A Cat Man leaped before her. The blaster burst caught him squarely in the chest. With a terrible scream, he fell.

A sound, a quick intake of breath, was her only warning of her next attacker. She wheeled around, but it was too late. The blaster was wrenched from her grip with a strength both superhuman and blindingly quick. A hand, claws unsheathed, swung toward her, striking her alongside the head. She saw stars, bright lights, then a roiling mist. With a cry of bitter frustration, Rissa fell.

Fighting frantically against the blackness she shoved herself to her knees. Sounds, awful growls and snarls, harsh intakes of breath drawn in pain, filled the air, surrounding her in a cacophony of animalistic battle. "N-Naren," she moaned. "Naren . . ."

Her arms were jerked roughly before her and bound. Rissa blinked fiercely, clearing at last the haze that shimmered before her eyes. She flung back her hair and tried to rise. A hand shoved her down, entangling cruelly in her hair to hold her there.

She saw, however, the scene of vicious, desperate battle being played out just ten meters away. Wounded and panting heavily, Limos and Cradoc circled a profusely bleeding Naren. The black-haired Cat Man dodged his two opponents' thrusts and feinted, but he was outnumbered. Though Limos was hardly his match, Cradoc was.

Repeatedly, Cradoc leapt at Naren. In defending himself against his opponent's attacks, Naren momentarily left himself open to Limos's slashes. He recovered fast enough to avoid a fatal blow but received another painful, debilitating rake of claws for his efforts.

It was but a matter of time, Rissa realized, before Naren weakened and they overpowered him. She struggled futilely in her bonds, a fearsome rage filling her. Gods, she had to go to him, help him! To watch him slowly be slashed to death was a horror beyond endurance!

In response to Rissa's crazed struggles, her captor's hand clenched only tighter in her hair. She bit back a despairing cry. *Naren!*

As if he'd heard her heartfelt call, Naren lunged for Limos. It was a desperate ploy, to eliminate one opponent while leaving himself open to the other, but Naren's only chance. He tackled Limos and brought him to the ground. Before the Cat Man could regain his balance and strike back, Naren slashed him, deep and hard, across the throat.

With a strangled scream Limos fought back, but it was already too late. Bright red blood spurted from the severed arteries in his throat. He choked, flailed frantically, then fell.

Before Limos even struck the ground, Naren was back on his feet. He whirled around. Cradoc slashed viciously across his face. As the blood welled, blinding him, Naren lunged for the other Cat Man. He groped wildly, finding only thin air where Cradoc had once stood. He flung himself around, clawing sightlessly.

"Naren, behind you!" Rissa screamed knowing, even as she did, the end was near.

Naren staggered around. A powerful arm snaked about his throat. A hand ensnared in his hair, wrenching his head back. Naren fought like a man crazed, but to no avail. Razor-sharp claws dug into his throat, ripping it asunder.

"Die!" Cradoc snarled victoriously. "Die, fool that you are. Your loyalty to Morigan was always misplaced. Always!"

"No! Oh, Gods, no!" Rissa shrieked, fighting like a wild cat against her captor's hold. "Naren! *Naren!*"

He turned to the sound of her voice. He reached out for her. Then the blood welled from his throat, coursing down into his lungs, strangling him. The proud strength and vitality that had always been his ebbed with each faltering beat of his heart. Naren slumped, held upright only by the grip Cradoc had of his hair.

As Rissa watched in tear-filled horror, Cradoc released Naren and shoved him away. He sank to the ground.

She screamed out her pain and rage, caught up in a maelstrom of agonized hysteria. The sounds were tormented, primal, as Rissa keened over and over, her cries reverberating off the foothills and forested mountains, reaching clear to the storm-fouled peaks and beyond.

Twenty

The storm followed Morigan as he raced through the mountains, nipping at his heels with icy glee, howling, and tugging at his cloak as if to pull him back and encompass him in its foul, swirling, snow-laden grasp. To tarry a moment, though, would force at least a night if not a day or two holed up in a cave waiting out the storm. That realization only quickened Morigan's pace. There was too much at stake, too much precious time already squandered, to allow the erratic elements of nature to interfere now.

Lisan and the others, however, would most likely be caught in the storm. The time needed to gather the men and necessary equipment would slow their trek after Morigan by at least an hour or two. Long enough to trap them in the storm's blinding grip. He'd get no assistance from them, he feared, when he might need it most.

The odds were strong he'd face Cradoc and the others alone, unless Naren managed to hold them off long enough for Morigan to reach him or killed a few in the meantime. He knew his friend, knew he'd not go down easily, but knew as well Cradoc's craftiness and determined intent. As powerful a fighter as Naren was, four Cat Men against one were crushing odds.

The hours wore on. The chill blanket of night settled over the mountains, freezing the sweat pouring from Morigan's body as he struggled up over rocky trails and ever deepening snow. The triple moons gradually rose in the ebony sky, illuminating the wintry landscape with an eerie, silver light. He glanced up briefly. The sight sent a chill of an entirely different kind rippling through him.

The triple moons neared their triennial alignment. It was but another six or seven days before the mating urge overcame the Cat People. He must be back in the lair by then, as must Naren, Lisan, and the others, or they risked certain death. He'd had no qualms about Naren's timely return. The journey to Primasedes would take five days, slowed as he was with Rissa. The return to the lair, even in the snow, would take an unencumbered Cat Man but an easy three. If all went well, Naren and Rissa should have reached Primasedes by the day after tomorrow.

But now, with Cradoc hot on their trail, perhaps even caught up with them, there was no telling where they were. Curse Cradoc! All Morigan's careful provisions to see to the mating needs of the Cat People when the night of the triple moons arrived, thanks to the self-serving ambitions of one man, were now in danger of coming to naught. Now, not counting himself, there were ten Cat Men out in the mountains within a week of the moons' alignment. Men who might well be without a mating partner when the time came.

The doubts, the worries, followed Morigan as he drove himself relentlessly through the night. Never slackening his pace, he ate and drank what he'd hastily prepared for the trip on the run, ignoring the aching muscles and burning lungs, the bitter cold. Finally, a numb euphoria drove him. Dawn rose over the mountains. cold and brilliant, as he traveled eastward. Behind him, the storm lowered ominously, engulfing the peaks and valleys in thick, gray, snow-laden clouds.

By sunset, the path led downward at last. He'd been on

the trail over twenty-four hours, and there was yet no sign of Naren and Rissa or Cradoc and his men. Their spoors still mingled, however, which squelched any hope Cradoc had purposes other than the pursuit of Naren and Rissa. The realization grasped Morigan's heart in a claw of anguish. Gods, if only he didn't reach them too late!

On and on, he drove himself, cursing his stupidity in sending Naren out with her alone, of not anticipating Cradoc's move, of ever agreeing to let Rissa leave at all. If only he had it to do over again, he'd defy the Council and demand the right to keep the woman he loved. If only . . .

As dawn once more streaked the sky, Morigan, his body trembling in exhaustion, gazed finally on the distant foothills leading to the winter-browned plains. With his acute Cat's vision, he blearily scanned the land. He saw nothing to fuel his strength or freshen his hope. Then, the faint sounds of battle reached him.

The cries and primal noises were unmistakable. With a low growl, Morigan sped down the trail, terror vibrating through him. Hold on Naren, he prayed, repeating the words with each beat of his pounding heart. *Hold on!*

The minutes plodded by, then a quarter of an hour, and still the battle raged on. Snarls rose ever loudly to his ears, rising in a fearful, savage cacophony. Gods, if only he could reach them in time!

Then, everything went quiet. Morigan groaned in despair. The silence dragged on, heavy, ominous.

A scream of pain, of rage, of unutterable loss reverberated through the air.

Rissa!

Morigan scrambled up that last hillside, grasping frantically at boulders to tug his tortured body ever onward. He stumbled; he slid back, scrabbling over dirt and rock until he finally reached the summit of the hill blocking his view—and looked down on a heartrending scene of blood and gore.

Limos lay sprawled below, his throat ripped out. Nearby, lay the blaster-scorched body of another Cat Man. Morigan's fevered gaze took both in and quickly moved to where Cradoc stood, Naren's body at his feet. As he watched, his cousin lifted his arms to the sky, threw back his head, and gave a roar of primal victory.

The harsh, terrifying sound rose in volume and stridency with each breath Cradoc took. Morigan's hands clenched at his sides; his big body shook with grief. Then, as Cradoc's jubilation faded at last, Morigan roared down his reply, a challenge rife with terrible promise. A promise that one, and only one, would survive the battle to come.

At the unexpected sound, Cradoc's head jerked up. For an instant, he stood there, transfixed. Then he set his hands on his hips and laughed. "Come too late, haven't you, Cousin?" he smirked, shoving Naren's bloody, lifeless body over with his foot. "Always far too late to save the ones you love."

Morigan's chest heaved at the sight of his dearest friend lying there, his body covered with fearsome wounds, his throat clawed away. For a fleeting instant his resolve faltered beneath the pain of yet one more loved one lost. Then he remembered Rissa.

"Where is she, Cradoc?" he snarled, a renewed sense of purpose fueling him. "What have you done to Rissa?"

Cradoc made a sharp motion. From below and out of sight of Morigan's position, another Cat Man dragged a bound and weeping Rissa into view. "Bring her to me," Cradoc ordered. "Let Morigan see his mate. Alive and well . . . for a brief time more."

As Morigan watched, every muscle in his powerful body gone tense, Cradoc grabbed Rissa by the hair, twisted his hand viciously, and forced her to her knees before him. He shot Morigan a wolfish grin. "Still want her, do you, Cousin? Then, come down and get her."

Morigan swung the blaster into firing position.

"I wouldn't try that," Cradoc growled, his voice low with warning. "I could slash her throat as easily as I did Naren's before you finished me with the blaster. But, then, perhaps she's no longer of use to you? Perhaps she's no longer worth risking your life for?" He cocked his head in mocking speculation. "But, of course, I'd forgotten. The female means nothing in light of the welfare of our people. And, to save yourself, to remain Lord, she must be sacrificed, mustn't she?"

He unsheathed a claw and pressed it to Rissa's neck. "Say the word, Morigan. Shall I slit her throat and be done with it? Eh, Cousin?"

Morigan's glance slammed into Rissa's. Tawny brown eyes, full of an anguished love, locked with his. Impotent frustration welled in his gut.

Once again, he was forced to choose between Rissa and his people. If he went down for her, he would place himself at Cradoc's mercy—a mercy that would last just as long as it took for his cousin to kill him. Yet, if he didn't, Rissa would surely die.

Either way Cradoc won, and he knew it. He would have Morigan's life, or Rissa's. And with Rissa's, he'd destroy the last vestiges of the essence that made Morigan what he was. That realization was more than the Cat Lord could bear.

A fierce battle waged within him and, for once, his concern for his people didn't prevail. Never again, he vowed savagely. Never again would he sacrifice Rissa. Naren had died trying to protect her. He could do no less.

Morigan flung his blaster aside. "I'll come down, Cradoc. Just don't hurt Rissa."

"No, Morigan!" she cried, struggling wildly. "Don't! Cradoc means to kill me, one way or another. Go, get away while you can! You can't save me no matter what you do."

"And I can't live with myself if I do anything else, sweet one," he called out to her as he climbed down the hillside and came to stand before Cradoc. Cradoc's compatriot, whom Morigan now recognized as the Cat Man, Zandar, leveled a blaster on him.

"Let her go," Morigan demanded, his voice raw, ragged.

He looked awful, Rissa thought, gazing up at him. Dark circles of exhaustion smudged the skin beneath his eyes. His leather clothes were torn, his hands abraded, and his hair tousled and tangled. From the looks of him, he hadn't slept in days, had been on the trail in their pursuit for probably as long. Despite the proud tilt to his chin and the piercing stare he riveted on his cousin, Rissa knew Morigan was spent.

"Not so fast, *my Lord*," Cradoc drawled, as Morigan reached out for Rissa. He jerked her by the hair closer to him.

His glance swept Morigan's, and his gaze narrowed. Rissa, glancing up at Cradoc, knew he, too, had taken in the significance of Morigan's appearance. A chill of premonition prickled down her spine.

"If you want her so badly, fight for her," the auburn-haired Cat Man said. "Fight for her and the Cat Throne."

Hope leapt within Morigan. Cradoc wouldn't spare Rissa if he won, and there was still Zandar if *he* managed to kill Cradoc, but the possibilities of combat offered promise nonetheless. "You'd let a fight between us determine everything?"

"I want the Cat Throne, but only by taking it from you,

Cousin," Cradoc said silkily. "It holds little value unless I kill you in the process."

"And what of Zandar?" Morigan gestured toward the other Cat Man. "He still has a blaster. How am I to trust that, if I win, he won't still use it on me?"

Cradoc shrugged. "I can speak only for my own honor. Zandar must face his as he would." He jerked Rissa's hair again, hard, wringing a gasp of pain from her. "Make up your mind, Morigan. You've heard my terms. They are more than fair. Do you accept them or not?"

"Yes." Morigan slung his pack from his back and laid it on the ground before Rissa. His eyes met hers briefly, then slid back down to the pack.

"Good. Good. Now, move away from us. Stand over there." Cradoc indicated a small pile of boulders about twenty meters away, near the edge of a steep drop-off.

Morigan shot him one final, blistering look, then did as directed. Once he was safely out of easy striking range, Cradoc motioned Zandar over. "Take the female and don't let her go. At no time during the battle are you to interfere. Do you understand?"

His compatriot nodded. Slinging his blaster over his shoulder, Zandar took Rissa from Cradoc. He jerked her to her feet and, twisting her arm, pulled Rissa to him. As Cradoc strode over to Morigan, Zandar whispered in her ear. "You're quite lovely. When Cradoc's done slicing Morigan to bits, I've a mind to ask him for a piece of you—before he kills you."

"And if Morigan wins?" Rissa hissed back. "What will you do then?"

"My life's worth more than my honor. What do you think I'll do?"

She had her answer. Somehow, she must find a way to

thwart Zandar. Rissa glanced down at the pack. There was something about the pack Morigan had been trying to alert her to. But how to get to it?

"Ah," Zandar breathed in eager anticipation, "the battle begins!"

She jerked her attention back to the two Cat Men, now crouched low, circling one another. Claws bared, low growls rumbling in their throats, and manes wild and awry, they looked the epitome of the savage animals they were fabled to be. Rissa's pulse pounded in her breast. Her fisted palms went clammy. A fierce, bittersweet exultation filled her.

Morigan, her mate, fought for her. He'd come through the snow and night and mountains to rescue her. Despite his act in sending her away, despite the cruel words they'd shared that morn she'd departed, and despite his personal fears and devotion to the will of his people, he'd still come. Though there was little she could do to assist him in this most terrible of battles, she would be with him until the end. She'd already lost Naren. Whatever happened, Rissa refused to lose Morigan as well.

Cradoc struck first, claws ripping and tearing as he leapt. Morigan jerked aside. His own claws left a glancing slash across Cradoc's face.

His opponent snarled in pain, pivoted, and sent a roundhouse kick to Morigan's gut. The Cat Lord caught his leg just before it made contact and shoved upward with all his strength, throwing Cradoc off balance. The Cat Man somersaulted into the air to land agilely on his feet. He flung his mane from his eyes, glared at Morigan, then proceeded to feint and dodge in relentless, dizzying moves.

The game, meant to wear Morigan down, did just that. As time passed, he evaded Cradoc's slashes with less and less speed, receiving increasingly severe wounds. Morigan cursed his slowed reflexes, knowing Cradoc risked little against him in his currently debilitated state. The realization angered Morigan, but he fought past it. He dared not waste precious energy on useless emotions, nor on foolhardy attempts that would gain him nothing.

Rissa, Morigan thought through his tormented haze as Cradoc inflicted yet another agonizing wound. He must fight on for Rissa.

Sweat dripped from his brow, bathing his body to mingle excruciatingly with his gaping wounds. His strength faltered. Dizziness consumed him. Desperation fueled his efforts now. Gods, there had to be some way to bring this battle to a close before it was too late! But how? How?

Blearily, he glimpsed sight of the cliff that lay thirty meters behind Cradoc. A desperate plan formed in his mind.

Step by agonizing step, Morigan forced Cradoc to the ledge. A deep ravine lay below, the drop sheer and long. At its bottom, large, sharp rocks jutted from the ground.

It was a desperate ploy, this hope of toppling Cradoc over the cliff—a ploy that could just as easily end in his own death—but all the chance he had. There was no other way . . .

Morigan and Cradoc battled to the very edge of the ravine. There, the two men grappled, feline claws raking each other with savage fury as each struggled for the advantage, for the final victory. Morigan's face contorted with the sheer effort it took to meet and hold back Cradoc's mighty assault, straining with all the strength left in his body.

And, just when it seemed as if Cradoc's greater power and stamina would at last prevail, Morigan let his knees buckle. Cradoc, caught by surprise and by the claw-deep hold he had on Morigan, lost his balance. It was all the opportunity the Cat Lord needed.

Dropping to the ground, Morigan flipped Cradoc over his

head. With a roar of outrage, his opponent sailed out and past the edge of the ravine. Arms and legs flailing, Cradoc grasped at Morigan, for any kind of purchase—and found none. Screaming in impotent fury, he fell, striking the rocks far below.

Morigan was immediately on his feet, racing toward Zandar. The Cat Man, however, had guessed the battle's outcome just a moment earlier. He swung his blaster down and fired.

The blast caught the Cat Lord in the shoulder. The stunning force of the impact sent him tumbling backward. Backward . . . over the edge and into the ravine.

"Morigan!" Rissa screamed. She leaped up, wild in her fear, slamming her shoulder hard into Zandar's momentarily unguarded belly. He gasped, staggered backward, tripping over Naren's body and fell, his head striking a sharp rock.

Sobbing, Rissa climbed to her feet, stared down at Zandar's motionless form, then glanced about for some way to free herself from her bonds. Her gaze settled on Morigan's pack.

Racing over to it, she frantically dug inside. Rope . . . food . . . a water flask. Her fingers glanced off something sharp. A dagger! Relief rocketed through Rissa. A moment later, and she'd sliced her bonds free.

She flung them aside and ran to the ravine's edge. Far below, Cradoc's body sprawled grotesquely on the sharp rocks, impaled and lifeless. Her glance swung from the fatally wounded Cat Man to seek out Morigan. He was nowhere to be seen.

"R-Rissa," came a harsh whisper. She glanced down. Morigan hung by one hand to a dead tree root just a meter below.

"Gods, Morigan!" she cried, horrified. "Wh-what shall I do?"

"M-my pack. I've a long coil of rope in it. T-tie it to the nearest boulder then . . . then lean down and tie the other end about my waist. Once the rope's secure . . . I can let go of this root and grasp the rope."

"Maybe I can pull you up instead." She grabbed him by the tunic and tugged. He moved upward slightly but couldn't gain a foothold in the unstable dirt.

"No, femina," Morigan rasped. "It won't work. My left shoulder's . . . useless and so's my right leg. I'm too big for you to pull up . . . by yourself. Get . . . get the rope. Hurry! I can't hold on much longer . . ."

Rissa leapt to her feet and ran for the pack. Grabbing it, she sped back to the ledge.

A large boulder, about five meters from the edge of the ravine, looked buried solidly enough in the ground to bear Morigan's weight. Rissa quickly tied off one end of the line around it, then scrambled over to the edge of the ravine. Leaning down as far as she dared, she was just able to tie the other end about Morigan's waist and knot it securely. Then, again grasping him by his tunic, she cried, "Now, Morigan. Grab hold of the rope now!"

He hesitated but an instant, then released his grip on the tree root and grabbed for the line. With a powerful surge of Cat-potent muscles, Morigan laboriously inched his way up the rope.

Long, torturous seconds passed as he strained to his utmost limits. Sweat sheened his brow. His breath rasped hard and ragged in his chest. Rissa pulled with all her might and was rewarded with a gradual upward movement. Bit by painful bit, Morigan finally made his way to the top of the ravine and over it.

She dragged the exhausted Morigan the rest of the way, pulling him safely away from the ledge before she finally

let him go. Then, turning him over, Rissa untied the rope
about his waist and tore his ruined tunic apart.

Blessedly, the blaster wound had been but a glancing
surge. His left shoulder was badly injured, his hand and arm
useless for a good while to come. His right leg lay limp and
motionless from what looked like a bruising blow to his hip
when he fell, but there seemed no permanent damage. His
other injuries, though painful, would heal as well.

"Will I live?" Morigan asked as she stuffed a torn piece
of his tunic over the wound.

"Yes, I'd wager so. It'll need—"

A low groan rose from behind them. Two pairs of eyes
jerked up and around. Zandar groaned again and moved
slightly.

"Quick, Rissa!" Morigan hissed. "Get the blaster!"

Her heart in her throat, Rissa leapt to her feet. She raced
toward the blaster that lay within arm's reach of the fallen
Zandar. Even as she neared, the Cat Man levered himself to
one elbow and shook his head, dazed.

Rissa dived for the blaster, rolled over, and shoved herself
to her knees. Zandar, realizing his danger, lunged for her
with a savage snarl.

"Rissa!" Morigan cried.

In that instant between realization and reaction, instinct
took over. Rissa fired. Blue flame spewed from the blaster,
catching Zandar full in the chest. With a strangled scream,
he toppled over.

She rose, walked over to him, and nudged him with her
foot. The scent of charred flesh filled her nostrils. Zandar
was dead.

Dead. All were dead, save she and Morigan. Broken,
bloody bodies lay all around. Zandar, Limos, Cradoc, the
Cat Man she'd first killed, and Naren.

Naren.

There'd been no opportunity, from the first shock of his death to the rescue of Morigan, to go to him. But now, finally, there was time. Time to mourn the good, brave Cat Man who'd been her friend. The blaster dropped from Rissa's hands. Her knees buckled and, with a whimper, she crawled over to Naren.

She touched him gently, hesitantly, smoothing away the blood-matted hair that clung to his face, dabbing at his wounds as if to staunch their flow. But there was no flow, no heart beating to pump the blood through his body. No breath, no life . . . nothing.

"Gods, Naren," she whispered achingly. "Why you? Ah, why you?" Rissa pulled him into her arms. His blood soaked her tunic. Its metallic scent filled her. She didn't care. As the tears began to flow, flooding her eyes, coursing down her cheeks to mingle in a pink river with his blood, Rissa rocked him to and fro.

Naren. Sweet, gentle, laughing Naren.

"R-Rissa?"

She turned. Morigan painfully crawled over, propelling himself by sheer dint of the strength of his opposing good arm and leg. At last, he reached her.

Shoving himself to one elbow, the Cat Lord stared down at Naren. Something flickered briefly in his eyes, then was gone. The emotionless mask fell, once again, into place.

He glanced up at Rissa. "I haven't the strength to bury him. We'll have to burn his body."

Pain slashed through her, then total disbelief. "B-burn him? Is that all you have to say? Don't you care he's dead? Doesn't it matter?"

He shot her a sharp, irritated look. "Of course, I care. But there's work to be done, my wounds to be tended, and a storm," he added, glancing over his shoulder at the fast-approaching clouds, "on its way. If we don't see to him soon, we'll be forced to leave him to the scavengers. And I won't let that happen to Naren.

"Now, could you gather the necessary wood?" Morigan continued on, seemingly oblivious to her growing horror. "I'm sorry to be of such little help but, in the meanwhile, I'll get a fire going. If you'd just hand me my pack, there's a tinder box—"

"Curse you, Morigan!" Rissa cried. "I've never met a more cold, heartless man in my life!" She grabbed his hand and placed it on Naren's brutalized face. "This is Naren. Your dearest friend in all the world. It's all right to mourn him, to even weep! He deserves that much from you. He died protecting me because I was yours, because you trusted him to see to my safety. He could have left—Cradoc said he could—but he didn't. He didn't, because of his loyalty and love for you!"

For a long moment, Morigan's hand lingered on Naren's face. A shudder vibrated through him. Then he jerked his hand away and shook his head. Hard, flat eyes lifted to hers. "I know what he did, what he was to me," he snapped. "I don't need you telling me. Now, will you gather the wood, or do I have to drag myself out to get it?"

"No. No, I'll get it." Ever so gently, Rissa laid Naren back on the ground and rose. She glared down at Morigan, knowing he loved his friend, knowing his stoic acceptance of his death was but his way of dealing with the pain, but unable to keep from lashing out nonetheless. She was tired, sick to death of his stubborn refusal to show emotion—if not for losing his family, if not for giving her up, then for dear, sweet Naren.

"He shouldn't have wasted his life for you," she hissed,

her face gone white, her mouth tight. "You've never been worthy of him. Never!"

She turned then and stomped away, leaving Morigan to lie there beside Naren, his heart twisted so tightly in his chest he thought he'd die from the pain.

They burned Naren at midday, just as the clouds and wind swirled down the mountains to reach them. The flames rose high, crackling in a fiendish delight, licking greedily at the body of the Cat Man placed upon the wood-heaped pyre. Smoke billowed. Sparks scattered. The scent of burning flesh filled the air.

Rissa stood before the pyre apart from Morigan, her arms clasped tightly about her, immersed in her own private grief. A grief not only for the loss of a fine man, but for the other man, as well, the man she still loved yet knew she dared not let herself want.

A bitter sadness welled in her. Naren, who could love and wanted to, was dead. Morigan, who refused to let himself love or feel too deeply about anything, lived.

If the existence he'd chosen for himself could truly be called living.

It was all too sad, too far beyond anything Rissa had ever known or had any experience of. She felt helpless, hopeless. Despair wound its tendrils about her and squeezed mercilessly, until all emotion, all sensation was gone.

The wind surged down, whipping her cloak about her. The first fat flakes of snow began to fall, brushing her face, melting to trickle down to mingle with her tears. The fire engulfed Naren now with a roar, totally consuming him.

Rissa watched for a few moments more, imagining his soul finally freed of the brutalized confines of his body, wending its way upward into the vast expanse of the heavens. She followed the sparks into the graying sky, silently calling out her farewell. Promising to meet him again, someday, somewhere. And vowing, in the interim, to never, ever forget him.

Then, she turned to where Morigan sat awkwardly propped against a nearby boulder. His head was lowered, his thick, brown mane cascading forward to hide his face. Rissa walked over. "Come, the storm approaches. Let me help you back to the cave."

His head jerked up. His eyes were shadowed, his mouth grim. "Yes," he ground out the word. "There's nothing left us here."

She squatted beside him, handed Morigan the stout walking stick she'd made, then helped him stand. He nearly fell before he gained his balance. Rissa quickly slipped around to grasp him about the waist. In slow, awkward steps, they made their way to the cave.

The storm roared down with a vengeance now. The snow fell with a thick, swirling intensity, blowing into Rissa's eyes, blinding her. She lowered her head against the frigid onslaught. Beside her, Morigan struggled silently on, the taut look to his face and quivering muscles the only evidence of the effort it cost him.

He staggered and, despite Rissa's attempts to prevent it, fell heavily just inside the mouth of the cave. She scooted beneath him and tried to help him back to a sitting position. He went limp in her arms. "Morigan?" she cried. "Please, just a few meters more, and I'll have you on your bed and beside a warm fire. Help me!"

"No," he whispered. "Leave me here."

His voice was raw, bleak. He was at the end of his strength.

"I can't leave you here," Rissa protested. "You'll freeze to death."

"Leave me," he replied listlessly.

Curse him, she thought in growing anger. If he thought now to die on her as well, after all she'd done and Naren had sacrificed, he thought wrong. She grasped him beneath the arms, rose to her feet, and dragged him, millimeter by agonizing millimeter, across the cave's stone floor. Never once did he utter a word or protest her actions.

A cold chill of premonition wafted through Rissa. More than just Morigan's physical strength had fled him. His will to live, the proud, stubborn essence that had always made him the man he was, seemed gone as well. Though he chose not to admit it, perhaps Naren's death had been the last burden on Morigan's already overburdened shoulders. The burden that had finally broken him.

Rissa had no way of knowing. There was just too much hammering at Morigan right now. The exhaustion of his long journey to reach them, his brutal injuries, some of which might still be hidden to her, and Naren's death. Only time would reveal the truth.

In the meanwhile, she must keep him alive. Rissa dragged Morigan over to the bed she'd slept in but a night ago, wrapped him snugly in the blankets, then turned to start a fire. Once the fire was blazing nicely, she rose and went outside to gather as much wood as she could before the ferocity of the storm drove her back inside.

She shoved the big boulder that sat outside the entrance across the cave's opening. Thankfully, it blocked a good amount of the wind. The cave wouldn't be cozy warm but, with the large amount of wood she'd been able to stockpile, they should manage through the night. On the morrow . . . well, she would deal with it when the time came.

Morigan lay silent and apathetic through the rest of the day and into the night. He said nothing, didn't react when she cleansed his wounds, sprinkled on some of Agna's healing powder, and bandaged them. A thorough examination revealed no additional hidden injuries. He wouldn't be traveling anywhere for at least a week, maybe two, though.

Her attempts at getting him to eat or drink were futile. Morigan simply shook his head and closed his eyes, effectively shutting her out. His body, when she finally crawled in the bed beside him to conserve their warmth, was cold and unyielding.

Morigan's mood was no better the next morning. He refused breakfast and accepted a swallow of water only after Rissa all but poured it down his throat. She cleansed his wounds, noted with satisfaction they looked clean and weren't festering, then rebandaged him.

As the storm raged on throughout the day, she managed to gather enough wood to keep the fire going. Near noon, Rissa prepared a passable soup from meat sticks and some dried vegetables and seasoning. Once more, Morigan refused to eat.

It was the last straw. "What, by the five moons, are you trying to do?" she raged, all the pent-up fear and frustration finally boiling over. "Kill yourself, you stubborn son of a subterranean sand worm?"

"Leave me alone," he growled darkly.

"No. No, I *won't* leave you alone." Rissa set aside the bowl of soup she'd just dished up for him and scooted over to his side. She took his face in her hands, anchoring him by his hair. "Have you forgotten you're Lord of the Cat People? That you've a sacred duty to stay alive to serve your people? You've sacrificed everything else for their welfare. This is no time to fail them now!"

He glared up at her. "What do you care what I do or don't do for my people? You've hated it every time I chose them over you. Let it be. I'm done, spent. I haven't anything more to give—to anyone."

"So, you'll lie here and die, will you?" Her voice rose on a thread of hysteria. "You can't face anything, can you, Morigan? Even now, you choose death over dealing with life. Gods, how could I ever have loved such a coward!"

"Stop it, Rissa. I can't take much more. If you've even a shred of compassion left for me—"

"It's because I *have* compassion that I fight so hard for you, beating against that wall you've built around your heart. That wall . . ." Her voice caught, " . . . that wall that keeps everyone out . . . even me."

"Perhaps, it's time you gave it up, then."

Her tear-filled gaze riveted on his face. He stared stonily up at her. "Is that what you really want, Morigan?"

His eyes slid shut. For a long moment, he didn't answer. "I don't know what I want anymore. It's that simple. I-I'm just so very, very tired."

Rissa stroked his face, his hair. "I know. I know. Sleep now. The soup can wait. Just sleep."

He sighed, then turned his face into her palm, nuzzling it as if there, in the sweet comfort of her hand, he'd find the solace he searched for. As the day wore on into night, Morigan slept, the healing sleep of the body if not the soul. Yet, it was his soul, Rissa realized sadly, that was far more wounded than his body. Wounded at last, perhaps, unto death . . .

A soul that might never heal again.

Twenty-one

Morigan woke in the early evening and, solely to please Rissa, took a few spoonfuls of soup and a cup of water. Then, after a grudging thank you, he turned and went back to sleep. He slept through all of the next day, rousing only for a short while at supper to take another swallow or two of soup and some water, then dozed off again.

Near dawn of the third day, Morigan came awake, stirred by a disturbing sensation that, as full consciousness returned, intensified into prickling bursts of heat coursing through his body. For a moment, Morigan imagined his wounds had festered and he'd taken with a fever. The unpleasant sensations only continued, however, rippling through his body, stimulating a restless unease. The blood pooled in his groin, congesting it, making it feel hot and heavy.

With a savage curse, Morigan rolled over onto his back. He gained nothing from the effort but a sharp pain in his injured hip and shoulder. Curse it all, how many days had he slept away? Were the triple moons already in alignment? Was tonight the night?

His glance found Rissa, sleeping beside but not close to him. He couldn't blame her after the way he'd shut her out of late.

He scanned the cave. From the looks of it, the fire had died several hours ago, yet the chamber seemed comfortably warm. Then, the faint sound of water, trickling and dripping outside, caught his attention. The snow was melting.

The storm was over; the weather had changed at last. Lisan and the others would be able to make it through the passes and reach them soon. Morigan only hoped they'd returned to the lair instead and would remain there now until the night of the triple moons passed. He prayed his grandfather, in his absence, would take command and refuse to let the search party out of the lair until then. Morigan didn't know what he'd do if he lost yet another six Cat Men in this ill-fated undertaking.

Not that he should let it matter, let it add yet another worry to his already overburdened conscience. He didn't want to face that—or anything—anymore. Naren was dead; Rissa, though he'd saved her from Cradoc, must still go back to her father. There was nothing left fighting for.

He knew, intellectually, there was still his people. His mother, Agna, Lisan, Ardan, and all the rest. But there was no fire, no will left in him to fight on. The realization frightened Morigan, yet, on another plane, he found he no longer cared.

With adequate food supplies and the blaster, Rissa was safe here until Lisan and the others arrived. They would carry out the Council's decision. He'd only to endure the agony of the mating urge until it drove him mad and killed him. Then, it would all be over.

Only another day or so, Morigan thought. He could endure until then. It might well be a coward's way out, but he at least had a choice in choosing his own death. A choice, fatal though it was, at last.

The heat rose, pulsing through him. He glanced over at Rissa. She looked so lovely lying there. Her lips were soft and full, her expression sweet, peaceful. His gaze dipped to the rounded fullness of her breasts, a fullness that even the leather tunic couldn't hide. A longing, to touch her, to pull up her tunic and suckle her breasts, filled him. Gods, but he wanted her so!

Tonight. The moons would surely align tonight, if the intensity of the hunger, the burning ache spiraling within him, were any indication. And he knew they were. He'd lived through four moon alignments since he'd come into his sexual maturity. No Cat Man forgot the unique fire that consumed him then.

As the sensations increased, he'd have to warn Rissa to stay away from him. Luckily for her, his mobility was severely limited. She could easily evade his advances when the hunger grew out of control, when he became so lust-maddened he no longer knew what he was doing. She, at least, would be spared.

Rissa wouldn't like seeing him suffer, though. Morigan knew her well enough to realize that. But there was nothing she could do. It was his decision, his choice.

He feigned sleep when Rissa stirred. There was nothing more to say until his mating urge became so unbearable he could no longer hide it. By then, if all went as he hoped, the end would only be hours away.

She rose, washed herself, then went outside for a time. When she returned, the scent of sempervivus wood and fresh air filled the cave. Soon, she had a new fire blazing. The sounds of Rissa cooking breakfast warned Morigan she'd soon be waking him. After last night, he was certain she'd try to force more food into him.

A few minutes later, a hand gently touched his good shoulder. "Morigan?"

He continued to pretend deep sleep. She grasped his shoulder and shook him. "Morigan? Wake up."

With a groan, Morigan opened his eyes. "I'm not hungry."

Rissa's mouth tightened. She cocked a slender brow. "Indeed? Try again, Morigan. You've gone three days without food. And I don't call an occasional bit of soup, food," she said, quickly cutting off his attempt at protest. "You aren't going to heal if you don't eat."

"Let it be, Rissa," he growled, surprisingly irritated at her. It was the mating urge, he realized. It plucked at him relentlessly, setting his nerves to tightening as taut as the strings of a Cygnian war harp.

"No, I won't let it be." She released his shoulder and sat back, settling comfortably on the ground beside him.

Morigan knew what that lifted chin and resolute stare meant. She was readying for a battle. And knew, as well, he hadn't the strength to best her this time. "Fine," he muttered. "Give me something to eat. Then leave me alone."

A look of puzzled hurt flared in Rissa's eyes, then was gone. "Morigan, please. Won't you talk to me?"

"What's there to talk about? You said it all the other day. And made quite clear what you thought of me, too."

She flushed. "Oh, that. I was angry, confused, and half-crazed with Naren's death. And I didn't understand why you . . ." Rissa inhaled a shuddering breath. "I thought about it a lot in the past three days. I'd plenty of time for thinking, with you sleeping so much of it. And I decided I've no right to dictate to you how you mourn or deal with your pain."

"Indeed?" Morigan's mouth twisted. "And if I choose not to mourn at all?"

Rissa eyed him uncertainly. "I can't believe you didn't feel something, seeing Naren, watching his body burn."

"Feelings like sorrow, loss, and pain accomplish nothing save to incapacitate a person. Besides, they're a luxury I've never had time for."

Her hands clenched in her lap and her shoulders went rigid. "I don't believe that. You say these things to hurt me, to turn me from you, don't you, Morigan? Why?"

"Does it matter?" He gave a harsh laugh. "You're lost to me anyway—one way or another."

She swallowed and looked away. "So, even after what has happened, you still mean to send me back to my father? I thought . . ." Rissa shoved herself to her feet and walked over to where the pot of porridge cooked over the fire.

"What did you think, femina?" Morigan called after her, though he well knew he should let it be. Something inside him, however, wouldn't let him stop or let him temper his words. Better he drive her from him. It served his purposes well, for now, for tonight. "Did you think I came for you because I loved you? That I didn't want Cradoc to harm you?" He laughed again, the sound mocking. "No, femina. You tossed my love away, that day you left. I came because Cradoc had you and meant to use you against me. He threatened my position as Lord of the Cat Men. I had to stop him finally, once and for all."

"I-I don't believe you." For an instant, Rissa lowered her head and her shoulders sagged. Then she wheeled around. "Why are you doing this to me, to us? Curse you, Morigan! I can't bear much more. At least have the kindness to be honest, to tell me the truth."

A tremor rippled through him. The mating impulse burned hotter. Gods, Morigan thought, in his weakened state he'd never make it until tonight! And then to have Rissa standing there, to see her anguish and know he was the one flaying her heart alive . . .

"Then don't believe me." He lay back and closed his eyes. "Soon, it won't matter. I give you my oath on that."

Rissa stared down at him, her gaze narrowing. There was

something wrong, terribly wrong, with Morigan. Yet, he refused to let her in, to allow her to help him. Frustration welled in her. Curse him! Curse his stubborn pride and need always to remain in control!

He needed her now, more than he ever had. A fierce determination not to turn from him filled her. She'd discover the reason for his psychic barrier, sooner or later. In the meanwhile, she'd keep hammering away at that damned wall until it finally came tumbling down—once and for all.

She knelt by the fire, scooped out a healthy serving of porridge and grabbed up a spoon. Rising, Rissa strode back to Morigan. "Here." She shoved the steaming bowl in his face. "Eat your breakfast."

Morigan tossed restlessly on his bed, the sweat pouring from his body. His heart thundered in his chest. The pulse of blood in his head pounded rhythmic, loud. And the pain. He'd never known such pain!

Wildfire raged in his loins. His sex throbbed, the pressure building in his groin so acute he thought he'd explode at any second. His abdominal muscles clenched in an endless spasm until they quivered with the effort. He dug his claws through the blanket and into the earth in an attempt to contain the torment. It did little good.

He was dying, imprisoned in fiery bonds that chained him in excruciating torment. The blood surged in his head, growing louder, deafening him. He squeezed his eyes shut, blocking out the nauseating lights dancing before him. Yet, on and on and on, the pressure grew. There was nothing left him but escape into madness.

"M-Morigan? Rissa's sweet voice, clear as a freshened

breeze, pierced the mists of his agony. "By the five moons, what's wrong?"

She'd been away for the past several hours, out hunting game to supplement their dwindling stockpile of food, a mission Morigan had sent her on in the hope she'd stay gone until it was over. But it wasn't to be. The day had just grayed toward twilight; the three moons had yet to rise. As painful a realization as it was to accept, the mating impulse wouldn't reach its zenith until then.

And neither would his torment.

A cool hand touched his face. "Gods, you're burning with fever!" There was a flurry of movement, then a damp cloth pressed on his brow, his cheeks, and his neck. He grasped at it, caught her wrist, halting her.

"Don't," he groaned. "It-it's not fever. Just . . . just leave me. Go away, Rissa. Get out of here!"

"Why? By all that is sacred, Morigan, tell me what's going on!"

"Too late." He shoved onto his side, away from her. "Too late . . . just as I planned."

"Morigan!" Hands, surprisingly strong, grasped him, pulled him over onto his back. "Curse your stubborn hide!" She slapped him, hard, across the face. *"Tell me what's wrong."*

His eyes snapped open. Momentarily, surprise cleared the red-hot mists. "What do you think—?"

He bit back a groan as the fires flared again. He almost told her but knew, if he did, she'd try to save him. And could. No, just a little while longer, and it would be too late. Too late . . . even for Rissa.

"M-Morigan." Rissa's voice, wobbling on a sob, called him back once more. "You're dying. Gods, I know it. But why? How? Ah, can't you tell me? I can't help if you don't—"She stopped. Her grip on him clenched. Then, with a sudden cry, she released him and ran from the cave.

As Rissa hurried outside, the cool evening air wafted across her face. The golden light of the setting sun faded behind the mountains. She glanced wildly around, searching, praying for the answer to her heartbreaking dilemma. And, as the last bit of sunlight dissipated, she found what she sought.

Just above the horizon in the eastern sky, the triple moons of Agrica rose. Each full, each a luminous ivory, and each in perfect alignment with the other. The Cat Men's night of the triple moons, Rissa realized in rising horror, the night of their uncontrollable urge to procreate. And if they didn't mate . . .

Morigan's words that day in the valley, under the robur trees down by the stream, came back to her. *For a Cat Man . . . to deny himself . . . on that night is fatal. To fight the urges . . . becomes excruciating, driving one to a terrible, pain-maddened death.*

Her horror grew the longer she contemplated his words. Morigan meant for the mating urge to kill him. *Don't believe me,* he'd told her earlier. *Soon, it won't matter. I give you my oath on that."*

She'd thought he'd get better, that her care and concern, rest and food, would slowly ease the despair that had engulfed him since Naren's death. She'd been wrong. And now, she didn't know what else to do.

Tears flooded Rissa's eyes and coursed down her cheeks. Morigan. Gods, how she loved him, but she didn't know what else to do. He'd turned from her, shut her out just as surely as he'd shut out all emotion from his life.

Morigan. Her mate . . . her love.

But, now, she knew. Knew his intent and held the power

to prevent it. But should she? Perhaps, the kinder thing, in the end, was to allow him to do as he wished. To honor his request. He had the right.

Rissa gazed up at the mesmerizing sight of the triple moons, a savage, primal resolve growing within her. Morigan was her mate. She would fight for him until the last breath left her body. And this night, whether he wished it or not, she would join with him one last time. One last time—to save his life.

The musky scent of lust, of wild, fevered hunger, hung heavy on the air. Rissa could feel it, taste it, smell it. Her body responded on some primitive level. Her heart pounded. Her palms went damp. Her loins felt tight, hot, swollen.

She forced herself to enter the cave, to stride across the chamber and over to where Morigan lay, writhing on his bed. He was drenched in sweat, his leonine features contorted in agony, his big, naked chest heaving. The sound of ragged breaths filled the air, the only noise in the stone-silent cave.

For an instant more, Rissa gazed down at him. Then, with a resolute breath, she knelt, flung his blanket aside and, with trembling hands, tugged at the lacings of Morigan's breeches.

At her touch, Morigan froze. His eyes snapped open, impaling her with a blazing, green-gold stare. His good hand moved, anchoring her wrists in an iron clasp.

"What do you think . . . you're doing?"

She twisted in his grasp, attempting to free herself, sparing him not a second's glance. "What do you think I'm doing, you stubborn son of an elephas? You need to mate. I'm going to mate with you."

"No!" There was a frantic, agonized quality to his voice.

Rissa's gaze jerked to his. A tormented entreaty burned in Morigan's eyes.

"No, Rissa. Please."

He was so beautiful, she thought, even in his pain. His lips were full and sensual, even cracked and bleeding as they were. His sweat-matted mane still framed an exotically virile face of high cheekbones, bold spade of a nose, and firm, beard-shadowed jaw. The single aureum Cat's claw still dangled from his powerful neck, a neck pulsing vibrantly with life.

"I love you, Morigan," she whispered her reply. "I won't let you die."

"Even if . . . I want it? Even . . . if I ask it . . . of you?"

She smiled down at him, tenderly. "I cannot, my love. For the sake of your people, for the sake of Naren who sacrificed his life out of loyalty to you, for the sake of your father, and your dead wife and son, I cannot. In willing your own death, you dishonor theirs. I cannot let you do that. For their sakes, if not for yours."

He grimaced. His jaw clenched against the twisting, searing agony in his groin. "Gods," Morigan groaned, "don't talk to me of dishonor! Don't remind me of them!"

"And why not?" Rissa freed herself of his weakening clasp and took his face in her hands. "You're hurting, Morigan. You're weary. Your spirit is sorely wounded and nothing holds you to life just now. Yet, there are those who love and have loved you who want you to live. Let us help you in your time of despair. Let us give you what you so desperately need."

Her fingers gouged into his cheeks, forcing his fevered attention to remain with her. "For once in your life, allow yourself to feel hunger and take what you need. Allow yourself to lean on another, to accept solace and peace. You, who've always given it to others, even at the cost of your own heart."

He gazed up at her with pain-glazed eyes, his body wracked by a myriad of tiny tremors. "I-I . . . Gods, Rissa, I don't know what to do!"

She leaned down and brushed her lips across his. "The first step is always the hardest, my love. But we'll take it together." She released his face, then her hands moved back to the lacings of his breeches.

This time Morigan didn't stop her. His eyes clenched shut, blocking out the sensual image of her disrobing him. He couldn't block out the surging chaos of impulses battling within him, though, nor the painful visions of faces, beloved, yet lost, that flooded his mind. Winna, Calder, his father— and Naren. Ah, Gods!

Something rent within him, tearing open the tightly guarded sanctum of his pain and loss. Something cool and liquid poured out, drowning the burning agony, the soul-devouring memories of people never mourned or put to rest. His body heaved. A soft moan, then another and another, split the air.

"Morigan, my love." Rissa's sweet voice reached him through the mists of his torment. "Let it go. Heal yourself."

He opened his eyes. He was crying. Shame flooded him. Gods, he was a Cat Man, Lord of his people. He shouldn't be crying!

Yet, gazing up into the warm, brown depths of Rissa's eyes, Morigan knew he could no more stop the tears than he could kill Rissa's love for him. Despite the mating urge still burning through his body, the tears felt soothing, liberating. He found himself surrendering and, with that surrender, began to heal.

Cool air rushed over his fevered flesh and tautly swollen

sex as Rissa freed the last of his laces and spread apart his breeches. The tears, the pain of mourning faded, overcome by a fiercer, more intense torment. As Rissa tugged his breeches down over his hips his throbbing manhood sprang free, hot, swollen, and jutting. She brushed him accidentally as she worked. Morigan thought he'd go mad.

"Hurry, femina," he whispered raggedly. "Gods, I'm on fire. I need you. Gods, how I need you!"

"Yes, my love. Soon. Very soon." She leaned back, her hands going to the lacings of her tunic. A second later, and Rissa had the clothing pulled over her head.

Soft, white breasts and cold-hardened pink nipples filled his gaze. Morigan reached out with his good hand. He took a taut little nipple between his thumb and forefinger. "Lean down," he commanded hoarsely. "I-I want to taste you."

She did as he asked, her own breath as uneven as his. Morigan's mouth opened, engulfed the delectable nipple, sucking hard and deep.

A whimper of pleasure escaped Rissa. "Ah, Morigan. Morigan!"

Her scent encompassed him, ripe with a woman's desire. His need burgeoned. His organ swelled even more, the tip flaring with desire. If he didn't take her soon, his passion would surely send him over the edge.

He released her nipple and nuzzled his face in the velvety valley between her breasts. "Y-your breeches," he rasped. "Take them off. N-now," Morigan grabbed for her breeches, then halted. He shoved her away and groaned.

"What? What is it, my love?" Fear shot through Rissa at the difference in the sudden pain and frustration fueling the sound.

"M-my leg. It's still too weak, too unstable, for me to

climb to my knees, much less mount you. Ah, Gods, Rissa, I can't mate with you!"

For a terrified, chaotic moment, Rissa knelt there, her hands frozen at her breeches. Then, she relaxed, chuckling softly. "Ah, but you can, my Lord. There are other ways—"

"No, no." He shook his head in an agony of frustration. "The games I taught you when you were forbidden to me in your time of restriction aren't enough this night. I must mate with you, Rissa. I must place my shaft within your body, spill my seed. Anything less won't be enough to free me from this mating urge."

"And I say again," Rissa murmured as she slid her breeches from her body and came to lie, naked, beside him. "There are other ways."

"I know of no such 'other ways,'" he growled, suddenly wary. "Where have you learned them?"

"From Diona," she giggled. "The Cat Man's way isn't the only manner of mating, you know. According to Diona . . ." She paused, a becoming little flush sweeping up her neck and face. "Well, better if I just show you, I think, my Lord."

"And what . . . what would you have me do?" He stirred restlessly beside her, mastering the rising madness with only the greatest of efforts.

She grinned seductively. "Oh, nothing but lie there as you are. I think I can do the rest." Her hand went to his shaft. Her fingers curled about it, clasping it tightly, savoring the thickness, the hardness of him.

Morigan groaned. His hips arched, reflexively, thrusting himself more fully into her hand. "Rissa . . . have a care."

But she was already shifting into position above him, spreading her legs to straddle his thighs, then scooting up to encompass his hips. She reached between Morigan's slightly parted legs, raked her nails gently over his hair-roughened

sac and the base of his shaft, then grasped him tightly once
more and began to stroke him.

He blinked back the lust-red haze and stared up at her,
transfixed. Her perfect body rose like some fragile blossom
from the strong foundation of his own form, a wraith of
slender shoulders, firm, full breasts, narrow waist, and gently
flaring woman's hips.

Morigan glanced down his body to where his sex jutted
just a hairsbreadth from the dark, moist secrets of her
woman's sheath. He thought he'd explode. "Rissa," he hissed
through clenched teeth. "Gods, h-help me. Take me, now!"

His good hand snaked down to what her widely parted
thighs revealed. His questing fingers sought—and found—
the hot, slick cleft, spread the delicate petals and touched
the soft nubbin of flesh that was the seat of her pleasure.
She moaned, flexing her hips to grant him fuller access.

"G-Gods . . ." Morigan ground his teeth in violent frustration. He arched to meet her, rubbing his hot, aching shaft
against her. Wild tremors vibrated through him. "Please . . .
Rissa," he begged.

She took him then, guiding him to her sweet, secret core.
With a sharp jutting of her hips, she thrust him inside her.

Morigan went rigid. His head snapped back, the cords of
his thick neck taut and straining. His mouth opened in soundless agony. An agony that racked him from head to toe, slipping beneath his skin to ripple with bursts of white-hot fire
over muscle and bone and sinew. His release—he couldn't
contain it, couldn't hold it back a moment longer!

"Rissa," he cried. "I can't . . . Forgive me!"

"Take it, my love," she crooned above him, even as her
hips began gently to undulate, sliding her tight sheath down
the full length of him.

She gazed at Morigan, her mate, lying there so powerful,

so primal, so potent in every way. Yet, for once, so needing, and yielding to her as well. He was no longer in control. He was beyond the limits of his control, trusting her to take him safely to the release his body and mind cried out for.

An exultant sense of power filled Rissa. "Take me," she urged. "I give myself to you fully, joyously." The rhythm of her thrusting hips increased in power and speed. The tug of his big glans within her sheath excited her. She clenched about him.

He moaned, writhed beneath her, his face twisted in agony. With all the strength left in his body, Morigan plunged upward, deep and hard, filling Rissa to the depths of her being. His good hand clasped her hip, anchoring him to her, guiding her in the relentless riot of sensations. He gasped, arched back, his fingers digging in the soft flesh of her buttock. Tears poured from his eyes.

In one sharp, tormentingly beautiful explosion, Morigan came, spewing his hot seed into her. He roared out his release, shuddering wildly beneath her, his sweat-slick body wracked with that special ecstasy of fulfillment. Calling her name over and over in wonderment . . . and surrender.

A surrender of heart as much as body.

The rippling, pleasurable sensations pulsated through him, fading gradually to delightful little tremors, then utter peace. Morigan smiled. His lids lifted.

Rissa's gaze locked with his. Unguarded emotions swam in his striking eyes. Wonderment, a gentle yielding, relief. And overlaying it all was a joyous look of love.

"R-Rissa . . ." He expelled her name on a soft sigh of air. "Rissa, femina. I love you so."

She leaned down, her nipples glancing across him. Her velvet-smooth, highly sensitized flesh rasped pleasantly across his thick pelt of chest hair and bulging muscle. Her sheath clenched, sending a spasm of pure pleasure rocketing through her. "And I love you, my Lord."

He grinned up at her, drained, weak as a babe. "I liked this 'other way' very much. Have you additional surprises you'd care to share with me this night?"

A small frown knotted between her brows. "Aren't you sated? Haven't we fulfilled that infamous mating urge of yours?"

"Not nearly, sweet femina." Morigan pulled her down to lie atop him, their bodies still joined. "Give me but a short time to catch my breath. Then I'll pleasure you as you've pleasured me, while we thoroughly examine all your 'other ways.' "

She snuggled close in unabashed delight. "I think I'd like that very much, my Lord."

"As would I, sweet femina," Morigan gruffly replied. "As would I."

She rose late the next morning, covered Morigan against the chill, and dressed. For once, he didn't hear her. He slept on, his expression relaxed and unguarded in repose.

Rissa hesitated, then knelt and brushed a lock of hair from his face. Tenderness welled in her, threatening her composure and the precarious control she held over her tears. By the five moons, but he'd turn her into a clingy, weepy female if he kept up the way he was going. She didn't know how to defend her heart against him anymore—and no longer wanted to try.

With a soft sigh Rissa rose, picked up the blaster and water flask, and left the cave. Morigan would be ravenous when he woke. The lepus she'd caught yesterday would make a nice stew once it was supplemented with some wild tubers and seasonings. She recalled the tubers she'd seen when she'd been tracking the lepus, growing just a kilometer away beside an ice-cold stream. She'd only be gone a short time. If luck was with her, she'd be back and have the stew simmering before Morigan even awoke.

The day was cool but pleasant. The still damp earth smelled rich and musty, ready to burst with life. Though just the first of the new cycle, it was but a matter of weeks before the Agrican spring officially arrived. It even felt like spring, with the bright sunshine, balmy breeze, and the first shoots of yellow-green grass pushing their determined little way through the ground. Rissa felt wonderful.

She was in love and was loved by a good, brave man who'd finally fought past his fears to open his heart and life. All the shattering loss, the excruciating pain of the past cycle, would soon be behind him. Their life together was just beginning, full of promise and fulfillment.

He wouldn't send her back to her father now. She'd sensed that in him as the night had passed, as the intensity and commitment of their mating had grown. Somehow, someway, they would convince the Council of their love and the need to be together. And this time the Council would listen, understand.

The sound of the stream crashing over rocks as it made its merry way down through the foothills caught Rissa's ears. The watery cacophony intensified the nearer she drew, until it drowned out the agitated chatter of a long-tailed little sciurus overhead in a tall robur tree. Rissa grinned up at the pert-faced, toothy little creature. It flicked its bushy tail at her in an irate challenge, then scurried away. She knelt beside the stream and filled the water flask.

Once the leathern container was bulging with fresh water, Rissa set it aside and splashed some of the ice-cold fluid onto her face, scrubbing away the dirt and grime. Her skin tingled from the frigid water, but it, too, felt good. Every pore of her body tingled, if the truth be known. And tingled yet more when the memory of Morigan, lying naked and wild and passion crazed beneath her, filled her mind.

He was such a skilled and virile lover, Rissa mused as she climbed to her feet. She set her blaster beside the water flask and walked downstream to where she'd seen the wild tubers. The thought of mating with Morigan again, even after the extremely satisfying night past, sent a most pleasant shudder of anticipation coursing through her.

The tubers were just where she'd remembered, their fresh green sprouts poking from the earth at jaunty angles. She knelt, unsheathed her dagger, and began gently to dig them out. As she did, the sound of crackling twigs underfoot caught her ear. Rissa whirled about.

Towering over her were five men—Bellatorian soldiers from their uniforms. Five men with blasters leveled on her. Rissa's hand clenched around her dagger.

"I'd drop that while you still can." A man with braiding on his collar that bespoke his rank of captain motioned toward her dagger with the firing end of his blaster.

Wordlessly, Rissa let the weapon fall.

The captain eyed her. "Who are you, femina? You don't have quite the look of the humanoid Agricans in these parts."

Her throat tightened. What were Bellatorian soldiers doing here, so close to the mountains? Gods, if they made even a cursory search of the area, they were sure to find the cave and Morigan!

"I-I escaped," she began, knowing nothing but the truth would convince them and save the Cat Lord. "I'm one of the women the Cat Men captured . . . from the merchants' caravan."

"Indeed?" The captain arched a skeptical brow. His compatriots chuckled. "And how came you to have a blaster? Or even to have escaped from the Cat Men? I find it hard to believe a mere woman could outrun Cat Men."

"A Cat Man was bringing me back to my father, the Lord Commander." A sudden fear filled Rissa. Morigan might awaken and somehow drag himself from the cave to look for her. "There's a ransom out for my return, you know."

Surprise flared in the captain's eyes. "Are you claiming you're Rissa Lindatees, Fautor Lindatees's daughter?"

She nodded. "Yes."

He studied her intently. "Your looks fit the description." He shouldered his blaster and strode over to her. The captain extended a hand. "But time will tell the truth of your words."

Rissa eyed his proffered hand. "What do you mean to do?"

"What else, femina? Take you back with us to Primasedes."

With a heart gone dull and heavy, Rissa placed her hand in his and allowed him to pull her to her feet. *Morigan,* she thought on a fleeting wisp of pain. *Forgive me.*

Then, blocking his memory from her mind, Rissa squared her shoulders and faced what lay ahead.

Twenty-two

"She's gone, my Lord. The Bellatorians have taken her."

Morigan glanced up. Lisan's words confirmed what he'd feared all along. With a savage curse, the Cat Lord shifted slightly against the unyielding stone wall. Two days had passed since Rissa had left him, two days of tormenting worry and impotent frustration as he lay helplessly in the cave, praying she'd return. To know the truth was almost a relief.

"At least she's alive, then," he muttered hoarsely. "At least she's not lying hurt or dying in a ravine, or chewed to death by some animals."

"We found her water flask and blaster lying beside a stream, her dagger some distance away." Lisan shifted uncomfortably. "There was no sign of a struggle. It appeared your lady went with them willingly."

Morigan shot the young Cat Man a narrowed glance. "Did she, now? And there could be many reasons for that, couldn't there?"

Lisan's eyes widened. "Of course, my Lord. She . . . she could have gone with them to protect you."

"Yes," he snarled. "She damn well could have."

But even as Morigan spoke the words, the doubts and the pain churned anew. Rissa was gone. Whatever her motive, she was gone. Without farewell, without explanation.

He would've taken her back with him to the lair and defied the Council to send her away. He'd never believed Fautor Lindatees would keep his word at any rate.

But, now, there was no choice. Rissa was gone, back to her father and her own people.

He clenched his hands, shut his eyes. Frustration, deep and agonizing, roiled within. *Rissa. Gods, Rissa.*

From somewhere outside his tortured self-absorption, Morigan heard Lisan clear his throat. The Cat Lord's eyes snapped open. His compatriot smiled down, hesitant and uncertain.

"Er, the litter is ready, my Lord. If we want to make good time this day, we should be going."

Morigan glanced about the cave, the cave he'd shared with Rissa. Without her loving presence, it seemed cold, empty, nothing more than a hollow of dirt and stone. And no reason to linger a moment longer.

He tamped down the swell of bittersweet emotion and shoved it into some distant corner of his mind. "Then, let's get on with it." Morigan straightened and offered his hand to Lisan. "I'm needed back at the lair."

A wild mix of apprehension and anticipation pounded through Rissa two days later as she followed the captain down the hall leading to the Lord Commander's private reception room. Their booted feet rapped on the black-tiled floor, echoing off the mottled gray and white marmor stone walls, beating in staccato rhythm to her agitated heart. Gods, what would her father say? What would he do?

She must have a care what she told him about the Cat People and Morigan until she could discern his mood regarding them. She still hoped to serve as the Lord Commander's emissary to the Cat People, but no matter what happened, she wouldn't betray them. It was so little to give Morigan in exchange for leaving him, but it was all she had left. And the only comfort that remained with which to ease her aching, lonely heart.

The captain drew up before an imposing door of hammered metal aureum and snapped the door clapper smartly. The sound reverberated down the corridor, filling the air with a brittle, irritating noise. Rissa jerked from her miserable musings, suddenly seeing the rich, yellow-gold metal looming before her in a different light. Somehow, when placed against the context of the Cat People's suffering, the beautifully wrought door seemed an ostentatious travesty.

Rissa squashed the traitorous thought. She was being unfair. She owed her father a chance.

The realization of where her loyalties now lay startled Rissa. In just six weeks' time, her perceptions had swung about completely. Now, Primasedes and her own people seemed foreign to her, almost the enemy. And the Cat People . . .

The door opened. A thin little man dressed in shimmering brown serica cloth robes stood there. He nodded to the captain, then eyed Rissa with a curious, assessing glance. When he took in her dusty leather clothing and boots, his lip curled.

"Enter, domina." The man's gaze returned to the captain. "We thank you for your assistance. The Lord Commander may require your presence later, but for now . . ."

The Bellatorian soldier stepped back and bowed. "As you wish." He turned and strode away.

The man swung the door open wider. "Come, domina. Your father awaits."

Rissa shot the captain's retreating back a look of longing. As cold and briskly efficient as he'd become once he learned of her true identity, the man was the only person she knew in Primasedes. If only he could've—

A polite clearing of a throat wrenched her back to the moment at hand. This was ridiculous, she angrily told herself. She was Morigan's mate, the Lady of the Cat People. She'd endured hardship and braved the likes of Cradoc and his minions. There was nothing to fear in a meeting with her father.

Rissa turned, squared her shoulders, and strode past the doorman and into the room. A hard-featured man with silver blond hair sat in one of two, plush lounge chairs at a blazing hearth. A long table of red robur wood and six tall chairs set upon a huge, handwoven Moracan herder's rug dominated the chamber. Richly brocaded red curtains covered the windows, shutting out the light.

After the cooler, more airy lairs of the Cat People, the room seemed hot, dark, and stifling. A sudden surge of dizziness engulfed Rissa. She inhaled several deep, steadying breaths, then walked over to the hearth. "Father?" She smiled uncertainly at the man sitting there. "It is I, Rissa."

His gaze never leaving her, he motioned to the other chair positioned across from him. "Welcome, child. Sit."

Somehow, the greeting lacked the warmth Rissa had expected. She took the chair as requested. Glancing up at her father, Rissa calmly met his gaze.

At closer scrutiny, his blond hair was heavily streaked with gray. Deep lines feathered the edges of his dark brown eyes, furrowed his brow, and dragged down the corners of his mouth. He was fit enough and dressed in the finest of fabric and style. Yet, for all his impressive bearing and clothing, there was an air about him of restless discontent. Something else besides wealth and power fired the man and fueled his resolve, something hard and smoldering that gnawed incessantly just below his thin veneer of breeding and power.

With an inward shudder, Rissa shook the uneasy impression aside. He was her father. Surely, it was just the unfamiliarity of him and the situation that unnerved her so.

"You are well, child?" he asked, his voice cool but gentle.

Rissa smiled and leaned forward. "Oh, yes, Father. I'm fine."

He leaned forward as well and templed his fingers beneath his chin. A speculative light gleamed in his dark eyes. "The Cat Men. Do you know where their lair is hidden in the Serratus Mountains? Can you lead us to it?"

Rissa drew back, suddenly wary. Here it comes, she thought. She shook her head. "No, Father. They blindfolded me, both going to their lair and bringing me back here."

He smiled thinly, never shifting his gaze. "It was to be expected. No matter. They can't escape my patrols forever." Fautor Lindatees paused. "Why did the Cat Men take you and the other women?"

She hesitated but an instant. "They needed breeding females to replace the ones our soldiers killed in the massacre a cycle ago."

"Good, good." Her father's smile widened. "I knew we hadn't exterminated them all, even as carefully planned as the ambush was. We slaughtered quite a few, though, if the Cat Men are now forced to steal breeding females. They're on the verge of extinction, aren't they?"

Yes, they are, Rissa silently replied, but if any species can come back from the edge of total annihilation, the Cat People can. You never bartered on going up against a man like Morigan.

The words hovered on her lips, but she choked them back. She must have a care. "Why did Bellator order the massacre,

Father?" Rissa asked instead. "It seems such a harsh punishment to exact on anyone. What did the Cat People do to deserve such cruelty?"

"Cruelty?" Lindatees's gaze narrowed. "And why do you care, child? Since when does a loyal Bellatorian question anything Bellator orders?"

"The Cat People treated me and the other women kindly. They're not the savage animals the tales make them out to be."

"You defend them, then?" The skin over his face grew tight, flushed.

Gods, Rissa thought, she'd been with him less than five minutes and already she was angering him! She wet her lips carefully. "I only ask why, Father. I only wish to understand, so as to better serve you and Bellator."

He arched a graying blond brow. "Indeed?" Lindatees turned to the small side table beside his chair. A finely wrought argentum wine flask and four cups sat on a small tray atop the table. "Would you like a cup of wine, child?"

Rissa eyed the flask, then nodded. Perhaps, a cup or two would ease the bow-strung tautness within. "Yes, please."

Fautor Lindatees poured out two cups, then handed Rissa hers. As her fingers curled about the silver vessel, her father covered her hand with his. "Has a Cat Man had you, child?"

The breath froze in her throat; her heart skipped a beat then commenced a wild pounding. Rissa's gaze dropped momentarily, then lifted to meet his. There was no point served in lying.

"Yes," Rissa softly replied. "That *was* the purpose of my capture, wasn't it?"

"Yet, you look quite normal." Her father cocked his head. "I see no scars, no bruises, no emotional trauma of any kind."

"He . . . he was gentle with me."

"Was he, now?" He released her hand.

Rissa's fingers clenched, knuckle white, about her cup. "Yes."

"And I think you're being too kind." Once more, Lindatees paused. "Do you carry the Cat Man's child?"

Tendrils of unease tightened within Rissa. "No, Father. I managed to obtain a contraceptive. I bear no one's child."

He smirked. "Good. At least you had the presence of mind not to get yourself pregnant with one of those alien's spawn." He glanced down, stroking his chin in careful consideration. "There's still a chance, then, to pass you as a maiden." Cold, dark eyes lifted, locking with hers. "You're not to tell anyone you were raped. Do you hear me? Trelan, the young officer I'd promised you to, will still take you to wife if he thinks you untouched. There's still a chance to salvage your future here—*if* we work fast."

Rissa wanted to tell her father she hadn't been raped, but the set, calculating look on his face warned her that, for now at least, the attempt would be futile. First, she must gain his confidence and trust. Then, her words might carry weight with him. In the meanwhile, she didn't need things complicated with a husband. Especially when even the thought of another man touching her filled Rissa with loathing. All she wanted was Morigan. If she was fated never to have him, she wanted no one.

"Please, Father," Rissa said. "I-I don't want to talk about a marriage right now. I've been through too much of late. I need time . . . to think, to work it all out."

He leaned over and patted her on the knee. "I understand, child. I'm not totally insensitive to the horrors you went through, man though I am. But it's all over now. You're safe. No Cat Man can touch you here." He smiled. "And we'll have time, at last, to get to know each other. I've missed you, child."

Rissa managed a wobbly little smile. "And I have missed you, too, Father."

Lindatees lifted the armrest of his chair and pressed a button on the inset control panel. "I've sent for your new serving maid. You must be weary after your journey. Enjoy a hot mineral bath, take a nap, and this evening we'll sup together. Time enough then to talk—about your life here, my plans for you. You'll be a valuable asset, with your special knowledge of the Cat People."

"I'd like to help you with them, Father." She took a sip of her wine and smiled. "Now that you've granted them amnesty for my return."

"Amnesty?" Fury flared in Fautor Lindatees' eyes. "How can you, of all people, expect me to honor that offer after what they did to you?"

"Yet, I do want that, Father. Bellator's word, once given, is irrevocable."

"Not in this case. And not with such ignorant and barbaric aliens. There'll be no amnesty or mercy shown these savages. You have my word on that, child."

A soft knock sounded on the door. As the brown-clad servant hurried over to answer it, Lindatees rose and offered Rissa his hand. She set down her cup of wine and stood.

"Father, please, at least don't make a final decision on your offer of amnesty until we've more time to talk, to—"

He clasped her hands in his. "You're my daughter, my only child. The Cat Man who forced himself on you did so as insult to me. I cannot—I *will* not—permit that cruelty to you, my innocent child, to go unpunished."

"But, Father," Rissa hurried to protest, "he didn't—"

"Ah, here is your new maid, Jaranda," he smoothly cut her off. "Come, child, let me introduce you to her."

As he pulled her toward a middle-aged, narrow-eyed woman with dull brown hair and unremarkable features, frustration welled in Rissa. Frustration—and a rising fear.

Her father had been kind, solicitous of her, but his hatred of the Cat Men lay like a seething mantle about him. He wanted vengeance, yet, despite his protestations of outrage for what he envisioned had been done to her, Rissa wasn't convinced fatherly intentions fueled his need for retribution. Something else fed the smoldering fires of his obsession to annihilate the Cat People. Something deep and dark and old.

Gods, but she was so afraid, so alone and powerless! And she missed Morigan so badly.

Morigan.

To bolster her flagging courage and resolve, Rissa invoked his name like some prayer. *He* was why she was here, not only to protect him from the Bellatorian patrol, but to use whatever influence she had as Fautor Lindatees's daughter to save his people. The knowledge of her purpose in Primasedes would be small comfort in the lonely hours of the night when she woke, aching for him, but it was all she had.

Rissa clasped the thought to her. Plastering on her brightest smile, she walked with her father to meet her new serving maid.

"The Bellatorian patrols have returned with the good weather," Morigan muttered across the table, meeting his grandfather's dark gaze with an equally dark one of his own, "just as I predicted they would. Lindatees has never been a man of honor—and never will, no matter how much we concede him."

Ardan sighed and glanced down at the tabletop. "I feared as much, my lord, but still thought it was worth a try. I am sorry you lost your mate because of my foolish optimism."

Morigan rose and walked across his lair. He paused at the doorway to gaze outside. Late spring washed the valley in shades of rich grass-green, dark earth-brown, and a myriad of bright colors. A soft breeze wafted by, carrying with it the scent of fragrant blossoms from the budding fruit trees. Birds soared overhead and twittered in the trees.

It was a glorious morn, herald of yet another fertile Agrican summer. A summer of fertile Cat Women, as well. Ten more had finally conceived. He should be happy, but he wasn't.

"The decision wasn't just yours." He turned to his grandfather. "The entire Council bears the responsibility as well."

"Can you ever find it in your heart to forgive us?"

"Forgive?" Morigan gave a bitter laugh. "What does it matter? I'm Lord. I serve the will of my people. Besides, Rissa is back where she belongs. It's been two months now, and she's sent no word. Despite the difficulties in doing so, she could have if she'd wanted to. I know her well enough to know that." He strode back to the table and sat again. A hard look darkened his eyes. "The Lord Commander knows now we live and thrive. Knows as well we'll continue to be a thorn in his side. He'll only redouble his efforts to find and kill us this summer. I've no time—"

"My Lord?"

At the sound of the voice at the doorway, Morigan whirled around. Brandar stood there. He motioned him in. Despite his words of resignation to his grandfather, he'd sent Brandar to Primasedes once more, specifically to check on Rissa. Morigan wanted assurance she was safe and happy, before he shoved further consideration of her forever from his heart and mind. He had to. He couldn't go on much longer enduring the agony of remembering, of needing her, knowing he could never have her again.

"Sit, Brandar," Morigan said. "Would you like a cup of wine to ease the dryness of your journey?"

"Yes." The big Cat Man grinned. "That would be much appreciated, my Lord."

The Cat Lord poured him a cup and shoved it over to him. Brandar tossed the contents down with one gulp, then wiped his mouth with the back of his hand. His gaze locked with Morigan's.

"I've news, my Lord. Good or bad, depending on how you choose to view it."

"Indeed?" Morigan forced down a surge of fear. "Rissa? How is she?"

"She looks well enough, though a bit thinner and paler. She has freedom to come and go in the palace and Primasedes as she wishes, but she's always followed." Brandar shoved his cup over. Silently, Morigan refilled it. "I don't think her father trusts her."

"That may come in time," Ardan offered hopefully. "And as long as she is safe and treated well . . ."

Morigan shot his grandfather a quelling look. "Her happiness is of equal importance to me." He turned back to Brandar. "Did she seem happy?"

"It's difficult to tell. In one sense at least, I think, yes." Brandar smiled. "She's breeding, my Lord."

The bottom dropped out of Morigan's stomach. He controlled his sudden swell of joy with the greatest of efforts. "How long?" he demanded hoarsely. "How far along is she?"

"Two months, I'd wager. The breeding aura is blossoming quite strongly about her." The Cat Man's gaze warmed. "She has one of the loveliest breeding auras I've ever seen in a female. It's quite striking."

"She carries my babe then. I thought, that night of the triple moons, she was fertile and ready for me, but . . ." He glanced at his grandfather. "She carries a Cat Child. My heir. Would you still keep her from me?"

"Not when a Cat Child is involved. You know how desperately we need children."

Something hardened in Morigan. "Yes, well I know. But know this as well. I want my mate, but I won't force her to return just because she bears my child. She must come to me willingly or not at all."

Ardan hesitated. "Perhaps that would be wise. Your mate has suffered enough at our hands. And there seems little point in continuing to honor our side of that ill-fated bargain with Lindatees. It's more than evident he has no intention of granting us amnesty." The old Cat Man smiled grimly. "Yes, I like it. You may have your mate again, as well as an heir, and we'll teach the Lord Commander the consequences of going back on his word to us."

Morigan rose. "I'll go for her. It's my right."

His grandfather stood. "I should advise against that. It will be dangerous to enter Primasedes and bring the female out. And you are our lord."

"But I will go, nonetheless." Morigan's jaw tightened. "I'll not risk even one more Cat Man on a quest that is mine alone to make. I have lost too much, too many already."

"Then go, my Lord," Ardan murmured. "Go now, before the Council knows and forbids it. I am old and walk slowly these days. If you hurry, I surely cannot reach the Council chambers nor call a special meeting before it's too late to stop you."

Morigan stepped around the table and grasped his grandfather's arm in a gesture of gratitude and farewell. "My thanks. You cannot begin to know—"

"You deserve your chance at happiness," Ardan softly cut him off. "You have never ceased to strive for ours." He squeezed Morigan's arm, then released him. "Now, go, and bring back our Lady to us. We need her as desperately as do you."

Yes, Morigan thought savagely, I *will* bring her back. But in the process, I'll also have my vengeance at last against the Lord Commander. A vengeance, he silently vowed, his hands clenching into rock-hard fists, for a massacre Fautor Lindatees won't live much longer to gloat about.

She was pregnant. There was no reason to deny the truth any longer. She carried Morigan's child, and she was trapped in a world that abhorred those of his kind.

Rissa rose from the stone bench in the palace gardens, gardens now resplendent with life and scent and color. Slowly, she walked back to her room, her mind awhirl. What would her father do when he discovered her precious secret? And secret though it might be for a while longer, as soon as the babe blossomed in her belly the truth would be apparent to all. What would she do then?

She wanted the babe with all her heart. She loved it already. It was Morigan's. It was all she'd ever have of him. But what would her people do when her pregnancy was finally known?

Trelan would turn from her. That fiercely proud and arrogant young officer would never tolerate a mate who'd lain with some loathsome Cat Man. In the past two months of his ardent courtship, Rissa had learned that much of him.

Not that his rejection of her would matter. She didn't want to wed Trelan, or anyone else.

All she wanted was to leave Primasedes and return to Morigan and the lair.

But that was impossible. Though her guards were clever, Rissa knew she was constantly followed whenever she left her bedchamber. Her father didn't intend to lose her again. And, even if she'd managed to escape, she didn't know the way back to the lair and wouldn't attempt it at any rate. Rissa knew she'd be followed.

No, she'd never risk inadvertently betraying the location of the Cat People's lair. Because of that, she was trapped. For herself, Rissa could accept the exile, willingly render the sacrifice, however painful, of never seeing Morigan again. But for her unborn babe . . .

A breeze, as soft as a feather's downy caress, brushed against her cheek. Rissa paused, smiled. Her babe . . . Her hand moved, unconsciously, to her belly before she caught herself in the revealing action. Too many watched and schemed in this palace of intrigue and self-serving ambition to risk giving anything away. And too many words of honor had been broken.

Her father had resumed his efforts to exterminate the last of the Cat People. His offer of amnesty had never been more than a bald-faced lie. Her sacrifice, and Morigan's, had been for naught.

She was nothing more than a political pawn in her father's hand, and had always been so. He'd no use for her other than to gain him further power and position by an advantageous marriage. All her dreams of serving at his side in the successful colonization of Agrica had been for naught. In his eyes, her only value lay in what her body could buy him.

The cruel irony of her situation both saddened and sickened Rissa. She'd raged against Morigan because she feared he meant to use her body. She'd fought him in every way she could because she was terrified she'd never matter to him or any of his people save for her breeding potential.

Instead, Rissa had found fulfillment, a sense of purpose, friends, and a gentle, passionate lover. A lover who needed her, who wanted her to stand at his side as his lady and help him save his people. A lover who'd finally, because of his love for her, opened his heart and allowed himself to begin to heal.

Yes, it was irony of the cruelest kind. But as much as she sometimes wished to die and escape her gilded prison, Rissa couldn't. Morigan had faced worse and somehow found the strength to go on. His love for her could allow him nothing less. Now, her love for him—and for their unborn babe— permitted her no other option, either.

Jaranda, her serving maid, appeared on the lower balcony at the back of the palace. When she caught Rissa's eye she waved, indicating she wished to speak with her. With a re- signed sigh, Rissa headed her way.

She neither liked nor trusted the woman. Jaranda was too inquisitive, nosing around in Rissa's belongings at every turn, watching her, and waiting. She knew the woman cal- culated the times of her monthly flow—and lack of it. Rissa's greatest fear was that Jaranda already knew of her pregnancy and that her father would soon know as well.

"You move more slowly of late, domina," Jaranda ob- served as Rissa finally drew near. "Are you ill?"

"No." Rissa forced her expression into one of bland friendliness. The other woman's gaze had narrowed specu- latively, and it wouldn't do to reveal anything. "It's just such a beautiful day, and I was but enjoying it." She cocked her head. "Did you desire something of me?"

The serving maid smiled thinly. "Not I, but your father. He wishes to see you in his reception chambers." She paused. "Now, if you please."

"Indeed?" Rissa's heart skipped a beat. Her father was a very busy man. He never asked to see her during the day. Their usual time together was at the supper meal, which was also routinely shared with the officious and utterly boring Trelan. But never, ever had they met during the day save for their first encounter. "Then it must be something of great import," she forced herself to respond. "I must not keep him waiting."

"Indeed you must not, domina."

Rissa climbed the broad stone steps leading up to the second balcony and main doors. The interior corridor was empty, quiet save for the tap of her sandaled feet upon the tiles. Her apprehension, however, didn't dissipate as she walked along. Something was wrong. She knew it.

The same, thin little doorman greeted Rissa's knock and ushered her into the reception chambers. This time, however, though the curtains were drawn and the room still dark, her father stood by the huge table. At her entrance, he waved her over impatiently, a hard, congested look on his face.

"Sit," he commanded when Rissa neared him, indicating the chair at the head of the table.

She quietly obeyed. Fautor Lindatees shoved in Rissa's chair for her, then stalked around to stand across from her at the table. He leaned over, his hands spread on the thick robur wood, and stared into her eyes.

"When were you planning on telling me you carried that alien's spawn?" he demanded harshly, without preamble. "When your belly swelled? When you thought it too late for me to do anything about it?"

The blood drained from Rissa's face. For a fleeting instant, the room spun wildly before her. She feared she'd be sick. Then, with several deep, determined breaths, Rissa squelched the nausea and dizziness. Someone had discovered her secret—Jaranda, most likely—and told her father. There was nothing to be done now but face him and the truth.

She met his blistering gaze squarely. "I was only recently certain of it myself, Father. I thought the stress of my recent months had delayed my woman's flow. I couldn't be certain."

"But now you are?"

"Yes, now I am."

"And how do you feel about this—this shameful set of circumstances?" He leaned back, his eyes feral, waiting.

Rissa wet her lips, frantically grasping at some reply that would be truthful but not anger him further. She needed to win his support for this pregnancy, not alienate him further. "The birth of a babe can never be shameful, no matter how it was conceived. The child, your grandchild, is as much mine as his. I want it."

"My gr-grandchild? W-want it?" The Lord Commander's face mottled with rage. "Don't try to distract me with sweet words at a time like this! I want no grandchild from a Cat Man's seed! What of my plans for you? What of your marriage to Trelan? Do you imagine he'll wish to take the filthy spawn of a Cat Man into his house?"

At his words, something snapped in Rissa. "I really don't care what Trelan wishes, Father! The babe is mine. It goes where I go!"

"Does it, now? I suppose that would be true, if you carried it to term." He smiled wolfishly. "But there's no need to carry this babe, is there, Daughter? There's still ample time to dispose of it. There's still ample time to hide the evidence of your pregnancy. Trelan and everyone else need never know. It can be our little secret."

Horror surged through Rissa. Blood pounded in her skull; dizziness once more engulfed her. She shoved back her chair and rose unsteadily, gripping the table edge to sustain her. "Never," she whispered, trembling with the intensity of her emotion. "I'll never end this pregnancy. The babe is mine. I love it. Love it," she said, her voice rising, "as I love its father. In your devious, dishonorable dealings with the Cat People, you've managed to take my mate from me, but you *will not* take his child. I forbid it!"

"You forbid? *You?"* Fautor Lindatees gave an unsteady, disbelieving laugh. "Gods, you're just like your mother—an alley walker at heart! You haven't a shred of decency or breeding in you. And just like your mother, you spread your legs for the first piece of alien manhood you ever came across." His hands clenched at his sides, and his whole body shook. "I was a fool to think it could be otherwise, you living with her all those cycles, listening to her poisonous venom about me. Just as I was a fool to think finding you a decent, upstanding young man with a fine military career ahead of him would turn you from your cheap, sordid ways."

"My mother . . ." Rissa shook her head, confused. "What do you mean my mother . . . spread her legs for . . . for some alien? She never told me anything about that, nor ever said a bad word about you. She never said anything at all about why you and she separated."

"Didn't she?" Lindatees snarled. "Well, that's not surprising, considering her shameful conduct. Do you wish to know who you've emulated all these cycles, whose steps you've followed in whoring with that Cat Man?"

"Yes," Rissa whispered. "I wish to know, once and for all, what happened between you and my mother."

"When you were two cycles old, I was posted to Arguila as emissary to the High King," her father said. "The Arguilian males are purported to be one of the most exotically handsome and seductively potent alien species in the Imperium. Equal to the fabled attractiveness of your savage Cat Men. And your mother, romantic, empty-headed female that she was, grew upset with the long hours I worked in the service of our king. Grew so upset she eventually sought out an Arguilian to take as lover."

"I-I don't believe Mother would do such a thing," Rissa whispered, shocked and suddenly sick to the marrow of her bones. "Not . . . not without a reason."

Fautor Lindatees laughed. "What does it matter the reason? She was unfaithful to me and, to add even further insult, the bitch got herself with the alien's child. I tried everything to make her dispose of it, threatening divorce, warning of the scandal, the shame it would heap on my name, on you, our daughter. But she stubbornly persisted in her determination to bear her lover's child."

Rissa frowned in confusion. "But there was never any child, any brother or sister." A rising presentiment filtered through her. "What happened to it?"

Her father shrugged, as if in the action he shed the responsibility for what came next. "I 'disposed' of the boy child while your mother lay weak in her childbed, then had her serving maid tell her he was stillborn." He smiled grimly. "Jaranda and I go back a long way. She's completely devoted to me. Why else would I have given her to you as your serving maid?"

"You killed . . . killed my brother?"

"Your half brother, and no son of mine," he corrected her with brittle certainty. "I've always had to be the one to oversee the errors of the females in my family, to smooth down their foolish, love-crazed mistakes. As I will yours, too."

Rissa's eyes widened in horror. Her breath shuddered through her in great gulps.

"Why so surprised, Daughter?" Fautor Lindatees glanced down casually to straighten the aureum braid trimming his tunic. "Did you think my hatred for the alien Cat Men had no basis? Think again. I'm a man of purpose and action. I saw the danger to Bellator from their seductive, exotically savage ways long before others of our kind did. I knew they, too, would seduce our women, steal them from our men." His voice rose, taking on a wild note as a fierce, almost maniacal light gleamed in his eyes. "I couldn't let that happen again. I couldn't let _them_ steal my wife, my daughter . . ."

He choked on a feral snarl, regained control, then shook the crazed aura of rage aside. "They dared resist me, dared defy Bellator's advances into Agrica. They were fools—fools who all but begged to be exterminated. When Bellator transmitted the order to control or eliminate them, I simply gave the Cat People what they asked for. As would any Lord Commander saddled with such an onerous task, you can be sure."

"You're mad," Rissa hissed. "You're not fit to serve Bellator, much less be Lord Commander of this planet! And you're the fool if you think to defeat the Lord of the Cat People. He's match for you and more!"

"Is he now?" A small smirk of dawning realization played about Lindatees's mouth. "You speak quite passionately of him. Is _he,_ perhaps, your mate? The father of the child you bear?"

Rissa blanched. "What does it matter who my babe's father is? He's a Cat Child."

"It matters little," her father agreed silkily, "save for the fact destroying the Cat Lord's child will but add to my pleasure. And destroy it, I will."

She stepped back from the table, her hands sliding down to meet across her belly. "No. I won't let you do it."

"And what say will you have, one way or another, Daughter?" His glance riveted on what her hands protected. "I am, after all, not only your father, but Lord Commander of Agrica. And I say, before the next day has passed, you'll carry that vile seed of a Cat Man no longer. Whether," he added viciously, "you wish it or not."

Twenty-three

Rissa leaned back in the bathing tub and savored the warm mineral bath. After the horrors of the day, after her father's heartless words and threats to take her babe from her, it was all the comfort left her. She'd refused the evening meal, fearful it might contain some harmful drug or hypnotic. She wouldn't last long without food and drink but, for now, it was the only defense she had. There was no hope of escape. Until a better option presented itself, she'd defend her babe as best she could.

Jaranda reentered the bathing room with a container of a floral-scented shampoo and knelt beside her. "Come, my lady." She spread a generous amount of the thick, liquefied soap in her hands and rubbed them together. The perfume of arosa flowers filled the air, light and delicately fragrant. "Let me wash your hair. Then, it'll be time to put you to bed."

Strong fingers threaded through her hair, expertly massaging the shampoo into Rissa's scalp, then sliding down to lather the length of her tresses. From time to time, Jaranda paused to rinse her hands, before once more continuing with the shampoo.

As the woman worked, a heavy drowsiness gradually encompassed Rissa. She relaxed beneath Jaranda's ministrations. Yet, even as she did, a tiny voice cried out a warning not to lower her guard against the treacherous maid servant. A maid servant in her father's employ.

Rissa tried to fight past the encroaching lassitude but failed. Something pulled at her, drawing her down into a hazy languor. Her arms felt heavy, her lids weighted, her breathing slow and deep. Why? she thought. Why did she feel this way?

Warm water flowed over her, down her face, into her eyes and mouth. Jaranda . . . rinsing her hair. With a choking sputter, Rissa tossed the water aside. Fingers plucked at her hair, smoothing it back from her face.

The maid servant paused at the side of the tub to slather a thick lotion on her hands and arms, then moved back to Rissa. "Come, domina." She tugged Rissa to her feet. "Time to dry you and put you to bed. Tomorrow will come soon enough."

"Tomorrow?" Rissa stepped from the bathing tub.

Jaranda began to rub her dry. "Yes, tomorrow. Everything will be better on the morrow." She slipped a sheer, sleeveless nightgown of ivory serica cloth over Rissa's head. With the faintest of whispers, it slithered down her body. Then, the serving maid was pulling on her arm.

Rissa turned to the older woman.

"Come to bed now." A look of irritation fleetingly tightened Jaranda's features. "I'll brush out your hair, then you can sleep."

Obediently, Rissa followed her to the bed and sat. Jaranda was none too gentle in smoothing out the tangles in Rissa's wet hair, but Rissa didn't care. She was just too . . . tired . . . to care. At long last, the serving maid was done.

"To bed with you now." Jaranda shoved Rissa onto her back and pulled up the down comforter. Tucking the covering about Rissa's shoulders, Jaranda paused, smiling down at her.

Even in her lethargic state, Rissa sensed something unsettling in the woman's expression. Something soulless, malevolent. Rissa blinked, attempting to clear the mist clouding her vision. She reached out, grasping at the other woman's arm.

With a low chuckle, Jaranda evaded her outstretched hand. "Sleep, now, domina," she crooned. "Sleep the deep sleep, and when you awake, the evil spawn of your body will be gone. Gone, like some nightmare you only imagined in your dreams." She moved back from the bed, edging her way to the door.

"J-Jaranda." Summoning all the strength within her, Rissa shoved herself up to her elbows. Her muscles rebelled, went limp and floppy. With a tormented groan, she sagged back onto the bed.

She was drugged, Rissa realized despairingly. There was no other explanation. But how? She'd not eaten or drunk anything since she'd last seen her father. And any sedating vapor sent into her room just now would've affected Jaranda as strongly as she.

The shampoo. It was the only explanation, and why Jaranda had repeatedly rinsed her hands and applied the lotion immediately after finishing washing Rissa's hair. Something in the shampoo had permeated her skin and entered her bloodstream.

She watched Jaranda open the bedchamber door. Fautor Lindatees slipped in, a large black case in his hand. He exchanged a taut, conspiratorial smile with the serving maid.

Tears of impotent rage, of searing frustration, and shattering sorrow, welled in Rissa's eyes and spilled down her cheeks. Her father had come to take her babe. Her and Morigan's babe. Ah, Gods . . . Gods . . .

* * *

Cloaked from view, he slipped through the main gates of Primasedes just as they were closing them for the night. His Cat's powers served him well. No one noted his passing.

Once inside, Morigan headed to the thick, stone parapets, passing heavily armed guards walking their rounds, his gaze and intent fixed firmly on finding the most unobtrusive spot from which to escape the Agrican capital with Rissa. His cloaking abilities weren't sufficient to cover her as well as himself when they departed Primasedes. They would need an alternative escape route—over the city walls.

He finally found a protected area alongside one of the guard towers. Once they were behind it, no one could see them until a guard passed directly in front. If Morigan timed everything well, there should be adequate opportunity to lower Rissa and then follow her.

The next requirement was a rope. He found a sturdy coil of sufficient length in the main guardhouse, quickly confiscated it, then carried it over to hide near the site of his planned escape. That done, the Cat Lord slipped down from the parapets and headed toward the center of the city—and the palace.

Primasedes was an ancient metropolis, built from the thick, rose-colored marmor stone that so abundantly covered this part of Agrica. The streets were cobbled, the shops and houses of fine timber that, as one drew closer to the heart of the city, became imposing buildings. The palace, once home to the hereditary rulers of Agrica, was now headquarters for the Bellatorian invaders. It was home, as well, to the Lord Commander and his daughter.

The flickering light of perpetual torches lit Morigan's path as he hurried through the narrow streets and up to the broad expanse of steps leading to the palace itself. It was late. There were few about save an occasional guard, giving an eerie, deserted feel to the area. Such carelessness was but another aspect of Bellatorian arrogance, Morigan thought in disgust. They imagined themselves safe from attack or subterfuge. This time, however, the Lord Commander's arrogance would be his death.

Morigan made his silent, stealthy way up the steps, passed two unsuspecting guards stationed at the open doorway, and slipped inside. Though his first impulse was immediately to seek out Fautor Lindatees, he tempered that with the need to find Rissa and ascertain she was safe. Once he found her, he could set her about preparing for the journey while he went in search of the Lord Commander. Then, before anyone even realized the full extent of what had transpired, he and Rissa would be gone from Primasedes.

The stone corridors were long and empty, devoid of any ornamentation even remotely reminiscent of the ancient rulers. As sparse now as the militaristic Bellatorian outlook, the palace was cold, hollow, and strangely melancholy. He wondered how Rissa had endured even two months within these confining and depressing environs. But then, Rissa was Bellatorian.

The reminder sent a tremor of doubt rippling once more through Morigan. What if Rissa had readapted to her former life and wished to stay? What if she'd acquiesced to her father's wishes and had succumbed, once more, to the Bellatorian dogma of unthinking obedience? What if she no longer loved him? Did he still have the right to take her away with him then?

She carried his child—his heir if it were a male. There was right enough in that to force Rissa to come with him if their love was no longer sufficient. Yet, even the thought that Rissa might have ceased to love him filled Morigan with pain. He couldn't believe she would ever stop loving him.

Not after all they'd endured for their love, not after the battles fought and won in the name of that love.

No, Morigan firmly reassured himself as he made his silent way through the palace to the living quarters, Rissa loved him and always would. If any doubts lingered in her mind about returning to the lair, he'd soon banish them. Just as soon as he held her once more in his arms, pressed her soft, woman's body against his and kissed her. She'd remember; she'd yield, just as she always had.

He found her room before he turned down the last corridor. Morigan sensed a wild surge of terror, as a mind struggled against a drug-induced stupor. It was Rissa. With his heightened Cat senses, he heard the sounds of battle behind the thick stone walls. His pace quickened.

The door to her bedchamber was secured by two well-armed guards. Still cloaked, Morigan flung himself at the nearest man, knowing his time to reach Rissa was short. The element of surprise aided his swift attack. The first guard fell only a second after the Cat Lord's form once more came into view.

The second guard, a big, brawny man, went down only after a vicious battle, his throat slit to preclude him sounding the call for help. Quickly, Morigan bent, searched the guards until he found the key control to Rissa's door, then shoved it into the wall slot beside the door. The portal slid soundlessly open. Morigan stepped in. The sight of Rissa, a man and woman leaning over her on the bed, fighting to tie her down, stopped him cold.

"Don't!" she wept, twisting and writhing on the bed, her words slurred but pleading. "Ah, Father, please don't take my babe. I-I beg you!"

Lindatees, Morigan thought with a furious exultation. At long last, he'd found the man responsible for the brutal slaughter of his people. At long last and just in time to find him preparing to kill again. Preparing to brutalize Rissa and murder his child.

With a savage snarl, Morigan flung himself across the room. Fautor Lindatees must have heard the sound, for he turned, gasped, and staggered backward. Morigan slammed into him, toppling them both to the floor.

Jaranda screamed. The sound moved Rissa to action. She must quiet the maid, she thought groggily, before the woman alerted the guards. She must . . . help Morigan . . .

Fighting past her drugged lethargy, Rissa grabbed Jaranda, pulled her down onto the bed and threw the full weight of her body atop the woman. She flung a pillow over the serving maid's face. Jaranda screamed again and again, the muffled sounds fading to crazed little mews as the lack of air slowly robbed her of consciousness.

Rissa lay there until the serving maid's body went limp, panting, battling the drug that was still strong within her. Finally, with a superhuman effort, she rolled off her. Her movements awkward and fumbling, Rissa tied and gagged Jaranda in the ropes originally meant for her, then shoved herself unsteadily off the bed and turned to the sounds of fearful struggle.

"Vile, filthy alien!" her father cried. "I'm not afraid of you. Kill me, if you dare, and be done with it!"

She staggered over to them and sank to the floor beside Morigan. He straddled her father's form, his hands pinning the Lord Commander's above his head. The Cat Lord's chest heaved, his body shook, and his eyes clenched shut in a face contorted in agony.

For an instant, Rissa thought Morigan had suffered some hideous wound, but he was unharmed. Fear rocketed through her, clearing at last the drug-induced stupor. "Morigan?" She touched him hesitantly on the shoulder.

He didn't respond, so caught up was he in some anguished, internal battle. She glanced down at her father. A triumphant smile twisted his lips.

"Kill me, Cat Man," he sneered. "What are you waiting for? Kill me, or slink back into the cowardly hole from whence you came. Either way, I win."

"Gods . . . ," Morigan moaned, even as one of his hands moved, releasing Lindatees wrists to slide down to encircle his throat. His claws sprang out, pricking his opponent's exposed flesh, bloodying him.

How he needed, hungered, *ached* to kill the man lying before him. It was a pain that had haunted him for over a cycle now, overshadowing his every thought and action until it had nearly consumed him.

It would be so easy. The man was soft, weak. The need for revenge flamed hot and searing, joining with all the Cat dead who cried out for retribution. It was his duty, as Cat Man and Lord of his people. Morigan's fingers tightened, squeezing the life from Lindatees.

"Morigan, don't, I beg of you. Don't kill my father!"

The sweet voice pierced the mists of his anger. Rissa. It was Rissa pleading with him. Pleading with him not to kill, to fight his rage, his need for vengeance. Gods, he wanted to give her what she asked, but it was so hard! So much called him to the blood churning within, consuming his soul. So much . . . too much . . .

"Morigan, please. He's not worth it. Don't let him destroy what you've fought so hard to preserve—your pride, your courage, our love."

Our love.

Morigan's eyes opened. He turned to Rissa; his gaze softened. Gods, but he loved and needed her. Though his people must always be foremost in his heart, she, too, held a precious value. She'd brought light and hope back to his life, had forced him to face his fears, and shown him how to love again. She was everything good and bright and pure. His need for vengeance, on the other hand, however justified, was dark, bitter and soul-rotting.

Zada's words came back to him, that day they'd rested in her hut. *You must let it go, sooner or later, or buy that dearly desired revenge with your very soul.*

His soul. The healer's dire warning had meant little to him that day. He hadn't thought ever to care or love again. But, now . . . now, there was Rissa.

He couldn't risk it. As much as he craved the pleasure of killing the Lord Commander, Morigan knew now he dared not give into it. Not and possibly lose Rissa and his unborn child in the bargain. Not and lose his soul.

The Cat Lord loosened his grip about Fautor Lindatees's neck. "You haven't won, Lindatees," he snarled. "And you won't. Even now, we draw others to our cause—the females we captured, your daughter. Our children grow; our Cat Women are fertile once more. And my seed thrives in Rissa."

"She's an alley walker, just like her mother!" the Lord Commander hissed. "You'll regret taking her to mate. See if you don't."

Morigan smiled. "On the contrary. What you've destroyed, she has salvaged. I've never been happier. You've failed, Lindatees. And you'll never destroy the Cat People. Never."

With that, Morigan lifted his fist and slammed it into the other man's jaw. The Lord Commander gasped, then went limp. Morigan released him. After tying and gagging the unconscious man, he climbed to his feet. His glance locked with Rissa's.

Uttering a soft cry, she ran to him. He welcomed her into the protective clasp of his arms, pressing her tightly, hungrily to him. "By the three moons, but it's good to hold you again," he groaned. "I've missed you so!"

"And I, you, my Lord." Rissa choked back a sob. "Ah, if you hadn't come when you did . . ."

"But I did, sweet one," Morigan soothed, stroking her hair, her face. "Did you think once I knew you carried our child I wouldn't come?"

She leaned back, puzzlement in her eyes. "But how? How did you know?"

He smiled. "I sent Brandar to check on you. We Cat Men can sense when our females are breeding." His smile widened. "As we do everything that happens to our mates."

Rissa scowled. "There are some things we women would prefer to keep to ourselves, at least until the time is right."

"Perhaps." Morigan shrugged negligently. "But the same psychic closeness that brings us mutual pleasure also intrudes on our privacy. It's a trade-off, I suppose." His glance swung to the door, and he gently pushed Rissa from him. "A moment, sweet one. I need to complete a bit of unfinished business."

Morigan strode to the bedchamber door, pulled in the two dead guards, and locked the door behind him. He returned to Rissa but, when he made a move to take her back into his arms, she halted him.

"Did you come solely *because* I was breeding your child?" she demanded warily. "Tell me true, Morigan."

"Not solely." He saw the doubt creep into Rissa's eyes. "Truly, it mattered not to me. Whether you carried my child or not, I wanted you back. I just thought perhaps you might feel differently, as well, once you knew you were breeding. That you might now wish to come back with me . . ."

He inhaled a shuddering breath and forged on. "I love and need you, sweet femina. In the end, though, it's your choice. I want you and our child, but I won't force you."

Her gaze moved to where her father lay, still unconscious. "Well, I certainly can't stay here. My father will never get over his hatred for the Cat People. And he won't listen to me."

Morigan's glance followed hers. "He'll also not cease his vendetta against us. We'll be in danger as long as he lives."

"But he won't succeed against you," Rissa whispered, moving back to rest her cheek upon the broad expanse of his chest. "He won't win. Now, you know him for the madman he is. Now, you'll always be prepared against him."

"Prepared against him in every way, sweet one," Morigan agreed softly. "I've regained everything he took from me, and more. Everything, save one." He paused. "Will you come back to the lair with me, femina?"

She lifted her gaze to his. "Perhaps." An impish look danced in her eyes. "If I do, will you at last be my most obedient slave? Swear to fulfill my every whim or desire?"

He eyed her for a long moment. Then, with a sudden radiance like the sun breaking through the clouds, Morigan smiled. He pulled Rissa to him until their lips hovered but a hairsbreadth apart. "In the mating bed, yes. It's naught more than my duty—a duty I'll endeavor always to fulfill with the greatest diligence and pleasure."

"And the rest of the time?" Rissa prompted. "What of that?"

"The rest of the time we must deal with as the occasion presents itself," he growled. "I'm no fool, though, to think I'll always get my way. Not with you, at least."

She smiled, a sweet, provocative, woman's smile. "You learn slowly, but well, my Lord. I'm content."

"As am I, sweet femina," Morigan whispered, brushing his lips over hers, his heart so full of love and pride and a fierce possessiveness he thought it would burst. "As am I."

He released her then, took Rissa by the arm, and led her across the room to the huge inlaid robur wood wardrobe. "Come, femina. You need better clothes for the journey ahead, and it's past time we headed home."

Home, Rissa thought. Home was where your heart was called, where your loved ones lived. And home, for her, was now with a brave, proud people . . . and an exotically handsome, if somewhat stubborn and domineering, Cat Man named Morigan.

Epilogue

The pain. Gods, but he'd never known such pain! It twisted within Morigan until his gut clenched in an endless, agonizing spasm, building, tightening until he thought it couldn't get any worse. Then, it did.

"Ahhh," Rissa cried, her voice piercing the torment that held Morigan equally as strongly in the throes of her labor. "I can't . . . it hurts! Gods, it hurts!"

"Push, my Lady," Agna urged, kneeling between her outspread legs. "I can see the head. The victory is almost upon you. Push, push, push."

"Y-yes, push, sweet one," Morigan whispered, fighting past the pain of their psychic union to lend his support. He clutched her to him, holding her upright in his lap. "I'm here. I won't leave you."

"Morigan! Ahhh, Morigan!" Rissa arched against him, went rigid, and, inhaling a deep breath, pushed with all her might.

"That's it, my Lady," the healer encouraged, excitement now edging her voice. "The head is almost out. The babe is—"

With a rush of fluid, the child slid from Rissa's body. Agna bent between her legs, wiped the infant's nose and mouth clean, then cut the cord. It was a male, big, red-faced, and strong. He inhaled a shuddering breath, then began to squall.

As Morgan held Rissa, Agna quickly moved from the bed to cleanse the child's body, wrap him snugly in a small blanket, and hand him to his mother. With a soft, happy cry, Rissa reached for her son and cradled him in her arms. She stroked him tenderly, crooning sweet words of love. "He's precious, is he not, my Lord?" Rissa glanced up at Morgan.

Tears flooded the Cat Lord's eyes. He shot Agna an imploring look.

The healer grinned and stepped back. "I'll give you a few minutes alone with your mate, my Lord, but the people grow anxious for the good news. We've an heir to the Cat Throne, you know."

"Yes, we do, don't we?" Morgan huskily replied. As Agna slipped from the bedchamber, he leaned down tentatively to touch his son's cheek. "You've done well, sweet one," he said, meeting Rissa's smiling gaze. "I never thought to be so happy, so complete, again."

"You've always deserved to be happy, my Lord. I'm so glad I could be part of that happiness for you."

"Part of it?" Morgan gave an unsteady laugh and blinked back the tears. "Femina, you're all of it! I took a she-cat, Bellatorian though she was, to be my mate and found she was everything I'd ever needed."

"You claim a bit too much credit for that," Rissa chided softly. "Naren was the one with the foresight, if I recall correctly, not you." She laughed. "Most definitely not you."

For a fleeting moment, the pain of old memories flared in the Cat Lord's eyes. "Yes, Naren was. And I'll always be grateful to him for it. And grateful, as well, for all he was to me." He gripped her hand. "Gods, I miss him so!"

"As do I, my Lord," she fervently replied.

The babe stirred, yawned hugely, and turned, nuzzling at Rissa's breast. Morgan chuckled. "A smart lad if ever there was one. He knows, even now, where his love and sustenance can be found."

"Then, he's already as wise as his father, isn't he, my Lord?" Rissa spread open her tunic and put the babe to her breast. With only an instant's hesitation, the heir to the Cat Throne found her nipple and began to suckle.

His greedy noises filled the room, the soft, smacking sounds one of the most soul-satisfying things Morigan had ever heard. "What shall we call this hungry little animal, do you think, sweet one?"

Rissa glanced down at her babe, a fierce mother's love welling in her. "Karic, my Lord. I think we'll call him Karic."

TURN THE PAGE
FOR AN EXCERPT FROM

ENCHANT THE HEAVENS
BY KATHLEEN MORGAN

SCHEDULED FOR JANUARY 1995

A Roman tribune. A Britanni maiden.
Roman Britain, 60 A.D.

It was an age of bitter conflict and of passionate love.
Journey back to a time of powerful rulers and intimate
betrayals where one man and one woman must overcome tremendous personal and political odds before they
can be free to experience the rapture of a true and
lasting love . . .

They strolled out upon the covered porch that opened onto
an enclosed courtyard. Though summer was fast fading, the
night was still warm, blanketing the little interior garden in
a comforting coverlet of darkness. Save for the silver light
of the full moon, it would have been impossible to see each
other as Marcus drew Rhianna from the noisy gaiety of the
room and farther into the tile-paved courtyard.

The fountain in the enclosure's center splashed and splat-
tered its contents into its seashell-shaped basin. From its
perch atop one of a twin pair of birch trees, a wren unexpectedly trilled as Marcus and Rhianna's approach awak-
ened it from its slumber. Realizing its mistake, the tiny
bird quieted.

Marcus smiled down at Rhianna. "You seem to bring out
the birds, no matter the time, nor place." He withdrew a
wrapped parcel from his toga and offered it to her.

She glanced down at the package, so small in the expanse of his large, callused palm. "What is it?"

"A gift I once tried to give you. Please accept it. It was always meant for you."

Rhianna eyed him warily, then took the parcel from his hand. With careful movements, she unfolded the covering. 'Twas the bone earrings he'd bought her at Lughnasa.

"They are yours, Rhianna," Marcus huskily explained. "Though perhaps I haven't the right to give them to you, they could never belong to another. No matter how you might fight against it, you're a woman who deserves women's things."

He silenced her protest with a gentle finger upon her lips. "You proved it that Lughnasa night. Proved it in my arms and in your passion when our bodies joined. Admit it, sweet lady."

"Aye, 'tis true," she whispered, lifting her gaze to his. "I have never denied my womanhood. My battle has always been against the woman's expectations placed on me. Expectations you place on me as well. But they, too, ended that Lughnasa night."

Gazing down at her, standing so near, so vibrant and alive, Marcus was nearly undone with the urge to take her into his arms and kiss her. Gods, if he could ease just once more the needs that had haunted him ever since that first night together! "Must it be over? I'm a practical man. I'll not force expectations you've no inclination to follow. But what we had was so special . . ." He stroked the side of her face. "So very, very special. I used to think once with you would be enough, but I'm no longer certain."

His hand encompassed hers, and he folded her fingers around the earrings. "Take the gift, Rhianna. They require no debt on your part, no expectations, save that you think of me when you wear them."

She sighed her defeat. "As you wish. I thank you for them."

"And does the acceptance of my gift also mean you accept its companion?"

Rhianna tensed, sensing his sudden change of tactics. "Ah, here it comes. I should have known—"

"No, it's not what you think. I only hope for the granting of what was also requested that Lughnasa day—your friend-ship."

Friendship, Rhianna thought. So simple a word, so fraught with complexities. Yet, had he not earned it time and again, with his kindness, his courage, and his willingness to sacri-fice himself for her?

Her gaze locked with his. "Aye, Marcus. For what worth there is in it, I'll be your friend."

He smiled. His large hand captured her chin. Marcus's head lowered, covering her mouth, the strong hardness of his lips melding with the yielding softness of hers.

Sweet spirals of delight shot through Rhianna. She gave herself up to the need to feel, yet again, the powerful strength of his arms about her.

With a small cry, she came to him, wrenching her mouth away to bury her face against the corded muscles of his chest. More than anything, more than life itself, Rhianna needed to touch him, to hold him. 'Twas more than just a simple desire for friendship—she knew this well—though friend-ship was all she could ever dare allow. Yet, still, she clung to him, savoring the deeply needed if forbidden solace of his body . . .

Marcus fingered a tendril of her hair. "This afternoon," his deep voice rumbled against her ear, "when your father said you'd journeyed here because you were worried about me, and then, you denied it—did you speak true?"

Rhianna's throat tightened. He'd so easily seen through her lie, had he? Yet, to admit it could reveal feelings best kept hidden. "Why would you have cause to doubt it?"

"No cause, just a foolish hope you'd come to care a little for me."

She struggled to raise her guard against him. He'd barely won her admission of friendship and now wanted more. Mayhap, she should laugh away his question, laden with its underlying implications, yet the dread of being cruel was more potent than her disturbing reactions to him.

"I care," she sighed. "Isn't it evident by my willingness to be your friend? Yet, what does it really matter—my caring, I mean? Do you still wish to bed me? You can have me for the asking, whether I care for you or not. 'Tis a spoil of battle, a privilege of conquering another nation, is it not?"

Marcus expelled a frustrated breath and gripped her arms, shoving her away from him. "Yes, it *can* be a spoil of battle. And, yes, I still wish to bed you." He stroked her arms in a sensual, stirring movement of fingers along soft flesh. "But don't bandy words with me, Rhianna. With you, I feel stripped of my rank and position. You are the conqueror, not I. Can't you look past your hatred of Rome and consider me as just a man?"

She stared up at him. "I . . . I don't know. 'Tis too hard to think when you hold me so closely."

"Stay here," Marcus rasped, his expression suddenly anguished, intent. "Be my lover. Your people permit their women to take other men before they wed. Stay with me until this fire cools between us. When it's over, I swear I'll let you go back to Cador."

A sudden rage engulfed her. When 'twas over, he'd *let* her

go back to Cador? The arrogance, the self-serving conceit of the man!

Yet, perversely, Rhianna found herself tempted to accept his proposition, as simultaneously attractive and hurtfully repulsive as 'twas. 'Twas too much to fathom. She had to put some distance between them, regain the perspective she so easily lost in his presence.

"Let me go!" Rhianna struggled in his grasp. "I should have known 'twould come to this! Let me go!"

In spite of her words, Marcus sensed she was near the admission he longed to hear. If he released her now, she might fly away forever. He pulled her to him. "No, Rhianna," he breathed into the fragrant cloud of her hair. "I won't release you until you give me the answer we both know to be true. The gods forgive me, but I want you. If you've any compassion, any pity—"

"And what of *your* compassion?" In spite of her best efforts, tears clogged her voice. "Can't you see that too much separates us? You've naught to lose. I have everything. Why must you press me? Aren't your own women enough?"

"No other woman is enough anymore!" Marcus cried, in a sudden outburst of agonized frustration. "Do you think I sought this torment, this confusion? Gods, Rhianna, meeting someone like you was the furthest thing from my mind." He made an exasperated motion with his hand. "This—you—were never in my plans!"

Plans.

What had Ailm said? Rhianna struggled to remember. *Love has its own pace and way of disrupting the best laid plans.*

Was this what it all came down to then? But Marcus didn't love her or she, him. 'Twas as he had said. He only wished to bed her for a time longer, to ease his lust, and naught more.

Yet, if this were only lust, why did it hurt so? There was no happiness, no peace in the revelation or its acceptance. And honor. Where was there any honor?

"Nay," Rhianna whispered, her determination growing with each anguished beat of her heart. " 'Tis wrong, no matter what you say, no matter what our customs might allow. I will not bed you again. Forget me, as I must you, for I won't betray my people, nor my vows to this land!"

She twisted violently until, to keep from hurting her, Marcus was forced to let her go. She fled him then, the bone earrings still clasped in her hand. Back to the brightly lit banquet room and the safety of the others, Rhianna ran. Back to a life familiar and comforting, if no longer so safe, so sure.

Yet, in her heart, she knew her flight accomplished naught. Naught . . . save the purchase of just a little more time.

Dear Readers,

HEART'S SURRENDER was a very special book for me in many ways. Not only was it my first futuristic romance for my new publisher, Pinnacle Books, but it was also the continuation of my hugely popular Cat Man futuristic romances. More than anything, I wanted not to disappoint the expectations of readers who'd grown to know and love Karic in *Heart's Lair,* as well as hopefully lure additional readers who had yet to give futuristic romance a try. Initially, the goal I set for myself both terrified and overawed me. Could I repeat the setting and pace, the primal tone and sensual intensity of *Heart's Lair?*

You, the reader, must be the final judge. All I know is *HEART'S SURRENDER* was one of the easiest and most enjoyable books I've ever written. The Cat People, the nuances of their culture and problems of life in their secret mountain lair, evolved so naturally as the story progressed. Instead of a scarcity of characters and conflicts, I found I almost had more than I could include. And all of them, from Morigan and Rissa to the most insignificant secondary character, came alive for me. I'll miss them all (especially Naren) . . . and look forward to the day I can again return to yet another tale of the Cat Men of Agrica.

I love hearing from my readers. If you'd like a list of all my previously published, available books and an autographed, excerpted flyer of my next romance, *Enchant the Heavens,* a historical romance set in Roman Britain to be published in

January 1995, write me at P.O. Box 62365, Colorado Springs, CO 80962. Please include a self-addressed, stamped envelope. In the meanwhile, Happy Reading!

Kathleen Morgan

Author Biography

KATHLEEN MORGAN lives in the Colorado foothills with her husband of fourteen years, two children, and various and assorted pets. A former army nurse with a master's degree in counseling, she now stays home to write full time. The proud recipient of a Romantic Times Career Achievement Award for Historical Fantasy, Kathleen also has four prior published futuristic romances, two fantasy romances, and one historical romance to her credit.

PUT SOME FANTASY IN YOUR LIFE—
FANTASTIC ROMANCES FROM PINNACLE

TIME STORM　　　　　　　　　　　　　　　(728, $4.99)
by Rosalyn Alsobrook
Modern-day Pennsylvanian physician JoAnn Griffin only believed
what she could feel with her five senses. But when, during a freak
storm, a blinding flash of lightning sent her back in time to 1889,
JoAnn realized she had somehow crossed the threshold into another century and was now gazing into the smoldering eyes of a
startlingly handsome stranger. JoAnn had stumbled through a rip
in time . . . and into a love affair so intense, it carried her to a point
of no return!

SEA TREASURE　　　　　　　　　　　　　　(790, $4.50)
by Johanna Hailey
When Michael, a dashing sea captain, is rescued from drowning by
a beautiful sea siren—he does not know yet that she's actually a
mermaid. But her breathtaking beauty stirred irresistible yearnings
in Michael. And soon fate would drive them across the treacherous
Caribbean, tossing them on surging tides of passion that tran-
scended two worlds!

ONCE UPON FOREVER　　　　　　　　　　　(883, $4.99)
by Becky Lee Weyrich
A moonstone necklace and a mysterious diary written over a century ago were Clair Summerland's only clues to her true identity.
Two men loved her—one, a dashing civil war hero . . . the other, a
daring jet pilot. Now Clair must risk her past and future for a passion that spans two worlds—and a love that is stronger than time
itself.

SHADOWS IN TIME　　　　　　　　　　　　(892, $4.50)
by Cherlyn Jac
Driving through the sultry New Orleans night, one moment Tori's
car spins out of control; the next she is in a horse-drawn carriage
with the handsomest man she has ever seen—who calls her wife—-
but whose eyes blaze with fury. Sent back in time one hundred
years, Tori is falling in love with the man she is apparently trying to
kill. Now she must race against time to change the tragic past and
claim her future with the man she will love through all eternity!

*Available wherever paperbacks are sold, or order direct from the
Publisher. Send cover price plus 50¢ per copy for mailing and handling to Penguin USA, P.O. Box 999, c/o Dept. 17109, Bergen-
field, NJ 07621. Residents of New York and Tennessee must
include sales tax. DO NOT SEND CASH.*